Point of No Return

Devlin drew a deep breath. "I call on Lord Kanjti as witness to my oath, and patron of my Choosing." As Devlin repeated the final phrase, a wisp of cold fire ran down the sword, then seemed to go through his arm and into his body. For a heartbeat his entire body was filled with icy fire. And then it was gone, and he felt nothing save the start of a throbbing ache in his head.

All was silent. Master Dreng had finished his chant and now regarded Devlin with a faintly quizzical look on his face.

Devlin lowered the sword. "Is it over?" He felt cheated, though he did not know why.

"It's done," the priest replied, sparing barely a moment to glance at Devlin before returning his attention to the altar. "You are now the Chosen One, champion of the Gods, defender of the Kingdom and its people, until your death."

From the sound of him he expected that Devlin would not last a week.

Devlin's Luck

The Sword of Change • Book 1

Patricia Bray

BANTAM BOOKS

DEVLIN'S LUCK

A Bantam Spectra Book / May 2002

ISBN 0-553-58475-8

Published simultaneously in the United States and Canada

Bantam Books are published by Bantam Books, a division of Random
House, Inc. Its trademark, consisting of the words "Bantam Books" and the
portrayal of a rooster, is Registered in U.S. Patent and Trademark Office and
in other countries. Marca Registrada. Bantam Books, 1540 Broadway,
New York, New York 10036.

PRINTED IN THE UNITED STATES OF AMERICA

OPM 10 9 8 7 6 5 4 3 2 1

To the two Jennifers

Jennifer Dunne, an extraordinary friend who set my feet
on this path when she told me it was time to stop dream-
ing and to begin writing the stories that were inside me.
Through the years Jennifer has always been there, provid-
ing encouragement, endless hours of critiquing, manning
the 1-800-plot-help line, and administering chocolate during the rough spots. I owe her more than I can ever hope
to repay.

And to my agent Jennifer Jackson, who believed in this
project, and helped make this dream happen.

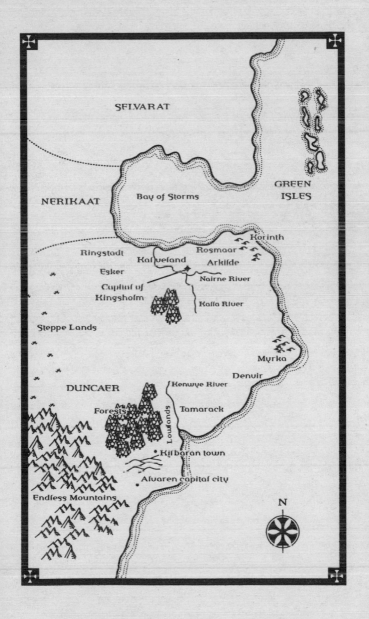

SELVARAT

GREEN
ISLES

NERIKAAT   Bay of Storms

Ringstadt   Kalvesland   Rosmaar   Korinth
                              Arkide
Esker   Nairne River
Capital of
Kingsholm   Kalla River

Steppe Lands

                                        Myrka

DUNCAER   Kenwye River   Denvir
          Forests   Tamarack
                  Lowlands
                  Kilbaran town
          Alvaren capital city

Endless Mountains

N

One

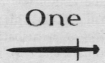

THE STRANGER ENTERED KINGSHOLM ON THE THIRD and final day of the midsummer festival. Lesser versions of the festival were celebrated throughout the Kingdom of Jorsk, but here in the capital city, the residents threw themselves into the celebration with an almost maniacal glee.

There was much to celebrate. Under the wise leadership of King Olafur, the residents of Kingsholm had enjoyed another year of peace and prosperity. Only the most bitter and contrary of the elders tried to dampen the celebration by pointing out that in times not so long ago peace and prosperity had been enjoyed throughout the Kingdom. Now, scarce a month went by that they did not hear tales of hardship from the distant corners of Jorsk, stories of failed harvests, attacking marauders, or uncanny plagues. But since these evils had yet to touch the lives of those who lived in the capital, they were deemed of little consequence.

At first the stranger, too, appeared of little consequence. He might have been any trader or farmer, come to Kingsholm to take part in the great celebration. But he did not mingle with the crowds, instead passing through them as if they held no power to touch him.

Devlin Stonehand regarded the celebrating townsfolk with a mix of impatience and dismay. In other circumstances he would have chosen to wait outside the city for another day, until the festival was concluded. But the choice was not his. Without coin in his pocket there was no inn where he could sleep or tavern that would feed him. He had not eaten in two days, and now he had a choice between begging in the streets or going forward to discover whatever fate awaited him at the palace.

As he stepped around a crowd of drunken revelers, Devlin could not help thinking how different it would be in his own country of Duncaer. There any stranger would find himself welcomed for the festival, and offered hospitality. His weeks of travel had taught him not to expect similar treatment in Jorsk.

He had reached the outskirts of Kingsholm at midday, although it was difficult to say where the city actually began, as outlying farms gave way to villages and small shops, which blended seamlessly into the outskirts of the city. It was only when the road widened and he found himself surrounded by crowds that he realized he had reached the great city.

Kingsholm was the most famous city of the realm, and drew people from all corners of the world. It was said that Kingsholm was not one city but three, consisting of the outer city, the old inner city, and finally the palace. Each was contained within the other, yet still held its own separate identity.

The outer city had sprung up around the walls of Kingsholm, as the population swelled beyond what the old city could hold. The nobles had left the inner city to build their grand houses on the north hill. To the east lay the residences of the merchants and most respected of the artisans. The south and west sides were given over to commerce, warehouses, and the large squares where markets and bazaars were held. It was here that the most raucous celebrations were to be found, and it was this quarter that he must cross on his way to the inner city.

Devlin wended his way through the crowds. He made a few wrong turns, and once had to retrace his steps to avoid a religious procession. But he was not lost. From any square he could look north to glimpse the white spires that marked his destination.

A granite wall marked the start of the old city. There was a gate, but no guards stood watch and the gate seemed permanently fixed open. Passing under the arch into the cobbled streets beyond, Devlin was struck at once by the change. Unlike the outer city of wood and brightly painted plaster, the buildings of the inner city were imposing edifices, made of gray and white stone. They were well built but had a dingy air, as if the buildings themselves knew that time and fashion had passed them by.

There were fewer people on the streets here, and those he saw did not seem to be actively celebrating.

Devlin paused to get his bearings. With the stone buildings looming over him, he could no longer see the spires of the palace.

An elderly woman followed him through the gates, then stopped. "Lost are you?" she asked.

"No," Devlin said shortly.

The woman regarded Devlin skeptically. "You are not here for the festival."

It was an easy deduction. Devlin had been traveling for near three months, and his cloak and boots showed every mile of his journey.

Devlin could make no guess as to the woman's station.

She appeared well-groomed, but he knew too little of the city to guess whether her clothes were fashionable attire or merely the livery of service.

"I need to find the palace," Devlin finally admitted.

The woman regarded him critically. "Of course," she said, with a decisive nod. "Dressed for hard travel, and not a smile on your face nor a glass of summer wine in your hand. It must be grim news indeed that make you seek the help of the Chosen One."

Devlin did not respond. Let her guess what she would. He had no desire to explain himself to her, or to anyone. He bent his head in courteous dismissal, and made as if to move off.

She stopped him, laying one hand on his arm, her eyes now filled with pity. "I did not mean to offend you. There is no Chosen in the city now. But if you go to the palace and ask for Captain Drakken, she will give you what help she may. Just follow this street till you reach the square of the fountain. Take the right-hand lane leading out of the square. Pass the Temple of the Heavenly Couple, then take your second left turning. It will be a wide boulevard and take you straight up to the palace."

"Thank you," he said stiffly.

He passed through two smaller squares before he found the large square with a fountain. Ornate residences surrounded the square, and from behind their high walls he could hear music and laughter and the sounds of families gathered in celebration.

He began walking more quickly, eager to have this journey over. He found the boulevard, just as the woman had said. It was paved with white stone blocks that looked freshly swept. Strange trees with golden leaves lined either side of the wide roadway, which led up the hill to the palace.

The palace dominated the central hill of Kingsholm. As Devlin approached, he felt a growing sense of his own insignificance. The palace was larger than many of the villages he had passed through on his journey.

This was no place for him, a simple man from a poor country. The residents of that splendid palace had no need for such as he. They would mock him, disdain his quest. He should turn back.

But there was nothing to turn back to. And so he plodded on.

At the end of the boulevard was a wide iron gate that opened onto the palace grounds. As in the city below, the gates stood wide open, but here they were flanked by two guards dressed in dark green uniforms.

"Halt," the guards said in unison, each leaning his spear so that they crossed in the middle, thus barring the way. The guards were both young men. Their uniforms were so well kept they looked new made, with every buckle gleaming. In addition to their spears, they wore short swords in their belts. They eyed him watchfully, but their posture was relaxed, indicating that they thought him no real threat.

Devlin came forward till just a single pace separated him from the guards. Then he stopped.

"State your business," the guard on the left said.

Devlin looked them over. The guards appeared to be the same age, but the one on his left wore a silver cord on his sleeve. At this range he could see they were very young indeed. Both their faces were unlined, and their eyes lacked the hardness that came with having seen battle.

"I am come for the Chosen One."

The two guards exchanged glances. "Another beggar," the younger guard muttered. "Will they never learn?"

"There is no Chosen," the senior guard said. "So be off now, and do not waste our time."

Devlin bit back an oath. He was hot and tired, and he could feel each of the miles he had walked in the aching of his legs.

"I will speak with Captain Drakken," he said. He was in no mood to argue his business with these young guards, only to have to repeat it again to their officer.

The senior guard shifted his arm so his spear was pointed slightly toward Devlin rather than simply blocking the path. Devlin knew better than to suppose this was by chance.

"Captain Drakken has better things to do with her time than to nursemaid the likes of you," the guard said scornfully. "There is no Chosen. Hasn't been one in months. So why don't you go back to whatever hole you crawled out from and tell your people that they'll have to find someone else to solve their problems?"

The senior guard had made a mistake when he shifted the spear, for now the way to the palace was no longer blocked. Devlin eyed the distance between himself and the guards. They had let him get in too close, and they were too relaxed, not expecting any trouble. If he moved swiftly, he could take the spear from the first guard, then use it to disable them both. Neither man would have a chance to draw his sword.

But he had not come here to teach guards the folly of trusting in appearances. No matter how foolish or discourteous they were.

"Captain Drakken," he repeated softly. He fixed the

senior guard with his stare, letting the young man feel the strength of his determination.

After a moment the guard looked away. "Private, go fetch Captain Drakken," he ordered.

"She's not going to like this."

"Not our worry. If she's angry, let it fall on him."

Devlin said nothing. It was enough that he had gotten his way.

The guard stared at Devlin, not bothering to hide his scorn. Devlin hadn't seen a mirror recently, but he supposed that he was an odd sight. Despite the summer heat, he still wore a long blue coat in the style of the Caerfolk. The coat was ripped and stained from travel, but it was as easy to wear as it was to carry. His boots were so dusty it was impossible to determine their original color, and the soles were as thin as parchment. In his left hand he held a long wooden staff. A tattered leather pack and transverse bow were slung over one shoulder. Underneath the coat he wore the shirt and trousers he had bargained for a few weeks back. The shirt was too big, and the trousers a couple of inches too short, but at the time they had been an improvement. His dark hair was indifferently cropped, and his complexion weathered from his journeys.

All in all he supposed he looked the part of a vagabond. He wondered what Captain Drakken would think of him, or how many other people he would need to see before he accomplished his mission.

The young guard returned, and with him came a woman who carried herself with such authority that he knew at once she must be the Captain. Her plain features gave the look of one who would brook no foolishness, while the gray in her blond hair spoke of years of experience. Her uniform was similar to the guards', save that her sleeve held two gold cords, and unlike them she wore no helmet. She carried no spear, but wore a long sword strapped to her waist. He had no doubt that she knew how to use it.

"You asked to see me?" She assessed him with a glance, but unlike the guards he could not read her opinions in her face.

"Yes," he said. "You are Captain Drakken, of the City Guard?"

She nodded, her fingers drumming impatiently on her sword belt.

He hesitated. Once he said the words there would be no taking them back. But the time had come. He could feel it in his bones. "I am come for the Chosen One," he said.

"I told you already, there is no—"

"Wait." Captain Drakken ordered, holding up her hand to silence the young guard. "Continue," she said, nodding in Devlin's direction.

The tradespeech was tricky at best. He tried again. "I know there is no Chosen," he said. "I am come to *be* the Chosen."

The two young guards stared at him, mouths agape. If he had been capable of mirth, Devlin would have laughed at the expression on their faces. As it was, he merely felt a grim satisfaction.

Captain Drakken rubbed her jaw with one hand. "And you think the Gods have called you to this?"

"Yes."

The young guards turned their faces slightly away, but she continued to look directly at him. "Well there is no doing anything today. It is Festival, in case you hadn't noticed. Come back tomorrow, and we'll take you for the oath."

"No."

The two guards stiffened, as if they were not used to people contradicting their commander.

"No," he repeated. He had not come this far to be turned away. Besides, not once in the ballads had they said the Chosen One had arrived, only to be turned away because it was not a convenient time. "I am a stranger in town, and have no coins to my name. There is not an inn or tavern in all of Kingsholm that will take me in."

"You can bunk down in the guardhouse for tonight," she said, with a strange half smile. "And tomorrow I will take you myself for the oath swearing. Fair enough?"

Despite his impatience to have the deed done, one more day would not matter. "Fair indeed," he said.

The senior guard raised his spear so Devlin could pass through the gate. His face held a strange mixture of pity and contempt. The younger guard would not look at him, but instead stared fixedly at the ground as Devlin passed.

The Captain set a brisk pace as she led him around the perimeter of the palace. They passed through a formal garden, an open courtyard whose purpose he could not discern, and then the stable block where his companion was greeted cheerfully by the grooms.

On the other side of the stable block were two buildings. The first was a long low structure of whitewashed plaster, with a row of small windows. He guessed it was a barracks of some kind. Adjacent to it was a small square building made of bricks, with only a few narrow windows set high up in the wall. A storage house, he surmised. But to his surprise the Captain passed by the barracks and led him to the smaller building.

She paused at the door and turned to him, letting him

see the same wry smile she had given him at the gate. "The guardhouse," she said.

He looked at her, and then at the small building. Now he was close enough to see that the windows of this building were barred with iron. It did not take a scholar to realize that his knowledge of tradespeech had once again tripped him up. The guardhouse was not where the guards stayed. It was where they put those they wished to keep their eyes on.

It was a gaol.

The door swung inward, confirming his guess. Two men sat across from each other at a table in the center of the room. One man was a soldier, and he stood to attention as the Captain entered. Looking around, Devlin could see that the building held six small rooms or cells, two on each of the three sides. The fourth side held the door through which they had entered, with a variety of manacles and weapons hanging on hooks.

Wooden doors, banded with iron, hung open, revealing that the cells were empty.

"I trust you have no objection to my hospitality?" she challenged.

He saw no reason to object. The place looked clean enough, and he was so weary that he would have cheerfully bedded down in the stable with the horses. "This will serve," he said.

Her eyebrows rose a notch and she looked at him, as if he had confounded her first impression.

"Sergeant Lukas, this one is a guest," she told the guard. "He can come and go as he pleases."

So he was not a prisoner. He had wondered about that, in a dim sort of way. Not that he cared one way or another.

He had used up all his strength to reach the palace, and now that he was here, he found he had no will to go farther.

"What about me?" the second man asked, standing and giving the Captain a courtly bow. He seemed more boy than man, despite the bruises that marred his countenance. He had a narrow, thin face, with light brown hair that hung down to his shoulders.

"*You* are going nowhere. You caused a near riot yesterday, and my guards have better things to do than rescue your sorry hide. You will stay put until Festival is over, or I will deal with you personally. Understood?"

The young man flushed. "Understood."

Captain Drakken turned her attention back to Devlin. "The Choosing Ceremony will take place tomorrow at midday. I will come for you then. But if you are not here, there is no shame."

"I will be here."

The Captain left, and Devlin found himself the center of attention. The soldier Lukas, a middle-aged veteran, regarded him warily, while the young man appeared fascinated.

"You are here to be Chosen?" the young man asked.

Devlin ignored him. Shrugging the pack off his shoulders, he set it down in the empty cell on his left. Then he untied his cloak and hung it on a hook. Entering the cell, he sat down on the bed and began to unlace his boots. Each movement was deliberate, requiring all of his concentration. It should have worried him, but it did not. He chalked up his weariness to the length of his journey, and to the strange sense of anticlimax he felt after having come so far, only to be greeted with less than welcome.

"Any hope of getting something to eat?" Devlin asked.

"You can go fetch something yourself, or they'll bring a meal here round sunset," the soldier said.

Devlin nodded. He pulled off his left boot, then his right. Those shreds of fabric around his feet had once been socks. He would have to do something about them. But not now.

"Wake me when food comes," he said, stretching out on the cot. After weeks of sleeping in fields and barns, his body eased itself into the welcome softness. By habit his right hand rested on the dagger he wore at his side.

"But wait. You can't go to sleep. Not now. It's midday. And I have so many questions to ask you," the young man said.

Devlin closed his eyes, and then his ears. The young man's voice was a distant hum, and then there was nothing at all.

When he woke, sunlight was streaming through the narrow slit window high up in the wall, crossing the small cell and bouncing off the wooden door. The door was closed, but through it he could hear the sound of voices. Devlin sat up, rubbing the last of sleep out of his eyes. A quick check showed that he still had all his weapons. His pack appeared undisturbed, which meant either they trusted him to a foolish degree, or whoever had searched his belongings was an expert at his job.

His boots were on the floor where he had dropped them earlier. He tried not to look too closely at his feet as he forced them back into his boots. Even his blisters had blisters.

Devlin rose and went to the door. He did not remember shutting it earlier. But it opened freely at his touch.

The veteran soldier and young man were seated at the table in the common room, along with another soldier whom he had not seen before. The young man had his back to Devlin, and was strumming a lute.

The veteran soldier turned as Devlin left the cell. "Good morrow," he said.

"And you," Devlin said courteously.

The young man put down his lute and turned to face Devlin. "Good morrow. I've been waiting for hours for you to waken. You scarce said two words at supper last night, and then you seemed like to sleep for a thousand years. I thought you were sick or dying, but Sergeant Lukas here said you were simply tired and I should not disturb you."

Devlin kept his face still. He did not remember anything of yesterday, after he had reached the guardhouse. And yet according to the minstrel, he had risen and supped, without ever truly waking. He must have pushed himself harder than he knew to have reached such a dangerous point of exhaustion. Worse yet, he had not realized it at the time. Such carelessness was foreign to his nature.

He looked around the room. There was a pot for kava by the fire. Devlin cocked his head in that direction.

"Help yourself," Lukas said.

Devlin selected a pewter mug from the shelf next to the fire and poured himself kava. Then he crossed to the table. The two soldiers had both chosen to sit facing the door. It was where he would have sat as well, but instead he compromised, picking a seat opposite the young man, which allowed him to split his attention between his companions and the doorway.

Devlin sipped the hot drink. There was an awkward silence, but he felt no inclination to break it. He wondered how long it would be till Captain Drakken came to fetch him.

There was a basket of breads and fruit at the far end of

the table. The second soldier reached out and pushed it toward him.

"I thank you," Devlin said. He took a roll in one hand, and began to eat, alternating bites of the sweet bread with sips of kava.

Lukas eyed him appraisingly. "I told young Stephen here that you had the manners of an old campaigner. Sleep when you can, eat when you can, and no complaining."

Devlin grunted noncommittally.

"Were you a soldier?" the young man asked.

"No."

Devlin fixed the young man with his best glare, hoping to discourage any conversation. But the young man was impervious.

"I am Stephen of Esker, a minstrel," the young man said. "It must be the grace of Kanjti that you came here yesterday. I am writing a ballad about the Chosen, which is sure to be my greatest work."

Lukas snorted. "It was no good fortune that got you stuck here. It was that riot you caused with your last song."

The young minstrel waved his hand. "Simply a slight setback. I did not realize that the yokels were unable to appreciate the subtleties of my interpretation of the legend of Queen Hoth."

"Hasn't been a Chosen One in nearly a year now," the second guard commented. "Not since that last one followed the witch Alfrida into a swamp and was eaten by a giant serpent."

"No, she was the one before. The last Chosen was torn apart by demon wolves," Stephen said.

"Right. Demon wolves it was," the second guard said. "He was a master of the blade, and yet he lasted all of a month. Wonder how long a peasant will last?"

Devlin did not reply. He knew the soldier was simply trying to provoke him. But he could not be provoked, for he did not care what they thought of him.

"You never gave us your name," Stephen said.

"Devlin. Devlin Stonehand." It was near enough to his own name that he had grown used to it in these last months.

The minstrel took a small leather-bound journal from his pocket, and a writing stylus. "Devlin Stonehand," he repeated. "From Duncaer?"

"Yes." It would be foolish to try and deny his origin, not with every word he spoke betraying his breeding.

"Good. Not that I'll use your name. The Chosen are always getting killed off before we can finish a song. Nowadays we just call them all the Chosen, to make it simpler. Not that much rhymes with Chosen. Except perhaps frozen, but that's not all that common either...." The minstrel's voice trailed off as he contemplated the difficulties of his profession.

Jorskians believed that the Chosen Ones were summoned by the Gods to service, and blessed by the Gods with extraordinary strength and courage. There were many songs about the Chosen Ones from the days of their glory, but few songs had been written in the hundred years since the passing of Donalt the Wise. Since his time men had diminished, or the dangers they faced had grown in stature. Whatever the reason, in these dark days the position of Chosen One had become nearly impossible to fill. Those that volunteered were invariably slaughtered within a few months of assuming their post.

In desperation the King had taken to offering large bonuses for anyone who would take the oath. Even that tempted fewer and fewer men these days. What use had a man for golden coins when he would not live long enough to spend them?

Devlin knew exactly what he would do with the promised treasure. And he had seen too much in these past months to be afraid of any foe, mortal or demon. If the people of Jorsk wanted to pay someone to play hero, then that was exactly what they would get.

Two

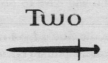

CAPTAIN DRAKKEN CAME FOR HIM AT MIDDAY. "You're still here," she said, her blunt features showing surprise.

"I said I would be."

"Yes, you did. I did not get your name yesterday."

"Devlin. Devlin Stonehand."

She looked him over skeptically. He did not blame her for her doubts. He had shaved and put on the cleaner of his two shirts, but it would take a long bath and a new wardrobe to make him even barely presentable.

"You are a farmer?" Her tone was courteous, but the word she used for farmer could also be used to mean the lowest of the low.

"Once." He did not elaborate. It was his future he had come to sell. These folk had no right to his past.

"I don't think we've ever had a farmer come for Chosen before. Soldiers, mercenaries, younger sons and daughters of the nobles. But not a farmer."

"There's never been a Chosen One from Duncaer province either," the minstrel Stephen said helpfully. "Devlin will be a first in many ways."

"I can take care of myself," he said, answering her unspoken question.

The Captain's face reflected her doubts. "If you become the Chosen One, you will have to do more than defend yourself."

If he was Chosen, he would have to risk his life again and again, until he came upon an enemy he could not defeat. "I have heard the last Chosen One was an expert swordsman, and yet he survived for barely a month. Leave it to the Gods to decide if my service is acceptable." His eyes bore into hers, refusing to back down.

"You have a sharp tongue for a farmer. But you are right. It is not for me to decide. Come and we will get this done with."

"What about me?" Stephen asked.

"Festival is over. You are free to go. But if you cause any more trouble, I will ban you from Kingsholm."

He nodded cheerfully. "There will be no trouble. I have learned my lesson. No more political songs. From now on I will stick to the heroic ballads."

Stephen followed as Captain Drakken led Devlin through the palace grounds to a small white stone temple. Frescoes over the entrance indicated that this was a royal temple, dedicated not to one God, but to all seven.

As they entered he saw two people inside, standing next to a stone altar. One wore the brown robes of a priest. The other was a lean man, just past his youth, dressed in wide trousers and short jacket in a style that Devlin had never seen before. His long brown hair hung in tangled locks, giving him an exotic appearance. Next to the two men was an altar holding a pair of candles, a silver sword, and a small wooden box.

Inside the temple it was strangely cold, despite the heat

of the summer day outside. Yet Devlin felt beads of sweat forming on his brow, as the inevitability of what he was doing came home.

"You can still leave now," Captain Drakken said. "Leave and return to your family. There are better things to do with your life than throw it away."

For a moment he was tempted, but the mention of family washed away all his doubts. The Captain was wrong. He had nothing to return to, and no better task for his life. Indeed, if he were killed during the Choosing Ceremony, there were none who would regret his death.

The priest paid him no attention, but the other man looked amused as he caught sight of Devlin. "This is the new Chosen? Captain, you got me out of bed for this?"

Now that they were closer Devlin could see that the man's face was pale, his eyes were bloodshot, his trousers were wrinkled, and there was a dark stain on the front of his jacket. He had the appearance of one rudely torn from his revelries.

"It's not my fault if you can't hold your liquor. The sooner this is over with, the sooner you can crawl back into your bed," Captain Drakken said.

Devlin wondered if such discourtesy was typical of Jorsk. After all, he had walked over two hundred leagues to offer his life to protect their Kingdom. Surely he was entitled to some respect. But instead they treated him as if he were an impoverished stranger, come to beg at their table.

"Brother Arni, Master Mage Dreng, this is Devlin Stonehand of Duncaer," Captain Drakken said, by way of introduction.

The priest nodded and then turned away. His back was to Devlin as he opened the small wooden box and began taking out objects, laying them on the altar. He arranged the items, then reached into the pocket of his robes and withdrew a small stone. Touching the stone to the first candle, he recited a brief prayer. The candle sprang alight.

Despite himself Devlin was impressed. He had never seen a firestone before. Only the wealthiest in Duncaer could afford them. Yet the priest treated it as if it was nothing, repeating the trick with the second candle, then placing the stone back in his pocket.

The priest turned back to face Devlin. "You understand that there are only two choices? Either the Gods accept your service as Chosen One, or you will be struck dead for your impertinence."

"I understand."

"I wager on dead myself," the mage said. "Anyone care to take me up on it? Say a silver latt?"

The minstrel Stephen spoke up. "I will," he said.

"But what do you have that is worth a silver latt?"

"I will wager my lute," Stephen said, his face flushed.

Master Dreng smiled mockingly. "Done. Your lute against my silver."

It was not a good bet. Devlin himself would not have taken it. He knew the Gods hated him. The question was, would they kill him outright? Or decide to prolong his suffering by letting him live as the new Chosen One?

He did not fear death. Haakon, the Lord of Death, had been close to him many times in these last months, but each time he had refused to take Devlin. No, if there was anything he feared it was the Geas attached to the Choosing Ceremony. Once the oath was sworn, the Geas would ensure that Devlin could not betray his service. In effect he would surrender his own will to that of the Gods. It was a prospect that would terrify a sane man, but Devlin was no longer certain he was quite sane.

At last everything was arranged to the priest's satisfaction. "You, sir, come stand here, in the circle, and place both hands on the altar."

Devlin stepped forward and did as he was told. The priest circled the altar so he stood facing him. The Captain moved to stand on his right side and the mage on his left.

"Captain Drakken is here as the King's representative, and Master Dreng will cast the binding spell," the priest explained. He had the air of a man who had done the same chore so often that he was simply mouthing the words. "If the Gods accept you as the new Chosen One, you will receive pardon for any crimes you have committed. But you must confess them now, in the presence of these witnesses."

"I have done nothing that requires your pardon."

The priest looked doubtful, but continued his explanation. "You will need to dedicate your service by your personal God. I assume you are a servant of Lady Sonja?"

"No." Cerrie had been a follower of Sonja, until the War Goddess had betrayed her. He would not swear by false Sonja.

"Very well, then Lady Teá."

"No." Teá was the mother Goddess, and known as the patroness of those who worked the land. She, too, had betrayed them.

The priest appeared confused. "Then who? The spell is not binding unless you invoke the protection of one of the Gods."

From the corner of his eye, Devlin saw the minstrel Stephen, and remembered that only that morning the minstrel had invoked the name of Kanjti.

Kanjti. The God of luck. A God with no temples or priests. Some called him the bastard god, the only one of the seven whose origin was a subject for hot debate. A God with no family for a man who had none. It was a fitting choice.

"Kanjti," he declared.

The priest looked over at Master Dreng.

"Kanjti will work as well as any," the mage confirmed. "Just give him the sword, and we can get this over with."

The priest picked up the sword from the altar. "Hold this between both hands, raised to the heavens," he instructed. "And repeat the oath of service."

The sword was clearly the work of a master smith. Long and tapered in the old style, it had a hilt of ebon, wrapped in silver wire. The blade shimmered in the candlelight, revealing a pattern of runes carved on one side.

Devlin accepted the sword from the priest with his left hand. It was an awkward grip, and as he tried to switch the sword to his right hand he fumbled and dropped it. The sword struck the marble floor with the ringing clang of steel upon stone.

He picked up the sword, suddenly curious. He examined the length of the blade, noting that the metal had the faint shimmering appearance that belonged to the finest steel. But somehow it did not feel right.

He was aware that the others were regarding him with a mixture of impatience and dismay, but he refused to be hurried. He ran his thumb along the edge of the sword, exerting just enough pressure to keep from drawing blood. Then he pulled his dagger out with his left hand, and struck the pommel of the dagger against the blade of the sword.

He heard it again, the faint note of wrongness. He replaced his dagger and shook his head uneasily. Should he speak up and risk revealing more of himself? Or keep silent as payment for the low regard in which they held him?

He struggled with his conscience for a moment, but in the end he could not keep silent. Honor was all he had left. "I will swear no oath on this blade," he said, placing it on the altar so that half its length extended over the edge.

"Why won't you use the sword? You've come a long way to change your mind now," Captain Drakken observed.

"Because any oath sworn on this blade would be as false as the blade itself." He placed his left hand on the hilt of the sword, holding it steady against the altar. Then he made his right hand into a fist and raised it over his head.

His fist came crashing down. The blade broke with a sickening crack.

"May all the Gods preserve us!" the priest exclaimed.

Captain Drakken's face whitened, her lips taut. Clearly she was imagining what would have happened had anyone trusted his life to that sword in battle.

Master Dreng appeared amused. He looked at Devlin, really looked at him for the first time. "Now I see why they call you Stonehand," he said.

Actually Devlin had taken the name from his father, a builder who had worked in stone. It served him as well as any other name, in this foreign land.

"How did you know?" Captain Drakken demanded.

"You called me farmer, but once my trade was that of a metalsmith. And there are some things you never forget."

"Now what will we do? We cannot complete the ceremony without a sword," the priest fretted.

Captain Drakken drew her own sword from her belt. "Will this do instead?"

He took the sword from her. It was a plain sword. A

soldier's sword. From the wear on the blade it had seen hard use. But the edge was sharp and, when he tapped it against stone, the metal rang true. "This will serve," he said.

At Brother Arni's gesture, Devlin raised the sword over his head, feeling vaguely foolish. But the feeling vanished as Master Dreng gestured with both hands and began chanting in a language Devlin did not recognize. As the mage chanted, a circle of light grew around Devlin, banishing the darkness and making it seem as if he were being inspected by the Sun himself.

Captain Drakken appeared impassive, but when the edge of the circle of light threatened to touch her, she took a hasty step to the right.

The priest began to pray, his high voice serving as counterpoint to the low chanting of the mage. He prayed for what seemed an eternity, till Devlin's arms began to ache with the effort of holding the sword aloft.

The priest looked up at him. "Now, repeat the oath after me." He rattled off a phrase in High Jorsk.

Devlin repeated the phrase, stumbling only slightly over the unfamiliar words. He spoke no High Jorsk, and wondered vaguely what he was promising.

"And now the same, but in tradespeech so you understand," the priest said. "Repeat after me. I, Devlin of Duncaer, promise to defend the King and people of Jorsk against all enemies both earthly and otherworldly...."

"I, Devlin of Duncaer, promise to defend the King and people of Jorsk against all enemies both earthly and otherworldly...." Although just what he could do against an unearthly enemy was a question that he could not answer.

"I swear to dispense the King's justice, and to enforce the writ of law and the will of the Gods. I pledge my life and soul in service of this oath."

No man could do all that. But he repeated the words anyway.

"I call on Lord Kanjti as witness to my oath, and patron of my Choosing." The priest looked at Devlin, then stared fixedly down at the altar. Captain Drakken and Master Dreng both turned their faces away as well, so they were not looking directly at him. He realized that they were afraid of what might happen next. Presumably this was the moment when the Gods indicated their displeasure with a candidate.

Devlin drew a deep breath. "I call on Lord Kanjti as witness to my oath, and patron of my Choosing." As Devlin repeated the final phrase, a wisp of cold fire ran down the sword, then seemed to go through his arm and into his body. For a heartbeat his entire body was filled with icy fire. And then it was gone, and he felt nothing save the start of a throbbing ache in his head.

All was silent. Master Dreng had finished his chant and now regarded Devlin with a faintly quizzical look on his face.

Devlin lowered the sword. "Is it over?" He felt cheated, though he did not know why.

"The ritual is complete," the priest replied, sparing barely a moment to glance at Devlin before returning his attention to the altar. "You are now the Chosen One, champion of the Gods, defender of the Kingdom and its people, until your death." From the sound of it, he expected that Devlin would not last a week.

The priest handed Devlin the gold ring that had lain on the altar during the ceremony. "Put this on."

Devlin slipped the ring on the middle finger of his left hand. It was a seal of some sort, with a blackish stone in the center.

"Now say, 'I am the Chosen One,'" the priest instructed.

"I am the Chosen One." Immediately the stone in the ring began to glow with a red fire.

"Neat trick, isn't it?" Master Dreng said. "The ring was sealed to you during the ceremony. Now no one but you can activate it. It's the symbol of your authority."

"Does it stop glowing?"

"Eventually."

The priest snuffed out the candles and began returning the ceremonial items to their wooden box. Devlin noticed that a second jeweled stone, which had lain on the altar during the ceremony, had now begun to pulse faintly with a reddish light. But the priest returned the stone to the box before Devlin could ask what its purpose was.

Master Dreng gave a half bow. "Chosen One, I must say this has been a most . . . interesting occasion. I look forward to hearing of your career. Brother Arni, Captain Drakken, I am off to seek my well-earned rest."

"Have you forgotten our wager?" Stephen asked, then took a hasty step backward as all eyes turned toward him.

The mage smiled, and reached into the purse that was tied to his belt. He withdrew a large silver coin and tossed it in the direction of the minstrel. "Take the new Chosen out and buy him a round of drinks. He'll need it."

Devlin turned toward Captain Drakken and held out the sword. "Thank you for lending your sword," he said.

She shook her head. "It is yours now."

"I have no use for a sword. I can use a war-axe and a transverse bow, but I have never learned the sword." At his age it was too late to start. Young warriors spent a decade mastering the sword.

"Nonetheless it is yours. Perhaps you will find a use

for it someday." She unbuckled her sword belt and held that out to him. "Here, you'll need this as well. Don't worry, this was but my practice sword. I have another in my quarters."

"Thank you," he said awkwardly. He was in her debt. He would have to find a way to repay her, for he had sworn never to be in anyone's debt again.

"So what happens now?"

Captain Drakken grinned. "You mean, do the Gods send an immortal emissary to announce your quest?"

The ghost of a smile touched his lips as he realized his own foolishness. Truly he had never thought about what would happen once he was Chosen. He realized that, deep inside, he'd never thought he would live through the ceremony. But it seemed that the Gods were not finished with him yet. He wondered what more they would require of him, before Lord Haakon would condescend to accept his death.

"Something like that," he said shortly.

"In theory, either the King or myself, as Captain of the Guard, can give you a commission. But for the most part the quests will find you. Some half-starved peasant will arrive at the palace with a story of marauders or magical plagues, and you'll find yourself compelled to go off and investigate."

Compelled. He repressed a shiver at the reminder of the Geas that now bound him to the service of this land and this strange people.

Captain Drakken must have sensed his change of mood. "No sense worrying; trouble will find you soon enough. For now I'd suggest you follow Master Dreng's advice, and get drunk. When you sober up, ask a servant to direct you to the chief steward of the castle. Show him the ring, and he'll show you to your quarters, and give you the first half of your reward."

The reward. He had nearly lost sight of the reason that he had come here. Ten solid gold disks for having passed the trial and been declared Chosen One. And another ten, payable on his death or retirement. It was a fortune, more coin than he could have earned in a dozen years as a metal-smith, or a lifetime as a farmer.

Devlin nodded.

Captain Drakken looked him over. "I'll give you one thing. You're the damnedest Chosen we've ever had. Whether that's a good thing or a bad thing is too soon to tell. But you're bound to cause a stir at court."

The sun beat down on the courtyard as Devlin left the temple, and he realized that it was still early afternoon. Strange, he could have sworn that the ceremony had taken longer.

Stephen followed him outside. "Chosen One, it would be an honor to take you for a round of the best ale or finest wine in Kingsholm." The young minstrel looked like a puppy begging for a treat.

"Not now," Devlin said. He looked around, but realized that he was lost. "First, can you direct me to the guard-house where we spent the night? I should collect my pack. And then I want to find the chief steward."

Stephen happily agreed to serve as his guide. He led Devlin back to the gaol, where Sergeant Lukas greeted their return impassively. He offered no congratulations on Devlin's survival, but handed over his pack without comment.

Next Devlin went to the Royal Steward's office. At first the steward seemed inclined to dismiss Devlin as a nuisance. Even when Stephen announced that his companion was the new Chosen One, the steward looked skeptical. Devlin finally had to produce the ring and invoke its power to prove his credentials.

Once he realized that Devlin was the Chosen One, the steward's attitude changed for the worse. He now treated Devlin as if he held a long-standing grudge against him. He tried to refuse payment of the reward, saying that Devlin should leave the coins with him for safekeeping. When Devlin insisted, the steward reluctantly counted out each of the ten gold disks as if they were coming from his own purse. In a pointed lack of courtesy, he summoned a servant to show Devlin to his new quarters, rather than taking him there himself.

The chamber assigned to the Chosen was located on the second floor of the east tower. It was a spacious chamber, with wide windows that looked over a courtyard where soldiers were drilling. The bed was large enough to sleep an entire family, but there was only a bare mattress.

"There's been no need for linens so they've all been put away," the servant explained. "Now that you're here, I'll send for the chambermen to put things right."

Devlin dropped his pack on the floor, then hung his newly acquired sword from a peg in the wall.

Across from the bed stood a tall wardrobe. Devlin opened the doors and saw that the wardrobe was filled with dark gray clothing in a variety of sizes and conditions. His gaze lingered on a gray jerkin that was stained with what could only be dried blood.

Next to the wardrobe was a rack, on which two swords were displayed, while on the wall hung a longbow and quiver. Beneath the weapons were two wooden trunks, each banded with iron. One trunk bore the name Sygfryd.

Unlike the rest of the room, which was well kept, a layer of dust covered the trunks and weapons.

"And these are?" Devlin asked, waving his arm to indicate the wardrobe and weapons.

The servant flushed. "They, er, they belonged to those that lived here. Before you."

"See they are taken away," Devlin ordered. He needed no such reminders of his own inevitable fate.

"At once, my lord," the servant said.

Devlin looked around, then realized that the servant was speaking to him. "My name is Devlin," he growled.

"Of course, my lord Devlin."

Devlin turned on his heel and left.

"Where are we going?" Stephen asked.

"You are going nowhere."

"But I promised you a round of drinks," Stephen said plaintively.

Devlin paused. He had no wish for companionship, or for the verbal fencing that conversation with the minstrel would involve. But there was much he needed to know about his new position, and the minstrel was as good a source of information as any.

"I have a few errands I must attend to," Devlin explained. "But I will meet you later, if you wish it. Name the place."

Stephen immediately brightened. "Of course. How about the Singing Fish, say around sunset?"

"Fine."

"The Singing Fish is in the old city, near the river. It's not fancy, but they have good food and a very fine cellar. Unless you'd prefer somewhere in the nobles' quarter?"

Devlin had no mind to rub elbows with the nobles of Jorsk. "The Singing Fish will do."

"It is very easy to find. Just leave the palace by the Queen's Gate, and then take Victory Lane. Then you need to turn right by the lesser temple of Haakon, and it will be at the third cross street. Of course you could start by the dyers' guildhouse and then go—"

"I will find it."

With some difficulty Devlin pried himself free of his eager young guide. Since the ceremony he had paid careful attention to his surroundings, and now he was able to find his way out of the palace, through the grounds, and out into the city.

The city had a somber air, as if the residents were still recovering from the celebrations of the previous three days. Traces of the festivities still remained; a crushed garland lying by the roadside, the smashed remnants of a wine jug a few paces away.

He walked some ways from the palace, till he was certain that he was not being followed. He did not trust these Jorskians, and from the treatment he had received, it seemed the suspicion was mutual. But if anyone was following him, they were too skilled for him to detect.

Satisfied, he made through the stone streets of the old city, past the permanently open gates, and into the new city. In the merchants quarter he found the festival booths had given way to market stalls, and commerce was brisk. First he found a money changer, who agreed to exchange one of the gold disks for forty silver latts. It was outrageous, but better than explaining how someone dressed like a beggar had come by the gold disk in the first place.

Next Devlin found a merchant who had clothing in his size. Devlin bargained for three shirts, two pairs of trousers, and a dark leather vest. At the merchant's suggestion, he added a half dozen pairs of socks and a set of smalls to his tally. The merchant seemed surprised when Devlin produced a silver latt, easily worth a dozen times the cost of the goods, but after much muttering produced the necessary change in coppers.

Flashing so much money was dangerous. He realized that he should have asked the money changer for some coppers to be mixed with the silver. Unused to such wealth, it simply hadn't occurred to him. He kept a wary eye on the crowds, but no one seemed to be paying him any special interest. And the pair of city guards in their green uniforms patrolling the bazaar gave him hope that he would not be accosted immediately.

He needed new boots even more than he needed new clothes, so Devlin took his time surveying the cobblers, passing by those whose displays showed cheap soles, thin leather, or sloppy stitching. Finally, he found one whose work seemed of good quality, and they struck a bargain for a pair of sturdy walking boots. The cobbler traced Devlin's feet onto a square of parchment, and agreed to have new boots made up within two days. He offered to deliver them, but Devlin, having no wish to disclose that he was residing at the palace, said that he would return for them instead.

As he went to leave, he saw that the cobbler had pouches that had been fashioned out of scraps of leather. They were too small to make proper purses, but would serve his purpose well. Devlin purchased three of them.

On the edge of the bazaar an enterprising scribe had set up a booth. Devlin bargained for the use of a pen and three pieces of parchment. Apparently the skill of writing was not common in Jorsk, for the scribe appeared astonished as Devlin sat down and swiftly penned three short missives.

Making sure he could not be overlooked, Devlin slipped three of the gold disks into the first pouch, then folded one of the parchment letters and placed it inside. He repeated this for the next two pouches. Then he pulled the strings tight and sealed the knots with wax.

Leaving the puzzled scribe behind, Devlin made his way across the square. He hailed the two guards as they passed by.

"Is there something wrong?" one of them asked.

"No. But I need someone to point me in the direction of the merchants who deal with wool," Devlin said. He had decided that the wool traders were his best bet. Trade with Duncaer was tightly controlled, and while there were other traders who journeyed between Duncaer and Jorsk, only the wool traders did so on a regular basis, seeking out the fine fleece that came from the mountain sheep. And with midsummer just past, the traders would soon be leaving on their annual journey.

Hearing his accent, the two guards exchanged glances. One of them glanced down at Devlin's hand, but Devlin had decided not to wear the Chosen's seal. Still there was speculation in the guard's eyes as he looked over Devlin and his sack of purchases.

"Most of the wool merchants live on the street of the Fourth Alliance. I can tell you how to find it, or summon a guide for you. Sir."

Flames! There was no reason for them to call him sir. Not unless they knew that he was the Chosen One. A very good description of him must be circulating already, for which he no doubt had Captain Drakken to thank.

Devlin listened carefully to the directions and then made a hasty retreat. He found the district of the wool traders with no problem, and entered the first shop he saw. Inside was a middle-aged man who regarded Devlin with suspicion.

"May I be of assistance?" the clerk finally asked, when he seemed to realize that his frowns alone would not make Devlin go away.

"Do you have wool from Duncaer?"

"But of course. The finest quality. Just look over there," the clerk said, waving to a pile of fleeces in the corner.

Devlin walked over and fingered the fleeces. They were the right color, but the wool seemed coarser than he expected. Still it might be from Duncaer.

"And do you trade for the wool yourself?"

"Yes, of course."

"And where in Duncaer is it from?"

"From Alvaren."

The clerk was lying. Alvaren was the capital of Duncaer, and the only city that most Jorskians had heard of. But Devlin had lived there, and knew that few foreign traders made the journey to Alvaren. Why should they? The wool trade, like most others, was concentrated in the trading town of Kilbaran, on the border of Jorsk and the endless mountains.

Devlin left without a word. He repeated his question at the next shop.

"Sorry, I have no fleece left from Duncaer," a white-haired woman explained. "What I brought back was already spoken for. But I have many other fine fleeces."

"No, thank you," Devlin said. He was not really interested in fleece.

"I will be journeying within the month to Kilbaran. I would be pleased to bring you back whatever you require," the woman offered.

Devlin looked the woman over. She appeared honest enough, if a bit old to be doing her own trading. "And who do you trade with in Duncaer?"

"I trade with many, but always with Brigia deMor, daughter of Nesta of the Mountains. She has given me the blessing of her name," the woman said proudly.

A blessing was a powerful thing indeed. In the literal sense, it meant that Brigia deMor regarded this woman as a member of her family. It was rare for any outlander to receive such an honor. It could be a lie, of course, but somehow he felt she was telling the truth. He made up his mind to trust her.

"I have a commission for you. I will pay you a silver latt if you take a small package to Kilbaran for me, and see that it is given to Murchadh son of Timlin, called Murchadh the smith from the city. Put it in his hands, and no other."

She looked at him shrewdly. "A silver latt is a great deal of money for such an errand."

"I expect fair service in return. And know this. If you betray me, I will see that you pay for the crime."

"I have never cheated a customer and I am not about to start, not at my age," she said tartly. She reminded him very much of his mother, who'd had a temper of her own. "Give me the package."

He handed the woman one of the leather pouches. In it were three golden disks, and a letter. He knew he could trust Murchadh to see that the money reached Agneta, and ensure that she did not reject the coins simply because they came from him.

"There are three golden disks inside," he told the woman. "Just so you know what it is you are carrying."

The woman looked at him carefully. "No insult meant,

but you do not look like a man who has three silvers to his name, let alone three golden disks."

"No insult taken," he replied. "But I swear to you by all the Seven Gods that the money is mine, and it is come by honestly."

Something in his voice or face must have convinced her, for she gave a slow nod. "I believe you," she said. "I promise to deliver this pouch when I reach Kilbaran. And do you wish me to bring back a message?"

"No." There would be no message. Murchadh would take the coins, but he would walk through fire before he acknowledged Devlin's existence.

"And if you guess who or what I am, you will keep it to yourself. Deliver the pouch, but tell Murchadh naught about who gave it to you, or where you met me." It was enough that Murchadh knew that Devlin had been exiled. There was no reason for Murchadh to know where he had gone, or what Devlin had become.

"I will not lie for you, but neither will I answer any questions."

It was as much as he could hope for. "Your courtesy does you honor," he replied.

Devlin visited several other establishments, eventually finding two other traders who agreed to execute his commission. Although neither inspired the confidence that he had felt with the old woman, the two men seemed honest enough, and both were leaving within the fortnight.

As he left the last merchant, he breathed a sigh of relief. It was as if a giant weight was off his shoulders. Now he had done all he could do. He had earned the money, and sent nine golden disks to his brother's widow, by three couriers. Even if only one of the packages made it to Duncaer, three golden disks would be enough to pay off their debts and keep her and the children in modest circumstances until they were grown and could fend for themselves. And, Gods willing, if all nine coins arrived safely, she would have more than enough to start over again anywhere she wanted.

It did not matter that earning the money would no doubt cost him his life in short order. Knowing that he had done his best to care for his brother's family would bring him a small measure of peace, and ease the burden that Devlin's soul would carry into the afterlife.

Three

STEPHEN WATCHED AS THE CHOSEN DEVOTED HIS full attention to the trencher before him. He ate methodically, in the manner of a man who ate because he must, not because he enjoyed it. Finally, the Chosen finished and laid down his utensils.

"A good meal," he said. They were the first words he had spoken in nearly half an hour.

"The honor is mine, Chosen One," Stephen replied.

His companion grimaced. "Call me Devlin, or not at all."

So the new Chosen One was not comfortable with his rank. Stephen added this to the little he had been able to glean regarding his companion. Earlier, when Devlin had arrived, he had noticed that the Chosen had found time to outfit himself in clothing more typical of Jorsk. But he had chosen to wear the clothes of a common laborer rather than one of the uniforms that the chambermen would have made ready for him. Interesting too that the Chosen was not wearing his seal, nor carrying his sword. No one looking at him would have taken Devlin for anything other than a laborer, or the smith he claimed to have been. Even his age was deceptive. At first glance the streaks of white in his black hair made him look like a man well into middle age, yet his features were that of a much younger man.

Seeing that Devlin had finished eating, a servingwoman came over to remove the trenchers. Turning to Stephen, she said, "The mistress says you are welcome to sing for your supper, but unless your friend has the voice of an angel, he'll have to pay good coppers, or help me wash up in the kitchen tonight."

Stephen flushed with embarrassment. "You should be honored to serve us. Do you know who this is? This is—" He broke off with a yelp as Devlin kicked him in the shins.

"What he means is that we are grateful for your fine food, and if the minstrel here is short of coppers, I have coins of my own," Devlin said, jingling the purse at his belt. "So we will have another round of this wine, if you would be so kind."

His tone was soft, but it had the desired effect. "Yes sir," the servingwoman said, and she returned with two more goblets of wine in the blink of an eye.

It must be something in Devlin's voice. In all the months Stephen had come here, not once had the servingwomen ever referred to him as "sir." Stephen stared at his companion, but he could not see what it was about Devlin that commanded respect. Indeed, even having witnessed the ceremony, it was still hard for Stephen to believe that this man was the Chosen One. He was nothing like the dashing, if doomed, heroes that figured prominently in the sagas and ballads. One could imagine trusting him to shoe a horse or to mend a kettle, but to save a Kingdom? It was not possible.

"Looked your fill? One would think you'd not seen one of the Caerfolk before."

Stephen felt the blood rise to his cheeks. It was true he had never spoken with someone from Duncaer before, but that wasn't the reason for his staring. "I am sorry. I was just wondering. I mean it seems so strange . . . well no, maybe not strange, but definitely odd, or perhaps surprising is a better word. You being Chosen and all."

Devlin took a careful sip of his wine. "And what is a Chosen One supposed to be like?"

"Well, er," Stephen paused. He'd never met one himself. He'd only been in Kingsholm a few months, and the last Chosen One had already been slain before he'd arrived. "Someone like Donalt the Wise. He was the last of the great Chosen. It was said that when he gazed on them, the guilty wept with shame and begged forgiveness. And when he drew his sword in battle, his enemies killed themselves rather than face the Sword of Light."

"Indeed," Devlin said, not bothering to hide his disbelief.

"The sagas tell us he was the greatest of the Chosen. And he was the last of the Chosen to retire from office and live out his days in peace and honor," Stephen insisted. He would not allow anyone, even the new Chosen One, to speak ill of the greatest hero that Jorsk had ever known. Donalt had been dead for scarce one hundred years, but many, Stephen among them, felt that the Golden era of Jorsk had ended with him.

"And since his time?"

"After Donalt came his daughter Miranda. She gave her life to save the young Prince Axel. I've written a song about her, and I could sing it for you—"

"No."

Stephen swallowed his disappointment. The ballad of Miranda's Sacrifice was Stephen's finest composition. He had sung it in this very tavern only a fortnight ago, and the patrons had seemed impressed. Well maybe not impressed, but definitely receptive. After all, they hadn't thrown anything during the performance, and surely that counted for something.

"If the position is so respected, how is it that the King must offer a reward for service?"

"It began in the time of King Olaven. The Kingdom was hard-pressed, and few felt the call to become the Chosen One. Some say it is because the Gods have turned their faces from us, others that we have no Chosen because our blood has grown thin. Whatever the reason, in the time of our fathers a year passed without a Chosen. Then a firedrake menaced the southern provinces. Noble Prince Thorvald demanded that the King allow him to become Chosen. But King Olaven refused to risk his heir and only child. Instead he named his son King's Champion and General of the Army. And he sent messages to all of the temples, asking the people to pray for the Gods to send a new Chosen One."

King Olaven had done more than offer prayers. He had also instituted a reward paid to any newly selected Chosen. Later he had expanded the largesse to include pardon for past crimes, along with a Geas which ensured that the Chosen used their powers only in service of the Kingdom.

Stephen saw no reason to mention these facts. His own father could go on for days, bemoaning the state of the empire, and how they had sunk so low that they could find no honest men, but rather needed to rely on criminals and mercenaries.

Stephen had disagreed with his father, certain that whoever the Gods called to their service must have some greatness within them, whatever their past misdeeds. Although so far the newest Chosen One was proving to be much less than he had expected.

"And this Sword of Light? Surely that was not the shoddy trinket that I saw this morning."

"No, that was just a copy. The Sword of Light was lost nearly fifty years ago, at the Siege of Ynnis. It is said..." Stephen let his voice trail off as he remembered that the Siege of Ynnis had been the bloody capstone to the conquest of Duncaer. As one of the conquered people, no doubt Devlin had his own view of the events surrounding the siege.

"A fitting end," he said. He leaned back in his seat, and folded his arms. "Fitting that you lost the sword, since you lost your honor there as well."

"I don't understand."

"Of course you don't. No doubt you sing about what happened on that day, hiding the truths behind pretty lies." Devlin's face darkened, and his eyes sparked with anger, and Stephen felt a tingle of fear. It seemed Devlin bore little love for those who had conquered his homeland, and yet, that made no sense. If he hated the Jorskians, then why would he have sought to become the Chosen One? And why would the Gods accept such a candidate?

Then Devlin shrugged, and the anger drained from his body like water from a cupped hand. "It does not matter," he said. "What was done was done, long before we were born."

"That makes it no less important," Stephen countered. As a minstrel, he knew full well how the deeds of the past resonated in the present. Why else would men harken back to the example of Donalt, or sing the songs of the time of Queen Reginleifar?

"My people have no love for yours, nor yours for mine.

What will they do when they hear the news that I am the new Chosen One?"

Stephen took a drink of his wine, as he considered how to phrase his response. He had no wish to provoke the Chosen One's anger for a second time. "Most will pay little heed to the news. In recent years, the Chosen have lost power and respect," he said.

No need to mention the obvious, that given the Chosen One's short life expectancy, even those who might object to a foreigner filling the post would assume that his tenure would be brief, and thus they would raise no objections.

"So I can expect neither help nor hindrance? It is as well, since there is no one here I would trust."

Devlin stared grimly at his wine cup, seemingly lost in thought. Then he lifted it, and drained it dry.

"Another? We have barely put a dent in Master Dreng's silver," Stephen said. And perhaps another round would loosen Devlin's tongue.

"No," Devlin said, beginning to rise. "It is late, and I must leave."

"But wait. You can't leave. You have told me nothing about yourself. What will I use for my song?" After two hours in his company, all Stephen knew was that his companion was from Duncaer and had once been a metalsmith. He had met clams that were easier to pry open.

Devlin hesitated, indecision written on his face. Then he resumed his seat. "Very well. I suppose I owe you that much. You may ask one question."

Stephen thought furiously. A dozen questions raced through his mind, but in the end there was one that overrode all others. "What was it that made you come all this way, to be the Chosen One?"

Devlin looked down at the surface of the table, and for a

moment Stephen feared that he would not answer. When he finally raised his head, his face was frozen, as if his features were cast in stone. But when he spoke, his voice was light and mocking. "It was in a place much like this. Having valiantly conquered nearly an entire cask of ale, I settled in the corner to sleep. Before I passed out, I heard a voice telling of the Chosen One. And I realized at once that this is what I was meant to do."

"You were drunk?" He had not meant to shout, but heads swiveled in their direction at his incredulous tone.

"You could call it that. I prefer to think of it as divinely inspired," Devlin said mildly.

Stephen could not contain his astonishment. "You journeyed hundreds of miles to offer up your life as Chosen One all because of a vision you had when drunk?"

"It is my life."

This would never do. He could not write a song about a man who became Chosen One because of a drunken whim. It just didn't fit the heroic mold.

Devlin rose from his seat. "Feel free to make up whatever tale you need for your song. It won't matter to me. And who knows? You may get luckier with the next Chosen One."

"Indeed," Stephen said, feeling his optimism returning. Devlin was right. The next Chosen One could be straight out of one of the heroic sagas, a perfect subject for immortalization. In his mind he began picturing how his new epic would be received.

Of course before there could be a new Chosen, the present appointee would have to be killed.

"Not that I wish any misfortune to fall upon you," he added quickly.

But Devlin had already disappeared.

Devlin returned to the palace and found his new quarters after only a few wrong turns. Dismissing the waiting servant with a growl, Devlin tried to settle himself for sleep. Instead he found himself seized with a strange restlessness. Going to the tavern with the minstrel had been a mistake. Though he had been careful to say nothing that would give away his past, still the conversation had stirred up old wounds. And the wine had not helped. Too little for oblivion, but too much to let his mind rest easy.

Ironic that he had slept as if enchanted the previous night, when no one, himself included, had thought he would survive the next day. Now, having survived the Choosing, and ensured that the reward would reach those he had left behind, he should be able to sleep without a care.

But sleep eluded him, and he began to pace around the chamber. The room that had seemed so grand earlier now seemed smaller than the cell in which he had slept the night before. As he paced, his gaze fell on his still unopened pack. Reaching down, he picked it up and carried it over to the scarred wooden table that stood under the window.

He opened the pack and began withdrawing the objects inside. They were few enough. A threadbare shirt, a small copper cook pot, a handful of spare bolts for his transverse bow. A leather pouch held his sharpening stones and oil. Underneath those was a large object wrapped in linen. He withdrew it and laid it on the table before him.

Unfolding the linen, he stared at the axe head thus revealed. Splinters of wood still clung to the socket, where the helve had been shattered in that final blow. He inspected the blade carefully, but the steel showed no signs of rust or corrosion. Once the mere sight of the axe had brought him pride, a testament to his skill in forging it. Now he looked at it, and all he felt was shame.

He should have left it behind. It had been folly to drag the axe head with him on this long journey. Useless weight—for without a helve, an axe head was just a lump of steel. There had been no need to carry it all this way. Kingsholm was a mighty city, and somewhere he could find a war-axe to his liking. A new weapon, one that did not carry a bloody legacy.

A sensible man would abandon such a cursed weapon. But instead Devlin found himself carefully picking out the splinters of wood that remained in the socket. Tomorrow he would find a weaponsmith and see about replacing the broken helve.

When he finally did manage to sleep, the dream came.

It was a morning in early fall, when the leaves had just begun to turn gold, and the fields were ripe, ready to be harvested. Cerrie emerged from the cottage, carrying their infant daughter in a small basket. Her movements were graceful and unhurried as she crossed the yard. Setting the basket down in the sunshine, she joined Cormack and young Bevan as they began to pick the red gourd fruit, stacking it carefully in baskets that would then be stored in the cold cellar.

It was a peaceful scene, and though the work was not easy, the three laughed and sang at their labors. They paid no heed to the dark woods that bordered the tiny clearing. Only Devlin saw the silver banecats as they left the woods and began their stalk.

He tried to move, but he was frozen in place, knowing the horror to come. "Cerrie! Cormack! The woods!" his dream self screamed, but they could not hear him. For he was not really there, just as he had not been there on that awful day.

At the last moment Cerrie turned and saw the approaching danger. She called out a warning, and seizing the small trowel, ran toward the basket where the infant lay. A banecat followed her. Cerrie turned and picked up a heavy gourd, hurling it toward the banecat with deadly aim. It struck the cat between the eyes, but the creature merely paused and shook his head before continuing its pursuit.

Then the banecat sprang. As Cerrie fell, she covered the basket with her body. She struggled desperately, but a digging trowel was a poor weapon, and no match for the power of that unholy creature. Devlin could not bear to watch and yet his visions gave him no choice, compelled to stand witness as her struggles ceased and her life's blood drained away in a crimson flood.

Bile rose in his throat as he turned and saw that the other two creatures had already killed the man and the boy, savagely rending the bodies limb from limb. He could bear no more, and yet the greatest horror was yet to come.

As her mother's blood dripped into the basket, the tiny infant began to wail. The banecat nudged Cerrie's body, then seemed to realize that the sound was coming from underneath her. Seizing Cerrie's arm in his great jaws, he tugged at her body until the basket was uncovered.

The baby continued to cry. Attracted by the noise, the other two banecats wandered over. The largest of them nuzzled the tiny body, then swatted the basket with his paw. Devlin's fists clenched in helpless rage as the basket tipped and the baby tumbled out onto the dirt.

One of the banecats began to bat the infant like a ball.

The others took up the game, toying with the child as if she were a helpless mouse. The baby's cries turned to shrieks of pain as their sharp claws pierced her skin. The banecats seemed to take a cruel delight in her torment, but eventually her cries weakened, and then ceased altogether.

Losing interest in playing with the tiny corpse, the leader of the banecats padded away into the tiny cottage, but there was no one within. He gave a disdainful sniff at the bleating goats and squawking chickens in their pen, but unnatural beast that he was, he had no interest in such easy prey. Returning to his companions, they briefly touched muzzles, then melted back into the forest.

Devlin found his dream self drawn to the corpse of the tiny infant. Kneeling down, he picked her up in his arms, straightening her limbs as if that would somehow make things better. Her eyes snapped open, and she looked at him with searing accusation.

"Why?" she asked. It was the first and last word she would ever speak.

He opened his mouth, but he had no answer. The spark of life faded from her eyes, and he was once again holding a corpse.

As suddenly as it had began, the dream was over, and he awoke. Slowly he unclenched his hands, feeling the pain where his fingernails had bitten into his palms. He rubbed the last of sleep from his eyes, not surprised to find the tracks of tears on his cheeks. Only in his dreams could he weep for those he had lost.

He felt an immense aching hollowness, as if all life, all feeling, had been drained from him, leaving nothing behind but a shell of a man. Against this hollowness, his grief and guilt were like two pebbles dropped into an enormous well. Nothing he did could change what had happened, or turn him back into the man that he had been before that day. He would never be free from his guilt, or from the horror of his dreams.

He should have been there. He should have saved his family, or died with them. He did not deserve to live.

The despair that was his constant companion rose up and threatened to overwhelm him. It would be so simple to give in to his demons and end his torment. Devlin fought back the despair, as he had on so many occasions before. *You cannot give in to your pain,* he reminded himself. *You have promises to keep.*

But he had paid his debts with the nine golden disks he had sent to Duncaer. He had kept his promise to see that Cormack's wife and remaining children would be cared for. There was no reason why he shouldn't give in to his craving.

A small voice whispered that an honorable man would not accept the King's reward, and then kill himself before he could fulfill his oath. The man that he had once been would never have contemplated such a dishonorable act. But the man he had become knew that the call of honor weighed little when measured against endless torment.

Devlin rose and picked up his knife from the table where he had placed it the night before. It was small, and served mostly as an eating knife. Nonetheless, like all his blades its edge was as sharp as he could make it.

Oblivion beckoned, but he paused for a moment, realizing that once he made this decision there would be no turning back. He searched his soul carefully, but found no reason why he should remain among the living. And all too many reasons why he should pay for his sins with his death. For though he had not killed them with his own hands, nonetheless he bore the guilt of their deaths. Wife, child, brother, nephew, all dead because of Devlin's mistakes and what he had failed to do. His sister-in-law Agneta had been right when she named him kinslayer.

He placed the knife back on the table and deliberately began to roll up the sleeves of his shirt. A cut the long way would kill him swiftly. Picking up the knife, he held it in his right hand, then placed it against his left wrist. Exerting a firm pressure, he began to draw the blade upward. But instead of cutting, the blade skittered along the inside of his arm, making only a shallow scratch.

Devlin stared for a moment. Never before had a blade turned in his hand. He tightened his grasp, and began again. This time the blade would not move at all. He swore, and strained with all the muscles his years as a smith had earned him. Beads of sweat formed on his brow, yet despite his fiercest determination, he could not make the shallowest cut.

It was as if his right hand had a will of its own. As soon as the thought occurred, he felt his concentration slip. In that instant he watched, a passive observer, as his right hand pulled the dagger away from his wrist and then flung the blade across the room, where it hit the wall, then fell to the floor. There it remained; for though he tried with all his concentration, Devlin could not will himself to pick it up.

He stood up. A sword would do as well. But as soon as the thought formed, his legs froze and he could not take another step toward the deadly weapon.

A cold shiver ran through him as he realized that there was only one explanation. The Geas. That strange binding spell that was part of the Choosing Ceremony. It was said that the Geas ensured that the Chosen remained faithful to their oath. And apparently this Geas held a dim view of anyone who would kill himself before embarking on his service.

So be it. He scowled, and kicked the knife away with his boot. The Geas wouldn't let him kill himself, but it couldn't prevent Devlin from being killed by an enemy of Jorsk. All he had to do was find that enemy, and he would earn the death that he craved.

Four

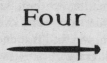

THE FIRST RAYS OF DAWN FOUND DEVLIN STILL seated in the wooden chair. The discarded knife lay on the floor next to him. In his hands he held the axe head, which he turned over and over, as if he could read his fate in the tempered steel. But there was nothing to be seen, save the reflection of his face.

He did not like what he saw. The man who looked back had the eyes of a haunted man, a man who had seen too much horror to be completely sane. And behind the horror he could see the shadow of fear.

The events of the previous night had shaken him. He had chosen death only to find that his own hands had betrayed him. All his strength of mind and will had been insufficient to wrest control away from the strange Geas that insisted he must live, in service of his oath.

It was not that he feared remaining alive. But what more would the oath demand from him? His body was no longer his to command. At any moment the Geas might assert itself. The knowledge was like a great pressing weight upon him. How could any man live with such a burden? No wonder the Chosen were killed so easily. They must have welcomed death, knowing that only death would free them from this ghastly bondage.

But death was unlikely to find him in this chamber room. He would have to leave here to seek it.

Rising from the chair, he crossed over to the wardrobe. The servants had removed the discarded clothing from his predecessors, and filled the chest with finely made shirts and trousers dyed a light gray color. A uniform, of sorts. He scorned these in favor of the plainer garb that he had purchased in the market.

Leaving his quarters, he realized that he was hungry. But he had no idea where to get food. Did they expect him to fend for himself? Or was there a common meal served that he was expected to join?

He left his room and made his way down the stairs to the ground floor. As he entered the main passageway, a woman walked by dressed in garb similar to the servants he had seen yesterday.

"Mistress," Devlin said. "Can you tell me where I might break my fast?"

"New here, aren't you?"

He nodded.

She shook her head in apparent dismay. "And fresh off the farm. What the palace is coming to when we have to hire such, I don't know. Still you'll be of no use to anyone till you're fed. Just go down the passage here till the very end, then turn left. The common room is midway down the hall on your right. It's late, but if you hurry there'll still be something for you to eat."

"I thank you for your kindness."

The common room proved easy enough to find. As he approached he heard folk talking, and the dull sounds of metal utensils scraping against wooden bowls. The room itself was enormous, easily the size of a guild hall. The room was only partly full. Men and women sat together at plain wooden tables. Some were talking, others were consuming their food with frantic haste. Many wore the livery of castle servants, while a few appeared dressed for outdoor labor.

Food of all sorts was laid out in bowls and pans on a table near the door. Devlin filled his trencher with something that looked to be made mostly out of eggs, and then added a chunk of bread. He poured himself a mug of kava, then took his food over to one of the empty tables. No one seemed to pay him any attention, so he settled himself down to eat.

He listened, but those few bits of conversation he heard made no sense. Someone named Emer was in trouble for having shirked her duties during the festival. A nobleman named Bozarth was in disgrace, having gambled away something while in his cups. There was no mention of a new Chosen One.

In the distance a bell sounded. From a table across the room he heard someone exclaim, "We're late!" A group of youngsters rose hastily and left, but the older ones stayed seated.

By the time he was drinking his second mug of kava, few diners remained. Two young girls appeared and began clearing away the dishes. Suddenly the room fell silent. Looking up, he saw Captain Drakken standing in the doorway. He did not rise, and after a moment she came over and slid onto the bench opposite him.

Those few who remained suddenly rose and left, as if they had just recalled urgent business elsewhere. Even the serving girls, after sidelong glances at Captain Drakken, left the room with the cleaning only half-done.

"You make them nervous," he said.

"Not half so nervous as they would have been, had they known that the new Chosen One had decided to dine among them."

He did not need to be reminded that the Chosen One was held in fear and contempt. His discussion the night before with the minstrel Stephen had told him all that he needed to know on that subject.

"A servant directed me here," he said.

"And if you had worn the uniform of the Chosen One, she would have directed you to the Great Hall."

"Is the food there any better?"

"No," Captain Drakken said. "But it is expected that the Chosen One will dine in the hall. It is a matter of custom and courtesy. But I did not come to speak of customs. I came to tell you about the sword you shattered."

"Indeed?" he asked, interested in spite of himself.

Captain Drakken leaned forward. "Two years ago, a smith made a dozen swords for us. Three were lost with their Chosen, and the fourth was the one you destroyed. After the ceremony I had a smith examine the eight that remained. Five of them had similar flaws."

There was a long moment of silence as he contemplated her words.

"This has no sense. Why spoil some of the swords and not all?" It could have been months or years before one of the flawed swords was put to use. What was the purpose of so chancy a scheme? Could the smith have been merely incompetent? Yet an apprentice should have been able to spot the flaw.

Captain Drakken shrugged and spread her hands wide. "I agree, it makes no sense. The smith who made the swords left the city soon after executing the commission. I have sent messengers out, but I doubt that we will find any trace of him."

"And how good is the smith that you had examine the swords? Can he be trusted?"

"Master Timo has served as armorer to the castle for twenty years. He made the sword that I gave you. Two years ago he broke his arm in an accident, which is why the sword commission was given to another."

He had no reason to question her judgment. And Captain Drakken's sword had been well made, which spoke for this Timo's skill. But he could not shake the sense that there was something more going on here than a few flawed swords.

"You should assume that all the swords are tainted, and have them melted down and reforged. And if your smith had a broken arm, no doubt there were other commissions that he had to refuse. Have your guards check every weapon they have for flaws. Ask everyone what else the traitor may have worked on, no matter how big or small, and if there is any doubt, have it forged anew," he said, his voice firm as if he were giving orders to one of his apprentices. Even as he spoke, he knew the words were not wholly his own. It was the Chosen One who spoke, and who felt entitled to give orders to the Captain of the Guard.

Captain Drakken gave him a measuring look, but he returned her gaze steadily.

"Do you truly think this necessary? It will mean a great deal of work, not to mention expense to the treasury . . ."

"Do it," he said sharply. "Even if you find nothing, it will reassure the guards. You do not want to lead them into battle when they are not sure if they can trust their weapons."

She grimaced. "I doubt very much that the King will let us see battle anytime soon. He holds us too close to the city, safe away from the disturbances that plague the out-lands. But I will do as you say."

He nodded. "And if you have no objection, I would speak with this smith myself."

The forge was located on the northern side of the palace grounds, just inside the inner stone wall. As Devlin stepped through the narrow entranceway, he was struck at once by the fierce heat. Against the far wall the fire bed glowed. Iron rang against steel as the smith expertly hammered away at a horseshoe. At Devlin's entrance the smith looked up but then returned his gaze to his work.

Devlin looked around, noticing that the forge boasted not one but four anvils, of differing sizes. There were two workbenches, each of which had an assortment of ham-mers, tongs, chisels, punches, and other tools for working metal. Raw bars of iron, steel, and other metals lay on racks, while near the door were shelves containing exam-ples of the smith's work, knives, buckles, saddle irons, and horseshoes.

Save that the building was made of wood, not stone, he could have been in his master's forge in Alvaren. A sudden wave of longing swept over him as he remembered how once he had dreamed of his own forge, and of the great work that he would do there.

The hammering increased in tempo as the shoe neared completion. Then the smith moved the shoe from the bick of the anvil to the flat face. Laying down the tongs, he picked up a punch in his left hand. Seven quick blows re-sulted in seven perfect nail holes. Returning the hammer and punch to the tool rack, the smith then used the tongs to pick up the shoe and douse it in the trough of water.

When the water ceased hissing he pulled the shoe out and turned it over in his hands to inspect it. After a moment he nodded, placing the shoe with a stack of others on the bench.

Only then did he acknowledge Devlin.

"Good day to you," he said.

"Master Timo, is it not?"

The smith nodded.

"Captain Drakken spoke well of you," Devlin said. "I have some work to be done, and will pay you well for the use of your forge and tools."

"You wish to use my forge, but to do the work yourself?"

"Yes."

"No." Master Timo shook his head emphatically. "There's not enough gold in the Kingdom to pay me to stand by while some fool who fancies himself a smith ruins my tools."

Devlin understood the smith's reluctance. If this were his forge, he'd feel the same. In his head a voice insisted that there was no reason to try and persuade the smith. As Chosen One, Devlin could simply order the man to obey. Devlin ignored the voice, and tried again.

"I apprenticed for seven years, and served as journeyman for three more. I understand your concern, and I would not ask if my need were not great."

"Let me see your hands."

Devlin shifted his pack on his shoulder, and propped his staff against the door. Then he held out his hands, turning them over so the smith could see the faint scars that he bore on both sides. Even the most careful of smiths had scars to show the risks of working with hot metal, and Devlin bore his fair share.

Master Timo grunted. "It has been a while since you

worked your trade. But those are the hands of a smith. I will not lend you my tools, but for sake of our craft, tell me what you want done and I will do it for you without cost."

Devlin hesitated for a moment, tempted. The task itself was easy enough, just fitting the axe head onto the new helve. Any reasonably skilled smith could do it. But it was no ordinary war-axe. Deep inside his bones he knew the weapon itself was cursed, and he could not ask this man to take the risk that the curse would fall on him as well.

"I thank you for your kindness, but I must refuse. There are some things a man must do for himself. If you will not reconsider, I will look for another." In a city this size, he was sure to find at least one smith who would have fewer scruples about lending his tools to a stranger. Devlin reclaimed his staff and turned to leave.

"Wait," the smith called.

Devlin stopped and turned back. The smith bore a faint frown as he regarded him. "As long as you are here, you can take a look at something."

He moved over to the workbench at the far corner, and motioned Devlin to join him. A copper armband lay on the workbench. Favored by soldiers as a luck token, this armband was marred by a crack that split it nearly in two.

"The owner offered me twice its value if I could fix it. I can't, but then steel is my specialty. If you can fix it, then I'd consider lending you a forge and some tools."

Devlin picked it up and turned it over in his hands. "Old work, this," he said. It was an elegant piece, showing a woodland scene in exquisite detail. The crack ran right through the central figure of a deer leaping over a stream. A border done in the old trefoil style ran along the top and bottom of the piece, framing the design. He guessed this piece had been made thirty or forty years ago, most likely in Duncaer. In a country where steel was rare, the Caer smiths had developed the art of working with copper to a high degree. Devlin himself had made dozens of similar pieces, before he had given up the craft to join his brother in the New Settlements.

"If I had my own tools, and a decent grade of mountain copper..." Devlin mused. "No, even then the chances are that I would destroy it entirely. You'd best tell the owner that it is beyond repair." Reluctantly he placed the armband back on the workbench.

The smith nodded in apparent agreement. "That is what I thought. It takes a good man to know when a job is beyond him, and an honest one to admit it. Here, my apprentice is gone for the day. You can use his bench and tools for whatever it is that you are so desperate to do."

His sudden agreement caught Devlin by surprise. "I thank you," he said.

Master Timo showed him the bench he was to use, then returned to his own work. Placing his pack on the floor, Devlin reached in, withdrew the axe head, and laid it on the bench. Then he set the staff beside it. The staff was black oak from the hills of Duncaer. It had withstood the long journey far better than Devlin himself. Now it would serve as the new helve.

First he trimmed the staff to the correct length. Then he used a chisel and awl to set the holes for the rivets. Taking a bar of copper the length of his hand, he heated it in the fire, then hammered it into a cylinder on the anvil. He then split the cylinder in two, forming the rivets. While they were still hot, he measured them against the holes he had made, and was pleased to see that they were a perfect match.

Now came the tricky part. If not done correctly, the

helve would shatter and he would have to start again with a new piece of wood. Carefully he placed the butt of the helve in the vise, then tightened it until it held firm. Then he lifted the axe head with the tongs and brought it to the fire. He held the shank of the blade above the edge of the fire bed, knowing that too much heat would ruin the temper of the blade. Just as the socket began to glow, he removed it from the fire. Then he turned and aligned the axe head over the top end of the helve. It slipped down the width of two fingers. Using the tongs in his left hand to hold it steady, he began to tap the top of the axe head with the hammer in his right. Slowly, almost imperceptibly, the axe head was forced onto the helve.

When he could see the top of the helve through the socket, he relinquished his tongs. But he kept hammering, checking the alignment with every blow, until the holes in the axe head had perfectly aligned with those he had drilled into the helve.

Unclamping the helve from the vise, he positioned the axe so that its head protruded over the anvil. He tossed the copper rivets into an iron cup, then set the cup in the fire bed. A few moments later the rivets were brightly glowing. Exchanging the large tongs for a smaller set, he pulled the iron cup from the fire bed, then grasped the first of the rivets. Aligning it over the hole, he tapped it into the socket with one blow. He then did the same with the second.

The rivets were just slightly longer than the width of the socket. With a few quick blows on first one side, then the other, he capped off the rivets at each end, completing the weld. As he finished, the metal had already cooled to the point where it no longer glowed with heat. He turned the axe over in his hands. The rivets appeared perfect, although he would need to test the axe to be sure. And last time it had been not the axe, nor the rivets, but the helve itself that had failed him.

Still it was done. He hefted the axe, trying to see it only as a weapon, once broken, now made whole again. But he could not, for the axe was bound up with his life. Seeing it, he could not help but remember the pride he had felt when first he forged the axe head, and set the blade on a helve. But that pride was overshadowed by the memory of all that had happened since that day, and of all that he had lost.

He stared at it, fighting the urge to toss the axe into the forge fire and to witness it burn into oblivion.

"That's an unusual design," Master Timo observed.

"It was meant for wood, once." Then feeling something more should be said, he added, "Your apprentice has fine tools."

Every smith made his own tools, starting as an apprentice. And the tools Devlin had used showed the quality of a journeyman, at least.

The smith beamed with pleasure. "He should. He's my son. He'll be a master himself, one day."

Devlin knew he should leave, but he did not. For all the strangeness of the wood building, it was indeed a forge, and it was the only place in this strange city that had the feel of home.

He glanced over at the racks of iron and steel bars.

"I need some bolts, as well. I would make my own, if you would let me pay you for the steel." He did not really need the bolts. He had a half dozen bolts in his pack, and as Chosen One could easily requisition whatever else he desired. What he needed was not the bolts, but to remember that once he had been something more than he was now.

"How many do you need?"

"A dozen should do. Steel, not iron, if you can spare it."

"All our weapons are made of steel," Master Timo said firmly. "I keep the iron for horseshoes and the like. Make a dozen for yourself, and four dozen for me, and we will call it a fair exchange."

"Agreed." Devlin selected two bars of steel from the rack, then placed them in the fire bed to heat. He used the opportunity to study the bolts that were set on the shelves near the door, noting that they were the same design he was familiar with, but longer by a good handspan. He brought one back to the bench to use as a pattern.

The steel was glowing red. He pumped the bellows till the fire was roaring. When the steel bar had turned white with heat he removed it from the fire and began to work. His body remembered his craft, and his arm swung with its old rhythm. Soon he was lost in his work, his mind shutting away all thoughts save those of the steel, and of the task before him.

Long unused to such work, the muscles in his back began to ache and then to burn. He ignored them, as he ignored the sweat that rolled off his body, pausing only to strip off his shirt. With each stroke of the hammer, sparks flew, and the metal rang in a sweet song that he had not known how much he had missed until he heard it anew.

It had been years since he had performed such simple craft, and yet his movements were swift and sure. He made the first dozen bolts for himself, as practice, and then began to work on the ones he had promised the smith.

Captain Drakken entered the forge, her eyes blinking as she made the transition from bright sunlight to the dimness inside. She saw Master Timo at once. He had a dagger and a sharpening stone in his hands, but it was clear that all his attention was on the apprentice at work in the corner.

Master Timo nodded as he saw her but did not speak. With a jerk of his head he directed her attention to the other occupant of the forge.

As her eyes adjusted she realized that the man at work was too large and well muscled to be Master Timo's son. And then she saw something that made her blink, and then blink again.

Terrible white scars ran down the length of the man's back. As he swung the hammer, she could see that the scars extended across his left side and chest. She did not know what manner of beast could have made those marks, save that it must have been larger than any creature she had ever heard of.

She had seen her share of deadly wounds, in the days before the King had confined the Guard to patrolling the city. But never had she seen anyone live who had been half so grievously hurt. By all the Gods, the man standing before her should have been dead a dozen times over.

She opened her mouth to ask Timo where he had found such an unlikely helper. Then the man turned, and she recognized the face of the Chosen One. She was shocked, then angry at herself for not having recognized him. Devlin Stonehand had declared himself a metalsmith only the day before. She should have known him at once.

But the man in the forge was not the same man that she had seen in the palace that morning. This man looked infinitely more sure of himself. And infinitely more dangerous.

"Captain Drakken," he said, inclining his head in the manner of a King receiving an audience.

"Chosen One," she replied, giving him the formal salute for the first time since the ceremony.

Her eyes were drawn back to the scars that were visible on his chest. Running in parallel tracks, they had the look of claw marks, although she fervently wished never to encounter a creature that could make those kinds of wounds. But apparently Devlin had, and somehow survived. And recently too. She would wager her Captain's rank that those scars had been made less than a year ago.

Her gaze seemed to discomfit him. He reached for the shirt that lay discarded on the workbench, then shrugged it on. She longed to ask him what had caused those scars, but sensed that this was not a question he would answer.

"The bolts are finished, although you will want to check them yourself after the last set has cooled," Devlin said, addressing Master Timo.

The smith nodded, but did not speak.

"You wished speech with me?" Devlin asked.

She shook her head. "No, I came to speak with Master Timo about what we discussed this morning."

"Then I will leave you to your duty. Master, I thank you again for the use of your forge and your son's tools."

Master Timo turned his head so he did not have to meet Devlin's gaze. "The Chosen One has only to command and whatever you need is yours," he said stiffly.

Devlin's face grew shuttered. He gathered up a handful of crossbow bolts from the bench, then picked up what appeared to be an axe, with the axe head wrapped in linen. "Let me at least pay you for the steel," he said, reaching into his belt pouch.

"I do not want your coin."

Devlin held out a silver coin, but the smith refused to

take it. With a curse, Devlin threw the coin into the far corner. "Tell your son it is for the use of his tools," he growled. Then he stalked out of the forge, without a backward glance.

Master Timo's rudeness surprised her, as did Devlin's angry reaction.

"So that was the Chosen One," Master Timo said. "He is not what I expected."

"Nor I." Devlin Stonehand continued to surprise her. Even after the ceremony she had dismissed him as another who would do more harm than good in the short time before he met his death. Now she was forced to revise her opinion. The man who bore such scars might have skills that she could use.

Turning her attention back to Master Timo, she explained her concern over what other mischief the traitorous smith might have caused, and commissioned him to seek out and replace anything that might have been tampered with.

"It will take weeks, if not months, to do this right. And cost more than you have in your budget for a year's worth of weapon work."

"Leave that to me. And if the steward complains, I will tell him that this is done by orders of the Chosen One."

The smith grimaced at the mention of the new Chosen.

"You do not like him? But you let him use your forge."

"That was before I knew who he was."

"And now?"

"Yesterday, when you told me of a man who had known that a sword was flawed simply by listening to the metal, I knew it must be a trick. Yet today, having seen him work, I cannot deny that he is a man of skill. Perhaps even a master, in his own country," Master Timo said grudgingly.

"And?" So Devlin had some skill as a smith. She did not see why that would make Master Timo angry.

"So why would a man with hands like that decide to become Chosen One? Any smith in the city would have gladly taken him on as a journeyman, even a partner in time." Timo shook his head. "I don't like it. It doesn't make sense. A waste of good talent, that's what I think."

It made no sense to her either. At first she had thought Devlin a farmer fallen on hard times, who had decided to try his luck as Chosen One. Yet from what Master Timo said, Devlin could easily have found work as a smith. So it had not been mere poverty that drove Devlin to seek the post. She prided herself on her ability to judge people, yet Devlin Stonehand continued to surprise her.

Perhaps she should stop trying to puzzle him out and simply make use of the tool that the Gods had placed in her hand. She would give him a task, and let him make of it what he would.

Five

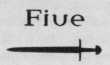

DEVLIN RETURNED TO HIS QUARTERS AS THE SUN was setting, carrying under one arm the newly reforged axe and the bolts which he had fashioned. The memory of the forge master's scorn lingered bitterly in his mind. Always before, a forge had been a safe haven for him, the one place he was sure of himself. But now even that was denied to him. Master Timo had made it clear that there would be no welcome for any man who bore the title of Chosen One.

As he turned down the hall that led to his quarters, a wave of hunger swept over him, and he realized he had not eaten since he had broken his fast that morning. Any hope of a quiet dinner was dashed by the sight of a liveried servant standing outside his door. The woman bowed as he approached.

"My lord Chosen One. The Royal Steward sends his compliments, and begs that you join the household in the Great Hall for the evening meal."

Devlin eyed her askance. He doubted very much that the haughty steward had ever begged for anything in his life. No doubt this was just a courteous turn of phrase.

"I am grateful for the honor," Devlin said carefully. "But I would prefer a quieter repast."

The servant shook her head. "But my lord, you cannot. To do so would be discourteous. All the King's court join in the weekly court dinner. It is the custom."

Courtesy. Custom. The two words bound him with chains as firmly as any Geas. The rules of hospitality were as much a part of him as the color of his hair or the cadence of his speech. He could not deny her request.

"Then it seems I have no choice," he said.

The servant woman smiled in relief, and Devlin wondered what would have happened to her if he had refused to comply. She reached behind her and opened the door to his chambers, then bowed, motioning for him to enter.

"I have laid out the garments for you to wear," she said. "Shall I assist you in donning them?"

"No!" he said swiftly, then in a softer voice. "No, I can dress myself."

He closed the door firmly behind him. A quick glance at the bed showed that she had laid out his formal uniform. First he placed the axe in the bottom of his wardrobe, then he opened his pack and stored the bolts in the holder within.

He stripped off his old clothes, piling them neatly next to his wardrobe. Then he turned his attention to his uniform, eyeing the unfamiliar garments with distrust. The gray silk shirt slipped over his head easily, and the buttons which held it closed were simple enough to figure out, though they ran across the shoulder rather than down the chest. Next he slipped on a pair of gray trousers made of leather that had been tanned to an unbelievable softness. The trousers were a bit loose, but a belt of silver links solved that problem.

But the gray half boots proved an impossible fit. His foot was too broad to fit into the narrow, pointed toes, and after two attempts he gave up in disgust. He would have to wear his own boots, no matter how disgraceful their condition. Fortunately the trousers were loose enough that he could pull them over the tops of the boots.

He regarded his appearance in the mirror next to the wardrobe. He looked like a damn fool. The shirt and trousers might be fit for a lord, but the weathered face and plain boots belonged to a countryman.

There was a rap at the door. "My lord? We must leave now or you will be late," a voice called.

"I am ready," Devlin said.

The servant woman escorted him through the castle. He recognized the hallway that he had seen that morning, but rather than turning right to the servants' area, his guide continued straight ahead.

At last they turned the corner, and before he knew it, he was standing at the entrance to a vast hall. At the far end, a long table set on a raised dais faced the occupants. Below, at right angles to the dais, were a dozen lines of tables. The room was lit by chandeliers, which hung suspended from the high ceiling. Bright banners decorated the walls, and silver plate shone on the tables.

There was room for a dozen dozen to dine, he thought, and then realized that he had underestimated. Perhaps thrice a dozen dozen could be seated at the benches, not to mention all the servants required to wait on them.

But his guide would not permit him to linger. "Come," she said, tugging on his sleeve when he proved reluctant to follow. "The steward instructed me to bring you to the gathering room, where you will join the others."

The gathering room proved to be a small chamber to

the left of the Great Hall. A guard came to attention as they approached, and after rapping once on the door, opened it. Devlin entered the room. When he looked back, he found that his guide had disappeared.

There were perhaps a dozen people in the room, standing talking in small groups. A few heads turned as he entered, but after a dismissive glance they returned to their own conversations.

"Finally. Have you no sense of time? His Majesty is expected any moment," the Royal Steward said, breaking away from one of the groups. His eyes swept over Devlin from head to toe, lingering on the shabby boots, and his lips pursed narrowly.

Devlin returned his gaze evenly.

"Well, I suppose it could have been worse," the steward said, shaking his head. "Come now, and we will fulfill our duties."

The steward led Devlin toward a small group of nobles who stood in a semicircle around a central figure dressed in brilliant white. The object of their attention was recounting a story, and some smiled politely, while others sipped a pale wine from slender glasses.

The steward waited, Devlin at his shoulder, until the nobleman had finished his story and the laughter had died away.

The nobleman turned toward the Royal Steward and raised an inquiring eyebrow.

"Your Grace," the steward said, with a slight bow. "It is my duty to present to you Devlin Stonehand of Duncaer, the new Chosen One. Chosen, this is Duke Gerhard, the King's Champion and General of the Royal Army."

Duke Gerhard barely glanced at Devlin. "I greet you, Chosen One, and welcome you to the King's service." The

words were gracious, but there was no true welcome in
his eyes.

Devlin decided that this man did not rate a proper
greeting. Instead he used a phrase he had learned in his
journeys. "The honor is mine," he said, giving a short bow
in the Jorskian style. Duke Gerhard acknowledged the bow
with a mere inclination of his head, then moved away.

With the air of a man performing a distasteful duty, the
steward introduced Devlin to the other occupants of the
room. Devlin acknowledged each introduction with grave
courtesy, then promptly forgot their names. To his eye, one
richly dressed Jorskian noble resembled another.

Even his encounter with the King proved a disappointment, for his fine robes could not disguise the fact that the
ruler of Jorsk was approaching middle age, with thinning
blond hair and the beginnings of a paunch. The King wore
the expression of a nervous and anxious man, and he acknowledged Devlin's introduction with but a wave of one
jeweled hand.

Or perhaps the wave had been a signal, for a moment
later the steward beckoned imperiously and two Royal
Guards opened the set of double doors that led into the
Great Hall. The King proceeded through the doors, followed by his courtiers.

As Devlin entered the hall, a servant stepped from the
sidelines and bowed to him. "Chosen One, I will show you
to your place," he said. Like the rest, he was careful not to
meet Devlin's gaze.

While the King and his intimates ascended to the dais
and took their places at the high table, Devlin was escorted
to the head of the table on the farthest right of the hall. A
servant poured a glass of wine, and Devlin sipped it slowly
as he watched the members of the court file in. Only half

the tables had been set for eating, and he realized why as he saw the number of empty seats. Either the King's court was smaller than it had been, or many of the nobles had chosen to stay at their estates rather than make their presence felt in the capital.

Two brightly dressed courtiers drew near, then stopped abruptly as they noticed his presence. After a whispered consultation, they took seats at the far end of his table. They were joined by an older woman in a plain dark gown and a young man garbed in a blue uniform the color of the summer sky.

"I am Lieutenant Olafson, aide to Duke Gerhard," the young man said, as he took the seat at Devlin's left. He was the only one to overtly acknowledge Devlin's presence.

"Lieutenant," Devlin replied, acknowledging him with a curt nod. Like the rest of his people, he had no love for the members of the army. Even after fifty years as a part of the Jorskian empire, Duncaer had yet to be assimilated. The army troops sent there knew full well they were not there to defend Duncaer's borders, but rather to control its native population.

The other diners ignored him, as if by refusing to acknowledge him they could pretend he did not exist. He made them uneasy, Devlin realized, as would any man who lived under the sentence of death. In their eyes he was already dead, and thus they treated him as a nonperson.

He found their lack of courtesy odd, but their rudeness had no power to wound him. Indeed he cared not what they thought of him. Those whose opinions mattered were hundreds of leagues away, and he knew full well how they regarded him.

Indeed, this custom of Chosen One was a strange one. As a foreigner in Jorsk his welcome had been cold. As the

Chosen One, his welcome was glacial. The strange folk gave him the title of lord, but treated him with scant courtesy. It was all show, and no substance beneath.

Servants bustled in with the first course, river fish garnished with summer vegetables. This was followed by a pastry shell stuffed with a meat he could not identify. Partridge perhaps, or some other fowl. Devlin ate what he could, but he could not do justice to the elaborate meal, although those around him seemed to have no such problem. The young lieutenant ate as if he knew this would be his last meal.

As he ate, Devlin caught scraps of conversation.

"A complete barbarian..."

"What else can one expect? In these times..."

"I heard Master Dreng is giving seven to one odds that..."

Devlin had a feeling that his survival was the subject of the bet. So the last wager had not been enough to cure the mage of his folly. He wondered if the sorcerer was now betting for Devlin's longevity or if he was wagering on Devlin's imminent demise.

The meal passed without incident. Devlin ate until he could hold no more, than began to refuse the dishes offered. The servants brought pitchers of pale yellow and strong red wine, but after two glasses he stopped partaking of these as well. He had no wish to spend the night with his wits fuzzed from drink. His attention turned first to the chandeliers, suspended on long chains that hung down from the high ceiling. The metal looked like silver, but only steel or iron could bear such weight. Although the chains could be silver-plated. He would have to find time to examine them someday.

His attention then turned to the courtiers, his eyes

wandering over the room. The gathering seemed strange to him. At first he thought it was because he was unaccustomed to seeing people dressed in such finery. Then he realized it was simply that there were no children. In Duncaer it would have been unthinkable to exclude the children of the guests. Even on the solemnest occasion, the babes might have been left with others, but those who had had their name day would certainly have been included. Yet in this gathering only the pages serving the royal table were below the age of adulthood. He shook his head, wondering what other strange customs these Jorskians held dear.

At last the King rose, and the court stood as His Royal Majesty left the room. Some of those present then sat down to resume their feast, but Devlin used the opportunity to slip away.

It was full dark, and it was nearly two days since he had last slept. But he felt no desire to return to his room, to face memories of what he had attempted the previous night. Instead he began to pace the corridors of the castle, exploring with no particular destination in mind.

It was nearly midnight when Captain Drakken found him. He had made his way to the battlements and stood at the edge of the parapet, staring out at the city revealed below.

The moonlight lent a silvery sheen to his gray uniform. For a moment she wondered what the King's Champion was doing here at this hour, and then realized from his dark hair that this was the Chosen One.

Captain Drakken had been on duty that evening, so she had missed the weekly court dinner. From his attire the Chosen One had been compelled to attend, and she wondered what he had thought of the experience. It was not every day that a peasant was invited to share the King's board.

As she drew near, she realized how dangerously close he was to the edge. One foot rested on the ledge, the booted toes projecting into space.

"It is a long drop from here," she said softly, not wishing to startle him.

"You need have no fear. The Geas will not let me jump."

His bitter humor caught her by surprise. She had not thought of his jumping, merely in terms of a careless misstep. If any of her guards had been caught in such a dangerous position she would have taught them a lesson they would not soon forget.

But Devlin Stonehand was not one of her guards, and so she waited patiently in silence. After a moment he stepped back from the ledge and turned to face her.

"Was there a reason you sought me out?" he asked.

Torches placed every ten paces illuminated the battlements, casting a flickering light that made it difficult to read his expression.

Now that she was faced with him, Captain Drakken hesitated. Who was Devlin Stonehand? Was he simply another in a long line of failures who would be lucky if he did not take innocents with him when he met his death? Or was there something more to him?

She rubbed her hand on her chin, as she often did when thinking. There was but one way to find out the mettle of this man, and that was to put him to the test.

She came to attention and gave the formal salute, thumping her fist on her shoulder. "Chosen One, I have a task for you."

Devlin nodded.

"There are reports of a band of marauders living in Astavard forest, who prey on travelers along the King's old highway."

"Why hasn't the local militia taken care of these robbers?"

"Astavard is part of the King's own lands, a royal hunting preserve grown wild in these uncertain times. The King journeys there no more, and thus has decided the road is of little importance. The councilors have agreed that there is no need to send anyone to investigate. Not until the losses grow more serious," she said, trying to keep the bitterness from her tone.

Fools! What would it take till they saw the truth? The roads were the lifeblood of the Kingdom. They carried taxes and royal decrees. Traders and noble councilors alike depended upon safe passage. As did the army, in times of war. They could not afford to lose control of the roads, and yet she could not convince the council to act. When it became clear that the Duke Gerhard was unwilling to commit the Royal Army, she had asked for permission to send a squad of Guardsmen, on the pretext of inspecting the royal hunting lodge, which fell under her purview as part of the royal residences. A training exercise she had called it, but that had been forbidden as well.

So far the bandits had been clever enough not to attack a noble, or a royal messenger, but she feared that it was only a matter of time until they did. Then and only then would the council be forced to heed her words.

"I see," Devlin said, after a long pause. "The army cannot be bothered with these marauders, so you are sending me instead. Tell me, do you have any reports as to their number? Is it a half dozen fools or a well-organized band?"

She shrugged. "There is no way to tell. But large parties

pass unhindered, so reason tells me this is a smallish group, or perhaps merely a careful one. The attacks go back at least a year, maybe longer, yet no one has found a trace of their victims, or their camp in the woods." This was the part that concerned her most. The thoroughness with which the bandits covered their tracks spoke of a highly organized group. "Mind you, if it is a large band, I do not expect you to take them on single-handedly. Survive to bear witness to what you have seen, and I will convince the King to send the Royal Army in pursuit."

It was a fool's errand, but she had nothing to lose. At best Devlin would find the proof she needed to convince King Olafur that there was a real and present danger. At worst he would be killed in the attempt, which would be a waste, but would certainly be enough to convince the King and Council that the marauders posed a serious menace.

She did not believe for a moment that Devlin would be able to defeat the bandits. Only in ballads did a lone hero take on overwhelming odds and emerge triumphant.

Devlin took a step closer to her, so that the torchlight shone full on his face. "I accept the task," he said, with no trace of expression. Even his gaze was strangely flat, as if he were looking through her rather than at her.

"I thank you," she said, feeling an uncomfortable twinge of pity for she knew he had no choice but to accept the task she had given him. The Geas would let him do no less.

She fought back an urge to countermand her order, having a sudden premonition that she was sending this man to his death. But she steeled herself against the impulse. She was the Captain of the Guard. Sending men and women to die was part of her job, as was protecting the residents of Kingsholm. And this man was not one of her guards, nor one of those she was sworn to protect. By his own choice he had made himself into a tool, and only a fool would refuse to make use of his services while he still lived.

"My Guard will help you with your gear, and the Royal Steward will provide anything else you need. You have only to ask."

"I thank you," he said. "And now, if you will excuse me, I bid you good night."

After his talk with Captain Drakken, Devlin had returned to his quarters. He slept only a few hours, rising before the dawn. But his rest had been blessedly free of dreams, and that alone had the power to grant him ease.

It was midmorning when he left. The guards at the main palace gate came to attention and saluted him as he passed between them. But there was no fanfare, no wishes for the success of his journey, no comradely encouragement.

By noon he had left the city of Kingsholm, passing out of the western gate. It felt good to be traveling again—whatever the reason. His new boots had been ready, and they fit better than he had hoped. But still they needed time to break in, and he planned on a short day's journey. He would stop before sunset rather than pushing on as had been his custom. All he wanted was to get far enough away from the royal city that buildings no longer crowded him on each side and he could see the land rather than being hemmed in by wood and stone.

The Geas dwelled in the back of his mind, and he felt its pull, urging him toward the west and on to his mission. But its compulsion was but a faint shadow of the burning need that had driven him to Kingsholm, to take this oath. He could bear it. For now.

His thoughts turned to Captain Drakken. He knew she did not expect him to succeed. Rather she saw him as a tool, an advantage to be gained in the world of court politics. If he returned with news of the robbers, well then, it was more than she had now. And if he failed, at least he had not taken any of her guards with him.

Some men might have felt insulted to be used in such a fashion, but Devlin found himself admiring her ruthlessness. She had the toughness needed to command. He suspected she did not like what she had done, and yet felt sure she would do it again if the opportunity arose.

Cerrie, too, had followed the warrior's path. There were times when he spoke to Captain Drakken when he caught a glimpse of what Cerrie might one day have become. If she had lived another fifteen years, tempering her courage with experience. If she had chosen to stay with the peacekeepers, rather than to resign and throw her lot in with him. If only—

He clenched his fist, letting the pain distract him from his unwelcome thoughts. He would not think of Cerrie, or of what might have been. The past was gone forever, and with it his future. There was only the present, a time that would be blessedly short, if the Gods had any mercy in their souls. He need only journey to Astavard, to face his destiny.

"He has left? Already? But I had no word, and he did not stop by the temple to beg for the blessing of the Gods. It is customary, you know," Brother Arni fretted.

Captain Drakken nodded, her eyes still adjusting to the gloom of the temple after the bright summer's day.

"I had a message from the guards at the West Gate," she said. "The Chosen One left the city on his quest before the noon bells rang."

"I do not understand. Surely he could have spared a moment to pray before he left."

"He left quite early," Captain Drakken said, trying to pacify him. "I understand he roused the Royal Steward out of his bed before dawn."

She suppressed a grin at the thought of the Royal Steward's reaction to such an impertinent request. He was an arrogant sod, and deserved to be taken down a peg or two.

The priest rubbed his chin thoughtfully. "Perhaps he wished to make his devotions in private, and visited the temple before I arose. Yes, that must be it. He is a foreigner, after all."

Captain Drakken doubted very much that the Chosen One had done any such thing, but she kept her thoughts to herself.

"Now he has left, would you fetch the stone?" Captain Drakken asked, coming to the point of her visit.

"Oh. Of course." Brother Arni turned and strode over to the altar. He bowed deeply before it, intoning a short prayer. Then he straightened up and approached the altar, taking from it the wooden box that had rested there since the time of the Choosing Ceremony.

As he slid the box open, she could see a ruby glow from inside. He lifted the soul stone reverently from the case and it pulsed with light, as if it were a beating heart. Turning, Brother Arni advanced to the wall in the back of the temple. An intricate mosaic covered its surface, mapping the imperial lands in exquisite detail. With a bow Brother Arni opened his hands and tossed the stone into the air.

The stone arced toward the wall, then clung to it, seeming to be as much a part of the mosaic as if it had always been there.

Captain Drakken stepped forward and peered at the mosaic. At shoulder height, she found the familiar double circle that indicated the city of Kingsholm. And, there, on the thin brown line that represented the Western Road, the soul stone was affixed.

She knew if she stayed there, she could trace the stone's nearly imperceptible movements as it followed the Chosen One on his journey. The stone had been sealed to him at the ceremony. It would mark his journey until his return to the city, when the stone would be replaced in the box on the altar.

If the stone grew dim, it meant the Chosen One was in mortal danger, though there was naught they could do about that from within the city. And if, or when, he died, the stone would turn black and fall to the floor, where it would shatter into dust.

She let her gaze wander over the mosaic. Over the years the mosaic had been added to as the Kingdom had expanded, concluding with the annexation of Duncaer a generation before. The realm looked impressive, but she knew it was a falsehood. The Kingdom was decaying, crumbling around them despite her best efforts. She had served in the Guard for more than two dozen years, rising in rank from private to Captain. And each year she had watched the Kingdom slip inexorably into chaos.

Piece by piece, the fabric of the Kingdom was being frayed away. Pirates preyed in coastal waters, so-called rogue soldiers from Nerikaat raided freely over the borders of the two countries, and the great southern swamp had risen, some say by magic, to overwhelm the Southern Road.

And still the King did nothing, as his advisors quarreled amongst themselves how best to meet these threats. If only there was an army arrayed against them, an enemy that they could see and understand, then surely the King would release the army to defend against their attackers. But the threat that faced Jorsk was far more subtle. A gradual decay, which had slowly paralyzed the Kingdom and its King with fear.

It was a hard thing, to realize that the King you served was afraid. Afraid of making the wrong decision. Afraid of committing troops to one battle only to learn the true enemy lay elsewhere. Afraid that he was not half the military commander that his father had been, when then Prince Thorvald had led the conquest of Duncaer. And Duke Gerhard played along with the King's fears, telling the King he was being prudent, and that his restraint was the sign of wise leadership.

So the Royal Army remained safe in its garrisons, while she and her Guard kept the peace in Kingsholm, and around them the chaos grew worse. Once confined to the borders, now the troubles were moving into the heartland. As witnessed by this robber band, which operated with impunity only a week's ride from the capital.

It was foolish to think that one man, even the Chosen One, could do anything about these troubles. She knew this, yet she had sent him anyway, for she had no other choice. She hated this feeling of impotence.

Her eyes returned to the soul stone, willing it to stay bright and beating. It had been years since she had begged a favor of the Gods, or indeed since she had put her faith in anything save her own competence and that of her guards. But in the coming days she knew that not even they would be enough to save the Kingdom from the dangers threatening it.

Conscious of Brother Arni's watchful gaze she muttered a short prayer for the Chosen One, and for her Kingdom, for now both would need the help of the Gods to survive.

Six

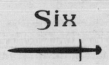

CAPTAIN DRAKKEN SHIFTED SLIGHTLY IN HER SEAT, trying to find a comfortable position. Not for the first time she reflected that the wooden council chairs would make ingenious torture devices. After hours of being forced to sit still in one of them, she herself was ready to confess to any number of petty crimes, if such would buy her freedom. But alas freedom was not so simply won, and she turned her wandering thoughts back to the debate.

Besides herself, thirteen other councilors sat on either side of the long oak table. At one end was the empty seat reserved for the King, flanked on either side by Duke Gerhard and Lady Ingeleth, the senior councilors. The remaining seats were filled by councilors in order of their rank. The vacant chair at the foot of the table was reserved for guests of the council.

She noticed that none of the other councilors seemed as ill at ease as she. Perhaps it was because they were regular attendees at council, while she attended only when requested to do so. Or perhaps they were as good at concealing their discomfort as they were at concealing their true motivations.

"So, we are agreed then? Lord Tynset's petition to acknowledge Jasen Storenson as his heir should be denied. Upon Tynset's death the Barony of Tamarack will revert to the crown," Lady Ingeleth said.

The elderly council woman's gaze went around the table, and watched as each head nodded, one after another.

Only Councilor Dorete, the most junior among them, spoke up. "It is a shame, truly it is. But if he wanted to claim Jasen as his son, he should have done so at birth, and not waited these dozen years," she said.

A dozen years ago, Lord Tynset had no doubt planned on one of his legitimate heirs inheriting. But that had been before a hunting accident robbed him of his virility. Now, with both his son and daughter dead in the strange epidemic that had decimated his people, the Baron had become desperate, and brought forward one of his by-blows.

There was precedent for such a thing, but it would have required wealth or political influence to sway the council, and Tynset had neither. Tamarack was a poor province and coping with the recent plague had emptied the Baron's coffers. And he had no political friends to help him. The traditionalists, to whom he owed his allegiance, were firmly against legitimizing a bastard, lest it call into question their own titles. And the more progressive elements had no reason to love Tynset, and every reason to hope that the King would name one of their own as the new Baron. Any fool could have predicted the council's response, but for form's sake they had debated the matter solemnly before casting their votes.

"But you agree that the petition should be denied, Councilor Dorete?" Lady Ingeleth asked.

"Yes, of course. If that is what everyone feels is best," Councilor Dorete stammered.

Captain Drakken bit back a sigh. Councilor Dorete was too young and inexperienced for her position, barely four-and-twenty. The traditionalists had championed her appointment to the council, to fill the seat her mother had once held. But Captain Drakken suspected their selection of Dorete had less to do with their respect for her late mother than it did with the knowledge that Dorete would make an excellent puppet, one who would do exactly as she was told.

"Let it be recorded that the council unanimously recommends that the King deny Lord Tynset's petition," Lady Ingeleth said, handing the scroll to the scribe who sat behind her. "Now, for the next matter, Captain Drakken wishes to address the council."

Finally. Captain Drakken rose to her feet and bowed to the assembled council members as required by custom, since they had been appointed by the King, while she was here merely as a courtesy to her position.

"At the last council meeting, I reported that the Royal Armorer had found five flawed blades among those set aside for the Chosen Ones. This was in addition to the one that the new Chosen had discovered during the ceremony. The records showed that during his time the false smith worked on a half dozen practice swords for the Guard, along with spearheads, a handful of shield bosses, and two gross of crossbow bolts. While Master Timo has found no flaws in these items that he can detect, at the command of the Chosen One he has undertaken the task of forging each anew. As well as forging new swords for the future Choosing Ceremonies."

Councilor Arnulf shook his head from side to side. "Are you certain this is necessary? It will cost a fortune to redo this work."

"It is better to err on the side of caution," Captain Drakken said. "I will not risk the lives of my guards by giving them equipment made by a traitor."

"But you offer no proof that this smith was a traitor," Duke Gerhard said. "He may be simply the victim of circumstances. Of poor quality steel, perhaps, that caused the swords to fail."

She ground her teeth. "A competent smith should have seen the problem at once. Master Timo had no trouble detecting the flawed swords."

"Is it possible that the swords were tampered with after they were made?" Lord Sygmund asked.

"A very good question. According to Master Timo it is most likely that the flaws were inherent in the manufacture of the swords. But a skilled smith could have altered the swords, heating them and warping the temper of the metal. Though it would take great skill to do so, and leave no visible sign."

From his seat across the table, Councilor Arnulf cleared his throat, and then waited until he was the focus of all eyes. "Perhaps the answer is right before our eyes. No doubt Master Timo was angry that such an important commission was given to another. He may have sought to discredit his rival by tampering with the swords. After all, he is the only one with anything to gain here. The commissions on replacing these weapons will fatten his purse, and he will keep his reputation as the foremost smith in Kingsholm."

"But why would anyone stoop to such a foul deed?" Councilor Dorete asked, her brow wrinkling in thought. "Isn't that treason?"

"If the blades were tampered with, then yes, that is treason," Lady Ingeleth said. "But I must disagree with

Councilor Arnulf. Maser Timo has no motive for such a deed. As Royal Armorer, he receives an annual stipend from the treasury. Reforging the weapons will cost him in time and materials, but will not add to his own fortune. Nor will it add greatly to his consequence, for surely there are those who will say that as armorer he is responsible for all weapons in the armory, regardless of whether or not he made them himself."

"And what does the Chosen One have to say? Why is he not here making his own report, since this was done at his command?" Lord Baldur asked.

"At my request the Chosen One is journeying to Astavard, to investigate the robber band that preys upon travelers through that forest," Captain Drakken said.

"And you did not see fit to consult us before sending him on this errand?" Lady Ingeleth asked.

Captain Drakken shook her head. "Such a task is within my authority. And since the council had refused my requests to send either army troops or members of the Guard to investigate, I took the initiative to send the Chosen One."

"You take much on yourself," Lady Ingeleth observed. "The royal roads are not the province of the City Guard."

Lady Ingeleth was no friend to Captain Drakken, but she was honest, and one of the few on the council who could be swayed by reason.

"The Guard is responsible for the security of Kingsholm, true. But we are also charged with the safety of the royal family. That includes securing the palace and the other royal residences. Including the King's hunting lodge at Astavard," Captain Drakken explained.

"Even if Astavard falls under your domain, the royal roads do not," Lady Ingeleth said.

"If not the Guard, then who else shall see to them?" Captain Drakken demanded. "Who will protect the King's own lands, and ensure the royal roads remain open? At least I am willing to do something."

"And just what is it that you think your guards can do?" Councilor Arnulf asked. "They are thief-takers. Skilled at breaking up tavern brawls, perhaps, but no match for warriors."

Captain Drakken fixed her gaze on Duke Gerhard, for she knew that he was her true opponent here. Arnulf was just his tool. "At least I am willing to commit my troops, rather than letting them molder away, unused."

"Show me an enemy I can face, and I will commit my troops to battle," Duke Gerhard said. "But I will not scatter my forces heedlessly around the countryside, chasing after every will-o'-the-wisp."

It was the same argument they had had many times before. The Duke, with the King's backing, insisted on holding the Royal Army in readiness, prepared for battle. They were fools, for they could not see that this enemy was different. There was no invading army, no great battle in their future. Instead, the Kingdom was dying from a thousand tiny pinpricks.

She knew some on the council saw the same dangers that she did, yet even her backers could not agree upon a course of action. They argued fervently in favor of their own interests, unwilling to put the Kingdom's welfare ahead of their own. And as for herself, she had a voice on the council, but no vote. She could only try to persuade and cajole, and hope that the council saw reason before it was too late.

"This matter has already been debated, and our decision stands," Lady Ingeleth said. "And while it would have been politic for Captain Drakken to consult us beforehand, she was within her rights to give this task to the Chosen One."

Duke Gerhard smiled mirthlessly. "And after all, should the Chosen One fail in his task, he will hardly be missed."

Lord Sygmund nodded, stroking the blond beard about which he was inordinately vain. "Now I see the urgency of replacing the ceremonial swords. Soon we will need a new sword, for the next Chosen One."

Captain Drakken felt ashamed, as she realized that their sentiments mirrored her own. She had given this task to Devlin precisely because he was expendable. And yet he deserved better than to be made the subject of the council's mockery.

"He may succeed at his task, and surprise us all," Captain Drakken said.

"Or he may wind up dead in some forest glade, and us the poorer by another ten golden disks," Councilor Arnulf argued. "Money that could be put to far better use. Even you, Captain, must agree that the Chosen One is a costly anachronism. How much lower are we prepared to sink? This man is a foreign peasant, to whom we have given not just money, but also rank and power. It is no wonder the Gods are deserting us in the face of such folly."

"The Chosen One is one of our most ancient traditions. King Olafur is ever mindful of our history, and rightly so," Duke Gerhard said. "Still, there is wisdom in what Councilor Arnulf says. There is much that could be done with ten golden disks. With such a sum you could recruit and equip another two dozen guards, could you not?"

"Easily," Captain Drakken agreed. With such a sum she could recruit thirty guards, furnish their equipment, and pay them for a full year. Last month she had begged the council for only half such a sum, only to be rebuffed.

But she knew better than to suppose that the Duke was serious in his suggestion. Should they abolish the post of Chosen One, there was little chance that any of the funds would wind up in her coffers. Instead it would be kept for the Privy Purse to be dispensed to the royal favorites, while she and the Guard were left to make do with their limited resources.

"Your views on the Chosen One are well-known, Your Grace," Lady Ingeleth said. "But we will not resolve this today, and so with your leave we will set this matter aside until the King is ready to debate it."

"Of course," Duke Gerhard replied.

"Captain Drakken, is there anything else you wish to add to your report?"

"No," she said.

"Very well. The council thanks you for your thoroughness," Lady Ingeleth said.

Captain Drakken gave another short bow and resumed her seat, uncertain if she had accomplished anything with her testimony. She had hoped that the council would be alarmed by the evidence of the false smith's treachery but they had not seemed overly concerned. Instead they were far more interested in continuing the endless debate over the need for a Chosen One. A debate whose politics had shifted with Devlin's selection. The conservative members of the council, who had been the staunchest supporters of the ancient office, looked askance at its current holder, a man they considered to be a foreign interloper.

Should the King allow the council to debate the subject, there was now a real possibility that they would vote to abolish the office. In which case Devlin would be the last Chosen One, and his death would mark the passing of an era.

Seven

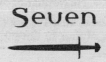

HE SHOULD HAVE TAKEN A HORSE. SERGEANT LUKAS had tried to insist, but Devlin had stood firm. Eventually the veteran soldier had been forced to concede, and had reluctantly helped Devlin equip himself for his journey with goods befitting a poor farmer.

Devlin had been troubled when the Sergeant shared what little was known of these forest marauders. Devlin made no claim as a tactical expert. Such was best left to professionals such as Lukas and Captain Drakken. But still, something about the seemingly random attacks had made him uneasy. Though he did not voice the thought aloud, it seemed as if whoever was attacking the travelers was selecting his targets very carefully indeed, choosing only those who were well pursed but not so well off that their disappearance would raise eyebrows in the capital. Such care spoke of inside knowledge.

Perhaps there was a spy in Kingsholm. If so, then there was no sense in his investigating in the persona of the King's Chosen. The raiders would either kill him swiftly or avoid him like the plague, and neither would let him fulfill his task. And as soon as he had reached this conclusion, the Geas chose to make itself felt.

Devlin would travel in disguise. He would take no equerries, nor servants. He would not wear his uniform, or even travel on horseback. Instead he would travel as he had on his journey to the capital, in the garb of a poor farmer, returning to his home.

He had thought of explaining to Lukas, but had realized that he did not know who in the palace he could trust. And as soon as he had that thought, the words had frozen in his throat. The Geas would not permit him to explain, merely to command. And so he had refused the offers of a mount brusquely, instead gathering a few supplies and slipping from the city as quietly as he could.

It had seemed a good plan. The nagging voice in his head had seemed to agree. But then the rains had come. For the past three days he had slogged on, ankle deep in muck. The torrential rains soaked his clothes, so that he was no drier wearing his cloak than without it. The straps of his pack dug into the muscles of his shoulders, and his calves ached with weariness at each plodding step.

A sane man would have taken refuge at one of the scattered farmsteads or tiny villages that he encountered along the road, and wait until the weather cleared. But the Geas allowed no such rest. He had a duty to perform, and the Geas drove him far more harshly than any earthly master.

Devlin's foot skidded across a slippery stone, and he flailed wildly before regaining his balance. At the start of his journey, this road had been paved with interlocking stones, with a raised crown that allowed water to run off into the ditches on the side. The farther he traveled from Kingsholm, the worse the road became. The stones showed signs of wear, then cracking, and then weeds had begun to appear. By now, nearly two weeks' journey from the capital, there were many places where the stones had vanished altogether. And the drainage ditches were choked with weeds and debris, so that instead of draining the water, the roads were covered with mud washed down from the fields on either side.

Slowly he became aware that there was another sound mixed with the driving rain. The faint jingling of metal on metal came to his ears, and then the rhythmic sound of hooves striking ground and the creaking of carriage wheels. The sounds were coming closer, and swiftly. Devlin turned, and saw a carriage emerging from the mist behind him.

"Ware! Ware away!" the coachman called.

Devlin leapt to the side, landing on his knees in the ditch. The coach, pulled by two highbred horses, swept by, splattering him with red mud without so much as an apology or even a glance backward from the coachman.

"Damn all nobles," Devlin cursed. "May your axle break, and may you be forced to tread in the mire like the rest of us poor common folk."

He tromped on in the mud. The fields of corn gave way to patches of rooted vegetables, and eventually those petered out until there were naught but overgrown meadows on either side of the road. Patches of scrub began to appear, and from time to time, as the road rose, he caught glimpses of a darker blur in the distance. It was the forest of Astavard, the reputed haunt of the robbers. He had not expected to reach the forest for a few days more, but the relentless pace of the Geas had driven him harder than he'd realized.

Once he reached the forest, his true work would begin. Perhaps it would be there, under the leafy bows of the alien pines, that the God of Death would finally see fit to accept the offering of his life.

His steps quickened. As if to mock his desires, the rain grew harder, and the wind began to blow, until the rain was falling slantways, lashing at his face. He struggled on, and slowly the gray day turned darker. The sun, hidden behind the rain clouds, began to set.

Devlin realized that he would not reach the forest today, not before night fell. He looked around, but there were no houses or cottages in sight. He'd passed the last village more than an hour ago. Hunching his shoulders, he contemplated the prospect of another wet night, spent out in the open.

He would walk a little farther, he decided. Perhaps he could reach the edges of the forest. The trees would prove better shelter than none at all.

It was full dark as he turned a bend in the road and saw the dim line that marked the beginning of the forest. But his luck had finally turned, for there, in a clearing at the edge of the forest, he saw a low building with lights in the windows.

The prospect of warmth and a dry bed quickened his steps and restored his flagging energies. As he drew closer, he smelled the acrid scent of burned timbers, and saw the burned-out shell of what must have been an impressive building—at least two stories tall, judging by the stone chimney that still stood, pointing forlornly toward the sky. Surrounding the chimney were piles of blackened timbers, which were slowly being overgrown by vines. The fire was not recent. At least a year; maybe two, if he was any judge. Strange that it had not been cleared away, even if the owners could not afford to rebuild.

A stone's throw from the burned-out hulk was a large barn that loomed over a single-story dwelling, shaped like an L. Light shone from the windows of the dwelling, and under the covered porch a sputtering torch did its best to illuminate a wooden sign that creaked on rusty fittings as it swung in the breeze.

An inn, or such as was left of one, Devlin thought, as he crossed the courtyard. His luck had indeed turned. No need to beg for hospitality from a suspicious farmer. This night he would rest under a roof, after eating a meal of hot food.

As he approached the inn, he saw that the carriage that had nearly run him down was drawn up next to the barn. It looked strangely out of place, like a noble come visiting to the poor quarters. The inn did not look like a place that nobles frequented, but perhaps they too had decided that any shelter was better than none.

Devlin climbed the steps of the inn and reached for the door handle. He pushed it, and found that it would not budge. Strange for an inn to have a locked door. It said little for the innkeeper's hospitality, but perhaps this was the custom in these parts. His own experience with inns was small, for in Duncaer there were few inns, and those that existed were run by foreigners for traders and the like.

Devlin struck the door with his fist, thrice.

After a moment, he heard footsteps, and then the door was pulled back, but only a few inches. The face of a young boy stared out.

"Open the door," Devlin said brusquely. "I want a room for the night."

The boy shook his head, his unkempt hair falling in his eyes as he did so. "I am sorry, but there is no room."

"I have money."

The boy glanced around behind him, and then repeated, "There is no room."

Devlin felt his anger rise. He was not begging for charity, but for the same right as any traveler who had coin in his pocket. He deserved better than this. Devlin put his left hand on the door and leaned some of his weight against it. Just enough so that the boy, leaning against the door with all his might, began to slide backward.

"You have room for Myrkan nobles, but not for a humble traveler, is that it? I need no fancy bed, but I will have a roof over my head, and I am coming in. Stand aside, boy."

Devlin took a breath, but before he could carry out his threat, a voice called out, "Jan!"

The boy let go of the door and turned to face whoever had spoken. Devlin pushed the door open, and stepped inside.

"Jan, what are you doing?"

"But Ma—" the boy protested.

"Enough. Go help your brother."

The woman who had spoken came toward Devlin, wiping her hands on her apron as she did so. She looked like any countrywoman in her dark dress, with her graying hair braided and wrapped round her head.

"I am Hulda, the inn-wife," she said. "Please forgive my Jan, he is only a boy."

An inn-wife. One who offered hospitality for coin. In this country it was an honorable profession. Devlin dipped his head in respect, as was proper.

"I am called Devlin," he said.

At the sound of his voice her eyes widened. "You are far from home," she observed, her gaze lingering on his black hair.

Devlin shrugged. The tradespeech came more easily to his tongue these days, but while his accent might have improved, there was no disguising his features.

"One goes where one must." Let her read into that what she would. "For this night, I need a meal, and a place to sleep. I have coin to pay," he said, placing his hand on his belt pouch.

"A meal you can have, but I regret there are only the two rooms, and they have been bespoken by noble travelers. As it is, my own boys will be sleeping in the barn tonight. You are welcome to sleep in the common room, if that is to your liking."

"Two rooms is not much of an inn," he observed.

Her eyes sparked with anger. "Once we were far grander. Then fire killed my husband and destroyed the inn, and now we must survive as best we can."

He felt an unwilling sympathy for this woman, though he sensed that she did not want his pity. "The common room will be far drier than a night spent outdoors. I thank you for your hospitality," he said.

"A half dozen coppers."

It was an outrageous sum for a man who would not even be given a bed. Still, what other choice did he have? He reached into his belt pouch and slowly counted out the coppers, leaving it perceptibly flatter than it had been before.

The inn-wife was not to know that he carried a much fatter purse, hidden in his pack. No sense spoiling the illusion that he was a poor farmer.

From the hall it was but a few steps to the common room. Once the parlor, or so he guessed, it now held four long wooden trestle tables with chairs of rough pine. An older man and a younger one, both in the silks of nobles, occupied one table. The inn-wife showed Devlin to the table farthest from the two. There Devlin unloaded his pack and stripped off his cloak, hanging it on a hook near the fire to dry.

"Good evening to you," he said. But the nobles, after a dismissive glance, said nothing, which suited him fine. After a few minutes, they rose and left the room. Their footsteps echoed down the hall as they headed toward their chambers. It was early to retire, but perhaps they were tired from their journey. Though how travel in a coach could be tiring he did not know. Surely the chance to sit in comfort would make any journey easy.

He dined on grilled rabbit in an herb sauce, with boiled red roots, and washed down his meal with several glasses of straw-colored wine. The food was far better than he had dared hope from the unprepossessing surroundings. The old inn must have been a grand place in its heyday. He said as much to the inn-wife when she returned to clear away the remnants of his meal.

"What's the use of fine skills, when there is no one to enjoy them?" she said. "Each year fewer come this way. Soon no one will travel at all."

His ears pricked up. "I had heard the road was dangerous," he said with feigned casualness. "Robbers or some such in the forest. But I thought that simply a tale."

"There are lawless ones everywhere," she said, flicking a cloth at the crumbs on the table. "I never thought I would live to see the day that the royal road was not safe. Who knows what will happen next? But the King does not care. He holds court in Kingsholm, far above the concerns of simple folk. He will take no notice until the robbers attack his own palace."

Just then a young man appeared in the doorway. "Ma, are you finished for the night?" he asked.

The young man was in his late teens, and bore a resemblance to young Jan. Another of the family.

"Go along, Paavo, and I will join you in a moment." Turning to Devlin, she said, "You can push the tables out of the way, and lay your bedroll by the hearth. Douse the lights before you sleep. The necessary is in the yard, past the stable. My sons and I were up at dawn, so we will retire now. If you need anything, my room is the first door down the hall."

He thanked her for her courtesy and bade her good night. It seemed early to retire, but his eyes were heavy, and his chin fell down on his chest.

He needed to move now, before he fell asleep in the chair. Devlin stood up, then gasped as a wave of pain contracted his stomach. Sweat broke out on his forehead and rolled down his back. He bent forward, grasping the table, as another wave of pain swept through him. It was as if a giant hand was squeezing his guts, and he could not prevent the gasp that escaped him.

He cursed as the pain subsided, for he knew that in a moment it would return. "Damned gray leaf," he growled, as the next wave of cramps began. Of all the ill luck! Even a single leaf could cause him to suffer, and from the symptoms he knew he'd had far more than a single leaf. Normally he avoided it, but the other flavors must have disguised it.

The cramps were getting worse. Now it felt as if he had poured molten metal into his guts. With a supreme effort, he straightened himself up and began to head for the door. With one hand around his guts, he used the other to open the door to the outside, then staggered out into the night.

Where was the damn privy? He could not recall what the inn-wife had said, and he had no time to hunt for it. He broke into a shuffling trot, and managed to make it to the burned-out ruins, just as his guts began to heave.

He fell down in the mud on all fours and vomited, enduring waves of fresh agony. It seemingly went on forever, until there was nothing left inside of him, and still he felt the urge to heave.

Slowly, he raised his head, then pushed himself up until he was leaning back on his heels. His head swam with dizziness, and his stomach ached but did not rebel.

He felt angry at himself, that he had made such a foolish mistake. But how was he to know? Gray leaf was native to Duncaer. Who would have thought a simple Jorskian inn would serve such an exotic spice?

He called himself twelve kinds of fool, and cursed himself with every epithet he knew as he waited for his stomach to calm down. His sweat-soaked body grew chill in the night air, and still the pains came.

Eventually the cramps grew farther apart, and less painful, and he risked standing. His head spun from the effects of the leaf, and from losing his dinner in such a fashion. Slowly he crossed the inn yard, and there, past the stable, he found the necessary. He used it, then splashed cool water on his face and rinsed his mouth out in the washroom next door.

Every bone in his body ached as he made his way back to the inn and into the common room. He barely had strength to push the tables aside and unwrap his bedroll. Spreading it on the floor made his head swim again and he lay down, not even bothering to take off his boots or to blow out the lamps.

His mouth was dry with thirst, but he knew from past experience that even a sip of water would be enough to trigger another series of spasms. There was nothing he could do save try to sleep it off and hope that he felt better in the morning.

Wrapping himself in his cloak, he closed his eyes and settled himself to sleep.

Sometime later, he heard steps in the hall, and the sound of the door being slowly opened. Wishing only to be left in peace, Devlin burrowed his head under his cloak.

The footsteps came closer, and then he felt a dull pain in his leg as someone kicked him. But he was too weary to react.

"He's asleep," said a voice that sounded like the young man Paavo. From the sound of it, he was standing right over Devlin.

"Of course he is," an older man's voice countered. "Ma knows her craft."

It took a moment for the meaning of his words to sink in. Herb lore was not his skill, but Devlin had learned from past experience that gray leaf could be mixed with kalanth berries to make a powerful sleeping draught. That is, if the subject did not have an aversion to gray leaf.

Paavo kicked Devlin again. "I would have taken care of him myself, but when I saw the lights I thought he was awake...."

Devlin kept himself very still, realizing that his life was in danger. For himself, he cared naught. He was ready to die. But his life was not his own to throw away. Even now the Geas prodded him, to stir and take action. It would not let him lie there passively and await his death. Not while there were other lives at risk. Not while he still had a task to fulfill, and a duty toward the Kingdom.

Still weak from the herb sickness, he did not know if he could even stand, yet he had no choice. He risked opening one eye and saw muddy boots before him. The intruder was between him and his axe, which was still strapped to his pack.

"He's a big one all right, but he's no threat. Finish him, and I'll do the others," the older voice commanded. "Unless you are too squeamish?"

"No, I'll do it," Paavo said.

Devlin waited as he heard the footsteps that signified the other had left on his deadly errand. He heard Paavo take a deep breath, preparing to strike.

In that moment he threw himself to the side, unrolling himself from his cloak as he did so. A long knife rent the air where he had been only seconds before as Devlin rose to his feet.

Paavo swore, his face white with fear and his eyes wild as he waved a butchering knife in Devlin's direction.

Devlin looked around, but there was no escape. The piled wooden tables boxed him in on one side, and the hearth on the other. He would have to pass his opponent to reach his weapons.

As Paavo made another wild swing, he attempted to grab the knife, but earned only a shallow scratch for his pains.

He was running out of time. In another minute the idiot would think of screaming for help, and Devlin would find himself trapped and outnumbered. And then he would have failed, and more innocents would be killed because of him.

So he did the only thing he could think of. Devlin took a few steps back, lowered his head, and charged.

His head hit his opponent's midsection with a satisfying thud as the breath was knocked out of Paavo. Devlin's momentum carried them several steps farther till they struck the opposite wall. The force of the impact stunned Devlin, and he bounced back a few steps.

His ears were ringing as he raised his head and watched as the hapless Paavo slid down the wall, collapsing at the bottom in a boneless heap. Devlin reached down, picked him up by the collar, and shook him, but Paavo's head rolled aimlessly on his shoulders. He was unconscious.

Moving to his pack, he unlashed his axe and tore off the protective wrappings. Pausing only to pick up the knife that Paavo had dropped, he thrust it through his belt.

He paused at the doorway, looking cautiously till he was sure that no one waited for him. Strange that the sounds of fighting had not wakened the noble guests, unless they, too, had been drugged.

Devlin made his way cautiously down the hall, sparing a bare glance to the empty kitchen opposite the common room. The next door was closed, and he recalled the inn-wife saying it was her room.

Two steps more took him to a corner, as the hallway turned and continued at a right angle. On the left-hand side, light spilled from an open doorway, illuminating the figure of a man holding a sack in one hand and a sword in the other.

"Halt or I will kill you," Devlin said.

The man turned to face him.

Devlin approached slowly, testing the weight of the axe in his hand. The walls of the narrow wooden hall seemed to press in on him, and there was scarce room for two men to stand abreast, let alone fight.

This opponent was older than Paavo, a man who had come into his full strength. And he was taller than Devlin, with long arms that would give him an advantage in reach.

"This is none of your concern," the man said. "Turn and walk away, and you may live."

"These men are innocent travelers," Devlin countered. "Killing them is a crime, and that makes it my affair."

"So be it," the man said. "Your death is on your own head."

He stepped back from the doorway and extended the sword.

Devlin held the axe in front of him as he advanced, moving the blade in short arcs. The hallway was too narrow for a proper swing, but the knife in his belt had not the reach to counter a sword.

The man retreated a few steps, then stopped. A skilled swordsman could have dispatched Devlin in moments, but the man holding the sword was barely competent. Still, it was more than an even match, under the circumstances.

He needed to tip the odds in his favor. "Awake, awake," Devlin shouted. He took his left hand off the axe, and began banging his fist against the wall. "In the name of all the Seven Gods, awake!"

Perhaps they had already been killed, and he had failed again. Devlin shook his head. No, he would not believe that. His opponent's sword was clean and unbloodied. There was still time.

He banged the wall again until it seemed the whole building shook. "Awake you miserable sods! Your lives are in danger!"

A groan came from the open door. His opponent's head turned toward the sound and Devlin saw his chance. Lunging forward, he swung the axe in a short arc, slicing across his opponent's middle.

The man screamed in agony as a line of crimson began to stain his slashed jerkin. His sword hand fell, but then he raised it back up and held the sword pointed in Devlin's direction, as he pressed his free hand to his stomach, to hold in his guts.

"You bastard," he hissed.

"What is happening? What is the meaning of this?" a weak voice called from within the open door.

"What are you called?" Devlin asked, never taking his eyes off his opponent.

"Dalkassar."

"Rise Dalkassar, and call to your companion. And arm yourself. This man tried to kill you."

His opponent's face shone with sweat, and his sword began to waver as the blood oozed out from between the fingers of his hand, staining his clothes a dark hue. He leaned heavily against the doorframe, still blocking the entrance to the lord's chamber.

"Eylif! Eylif!" The older man called again and again for his companion, and after what seemed an eternity, the door on the right-hand side of the hall opened. A bleary-eyed young man peered out, still dressed in a linen robe, and with bare feet.

"Uncle! What is going on?"

"This man tried to kill your uncle," Devlin said.

A voice came from behind him. "That is a lie," Hulda announced.

Devlin turned so that his back was pressed against the wall. There, at the bend of the hallway, stood the inn-wife, her young son Jan by her side. The inn-wife carried a deadly-looking cleaver.

"This peasant sought to rob you and your nephew, Lord Dalkassar," the inn-wife explained. "If not for my son's courage, you would have been murdered in your beds."

Lord Dalkassar appeared in the doorway of his room, foolishly coming within arm's reach of the wounded swordsman. He had taken time to pull on trousers, and clutched a dagger in his hand. But his eyes were dulled from sleep or drugs.

"Come now," the inn-wife urged. "What reason would we have to harm you, noble lords? This wicked villain has abused my hospitality and threatened my guests. Help us subdue him so you may return to your slumber."

The lord looked at Devlin, then at the wounded man, clearly confused.

"I don't know what to think," he fretted.

"You cannot think because you and your nephew were drugged by this evil witch," Devlin said. "To make it easier to slaughter you as you slept. If I were trying to kill you, then why am I standing here while this one's blood stains your doorway? Think carefully, for your life depends upon it."

For a moment Devlin thought he had convinced him, and then the noble shook his head. "No, you are clever-tongued, I'll give you that. But the inn-wife is right. You are the only one who has reason to harm us." He nodded decisively at his nephew, who vanished back into his room, presumably in search of a weapon.

Of all the cursed luck. Now the odds had changed, for it was three against one. Or four against one, if you counted the inn-wife, and Devlin did not doubt that she was the deadliest of all present. And he had no wish to battle the nobles, who did not deserve to die for their foolish trust.

There was but one way to regain control of the situation. "I will prove that I mean you no harm," Devlin said, catching and holding the gaze of Lord Dalkassar. With his free hand he reached under his shirt and took hold of the leather lanyard he wore. He fumbled for a moment till he found the ring, and then with a quick jerk he broke the lanyard and the ring came loose in his hand.

He slipped the ring on his finger as he said, "I swear to you, in the name of the Seven Gods, that I mean you no harm, for I am the Chosen One."

As he said the words, the ring began to glow with a brilliant red light, filling the narrow dark hallway until it was near as bright as midday. The wounded robber seemed to shrink in on himself.

The nephew Eylif gasped, and behind him he heard the inn-wife curse. But all of Devlin's attention was fixed on the older nobleman.

"My lord Chosen," the old man said, his eyes clear as the last vestiges of the drugs faded from his mind. "How may I serve you?"

Eight

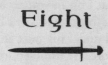

DEVLIN SAT IN THE COMMON ROOM, HIS ELBOWS ON
the table, cradling his head in his hands. The unnatural
energy which had sustained him through the fight had
drained away as soon as the villains had been disarmed—
almost as swiftly as the glow from the ring had faded. Now
he was left weary, and wishing there was someone, anyone,
to whom he could turn over responsibility for this mess.

But he had declared himself and seized command, and
now he must live with what he had done. And what he
must still do.

His eyes were closed, but he could feel the heat of the
inn-wife's gaze. He and the lord's nephew Eylif had
brought her to the common room and bound her in a
chair, and then done the same for the young man Paavo,
whom Devlin had knocked unconscious earlier. A bucket
of water had brought him back to wakefulness, but after a
quick glance at his mother, the young man had held his
tongue.

Lars, the wounded swordsman, had been dragged to
his mother's room and flung upon the bed. His mother
had shown no interest in her injured son, so it had fallen

to Devlin, assisted by the boy Jan, to bind up the wound which he had inflicted. The cut was not deep, but it was deep enough. The intestines had been slashed, and Devlin knew that he would not last for long. Still, he was capable of causing trouble, and so Devlin had taken the precaution of binding the outlaw to the bed, despite the man's curses.

Hinges squealed with the sound of rusting metal as the front door was opened and then shut. A single set of footsteps crossed the hall and entered the room. So Eylif had returned alone.

"Your coachman, he is dead?" Devlin asked, without opening his eyes.

"Yes, sir, I mean, my lord Cho—"

"Devlin will serve," he said, raising his head and finally opening his eyes. So another innocent had died because Devlin's heroics had come too late to save him. "I have no use for fancy titles."

Devlin looked around at the unlikely tableau. Hulda glared defiance, while her son Paavo merely looked scared—and far younger than the eighteen years he claimed to possess.

Lord Dalkassar had taken time to dress himself, in court silks no less, and sat calmly across the room from the villains. His nephew had moved to stand by his uncle's shoulder, refusing the offered seat. He rocked back and forth on his heels, as if too excited to stay in one place.

Devlin's own seat was squarely in the middle of the room. His gaze swept dispassionately over the innkeeper and her son on his right, and the two nobles on his left.

"Chosen One," Lord Dalkassar said, rising and giving a formal bow. "I must thank you for my life, and that of my nephew."

Devlin shook his head. "Only the Gods may give or take a life."

"But you were their instrument."

The praise made Devlin uncomfortable, because he knew he did not deserve it. A wiser man would have sensed the trap before it was sprung. A hero anointed by the Gods would have seen through the villains' disguise at once, and not consumed the tainted food. A true hero would have saved the hapless coachman.

"Say rather that you owe your lives to Captain Drakken, who sent me along this road to seek out the forest bandits who are said to prey on travelers. And to my aversion to certain herbs, which made me immune to the sleeping draught. When this one came to dispatch me"—Devlin cast a dark glance at Pavvo—"I was awake, and could defend myself. Fearing that you were the true targets, I sought out your rooms and found Lars about to enter. The rest you know."

Lord Dalkassar's brow wrinkled. "If you are hunting for bandits, then where are the rest of your men?"

"I came alone," Devlin said. "Bandits who know the terrain can easily avoid mounted troops, but what threat could one poor farmer pose?"

"But even the Chosen One is no match for a troop of bandits," Eylif blurted out. "I mean no disrespect, of course."

The young noble spoke the truth. The Chosen One had no special powers. If he had been confronted by armed bandits, then driven by the Geas, Devlin would have no choice but to fight until he was killed. He would have the satisfaction of knowing that he had fulfilled his oath, and he would have achieved the oblivion he craved.

But Fate had played a cruel game with him.

"It does not matter, for there are no robbers in the forest. Those that I seek are within these walls," Devlin said.

Disgust filled him as he looked at the inn-wife, and Devlin spat on the floor in rejection of her hospitality. In Duncaer such a gesture could touch off a blood feud, but in this case it was only fitting that he express his utter contempt.

"The Guard has long suspected that these robbers were no ordinary band of desperate souls. Their targets were carefully picked, travelers who had coin, but were not sufficiently wealthy or powerful that their disappearance would cause the King to take notice. Those who were traveling on confidential affairs, or whose arrival was not expected, also fell victim to these mysterious disappearances. A robber band does not have that knowledge, but an innkeeper? Who better to know the affairs of her guests?"

"My lord," Hulda said, ignoring Devlin and addressing her pleading words to Lord Dalkassar. "I do not know what this man is saying, or why he is accusing me. I am but a poor widow. My only crime is that I trusted my sons too much. I swear to you I did not know that Lars intended to harm you. He must have gone mad, and convinced Paavo to follow his lead."

"Enough," Devlin growled.

"The Chosen One is correct," Lord Dalkassar said. "It was not Lars or Paavo who prepared the food we ate."

"But I know nothing of a sleeping draught. They must have put it in the food without my knowledge. I ate that food as well. That is why I slept so soundly. I only awakened when I heard a voice call out." Her voice cracked, as if with tears. "When I came upon the struggle, I was certain that Lars was only trying to defend you. I knew nothing of this evil, I swear it."

Her words struck a chord with Lord Dalkassar, and he appeared troubled. His nephew was less troubled, but then again, he had been the one to find the body of the coachman. No doubt he had little sympathy left.

"What say you, Paavo? Is your mother telling the truth?" Devlin asked.

Paavo licked his lips, then looked at his mother. Under her fierce glare he seemed to shrink in on himself, and he hung his head as he replied. "I don't know. I don't remember anything."

"Nothing?"

"Nothing."

Devlin felt his frustration rising. He was convinced that the two were guilty not only of tonight's misdeeds, but of far worse crimes. And yet, what could he promise them to make them talk? They must know that their lives were hanging in the balance. Lars, as the one who had tried to murder a nobleman, would have to pay with his life. But the other two might escape with their skins intact.

He knew with bone-deep certainty that these two were guilty, and deserved to die, but he had no proof. All he had were his own suspicions, and those were not enough.

But there was one person whom they had yet to question.

"Fetch the boy Jan," Devlin said to Eylif.

He had not known what to do with the lad, whose youth made him the only innocent member of this family. In the end, he had settled for locking Jan in a storeroom, lest he be tempted to try and help his brother Lars escape. Devlin had no fear that the boy would try to run away. Where could he go? This was his home, and these foul creatures the only family he knew.

The boy came into the room, scuffling his feet. He was

pale, and his eyes were swollen as if he had been crying, but he lifted his head and met Devlin's gaze.

"Come here," Devlin said, pitching his voice low as if the boy were a frightened animal.

Jan came over and stood between his mother and Devlin. He darted nervous glances at his mother, seeking reassurance, but she had no words for her youngest son.

"Look at me," Devlin said. "Jan, you know that your brothers tried to kill Lord Dalkassar and his nephew tonight."

The boy nodded. "Aye," he said in a quiet voice.

"Did you know they would do this?"

Another quick nod.

"And how did you know? They have done this before, haven't they? Other travelers, who came for the night and never left."

Jan's eyes went wide, and he began to tremble.

"I know this is painful but you must tell us."

"Say nothing," Hulda urged.

"Speak the truth. You are a good lad and you know this is wrong. Tell me what they have done."

Jan's shoulders slumped in defeat. "Aye. They have done this many times before."

Devlin felt a savage burst of satisfaction. At last, here was the proof he needed.

"I am sorry, Ma," Jan said, turning to face his mother.

"You viper! You are no son of mine," she cried. She raised one arm and swung it, smashing her fist into the boy's jaw.

Jan flew back, and his head hit the fireplace with a sickening crack. Devlin leapt to his feet, but it was already too late. The boy's crumpled body lay on the floor, blood oozing from his skull. Frantically, Devlin pressed his fingers to the slender throat, then pressed his ear to the boy's chest. Nothing. He lifted his head, starting at the chest, willing it to rise and fall, but it was over. The boy was dead.

"What have I done?" he whispered.

Lord Dalkassar had risen to his feet. "Is he grievously wounded?"

"He is dead."

Lord Dalkassar's face darkened with anger. "Kinslayer," he said.

Devlin flinched, then realized that Dalkassar was berating Hulda.

"Foul creature who kills her own child," Lord Dalkassar continued. "I could not imagine worse evil."

Devlin rose, his gaze locked on Hulda. "I will see you hang for this. You and your sons."

"You would have killed us anyway," Hulda replied, still defiant.

"Yes. But now I will enjoy it."

"After that, there is little to tell. I buried the boy, and hanged the inn-wife and her second son the next dawn. By then the eldest son had bled to death, having ripped open his own wounds trying to free himself from his bonds. I sent the lord's nephew to fetch the magistrate from Skarnes. The magistrate brought laborers, and I stayed just long enough to see the work was in hand."

Devlin Stonehand, the Chosen One, shrugged his shoulders, as if dismissing the incident, then reached down to pick up his tankard. Two quick swallows drained what was left.

Captain Drakken stared at him, wondering how he could sit so calmly before her. The first reports she had received from Skarnes had been so horrific that she had instructed the guards at each gate that when the Chosen One returned he was to be brought before her without delay, no matter what hour of day or night. And yet here he was, his eyes as dispassionate and his voice as even as if he were recounting a minor skirmish with an alley thief.

She lifted the pitcher of citrine. "Another?"

He nodded.

As she poured, she took the opportunity to study his face. The Chosen One was weary from his journey, and yet that alone did not account for his calm. He had looked much the same before she had sent him on this fool's errand that had taken such a bizarre turn. She wondered if this was simply the resilience of youth, or if somehow the horrors he had witnessed had no power to touch him.

"I understand you found several bodies?" she prompted.

He took another sip of his drink, then narrowed his eyes. "More than several. One-and-twenty by the morning I left, but the magistrate's men had just found a second pit. And those are only the ones they found. A hundred men could dig for a hundred days, and you would still never be sure that you had found all there was to discover."

"Evil," she said, as a cold chill ran through her.

"Evil indeed."

"But what made you suspect the inn-wife?"

"It was not suspicion but merely good fortune that I was immune to her potions. And bad luck for her that I happened along that night. If I had come a day sooner, or a day later, I might have stayed there unscathed. The Myrkan nobles were her true targets. She only went after me because I had seen them there, and might raise awkward questions about their disappearance."

"Lord Dalkassar did not call it luck. His letter was effusive in his praise."

"Lord Dalkassar is grateful to be alive," Devlin countered. "And I will wager the missive the magistrate sent was no paean of praise."

Indeed it had not been. The magistrate's letter had been scathing, furious that Devlin had passed sentence and executed justice in the King's name without waiting for the magistrate to arrive. Never mind that such was the right of the Chosen One. The magistrate felt, perhaps with some justification, that if the villains had been kept alive then they might have been persuaded to reveal the full details of their crimes, and where their victims had been buried.

But in her heart, Captain Drakken knew that she would have done the same as Devlin. The inn-wife and her grown sons had deserved to die. Preserving their lives, even for a few days, seemed obscene in light of what they had done.

"The magistrate was distressed, but I'm sure he has had time to reflect on the wisdom of what you have done."

"I would have stayed to help, but they would have none of it. As if being Chosen One made me too grand to dig in the dirt," Devlin offered unexpectedly.

At every turn, Devlin deprecated his rank and accomplishments. It was as if he felt that he did not deserve such things. She added this tidbit to the storehouse of knowledge she had accumulated about the man.

This Chosen One was a puzzle indeed. The other Chosen she had known had reveled in their rank, even knowing that they were despised. The last Chosen, Gudbrand, had been a drunkard, and Asfid, who served before, had been a gambler. They had taken full advantage of their privileges, in their short careers. For like all of the Chosen in the last decade, neither had lasted longer than a season.

This man was different, and it had nothing to do with his humble origins. Rather she sensed a core of steel inside him, an inner strength to match the drive of the Geas and the power of the Chosen One's office. Her instincts said she could trust him, and yet her long years of service in the Guard had taught her to be cautious. Court politics was a deadly game, even for one who had achieved the rank of Guard Captain. This Chosen One was an unknown quantity, who could be of help, or set all her schemes at naught.

"I am grateful that the killings will end," she said. "But you did me no favors. If you had encountered a well-armed band of robbers, I might have been able to convince the King to allow the Guard to patrol the royal roads."

"I would rather have faced a band of robbers any day than the horrors I found," he said flatly. "I did not choose what happened. They did."

His eyes flashed with anger, and she knew she had offended him. She sought to lighten the mood. "You did well," she said. "Although I will think twice the next time I stay in an inn."

Devlin smiled so briefly that it might have been only her imagination. "In Duncaer we have no such customs as inns. I now see the wisdom of our ways."

This, too, she filed away, to think about later. She wished she had questioned him more closely when he first appeared in Kingsholm. But she hadn't really expected him to survive the Choosing Ceremony. No one had. And then when he was picked, she'd expected that he would prove as useless as his predecessors. So what need had she to learn of him?

But Devlin was a survivor. He had the scars to prove it; she had seen them herself. He had survived the Choosing Ceremony. And then he had survived the inn-wife's hospitality, as so many before him had not. She wanted to find out what else he had survived, but he had made it quite clear that he would not answer any questions about his past. And she could not risk alienating him by pressing him for answers.

Was Devlin typical of his people? She had scoured the King's court to find what experts there were on the Caerfolk, but their store of knowledge had proven pitifully small, and often contradictory. Few people had made the long journey to Duncaer in the years since its conquest. Despite nearly fifty years of occupation by royal troops, and a government controlled by functionaries from Jorsk, Duncaer was no closer to being assimilated into the Kingdom than it had been at the start of the occupation. The people of Duncaer clung stubbornly to their own traditions, and as long as they paid their taxes, the King left them in peace.

Still, she did know a few things, such as that Devlin Stonehand was almost certainly not the name this man had been born with. The Caerfolk had names that changed to reflect their owner's lives. By rights Devlin should have introduced himself by giving his birth name, trade, and the place where he resided. A formal introduction called for the names of his parents, and if married, equal honors to his wife and her family, and any children they might have.

And yet he had given but two names. One courtier had told her that this was simply a short name, used by those who had the most contact with Jorskians, and had adopted some of their customs.

This information was contradicted by a retired lieutenant, who had served in the occupying army. According to her, such a lack of names indicated a man who had been exiled for his crimes, or who had chosen to deliberately separate himself from society.

So which was he, this man who sat so calmly under her gaze, sipping at the tankard of citrine as if washing the road dust from his throat was his only concern? And how could she trust him, until she knew the truth? Or would she have to wait until he learned to trust her, and confided in her of his own accord?

Judging from the stubborn set of his jaw, that day might never come.

She sighed, and he apparently took that as a sign, for he rose to his feet. "I thank you for your hospitality," he said. "If you have no more questions, then I would seek my quarters. Even with the borrowed horse, it has been a long journey."

Captain Drakken nodded. "Of course. Do not forget to give the Royal Steward a list of your expenses, and he will reimburse you. Court is in session, so barring a new crisis that requires your attention, you will be expected to attend the major functions."

"Then I must hope I am soon called away," he said, with no trace of sarcasm.

"Be careful. Court intrigue can be lethal, and now that you have returned, there will be those that seek to use you, for good or for ill," she warned.

"They can but try," he said.

Nine

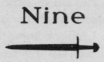

IN THE WEEK SINCE HIS RETURN, DEVLIN HAD DONE his best to avoid the royal court and its denizens. The one exception had been the weekly court dinner, where his presence had been mandated by custom. That dinner had proven even more uncomfortable than the first. Now, rather than ignoring him, the younger members of the court sought him out, ostensibly to praise his success. But he knew they meant only to mock him, and were competing among themselves to see who could deliver the most elegantly veiled insult.

He knew that many would be pleased if he simply stayed in his chamber all day and night, as if he were a tool that could be placed on a shelf until it was needed again. But he was a man, not a tool—no matter what he had done, or what the Geas had done to him. He could not sit idly in that room, waiting and thinking. Not when every time he closed his eyes he saw the faces of his dead. And now they had a new face to join them, as young Jan joined his accusers.

He took to exploring the palace grounds. He found the practice yards and watched the guards as they trained, finding an echo of familiarity in their ordered exercises and calm discipline. Though the weapons differed, the discipline was the same, and he knew Cerrie would have found kindred spirits there. Watching as they practiced with their short swords brought to mind the fight in the inn.

An axe was no weapon for a fight in such a confined space. It had been luck that had won that battle, not skill. But perhaps there was a way to tip luck in his favor, next time. He had not time to learn the sword, but there were other weapons that could be used close in. Weapons that he had once known, and could learn again.

Devlin paid another visit to the forge of Master Timo, the Royal Armorer. His reception this time was chilly, as he had known it would be. Yet Master Timo's skill was widely praised, and as the Royal Armorer he could be trusted to craft the weapons, and to keep silent about their existence. Until Devlin had a chance to regain his skill, it was best that no one know what he was planning. So he had invoked the power of his office to insist that the smith forge the knives to his specifications.

Two days later Devlin inspected the first of the knives that had been crafted, and pronounced himself satisfied. Master Timo promised the others would be ready within the day.

Returning to his chamber, he entered, then paused. Someone had been there, for a uniform had been carefully laid out upon the bed. A piece of parchment tied with a ribbon lay next to it.

The ribbon was silk, tied in an intricate knot meant to display the sender's skill at this royal art. One stroke with the new knife put an end to the foolishness, and Devlin unrolled the parchment and began to read.

"His Grace Duke Gerhard, King's Champion, General of the Royal Army, Defender of the Throne, invites you to witness an exhibition of skill at arms, in a courtly duel against the challengers from Selvarat. At the third hour, in the arms salon."

A courtly duel. No doubt it was nothing more than a few overdressed nobles, posturing with their swords. He released the end of the scroll, and it curled up in his hand. He began to crumple it, as he had discarded all previous invitations.

Yet something made him pause. He remembered Captain Drakken's warning about court intrigue. This duel would give him a chance to observe the members of the court, when their attention was on something other than his presence. And should Duke Gerhard suffer an ignominious loss, Devlin wanted to be there to bear witness. There had been something about the Duke that he had disliked from their very first meeting. It would be a pleasure to see such a one get his comeuppance.

At the appointed hour Devlin made his way to the salon of arms. He had discovered the salon earlier in the week, during his restless wanderings. It had been empty then, and he had spent a few moments marveling that so much expensive glass should be put to such a purpose.

The arms room was designed as a rectangle within a rectangle. The center rectangle was fifty paces in length and twenty paces in width, and its wooden floor was lightly dusted with fine white sand. Stone pillars linked together by finely wrought iron chains separated this practice court from the observation gallery that formed the perimeter of the room. Light streamed in from windows set high up in one wall, adding to the brilliance of the torches mounted on the pillars. All four walls were paneled with glass mirrors to twice the height of a man.

But he had not reckoned on the full effect. Now, with the room filled with richly dressed courtiers, the mirrors multiplied their reflections over and over, till he was nearly dizzy. From a corner of his eye he spied movement and turned suddenly, only to realize that he had been startled by the reflections of those who stood across the room.

Devlin turned left, and began to circulate around the room, receiving a few curious glances as people recognized the uniform of the Chosen One. But as he had expected, the forthcoming spectacle outweighed the novelty of his presence. Helping himself to a goblet of straw-colored wine from the tray of a passing servant, he continued his circuit. Snatches of conversation came to his ears.

"And that is why Lady Helga has repudiated the marriage—"

"No, no, that was his father. The son has never—"

"A petty noble from Myrkan. No one of importance. I daresay the court would never have noticed if he was gone."

At this Devlin pricked up his ears, realizing his recent errand was the topic of discussion. Turning his head, he identified the speaker as a plump elderly noblewoman, in conversation with a middle-aged man. The crowd swirled around him, and he discreetly edged nearer.

"And how humiliating to be rescued from an innkeeper. Not that I haven't had an encounter or two with an amorous inn-wife myself. But never one where I required rescuing," the nobleman said with a snicker.

"Baldur, you miss my point," the noblewoman said, tapping her companion's arm for emphasis. "It is we who are humiliated. The man is a foreigner. A commoner, fit only for public brawling. I would not have him as a servant, and yet now we must call him my lord, and give him the precedence accorded to the Chosen One. What was Captain Drakken thinking? He should never have been allowed to petition the Gods. In the old King's day this would never have happened. Someone should remind our King that Captain Drakken takes too much on herself."

"Lady Vendela, if you were still a King's councilor, I am sure this outrage would never have happened. But perhaps there is a way to turn this to our advantage. Surely after this debacle, the King will see how foolish this has become, and agree there is no need for the post of Chosen One."

Lady Vendela muttered something too low for Devlin to hear. Was she agreeing with this Baldur? He ventured a step closer, but the courtiers who had screened his view chose to move on, and suddenly he was in clear view of the pair.

Baldur caught sight of him first and whispered in the ear of Lady Vendela, who turned to look at Devlin. Devlin returned her glare steadily, and her face turned pale with anger or perhaps shame. After a long moment, he turned on his heel and walked away.

Silver bells rang, and at that signal, the courtiers began to gather around the perimeter of the practice area. Devlin positioned himself near the center of the bottom end, with his right side against a pillar. The space to his left was empty.

For the first time he noticed that three chairs had been set up at the top of the square. As the silver bells rang again, King Olafur appeared and took his place in the center seat. A young girl came and sat on his right, while a tall man dressed in a dark green brocaded robe took the seat to his left.

He recognized the foreigner as Count Magaharan, the Ambassador from Selvarat, who had been an honored guest at the last court dinner. The girl must be Princess Ragenilda, the King's only child and heir. From this distance it was hard to read expressions, but he got the impression of a solemn child.

Duke Gerhard then stepped into the square. "On behalf of our noble King Olafur, I bid you welcome. And we thank Count Magaharan for allowing his personal guards to participate in this exhibition of martial skills."

The Count rose and bowed to those assembled, who applauded softly in recognition of his contribution to the afternoon's entertainment.

Duke Gerhard stepped out of the square, and was replaced by a woman wearing the blue uniform of the Royal Army. "The first match will be between Vidkun of Jorsk and Teodoro of Selvarat, using the light swords."

The two combatants entered the square, bowed to the King and his guests, then turned to face each other. The dueling mistress stepped back a few paces, but remained in the square so she could observe the action.

The combatants drew their swords and saluted each other.

"Begin," the dueling mistress ordered.

The swordsmen began to circle around each other, their long slender swords flashing as they probed for an opening. Each parry was countered by a block, so smoothly that they might have been performing an elaborate dance.

"Only second-rank swordsmen," he heard someone complain. "It will be ages before the skilled fighters take the floor."

Around him, the courtiers began to drift away from the practice square, far more intent on resuming their conversations or seeking out acquaintances than they were in watching the duel. But Devlin remained, fascinated by the spectacle. He had seen sword practice many times before, but never had he seen anyone use swords of this type. At least two handspans longer than the broadsword with which he was familiar, the swords were incredibly thin and flexible. Light enough that the swordsmen could perform complex patterns with dazzling speed, and yet resilient enough that when the swords crashed together, they did not break.

He ached to get his hands on one of them, to see how it was made. How did they sharpen the edge without weakening the mettle? Or was the edge only sharpened for part of its length? Perhaps it was merely the point that was lethal, for the fighters' tactics seemed focused on point-first lunges rather than on the heavy killing stroke of a broadsword.

"Third point! Selvarat!" The dueling mistress called out, pointing to the foreign challenger.

The fighters broke apart. The foreign challenger raised his sword in victory while the Jorskman lowered his sword and bowed low in acknowledgment of his defeat.

A faint scattering of applause was heard as the fighters exited the square. The next pair, two women carrying short swords and round shields, took their places.

Devlin felt his attention begin to wane, as the short sword was nothing new to him. He watched for a few moments. The fighters were very good, but they lacked the indefinable spark of greatness. Cerrie could have defeated either of them without breaking a sweat.

It was interesting that the officials and duelists were from the Royal Army, which drew its officers from the ranks of the nobility, rather than from the City Guard, which was based on merit, and open to all. Did the King favor the Royal Army over the Guard? Perhaps that explained some of the remarks he had overheard earlier.

Or was it simply that Duke Gerhard was head of the Royal Army and had chosen his own to compete this day? How could Devlin tell what was significant and what was not in the morass of court politics and ancient loyalties? The members of the court had spent their lives learning the game of power, forming allegiances and learning whom they could trust and whom they should fear.

What Devlin needed was an impartial guide to the court, someone who could explain its factions. But whom could he trust? Captain Drakken had her own concerns and goals, which would color any advice she gave. And yet there were few others who would deign to exchange greetings with him, let alone trust him enough to exchange confidences about the other members of the court.

There was naught to do but see what he could learn on his own. Devlin turned away from the square and began to make his way through the crowd.

"Chosen One! Devlish Rockfist, or whatever your name is."

He turned, and saw Master Dreng standing near the mirrored wall. The court magician had a glass of red wine in one hand, and with the other he gestured imperiously for Devlin to approach.

Devlin remained where he was, ignoring the gesture. He still remembered the day of the Choosing Ceremony, and the role the mage had played. In other circumstances, a mage of such skill would inspire respect and a healthy touch of fear, but Devlin felt only anger as he contemplated the man who had used his craft to place the loathsome Geas upon him.

Seeming to realize that Devlin had no intention of coming at his call, Master Dreng excused himself from his companions and approached.

"Chosen One."

"Mage," Devlin said flatly.

"I must congratulate you on your survival, although you have cost me another wager." The mage's tone was light, but he inspected Devlin from head to foot, as if he was trying to divine the secret of Devlin's survival.

And perhaps he could. He was a master mage, after all. Who knew what he could do? Devlin repressed a shudder at the thought.

"I regret if my survival distresses you," he said. "I will try to be more considerate in the future."

Master Dreng blinked. "I believe you are mocking me."

"No doubt an unusual experience. But there is a first time for everything," Duke Gerhard said, as he joined them. "After all, who would have thought that one of the Caerfolk would be Chosen? What other new wonders will there be under the sun? Perhaps pigs will fly, or horses begin to sing."

The back of his neck prickled, and Devlin felt his muscles tense. Something about the King's Champion made him uneasy. Perhaps it was the way his cold green eyes belied his seemingly affable smile. Or maybe it was the way he seemed to regard Devlin as a nuisance, someone whose presence was unworthy of his notice. Or it could be simply Devlin's own ingrained dislike for the man who led the Royal Army. After all, the troops that garrisoned Duncaer called this man General, and followed his bidding.

"The report of your adventure in Astavard has reached even my ears," Duke Gerhard said. "What a formidable test of skill that was. An old woman, and two beardless young men? You are lucky you escaped with your life."

Devlin felt his anger rise. What did this posturing noble know of fighting for one's life? All of his battles had been fought on the sands of the practice floor. "The inn-wife and her family murdered over three dozen innocent travelers. What I did was justice. No more and no less."

"Of course," Duke Gerhard said, but his tone was disbelieving.

"And as for skill, there is a world of difference between a pretty duel and a fight for one's life. I would match my skill against anyone's on the killing floor," he declared rashly. Even as he said the words, he knew they were a hollow boast. His skills were no match for those of a master swordsman.

Duke Gerhard's eyes glittered. "Perhaps that can be arranged. I have always wanted to match blades with one of the Caerfolk."

"I am at your service," Devlin replied. His heart leapt with a fatalistic joy as he realized the Duke was seriously considering his offer. With luck he could goad the Champion into making a killing stroke, ending Devlin's torment. Devlin took a step closer so that he stared the King's Champion full in the face. "What better place than here, what better time than now?"

"No!" Master Dreng interjected, grasping Devlin by the shoulder and pulling him backward.

Devlin had forgotten about the mage. He glared fiercely at Master Dreng, as did the King's Champion.

"No, my lords, you must see reason," the magician said hastily. "The Chosen One is spellbound, under Geas. If he engages in a duel, I cannot predict the outcome. The risk to you, as the King's Champion will prevent him from defending himself. Your Grace, you must see how unseemly this is."

Duke Gerhard nodded. "Of course, Master Dreng. I was but toying with the idea, but naturally such a challenge could not be accepted. Not in light of the Chosen One's duty . . . and, err, skills."

Devlin felt a surge of disappointment as he realized that his wish was not to be granted. He allowed Master Dreng to lead him away from the confrontation, and when the magician thrust a goblet in his hand, he drained it in a single gulp.

"You were lucky today," Master Dreng said. "Even I would not lightly antagonize Duke Gerhard. The man is a master of the sword and a cold-blooded strategist. He has never lost a duel. Ever. That is why he is the King's Champion."

"It is not over between us," Devlin said. "Someday I will test his skill, and then we shall see."

Ten

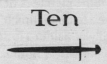

THE DUELING EXHIBITION WAS BUT ONE OF THE DI-
versions provided for the members of the royal court. The
courtiers' days were packed full, from morning until the
small hours of the night. Even Devlin came in for his share
of invitations, and slowly he began to accept a few. It was
not that he sought out diversion, for in truth most court
functions left him bewildered and bored. But rather he had
come to realize that his only hope of achieving the oblivion
he desired lay in finding a challenge that the Geas would let
him pursue. Such knowledge would not come to him while
he skulked in his room or haunted the low taverns. Instead
he would find it in the gossip of the courtiers, and their
tales of the troubles that beset the fringes of the empire.

Much to his surprise, Devlin found that the courtiers
gossiped quite freely within his hearing, seeing no reason
to conceal their secrets from him. Perhaps it was because
they realized he knew too little of the working of the court
to make use of what he learned. Or perhaps it was simply
that they did not see him as a person at all. In their eyes, he
was as invisible as one of the servants, or a piece of furniture. A tool, not a man to be reckoned with.

This day was no exception, and as he strolled through the crowds gathered on the grassy Queen's field to watch the races, he overheard snatches of conversation. But since he knew only a few of the members of the court, much of what he heard made no sense to him. It did him little good to know that the family of Baldur Hurlafson was rumored to be penniless, or that Mistress Botilda of the silk trader's guild had taken a lover half her age, installing him in her great new mansion on the eastern hill.

Of slightly more interest was the news that a young woman named Dageid had fled the capital after killing her opponent in an illegal duel. Should he ever encounter this Dageid, perhaps the Geas would allow him to challenge her to a fight, in the name of justice. If she was half as skilled as they claimed, he would win a mercifully quick death.

Devlin watched the first race, but found he had little interest in this artificial sport. The horses were strange, fragile-looking creatures, and their riders scarcely more than children. The races were as far removed from real horsemanship as the courtly duels were from a battlefield. And yet the crowds around him cheered passionately, as if this were a matter of life and death. It made no sense to him, and he resumed his wandering progress.

He strolled by one of the canopied tents on the south side of the field, erected to provide shelter from the heat of the sun. A few nobles stood within, sipping wine punch and talking desultorily. He overheard a woman musing that it was a waste to bet against the Countess of Rosmaar, for no one dared risk her wrath by defeating her favorite stallion. He had been beaten only once, but the owner of the winning horse had found his satisfaction brief. The Countess had thrown her support to his enemies, and he soon found himself friendless at court and forced to resign his seat on the King's Council.

Devlin had been warned that court politics could be a deadly game, and this tale seemed to bear out the truth of those words. He kept his ears open, but heard nothing else of interest until he heard his own name.

"Isn't that him? The Chosen One?" a young man asked.

"Yes," another replied. The second speaker sounded older.

Devlin paused, his back to the tent. He shaded his eyes, and scanned over the assembled crowds, looking for the green pavilion where he had been told he could find his host.

"Doesn't it give you the shivers when you see him? I can't imagine speaking to him, can you? It is as if you are talking to one already dead," the young man observed.

"Caution, he may hear us."

Wise advice, but the young man ignored it. "But you must admit it is strange. Alfrim said as much to me, at the last court dinner. How can we be expected to take pleasure in our repast, when he is there? When one speaks to him, it is as if one speaks to the Dread Lord himself. One is almost tempted to give him a message to carry into the dark realm."

The words struck an angry chord within Devlin, and he abruptly turned on his heel. He gazed into the tent and saw two men standing together. As Devlin caught his eye, the young lordling flushed red, and Devlin knew he had identified the speaker. Devlin made his way slowly into the tent.

"Your name?"

"Miklof. Miklof Serikson," the young man said, with a gulp. His fingers were white where they gripped the wine cup.

"I will remember your name, and give your greetings to Lord Haakon when I join his realm," Devlin said.

The older man drew in his breath with a hiss. "My cousin meant no insult—"

"Then he should take more care in what he says," Devlin answered. "My service prevents me from answering any insults to my person, but there are others who are not so bound, and who will be less forgiving than I."

Miklof now looked ill. No doubt he was contemplating the folly of having mocked both the Chosen One and the Death God. He opened his mouth to apologize, but Devlin was in no mood to hear whatever excuses he might make, and turned on his heel and left.

Leaving the courtiers behind, Devlin made his way through the crowds of commoners and merchants, until he reached the far side of the oval track and the fluttering flags he had spotted earlier. Here, on a slight rise, an elaborate pavilion had been set up, nearly fifty feet long, with cushioned seats for the assembled guests. Servants circulated among them, bearing trays of drinks and refreshments. Recognizing his uniform, a servant unfastened the silken rope as Devlin approached, allowing him to enter.

There was a roar of noise from the crowd, and Devlin looked over to see that the previous race had just finished.

Devlin made his way over to his host. Count Magaharan, the Ambassador from Selvarat, was a tall, ascetic-looking man, with shoulder-length brown hair pulled back in a silver clasp. Rather than court robes, he wore a simple tunic of pale green silk and dark brown trousers. But there was no mistaking his power. It was there in his eyes, and in the way that all present were turned so that at least some of their attention was focused on the ambassador.

The Count was conversing with Councilor Arnulf and

another noble, but when he saw Devlin, he abruptly broke off his conversation and came forward.

"Chosen One, I am pleased you saw fit to accept my invitation," he said, smiling as if he and Devlin were old friends. "A beautiful day for the races, is it not?"

"The day is fine," Devlin replied. "And I thank you for your hospitality."

The Count took Devlin's arm and guided him to a spot near the front of the pavilion. "Here, we will have an unobstructed view of the next race," he said.

Count Magaharan snapped his fingers, and a servant came over. "Will you take wine?"

"Citrine." On such a hot day even a small amount of alcohol was certain to go to one's head, and Devlin needed to keep his wits about him if he was to learn anything of use.

"For myself as well."

The servant fetched them two pale crystal glasses of citrine. Devlin took a sip, for the sake of politeness.

"So, what do you think of the races so far?"

"An interesting custom," Devlin answered. "I have not seen their like."

Count Magaharan's eyebrows rose. "Truly? But surely you have horse races in your own province."

"Not like this," Devlin said, waving his right hand toward the starting line, where a half dozen horses were being maneuvered into position. "Duncaer is a rocky place, and we have little flat land for such things as races. Our horses are bred for endurance, and for making the best of poor trails. Our contests are tests of skill and stamina."

The Count frowned. "You do not know what you are missing. True racehorses are among the most noble of all animals, and in my country they are greatly prized. See there, the gray mare on the end, with the crimson rider?"

Devlin nodded.

"Is she not beautiful? Her sire was bred in Selvarat, and sent here as a gift from our Emperor to King Olafur, to celebrate the birth of his daughter Ragenilda. Many great racers have come from that line."

"A creature fit for nobles, for no other could afford to keep something that has no use," Devlin observed. "Those legs are too delicate for rough country, and breeding a horse to win at short sprints is of no use when a battle-trained mount is needed."

The Count gazed at him in horror. "You have no soul," Count Magaharan declared.

A shout went up, and Devlin turned to see that the race was under way. He was amazed by the fervor with which the crowds cheered their favorites. Even Count Magaharan was not immune, calling, "Fly, Wind Dancer, fly."

Devlin took another sip of citrine, and in a few moments the race was over, the gray mare loping over the finish line several horse lengths ahead of the rest. A few hissed, but most cheered to see the favorite win.

"See, I told you she was a champion," Count Magaharan declared.

"The Jorskians agree with you," Devlin said, nodding to indicate the crowds that had advanced to surround the winning horse and rider. "Your people and theirs must have much in common."

"Yes, though it took us until the time of Emperor Jeoffroi to realize the folly of our old enmity and to make peace."

"But you are allies, are you not?"

"Now, yes," Count Magaharan said. "But that was not always so. It was nearly a hundred years ago that we put aside our animosity, and joined with King Axel to defeat the Nerikaat alliance. It was a glorious campaign and since that time we have been the firmest of friends."

Devlin shrugged. It was Jorsk's present that concerned him, not the past. His gaze wandered around the pavilion, noting those members of the court whom he recognized.

"Surely such a great event is still part of your history. You must have learned it as a child," Count Magaharan said.

"Their history, not mine," Devlin corrected. "I am of Duncaer."

"Ah yes. That is a province, to the south, is it not? I seem to recall it was annexed during the reign of the King's grandfather."

"It was conquered, not annexed." Even Devlin could hear the anger in his tone, and he took a deep breath to calm himself.

"And it seems you bear little love for those of Jorsk. So tell me, what is one of the conquered people doing as the Chosen One?"

Count Magaharan's tone was casual, but his dark eyes betrayed his keen interest, and Devlin knew that this was the reason why he had been invited to this event. Devlin was as much a mystery to the members of the court as they were to him. And in the Count's position as Ambassador, no doubt he wished to know as much as possible about his allies.

"Think of me as a mercenary," Devlin said.

"You must be the best-paid mercenary in history," the Count said, with a faint smile.

"Not yet. But I will be," Devlin added. Though the true payment he sought was not one the Count was likely to understand. And even if he tried to explain, he doubted he would be believed. How could anyone understand that the true reward he sought was not coin, but his own death? Only someone who had suffered as Devlin had would understand the impulse that drove him to seek his own destruction.

"I thank you for your hospitality," Devlin said. "But I have taken much of your time, so I will leave you now, to your other guests."

"The thanks is mine," Count Magaharan said. "I hope we can speak again someday."

"That is in the hands of the Gods," Devlin replied. And should Lord Haakon finally relent and accept Devlin's sacrifice, they would not meet again until Count Magaharan made his own journey to the Dread Lord's realm.

Three days after the races, Devlin received an urgent summons to attend the King's Council. The royal messenger made it clear that the summons brooked no delay, and Devlin speculated as to the cause as he accompanied the messenger through the palace. The council had been meeting daily now that the court was officially open, and yet his presence had never been requested before.

Could it be that they had an errand for him? An enemy that he could face? Any excuse to leave this strange and inhospitable place would be welcome.

Two guards in dress livery flanked the doors to the council chamber. Recognizing the Chosen One, or perhaps the authority of the royal messenger, they uncrossed their spears and opened the doors, bowing low as Devlin passed.

Devlin entered the room. The doors swung shut behind him.

"At last," a voice muttered, but Devlin did not know who had uttered the words.

His attention was fixed on King Olafur, who sat at the head of an oval table of richly polished heartwood. He had seen the King several times in the past weeks. But the King had barely acknowledged his existence. Until now. And as he had on their first meeting, Devlin found himself oddly disappointed by this man whom he had sworn to protect with his life. King Olafur was a man of average stature, with thinning blond hair and lines of perpetual worry on his face. Save for the golden circle on his brow he might have been any merchant or small farmer, facing hard times.

To the King's left sat Duke Gerhard, the King's Champion. To his right sat Countess Ingeleth, who was first among the King's councilors. Along the table sat a dozen other councilors and officials. He recognized the Royal Steward, and the gossipy Lord Baldur, whom he had overheard at the duel.

Captain Drakken was not there, but a lieutenant in the uniform of the Guard sat midway down the table.

The foot of the table held an empty chair.

Devlin took a step, then hesitated, realizing he did not know the courtesy and custom of this situation. Should he greet the King? Should he wait for the King to greet him? Was he expected to bow or to kneel in the fashion of the foreign courtiers?

The King gestured, a languid wave of one hand, and Devlin took this as a sign that he was to take a seat. He did so, with a slight nod of his head.

From the sour expression on Countess Ingeleth's face, he knew he had broken at least one of the rules of propriety. So be it. They had not sought him out for his advice on manners.

"Your Majesty summoned me?" he prompted.

King Olafur sighed, and rubbed his chin in thought.

"There is no need for this," an elderly councilor muttered.

Countess Ingeleth glared at the councilor, then turned her attention to Devlin.

"The King has received a petition from Greenhalt on Long Lake. Greenhalt is one of several small villages along the lake that make their living from fishing. It seems that something or someone is attacking the fisherfolk and devouring the fish in the lake. The villagers sent to Lord Brynjolf, the Baron of Esker, but he was unable to aid them, and so they have petitioned the King." Her tone was even, as if she were describing a minor nuisance.

"I tell you, it is all a ploy by that crafty Brynjolf. He's already behind in his taxes, and is hoping to use this as an excuse to avoid paying this year's harvest tax," the Royal Steward said. "This is a fool's errand. There is no creature. There is nothing wrong except lazy villagers and a feckless lord."

Well at least his opinion on the matter was clear.

"I don't understand why Lord Brynjolf doesn't send his own armsmen to take care of this, rather than come begging to the King," Lord Baldur said. "Surely even a petty lord can dispose of such a trifling disturbance."

The Guard lieutenant cleared his throat. "May I remind the councilor that Lord Brynjolf has already sent over half his armsmen to Ringstad, to help them patrol the border? The armsmen he has left are scarce enough to secure his own Barony."

"Indeed," Duke Gerhard said, with a touch of condescension, "there has been much restlessness along the borders. It is why I fear committing my own troops. Although, of course, should the King wish it, I would obey your royal command."

"No, no," the King said swiftly. "We need the Royal Army in garrison, ready for when our true foe shows his face. We cannot have them haring off all over the country. This creature could be an attempt to dilute our forces and distract us from the real danger."

Devlin leaned back in his chair, getting a grim pleasure as he observed the interplay of the court. He was learning more about allegiances in a few minutes than he had in the past fortnight. The councilors seemed stubbornly prepared to argue their positions, never mind that all present, including himself, knew what the answer would be.

"The Guard stands at your service," the lieutenant said. "I know Captain Drakken would approve of a plan to send a small party to investigate the problem, and to report their findings to the council."

Devlin did not like the sound of that. He did not want an escort. He did not want companionship of any sort. The guards would slow him down, and worse yet, their help might improve the chances of his survival.

"So now we have guards to spare? Only the other day, your Captain Drakken was in here arguing that we needed to fund more guards to keep the city secure. She will not thank you for making her look foolish," the Royal Steward said.

The lieutenant flushed.

"There is only the one monster in that one lake?" asked the woman on his left. "And no one has reported that it flies or hops on land?"

"It seems confined to the lake. So far," Countess Ingeleth said cautiously.

"Well then it is simple," the woman declared. "Instruct Lord Brynjolf to find other lands for his people, and if the creature wants that lake, leave him to it."

Devlin turned to stare at the woman. How could she be so callous? Didn't she realize what it would mean to these simple folk to give up their lands and their livelihoods? To lose the place where they had been born, where generations before them had lived and died? They would lose everything and be forced to become beggars, dependent on the charity of their lord and their countrymen. And from what he had seen, the charity of Jorskians would make cold comfort indeed.

"Enough," he said, rising to his feet. "There is no need to wrap it up in fine linen. We all know why I am here, and why the good steward there parted with ten golden disks in the King's name. If there is an evil creature in that lake, then it is the task of the Chosen One to destroy it."

As he said the words, he could feel the faint tickle of the Geas as its power stirred within his soul. He had committed himself to this quest, and unless a greater danger arose, nothing, save his own death, could stop him from seeking out the mystery of the lake creature.

"I am not certain this is wise—" the King began.

"I am." Devlin said shortly, ignoring the gasps that arose at his impertinence in interrupting the King.

His eyes swept the room, memorizing their expressions. Lady Ingeleth was calm, Lord Baldur appeared amused, and Duke Gerhard's face wore a subtle sneer. Only the face of the Guard lieutenant held any trace of sympathy—or understanding of what Devlin had committed himself to do.

"King Olafur. Gentle nobles. Is there anything more you can tell me about this creature?"

"I will send the reports to your chambers," Lady Ingeleth said.

"I thank you for your courtesy," he said. "And now I will away, to begin preparations. By your leave, Your Majesty."

He left the room without waiting for the King's response. He knew if he stayed he would be unable to hold his tongue, and would give vent to the contempt he felt for councilors who cared so little about the people they served. With the luck of the Gods this errand would be his last, and he would be free of these councilors and their ilk forever.

Lady Ingeleth had been as good as her word. She had sent along copies of the politely worded request from Lord Brynjolf, the Baron of Esker, and the less polished but more heartfelt pleas of the fisherfolk. The fisherfolk described the creature as a giant skrimsal, which seemed to be their name for a water serpent. Along with the petitions was a map of Esker, showing the location of Long Lake, with a circle marking the location of Greenhalt.

Devlin studied the documents with care, but learned little more than he had from the council session. The villagers were afraid. Their lord was concerned, but unable to help them.

The map proved more helpful. It showed that Esker lay to the northwest. He would have to travel along the Kalla River, through the province of Kalveland, and then cross another river before he reached Esker. His finger traced the route. Kingsholm was as far north as he had ever ventured, but the route did not look too hard. The country he would travel through was hilly, but that would be no challenge to one raised in the mountains of Duncaer.

Opening the cedar chest, he withdrew the saddlebags he had acquired on his last journey and placed them on the bed. Swiftly he began to pack. A spare uniform, two shirts, a set of smallclothes and several pairs of socks went into one saddlebag. In there, too, went spare bolts for the transverse bow, and a purse filled with the King's coins.

Into the other saddlebag went his cooking pot, utensils, and a firestone. He would draw upon supplies from the Guard's stores before he left.

A knock sounded at the door.

"Enter," he called.

The door opened, revealing the minstrel Stephen.

"Chosen One, I—" he began.

"I have no time for idle chatter," Devlin said. "You had best be on your way."

The minstrel flushed, but he raised his chin and came into the room. "I heard that you are leaving for Esker."

"You hear well."

"Then you will need a guide and companion. I am here to offer my services."

"I need no companion," Devlin said firmly. He did not need this young man, with his constant questions and absurd belief that the Chosen One was a mythic being. Especially when Devlin considered that anything he said or did was likely to prove fodder for the minstrel's songs. "If I need a guide, I will hire one when I reach Esker."

"But there is no need for that. I am of Esker. I know the roads and I know the people. With me as your guide, your journey will be faster."

The minstrel's words held a certain logic, but Devlin was not convinced. The advantages of the minstrel's presence were outweighed by the fear of having another person close to him for any length of time. Devlin had too many secrets to keep. He could not afford to get close to anyone, or to let anyone get close to him.

He opened his mouth to refuse, but instead heard himself say, "I accept your offer."

He closed his mouth with a snap. He could feel the Geas, asleep no longer. Its power had stirred to life once he had committed himself to this quest, and now it would not let him act to serve his own comfort and peace of mind. The Geas recognized only one priority, and that was the welfare of the Kingdom.

"You will not regret this," Stephen said, taking Devlin's hand and wringing it enthusiastically.

He was regretting it already. But he refused to explain to the minstrel that the Geas had been the one to accept him, not Devlin the man. There was no reason to reveal the extent of his weakness to another.

"You will need a horse," he said, instead.

Stephen nodded. "I had thought of that. I purchased a mount this afternoon, with what was left of Master Dreng's silver."

Had it ever occurred to the minstrel that Devlin might refuse? What had he been planning on doing then? Attempting to follow Devlin on his own? Skulking along the trail like a gangly wraith, waiting till Devlin changed his mind?

Had Devlin ever been that young or that hopeful? He tried, but could not remember such a time. There were less than ten years in age between himself and young Stephen, but that was as the suns counted. In terms of experience, Devlin was a thousand years older than the minstrel was, or ever would be.

"I will leave at first light. Meet me in the courtyard then, or I will set off on my own."

"I will be there," Stephen said, as he began backing out of the room. "And I thank you."

"You will not thank me when this is over," Devlin warned, but the minstrel had already disappeared.

Eleven

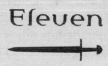

THE CHOSEN ONE ARRIVED AT THE ROYAL STABLES as the pale light of near dawn began to brighten the skies. If he was surprised to find that Stephen had preceded him, he made no sign. He waited calmly as the groom brought out his horse, then he inspected the horse from bridle to tail, lifting each hoof to check the fastening of the iron shoe. Tugging on the saddle to ensure it was tightly girthed, he then fastened two saddlebags to the front of the saddle and lashed on a sack of provisions and skins of water behind. Lastly a rolled blanket and cloak were tied to the back.

Stephen had already secured his own gear, but Devlin chose to inspect his mount as well, checking each strap and buckle. Stephen opened his mouth to protest, then shut it with a snap. There was no point in antagonizing the Chosen One. Not while he could still change his mind about allowing Stephen to accompany him.

They rode out of the palace and down to the docks, where they boarded a flat-bottomed river barge. Though the barge was only half-filled, a few words from Devlin in his role as Chosen One were sufficient to inspire the barge owner to begin the trip, though he cursed mightily under his breath.

They traveled downriver with the current for over a week. The passengers and crew ignored the Chosen One, a favor he returned. He also ignored Stephen's few attempts at conversation or comradeship, eating alone and spending most of his time checking and rechecking his weapons, or working on small scraps of leather that he was fashioning into a kind of harness. But when asked what the harness was for, he only grunted.

It was an inauspicious beginning for a glorious quest, and Stephen began to question the wisdom of his decision. Like most of the other residents of Kingsholm, Stephen had been astonished when the Chosen One had returned from his first errand still living, with barely a scratch to show for his adventures. Neither of the past two Chosen had lived through their first tasks. Though once the grim details began to emerge, Devlin's survival seemed less a matter of skill and more one of luck. And his feat could hardly compare to the glorious deeds of the past Chosen. Bringing cowardly murderers to justice was necessary, but not even the finest of minstrels could compose a glorious song about such a squalid affair.

On the other hand, the quest to defeat the creature of the lake had the hallmarks of a fine adventure. Whether Devlin defeated the creature or was killed in the attempt, it would make a glorious song—one which would win Stephen fame and the recognition he craved. For Stephen had found these months in the capital to be difficult. His talents for playing and singing, so highly praised in the province of Esker, seemed merely ordinary when compared to the skilled musicians of the capital. He needed something more to make him stand out.

He needed a song. A great song that other minstrels would play, spreading Stephen's name far and wide. And how better to write that song than to accompany the Chosen One on his journey and learn all about him? It was a good plan, but so far the Chosen One had refused to cooperate. Stephen could only hope that once free from the distractions of the river journey, Devlin would become more approachable.

After eight days, they disembarked at a small village. The rest of the passengers remained on the barge for the trip to the seaport of Bezek.

As they rode through Kalveland, Devlin did his best to ignore Stephen, speaking to him only when absolutely required. When afternoon wore into twilight, they found a small clearing and set up a camp for the night.

Devlin saw to their mounts, while Stephen, who had appointed himself as cook, prepared the evening meal, boiling preserved meat in water to soften it, then frying it with cut-up tubers. Devlin accepted his plate with barely a grunt of acknowledgment, and ate it with solemn concentration.

After the meal, Stephen took his lute from its case and began to tune it. Devlin frowned, but said nothing.

Devlin withdrew a piece of folded leather from one saddlebag and unfolded it to reveal a half dozen thin blades nestled within. Gathering the blades in one hand, he rose, then walked over to a young pine and scratched an X at eye level. He turned and walked away, stopping when he had reached fourteen paces. Then he turned back to face the tree.

Taking one knife in his right hand, he brought his hand up until it was next to his shoulder and let fly. The knife came to rest in the tree, about four feet from the ground.

An inch to the left and it would have missed the tree entirely.

Stephen watched, fascinated, his lute forgotten in his lap. He had never seen anything like it before. The second knife flashed through the air, turning end over end until the blade struck home. This shot was closer to the center, and slightly higher than the first. Four more knives flew through the air, the last one nearly on center.

"Well done!" Stephen said.

Devlin shook his head, as he walked over to retrieve the knives. "Too low. And off the mark by a handbreadth or more."

This time he held the knives in his right hand and prepared to throw with his left. The first shot went wild, missing the tree entirely. "Blast," Devlin muttered.

He gritted his teeth and tried again. This time he struck the tree, but with the haft of the knife, not the blade. The knife slid to the ground.

The third throw went better, and actually stuck in the tree. After he had thrown all six knives, Devlin retrieved them and began again. He practiced until the twilight faded and he could no longer see the target.

Returning to sit by the fire, Devlin began rubbing the first of the knives with a cloth, to remove the tree sap.

"May I see one?" Stephen asked.

Devlin flicked his hand, and the knife he had been cleaning embedded itself point first in the dirt next to Stephen's foot.

Stephen pulled the knife out and turned it over in his hands, marveling at its construction. In length it was similar to a dagger, but the blade was far narrower. And unlike a dagger, the blade had no hilt. Instead it was a seamless piece of metal, requiring Devlin to grip it between his fingers as he threw.

Stephen held it, as he had seen Devlin do, and aimed the knife at a nearby tree. He let it fly. The knife tumbled in the air and landed just a few feet from where he sat. Embarrassed, he rose to retrieve it, grateful that Devlin did not see fit to comment.

"I have heard of throwing knives, but never have I seen them used. You must be quite skillful."

Devlin shook his head. "Hardly. I barely managed to find the tree with my knives, and when I hit the mark it was luck not skill. And this is only a tree. A target that moves is quite a different thing. But with practice I can regain my old skills."

Those were more words than Devlin had said all day.

"You have used these before then?"

"A long time ago," Devlin said. "In Alvaren there are peacekeepers...I suppose you would call them guards. They practice with these, and when I was young and foolish I took a fancy to them as well. Ten years ago I could have hit that mark every time, with my eyes closed."

So Devlin had lived in Alvaren, the capital of Duncaer. And he had been friendly with the guards of that city. Perhaps that was why he was so comfortable around Sergeant Lukas and Captain Drakken. Certainly he had shown Captain Drakken more respect than he had shown anyone else.

"But what need is there for such a weapon? Wouldn't a bolt from the transverse bow serve equally well?"

"Neither bow nor axe can be used well in a narrow space, or in a crowded dwelling, as I found to my cost. A skilled knifeman can strike the enemy before he can draw a breath."

"Why don't you carry a sword?" Stephen asked. He himself was wearing a sword for the trip, a gift from his father.

When he had imagined Devlin as a farmer, or an apprentice metalsmith, then it had seemed fitting that he carried a bow and a war-axe, as did most peasants. But the more he knew of Devlin, the more he realized that this man was no simple farmer. And a man who had trained with guards would have learned to use a sword.

"My wi—my friend told me that I had no skill with the sword. I can recognize a good swordsman from a bad one. I can repair a broken blade, checking its balance and testing its mettle. I could even forge one, given good steel and the right tools. But when the apprentice guards were learning to drill and fight, I was learning metalcraft. And now it is too late for me to begin again."

"I see," Stephen said, nodding thoughtfully. It was true the sword was best learned at a young age. His own father had insisted that all of his children learn to use the short fighting sword and the long sword of courtly dueling. As a boy Stephen had hated those lessons, yet now he was grateful for his father's insistence.

He watched as Devlin unrolled his blankets and lay on top of them, checking first to make sure that his axe was within easy reach.

Stephen felt a trickle of unease. Did the Chosen One really expect that they would be attacked here, in this peaceful country? What danger could there be?

And yet, had Stephen visited that infamous inn, he would have seen no danger there. He might have been killed, like so many others, for the sake of his coins and possessions. He shivered.

Perhaps it was fitting that the Chosen One saw the

threat of danger everywhere and trusted no one. Such fears might well keep him and his companion alive.

Within moments Devlin was asleep, but it was a long time before Stephen found his own rest.

Devlin was never again as talkative as he had been that first night. Though he observed carefully, Stephen saw few signs that Devlin was cast in a heroic mold. Instead he discovered ordinary facts, as he would with any traveling companion. Devlin was surly in the morning before his kava, and only slightly less surly afterward. He showed little interest in their surroundings, or in conversing.

Every morning he practiced with the transverse bow, and every evening he practiced with the throwing knives. He began wearing two knives in forearm sheaths hidden under his shirt, and from time to time as they rode he would suddenly jerk his arm and a knife would appear in a fence post, a tree, or once in a rabbit that became their dinner.

Devlin allowed Stephen to direct their course, but he set a hard pace. Each day they began earlier and continued on later. Soon they would reach the border of Esker.

Stephen found his thoughts turning toward home. This was not how he had imagined his return. When he had left in the spring he had sworn he would not return until he was a famous minstrel, covered in glory. He had not really considered how long his absence would be. It might take a year, or two, or even five, for his talents to be recognized and to receive their due acclaim.

And yet here he was, a scant six months later. He wondered what his father would say? Would he be glad to see him? Or would he see Stephen's decision to accompany the Chosen One as still further proof of his youngest child's obstinacy and lack of sense?

In many ways his father and Devlin were alike. Both treated him as though he were still a child, someone who could be ordered around, instead of the man he knew himself to be. He longed to prove himself, but he could not see how. Improbable visions danced through his head, where he slew that lake monster single-handed, while Devlin and the fisherfolk watched with awe from the shore. Then he sighed. He knew himself too well to believe himself capable of heroics. When the lake monster appeared, he would probably run screaming in the opposite direction.

It was fortunate that no one expected a minstrel to be a hero. A minstrel did not perform heroic deeds; instead he was a witness bearer who ensured that the hero's glorious deeds (or tragic defeat) were set down in verse for all time. Now that was a role he could fill with relish.

"We are lost," Devlin declared, reining in his horse.

Stephen rode up beside him.

"No we are not. I know where we are."

Devlin shook his head. "You said that before."

"Well, yes. Then I was lost, I admit it. But that was different. The road I knew was impassable because the bridge was washed out. And the directions that farm woman gave us were incomprehensible. We never did find the stone marker she described."

That had been three days ago. Once they realized that they had missed the turning, they had compounded the mistake by trying to take a path that led in the direction they were headed. However, the path soon narrowed to a game trail, then disappeared altogether. They had spent most of the day retracing their steps, only to wind up where they had started. This time it had been Devlin who inquired of a local resident on how best to get around the bridge, only to learn that there was a passable ford just half a mile up the river.

Devlin had barely spoken to Stephen since. The delay had chafed at his nerves, already worn raw from the strain of the Geas. Each day of the journey the pull of the Geas had grown stronger, driving him until he could not rest. He set a pace that taxed the limits of his endurance and that of his mount. And although the minstrel had complained about the brutal pace, he had not fallen behind or turned back. There was more to the lad than met the eye.

Even when they stopped for the night, Devlin could not find peace. He slept fitfully, waking early and forcing himself to wait until there was light enough to travel safely.

They had crossed the border into Esker in the morning. From there, Stephen had claimed it was but four days' journey to the lake. That is if his guide knew where they were, something Devlin was beginning to doubt.

"You said nothing about a fork in the road," Devlin said. "And we should have reached the village of Zimsek by now, if we were where you said."

He reached into his belt pouch and unfolded the map that Lady Ingeleth had given him. Not that he had much faith in the map. The major roads were still there—for the most part. But many of the smaller roads shown were no longer passable, while others had sprung up that the mapmaker had known nothing about.

"I did not mention the fork because it is unimportant," Stephen said. "If you journey to the left, you will join a larger road, which eventually will take you to the manor of

Lord Brynjolf. We will take the right-hand side, which will lead us to Zimsek within the hour. From Zimsek we will take the trade road, and from there will find a path to Greenhalt on the Lake."

Devlin peered at the map, then folded it, dismissing it as useless. He looked ahead. Both roads curved off among the trees, a faint layer of dust covering wheel ruts and hoof-prints, showing that they were well used. Then he looked over at Stephen, who was regarding him earnestly, appearing absolutely confident.

Traces of dust appeared on the left-hand road. "Riders," Devlin said.

He flexed his arms, checking that the knives were still in their wrist sheaths, then loosened the bindings of his axe. He expected no danger, but it was best to be ready for anything.

As the riders drew closer, Devlin could see they were dressed in dark green, with bows on their saddles and quivers on their backs. Each also wore a short sword for good measure.

"The Baron's riders," Stephen explained.

Devlin waited impatiently for the riders to reach them. There were two, a man and a woman, both dressed in dark green shirts, with brown leggings and high-topped boots. Their swords were still in their scabbards, but unlike the city guards', the weapons had the look of ones that had seen hard use.

"Greetings travelers," said the man. He smiled affably, but his eyes swept over the two of them, assessing them as if they were a threat. His gaze was cold on Devlin, taking in the uniform of the Chosen One, but his gaze lingered even longer on Stephen, who seemed to shrink under the scrutiny.

"Chosen One. Stephen. What brings you to Esker on this day?"

"We—" Stephen began.

"Our business is our own affair," Devlin interrupted. "We will continue on to Zimsek, and you may be on your way." He found it strange that these armsmen recognized Stephen at once, and that Stephen appeared unhappy to see them. He wondered for the first time if Stephen's absence from his homeland was by his own choice. And yet if Stephen was an exile, surely the talkative minstrel would have said something before now.

"Lord Brynjolf's manor is but a short ride," the female guard said. "He would welcome the opportunity to provide hospitality for you both."

Devlin shook his head. "We must refuse. Our errand brooks no delay."

The two guards exchanged glances.

"You are come for the creature in Long Lake," the first guard said.

"Yes," Stephen said.

Devlin gave the minstrel a sharp look.

"Then you must make Lord Brynjolf aware of your arrival," the first guard continued. "The lord has sent guards of his own to try and deal with the creature, but they failed and had to return. Surely your quest will benefit from talking to those who had tried before you."

"No," Devlin said sharply. The guard's words made sense. This was Lord Brynjolf's domain. Courtesy demanded that Devlin inform the lord of his presence and gain whatever knowledge of the creature the lord could share. But courtesy meant nothing when balanced against the pull of the Geas in his mind. The earlier detours had cost him dearly, for with each day the Geas grew stronger and his ability to control it grew less. Even now, it chafed against the small delay, urging him to ignore them and ride onward.

"Perhaps you would like to confer with your companion," the female suggested. The two guards backed their horses a few steps away.

"There is reason in what they say," Stephen began. "And I know Lord Brynjolf will welcome us and treat us well."

Hospitality. Clean bedding, food that he neither had to hunt or prepare, and warm water for bathing. It was a tempting thought. And what matter a delay of a day or two? The creature had been there for months. Another day would make little difference.

But there was no giving in to such temptations. Not while the Geas held him in its grip. Duty called him in one direction, and one direction alone. It would not permit him to choose another path.

"No," Devlin said. "I cannot."

Stephen glared at him. "You mean you will not."

"I cannot," Devlin said, grinding the words out between his teeth. "I must journey to the lake. Nothing must come between me and my task." His hand went to the axe by his side. "Not Lord Brynjolf, not these guards, not even you. Do you understand, minstrel?"

Beads of sweat formed on his brow, as he clenched the handle of the axe in his fist, and for the first time Devlin felt a trace of fear. Not fear for himself, but for what the Geas might force him to do. There was no reasoning with this force. The voice whispered that anyone who sought to delay him was an enemy, an obstacle that he must overcome.

Something of his desperation must have gotten through, for a look of pity appeared on Stephen's face. In that moment Devlin hated himself for showing such weakness before another.

Stephen rode over to the guards, and Devlin kicked his horse into a trot, turning down the right-hand path. He expected the guards to call him back, or try to intercept him, but they did nothing. As the moments passed, he could feel the awful tension that had built in him begin to drain away, as the Geas accepted that its pawn was once more continuing along the path that had been set for him.

A short time later, he heard a single set of hoofbeats, and turned his head as the minstrel drew his horse alongside.

"What did you say to them?"

"I told them they had no reason to delay us, and that they could inform Lord Brynjolf of our presence if they so wished."

Devlin waited for Stephen to comment on his behavior, but for once the minstrel forbore to question him. Instead he talked about their route, saying the guards had confirmed that the dry summer had left the roads to Greenhalt in fine shape, and they should reach their goal with ease.

And then, with luck, it would be over, and he would be freed from his burdens forever.

Twelve

DEVLIN SAT PERCHED ON A ROCK AT THE EDGE OF Long Lake. From his vantage point the lake looked deceptively peaceful, with still, blue waters and tree-lined shores that gradually curved away in the distance.

To his left, on a narrow strip of sand, there were two rows of small boats, lying idle and useless though the day was fine. Next to the boats were empty wooden racks that should have been full of fish drying in the sun. Behind him, to his right, was the village of Greenhalt, three dozen or so cabins nestled among the fir trees.

Greenhalt was located at the narrow end of Long Lake, and was the largest of the seven communities that made their living from the lake. The other settlements looked to Greenhalt for guidance, and thus it was Greenhalt that had petitioned first their lord, and then their King.

The villagers had greeted Devlin's arrival with initial disbelief, followed by an enthusiasm that made him squirm. Their confidence in the power of the Chosen One was absolute. They seemed to think that Devlin had but to swim out to the center of the lake, challenge the creature to

single combat, and with one mighty blow rid them of its
evil presence.

As a plan it held all the subtlety of a berserker charge. Its
only virtue was that his death would be swift—either from
the monster or from drowning, since Devlin had never
learned to swim. The Geas, which had driven him so hard
to arrive, apparently agreed with this assessment, for it refused to consider such a plan. Instead it allowed him to
keep his mind clear, and to form the outlines of a plan that
had at least some chance of succeeding.

The villagers described the creature as a giant skrimsal,
a creature from their ancient legends. The head alone was
as big as a man, on a long snakelike neck, connected to a
massive body. Four triangular appendages, two at the front
and two at the back, served to propel the creature through
the water as swiftly as a bird could fly.

The skrimsal could swim underwater for great dis-
tances, surfacing only at the last moment before it struck
its prey. The massive jaws could reduce a boat to splinters
or devour a man whole.

The guards had tried attacking the creature with bow-
shot, but the creature had simply dived under the waters
and swum away. The size of the lake meant it was impossible for the guards to patrol all of it, so while Greenhalt
was protected, the lesser villages at the northern end of the
lake came under attack. When the guards moved north,
the monster moved south. Eventually the guards had realized they did not have sufficient force, and had conceded
defeat.

Turning the problem over in his mind, Devlin had realized that the key to defeating the creature was to somehow
capture it, to force it to remain on the surface long enough

for the archers to do their work. And so he had devised his scheme, and set the villagers to work.

"The fisherfolk are nearly finished with the net," Stephen said, as he climbed up on the rocks.

"Good. Let me know when it is ready, and I will try a few practice casts."

To capture the creature, Devlin had devised a scheme that was daring in its boldness, or stupidity. The fisherfolk were to take nine of their largest nets and sew them together. Small rocks were to be tied into the edges to give the net the necessary weight. Finally, cordage was spliced into two long ropes, to be attached to opposite sides of the net.

The ends of the ropes would be anchored on the lakeshore. Devlin would venture out in a boat as far from shore as their length allowed. When the skrimsal appeared, Devlin would throw the net, hoping to catch the head ridges or one of the fins. Once the creature was caught, the fisherfolk would open fire with their bows from the shore.

There was just one flaw with the plan. Well two, actually, if you counted Devlin's probable demise at the hands of an irate lake creature.

"Who have they found to row the boat?" Devlin asked.

Stephen cleared his throat. "No one," he said. "It seems they are all afraid."

Of course they were afraid. All folk were afraid, when it came to the test. But the mark of a people was how they behaved in such moments. All told, the creature had already claimed more than a dozen lives. If left unchallenged, it would no doubt claim more. And yet no man or woman among these folk had the courage to risk their own life for the sake of their kin and neighbors. Devlin turned his head and spat on the sand in disgust.

He did not understand these folk. When the banecats

had appeared in Duncaer, never had it occurred to him that he should call upon another to destroy their evil. He would have been ashamed of himself if he had sent to the King for help rather than pursuing them himself. It was not the way of his people to rely upon others. In his eyes these Jorskians were as sheep, witlessly awaiting their slaughter.

Stephen interrupted his musings. "When I was a boy, I learned to row boats on a pond near my father's home. It would be an honor to serve you this day."

Devlin turned his head so suddenly he nearly snapped his neck. He regarded Stephen, certain he must be joking. But though the minstrel's face was white, he raised his chin and met Devlin's gaze squarely.

"Show me your hands," he ordered.

"What?"

"Show me your hands."

Stephen held out his hands. Devlin took them in his and turned them over. The minstrel's fingers had calluses on the fingertips from playing, but they were a far cry from the horny palms that Devlin had seen on every member of the fisherfolk.

"No," Devlin said. "Your offer shows a good heart, but there is no reason for you to ruin your hands for such foolishness."

"This is not foolishness," Stephen said, pulling his hands free. But the color came back to his cheeks, and he appeared relieved that Devlin had rejected his offer.

"No, it is not," Devlin said. "But it is their kinfolk I go to avenge, their livelihoods I will risk my life to defend. The blood price cannot be mine alone. Go back and tell them that they must find a rower within the hour, or I will leave them to their fates."

"Would you really do that?"

"You know I cannot," Devlin said. "But they do not know, and so will believe."

The bright afternoon sun beat down on Devlin, reflecting off the water until his eyes were dazzled. He put one hand to his brow and strained his gaze, but the surface of the lake was still. No sign of the creature.

"Again?" asked Eynar, the grizzled old fisherman who had finally been chosen as Devlin's rower.

"Again," Devlin said.

Eynar lifted his left oar and used the right oar to turn the boat around, careful not to foul the lines that tethered them to the shore. Then he dipped both oars in the water and began to row.

They had been on the lake for nearly three hours, rowing back and forth in an arc across one end while the villagers watched anxiously from the safety of the shore. Perched along the rocky sides were two dozen men and women equipped with a variety of small hunting bows and ancient longbows. Devlin's own transverse bow, with its metal bolts, was in the hands of the minstrel Stephen.

From the shore, the odor of frying fish wafted toward him. Devlin had ordered the villagers to dig into their precious stores and cook the fish, in the hope that the creature would be attracted by the smell.

He bent to examine the folded net, which lay in the bottom of the boat, and the coiled ends of the two ropes that stretched toward shore. The ropes, which had looked so long on land, now seemed a pitifully short tether. Yet Eynar had assured him that the monster had been known to come nearly to the shore in search of prey.

The minutes dragged on, and Devlin's nerves stretched taut. He hated this inaction. Yet he knew he had done all he could. Now it was up to the creature to make an appearance.

They reached the end of the circuit, and Eynar turned the boat around. Devlin glanced at the lake, then at the sun, which was swiftly approaching the horizon. It would be twilight soon, and the fading light would make it difficult for the archers.

"Another time across," Devlin said. "And then we will return to shore and try again on the morrow."

"Could have told you nothing would come of this," Eynar muttered. But he bent his back into the oars with a will, speeding the boat across the surface of the water.

What would he do if the monster failed to appear tomorrow? Should he try again at a different section of the lake? Devlin allowed his mind to drift as he considered the possibilities.

Suddenly the boat rocked back and forth as a wave rippled through the water. Devlin grabbed the sides just as the skrimsal began to surface, not ten yards from the tiny boat. First to appear was a monstrous head, easily the size of a grown man, with two great horns, large yellow eyes, and teeth like ivory daggers. Lifting its head on its long snakelike neck, the body of the creature appeared on the surface of the water. The sunlight shone off the skrimsal's glistening deep blue scales. It would have been a wondrous sight if not for the malice that lurked behind its gaze.

Devlin froze as the creature raised its head to its full extent. Nothing the villagers had told him had prepared him for what he saw. The great head swiveled around, then fixed its attention squarely on the boat. With a gentle stroke of its flippers, the skrimsal began to glide toward them.

They were doomed, a small voice in the back of his mind gibbered. No one could defeat such a creature. But the Geas held him firmly in place, patiently waiting until the creature was within range.

Eynar gave a frightened cry, then jumped into the water and began furiously swimming toward shore. His panicked flight caught the attention of the creature, which swiveled its neck to pursue.

Devlin saw his chance. He gathered the net in his hands and, just as the creature glided by, Devlin made his throw.

The net sailed through the air, catching the creature squarely on the head, which had been lowered in its pursuit of the fisherman. The ropes caught over one of the great horns and around the neck ruff, the weighted rocks pulling the net down toward the water.

The creature hissed with displeasure and raised its neck. Devlin grabbed his axe from the bottom of the boat and tore off the leather covering, ready to strike should the creature venture near.

"Now!" he screamed, but the archers needed no signal, for the first arrow flew over his head and splashed harmlessly into the water near the skrimsal.

A volley of half a dozen arrows followed, and then another. Most arrows fell into the water or bounced off the creature, but a few managed to penetrate its iridescent scales.

He felt a fierce satisfaction as he realized his plan was working.

The creature thrashed its head back and forth, trying to cast off the net. There was a loud crack as the first of the ropes holding it to shore parted. He watched in horror as the suddenly slack rope fell across the boat, the end disappearing into the lake.

He realized it was only a matter of time before the other rope broke, and the creature broke free.

"No!" This could not be. Not when he had come so close to success. If the creature escaped, it would be free to continue its deadly rampage. This might be their only chance, for both him and for the people of the lake. And he refused to acknowledge the possibility of defeat.

Thrusting the axe through his belt, Devlin stood up and grabbed the dangling rope in both hands. The creature thrashed, and he was jerked off his feet, flung high in the air, then dunked into the water before rising once again. As the creature continued its struggles to break free, Devlin slowly began to climb the rope, which swayed and twisted like a wild thing, trying to throw him off.

As he climbed, the skrimsal twisted its head to snap at him, but its own momentum swung the rope and carried Devlin out of harm's way. A lucky arrow shot pierced the creature's chin, and hung there like an absurd splinter. The skrimsal turned to locate this new threat, and Devlin resumed his ascent.

He felt a burning pain in his left leg and looked down to see that an arrow had pierced him in the calf. Red blood streamed down his leg.

His arms ached by the time he reached the first of the joined nets. Gratefully, he caught his feet in the lower netting and grasped hold of it with his hands. He clawed his way along the nets until he was perched on the back of the creature's neck, just below the horny ridges of the neck ruff.

The creature continued its struggles, but Devlin could see that the arrows were doing little damage. The villagers' bows were meant for small forest game, and most bounced harmlessly off their target. If only he had brought trained archers with war-bows, or a squad of peacekeepers with their transverse bows, then they might have had a chance of felling the creature.

He heard another loud crack, and realized that the second rope had broken. Any moment the creature would dive under and swim away.

Holding tightly to the nets with his left hand, Devlin reached into his belt and withdrew the axe. Drawing back his right hand as far as he could, he swung the axe, and it embedded itself in the creature's neck with a solid *thunk*.

Dark purple blood oozed from the gash, but he knew it was no more than a flesh wound. It would take many more blows to kill the creature. Surely there must be a vulnerable spot. He tugged on the axe, preparing to make another try.

The axe did not move. He tugged again, but still it would not come out.

"By Egil's forge," he cursed. He needed that axe. Balancing himself on the precarious netting, he let go of the net and grabbed the axe with both hands.

The creature swung its head, and Devlin felt himself losing his balance, but he refused to let go of the precious axe. His legs swung out from under him, then he felt the axe begin to move, carving a slice in the creature's neck. The skrimsal shrieked and began to roll over as the axe, propelled by Devlin's weight, continued to carve a bloody trail down the skrimsal's neck.

Hot blood gushed from the open wound, drenching his hands and forearms. The blood burned like acid, but despite the pain he grinned, for he knew that he had given the creature a death blow.

As he continued sliding down the neck, Devlin also

knew his own death was certain. The creature would crush him in its death throes, or he would drown in the lake. It did not matter how he died. What mattered was that he had completed his task. He had served as Chosen One with honor, and now he would receive the one boon that he truly craved.

Cerrie, he thought, as his wife's face swam before his eyes.

With a final convulsion the creature thrashed from side to side, and Devlin was flung free. He felt himself sailing through the air, and then he knew no more.

Thirteen

"CHOSEN ONE?" STEPHEN CALLED AS HE ENTERED the room. "Devlin, they are all waiting for you."

Devlin looked up from the bed, where he sat propped up against the headboard. He still could not comprehend how he had survived. One moment he had been sure he was going to die, then he was lying on the sandy beach, retching as he vomited up the lake water he had swallowed.

Too weak to move, he'd been unable to do more than utter a token protest as the villagers had carried him to the nearest cottage and installed him in the owner's bed. Grumbling, he had permitted the village herbalist to dress the arrow wound on his leg. But the man's obvious hero worship had disturbed him, and Devlin had ordered the herbalist to leave as soon as his task was done.

Stephen had then arrived, eager to tell the tale of the monster's death throes. In those last moments, the creature had thrown Devlin into the shallow waters near the village shore. Two foolhardy youths had ventured in to save him as the creature had flailed in its death agonies, its lifeblood pouring into the lake and turning it black.

Stephen had wished to linger and recount the glorious

struggle, but Devlin, once he was certain the creature was indeed dead, had no interest in hearing the minstrel's tale. So Stephen had left, seeking a more appreciative audience.

But now Stephen had returned.

Devlin stroked his axe, which lay on the bed beside him. Even at the end he had not lost his grip, and the villagers had had to pry it out of his hands. Then they had lovingly cleaned it and coated the blade with oil, before restoring it to a place of honor by Devlin's side. Somehow it seemed only fitting that as Devlin had survived, so too had the weapon that was bound up with his life.

"They have a feast prepared," Stephen said, breaking into his musings. "They want to show you their gratitude, and to celebrate the death of the monster."

Devlin shook his head. "No. I am in no mood for celebrations."

"But why not? You are a great hero. You saved these people. You saved their lives and their livelihoods, and now they want to thank you. What could be wrong with that?"

He was not a hero. He had simply done what had to be done, spurred on by the Geas which could not fathom defeat. He had leapt not out of courage, but because he had no choice, comforted by the knowledge that he was going to his own death.

But he knew he could not explain these things to the minstrel. Stephen's eyes were shining with excitement, and a touch of the same hero worship that had infected the villagers. Devlin felt an enormous weight pressing down on him. He could not bear this. Not when he had yet to reconcile himself to the fact that he was still alive.

"Tell the villagers that I am weary," he said, and it was no more than the truth. "My wounds are paining me, and I must rest."

Stephen's eyebrows drew together in a look of concern. "Is it your leg? I will run to fetch the herbalist."

It was not just the arrow in his leg. There was a litany of injuries that he'd refused to share with the herbalist. His right side ached, and it hurt to breathe. He'd probably cracked a rib or two. His arms and hands were sore, and there was a soft spot on his skull where a bruise was forming. But all told he'd come through the ordeal far better than he'd had any right to expect. Many would call him lucky to be alive.

"No," Devlin said. "I do not need a healer. I just need rest. But you go and join the fisherfolk at their feast. They need to celebrate, to remember that they are alive, and to convince themselves that the monster is truly gone. And for that they deserve the talents of the finest minstrel in Kingsholm."

"If you are certain," Stephen said, preening under the flattery.

"Go," Devlin ordered.

After Stephen left, Devlin allowed himself to sag back against the bed. Even that tiny movement caused pain to shoot through him, and he swore softly under his breath. Still, he had endured worse before and lived. In time the wounds would heal and the pain fade away to a memory.

Once again the Gods had spared him. He cursed them, even as he wondered what they intended for him next.

The celebration lasted far into the night. From his cottage Devlin could hear the sounds of the revelers. But he did not envy them, for a thoughtful soul had supplied a tray of the finest food the village could offer and a clay jug filled with a clear liquid called kelje. The seven different forms of fish that were offered reminded him unpleasantly of the skrimsal's flesh, and he had pushed the tray aside without eating. But the kelje had proven a welcome surprise. Clear like water, it burned his throat like fire and settled into his stomach with a comforting warmth.

The next morning he was paying for his indulgence. His head was heavy, his eyes sore, and he could barely manage to stand and dress himself. But he would not stay another day in the village, and had sent the woman of the cottage in search of Stephen, to tell him to make preparations to depart.

As he stepped outside, the sunlight made his eyes water, and he lifted his hand to shade them.

"Hail to the victor of the lake," a voice shouted, and then a multitude of voices echoed, "Hail!"

Devlin flinched. It seemed the entire village had assembled to see them off.

Some of them looked a little worse for wear, as if they, too, had overindulged in spirits last night. But most faces wore the same expression of awe and fear that he had seen on the face of the herbalist the day before. His skin crawled as he realized that, though they looked at him, they did not see the man. Instead they saw a legend brought to life. No mortal man could live up to the image they had created.

The village speaker advanced from the crowd, then bowed low, as if to the King. "Chosen One, the Gods sent you to aid us in our time of great peril. We will be forever in your debt, and we will sing your praises to the Gods each feast day, from now until the end of time."

Devlin felt nauseous. "I am but a man," he protested. "Any could have done what I did."

The speaker shook his head. "You are modest but we all bore witness to your great deeds. Only a man with the heart of a wolf, the courage of a she-lion, and the strength of a river could have done as you did. Truly you are blessed by the Gods."

The heart of a wolf? The courage of a she-lion? Those phrases had the ring of minstrelsy. Of bad minstrelsy. Devlin's eyes searched the crowd, and found Stephen standing at the edge, holding their two horses. He caught the minstrel's gaze, with a look that promised later retribution.

"I thank you for the gift of your hospitality," he said to the speaker. "But we must travel onward now. Troubles wait for no man."

The villagers beamed at this fatuous bit of wisdom.

Devlin beckoned Stephen, who led over the horses. His packs had already been loaded. Impatient to be gone, for once Devlin did not check the harness. Instead, he placed his left hand on the pommel, gritted his teeth, and with his right hand pulled himself into the saddle.

Air hissed between his teeth as his ribs complained of the maneuver, but he forced himself to sit upright as if nothing was wrong. A woman handed him his axe, which he fastened to the saddle. Stephen mounted his own horse, and after another exchange of flowery compliments they were finally allowed to depart.

They set off at a brisk trot, which made his head twinge with every stride. A band of young children ran after them for a short distance, but after a while even the hardiest of them turned back. When he was finally certain they were no longer being observed, Devlin eased his horse into an ambling walk and allowed himself to slump in the saddle.

"Chosen One?" Stephen asked.

"My name is Devlin," he said, unwilling to put up with this nonsense. "Use it, or call me not at all."

"Devlin, then. You look ill. Are you sure we should leave

today? Perhaps we had better return and rest until you are well."

"I am not ill. I have drink taken."

"You have what?"

"Last night. That kelje. I must have had the whole jug before I fell asleep."

"You were drunk," Stephen accused.

"Yes. And now I must pay the price for my misdeeds. So please, speak softly. And no singing. No playing your lute. Just... quiet."

They rode in silence for the rest of the morning, pausing only at noon to rest their horses and to eat the fish pastries the villagers had prepared. Devlin found the food dry and tasteless, and consumed no more than a few bites. Remounting his horse was harder than it had been that morning, but he managed it without letting Stephen see how much the effort cost.

By now his head was throbbing, and there was a mist across his vision. Where the creature's blood had splashed him, his skin was turning red and peeling as if sunburned, and it itched ferociously. He wound his hands tightly in the reins, trying to resist the urge to tear at his flesh.

This was no simple hangover. And he was getting worse, not better. He opened his mouth to call out to Stephen, who had ridden ahead, then closed it. What would he say? If he confessed his weakness, the minstrel would insist that they return to Greenhalt. And he would not do that. He refused to return to that place, which insisted on treating him as both less and more than a mortal man.

Devlin would take his chances on the road. Either the fever would pass, or it would not. Perhaps the monster had killed him after all. It was just taking Devlin's body time to realize it had received its death blow.

It was the third day since they had left Greenhalt, and by now Stephen had realized that something was dreadfully wrong with his companion. Devlin's excuse of a hangover had seemed reasonable on the first day, and his fatigue that night explainable as a result of his ordeal.

On the second morning, Devlin had appeared worse than the first. He had refused to eat. And yet he had insisted they journey onward. Stephen knew he should have demanded that they turn back, but he had allowed himself to be overruled. That night Devlin had practically fallen out of the saddle. He had blamed his weakness on the arrow wound in his leg, and Stephen had believed his excuse.

By the third morning, there had been no hiding his illness. Devlin's face was white and covered with sweat, his eyes dull and sunken. His hands and arms were bleeding where he had scratched at the peeling skin during the night. He'd allowed Stephen to bind them up in linen, and this worried Stephen most of all. Such docility was not like Devlin.

Stephen fretted as he wondered what to do. Should he stay here and hope that rest would enable Devlin to regain his strength? Yet the little he knew of healing told him this would be folly. He had willow bark for fevers, but no other herbs. What the Chosen One needed was a skilled healer.

And skilled healers were scarce in the country provinces. The nearest one lived at Lord Brynjolf's keep. If he and Devlin stayed on the road, they would reach Zimsek within a day. From there he could send someone to fetch the healer, but it would take at least another day for them to go and for the healer to return. Two days, then, before Devlin received help.

Devlin did not look as if he would last two hours, let alone two days.

Stephen cursed himself for his foolish blindness. He knew he had only his own selfishness to blame. How proud he had been of the fight against the skrimsal and the role he had played. With his own hands he had shot metal bolts from the transverse bow and seen them pierce the creature's scaly hide. And he had been there to witness Devlin's heroics as the Chosen One had struck the death blow.

He'd felt as if he were in a legend come to life, and was already hard at work at a glorious song that would commemorate the event. A song that would bring him fame and fortune.

He had been so wrapped up in his music and his dreams of glory that he had paid little heed to Devlin's rapid decline. Only when it was almost too late had he realized his mistake.

Two days was too long, he decided. But there was another way. Yesterday, just before they had made camp, they had passed the start of an old forest trail, one that Stephen had known as a boy. The trail led through the forest, to Lord Brynjolf's keep. If the trail was passable, he and Devlin could reach the keep, and its healer, by sunset.

He knew it was a gamble. Falling trees, flooded streams, or mud slides could have altered the trail, or rendered it impassable, in which case he would have to retrace their path and try the main road. Already on their trip he had confidently guided them along a road he knew well, only to find it washed out by floods. And it had been many years since he had ventured on the forest trail. But it was a gamble he had to take. Better by far to gamble than to take the safe way, only to watch Devlin die because no healer could be found in time.

He lifted the cup of willow bark tea from the ground, where it had been brewing, and thrust it into Devlin's hands. "Drink," he ordered, his own hands wrapped around Devlin's as he lifted the mug to his lips. Devlin's hands shook, and he spilled some of the tea, but he managed to swallow most of it. Stephen decided to take that as a good sign.

"We cannot stay here," he said. "Can you ride?"

Devlin nodded, his eyes focused on the air to Stephen's left. "I can ride," he rasped.

With difficulty he rose, and allowed Stephen to lead him to a flat rock, on which he stood. Stephen brought over his horse, and, with Stephen's help, Devlin managed to pull himself into the saddle. Barely.

"No need," Devlin objected, as Stephen unbuckled the war straps and used them to tie Devlin's legs to the sides of the saddle. Stephen ignored his objections and took the strap from the high-backed cantle and ran it around Devlin's waist, buckling it firmly. There. That should keep him on his horse.

Taking the reins of Devlin's horse in his hand, he mounted. "Stay with me," he said. "Stay with me and I promise today will be the last of our travels."

A faint smile touched Devlin's lips. "The last day," he muttered. His eyes half closed, and he slumped in the saddle. "What a tale you will have to tell, minstrel."

Stephen kicked his horse into a walk, and Devlin's horse followed obediently behind. After an hour's ride back along their route, they reached the clearing that marked the start of the old forest trail. He turned to check on his companion, but Devlin looked no worse than before. It was now or never.

"I will not fail," he vowed, turning their horses onto the trail. He could not. He promised the Gods he would give everything he had, if only they would grant him this one boon.

"In the name of King Olafur and his people, I call upon Teó, the Great Father, and Teá, the Great Mother, to bless us. I call upon Lady Sonja to bestow courage upon your people. Lord Haakon grant us justice, Lord Egil bless our work, and Lady Geyra heal our hearts. And may he who is not named favor our endeavors."

As he finished the dawn prayer, Brother Arni bowed low seven times before the altar, then knelt to the ground and prostrated himself for a count of one hundred heartbeats. Then he arose.

"In the name of all the Gods, I greet this day," he said, invoking the traditional dismissal at the end of the service, though he knew there was no one in the Royal Chapel except himself. Still, there were the dignities to be maintained.

He sighed. Nowadays few people came to the Royal Chapel. In these troubled times, most chose to dedicate themselves to one of the seven, as if that would grant them additional protection. In the city, the temple of the Heavenly Pair, devoted to Father Teó and Mother Teá, was filled each rest day, and never lacked followers for the dawn services. Many of the courtiers worshiped there, or made the trip into the old city to pay their homage to Lady Sonja, Goddess of War.

In his youth, Brother Arni had considered devoting himself to the service of Lady Geyra. He'd always felt a special kinship for healers. But instead his mother had convinced him that the wisest path was to follow her own vocation, and to serve all the Gods equally.

Not that he regretted his decision. Oh no. He took pride in his faithful service, and in quiet meditations of devotion. Still, it would have been nice, from time to time, to lead others in prayer.

Yet that was not to be. The Royal Chapel came to life only once a year, when the King led the midsummer service. The only others who ventured in were the ones who would be Chosen. And even those were all too rare these days, although he was afraid there might be a need for a new Chosen One soon.

He ventured over to the map wall, his fingers tracing the mosaic. The soul stone that represented the Chosen One no longer shone with a ruby light. Instead it was dim and barely flickering, revealing that the Chosen was near death.

"Brother Arni," Duke Gerhard said.

He whirled around, startled. He had not heard the Duke's approach. But there he was, the King's Champion, bowing perfunctorily before the altar.

"Your Grace," Brother Arni said. "How may I serve you?"

The Duke made a wide circuit around the altar and came to stand beside him. His arm gestured to the map. "I had heard that the Chosen One was faring ill, and I came to see for myself."

Brother Arni blinked at this unusual show of concern. Duke Gerhard had never before expressed an interest in the fate of any of the Chosen. It had always been Captain Drakken who was charged with overseeing their Choosing and, in time, recording their deaths.

But perhaps this concern was understandable, since the

Chosen One had been sent on his errand by the King's Council. As one of the chief councilors, Duke Gerhard was naturally interested in the success of the venture.

"The situation appears grave. But see here." He gestured to Long Lake, then allowed his fingers to trace the route to the Chosen One's present position. "I have watched faithfully every day. The Chosen One arrived at Long Lake, and has now made his departure. The Geas would prevent him from leaving until he fulfilled his mission, so it seems he has indeed destroyed the monster."

"Would that were so," Duke Gerhard intoned gravely. "But it could easily be that the monster has struck down the Chosen, and his companions are carrying him away to die."

That grim interpretation had not occurred to Brother Arni.

"Send word to me when the Chosen is no more," Duke Gerhard added.

"As you wish," Brother Arni replied.

He waited until the Duke left, then turned his attention back to the map board. Had the stone grown darker or was that only his imagination? "I will pray that the Gods spare you," he whispered, as if somehow the Chosen could hear him through the soul stone. Returning to the floor in front of the altar, he prostrated himself and began to pray.

Fourteen

DEVLIN WANDERED IN BRIGHT FEVER DREAMS, LOS-
ing himself in the memories of precious days long past,
when a youthful metalsmith had courted the proud Cerrie.
They wandered hand in hand through the streets of
Alvaren, secure in the belief that nothing could ever part
them. He crafted beautiful jewelry and lethal weapons in
his forge and gifted them to his love, taking fierce pride in
her deadly skills. She inspired him to new heights of arti-
sanship. His reputation grew, and the master smiths began
to speak of admitting him to their ranks.

He ached to lose himself in the memory of those happy
days, when the future had seemed full of promise. Before
they had heard of the New Territories. Before he had made
the fatal choice that damned them all.

But each time the memories turned dark, and he was
forced to relive the moment when he had returned, to find
their bodies in that blood-soaked field. "No!" he cried, but
his demons gave him no rest, as he relived the horror again
and again.

Hours or perhaps days later he awoke. He moved his
arm restlessly and felt silken sheets under his hand; he

realized that he was lying on a soft bed. He opened his eyes, and saw a green canopy overhead.

He heard the sounds of someone moving.

"*Ni?*" he called out.

An elderly woman, dressed in a lavender robe, bent over him.

"*C'raad? Cionnas?*" he asked.

The woman smiled and shook her head. "I am sorry, but I do not speak your language," she said, placing her hand on his forehead.

He forced his mind to think a moment. "Where? How?" he asked, repeating his questions in the trade tongue.

The woman withdrew her hand and nodded. "The fever is gone," she said. "You should rest easy, and not trouble yourself. For now it is enough to know that you are in the keep of Lord Brynjolf, and that you have been ill but will soon be well again."

His memories returned in a rush. The lake. The battle with the skrimsal. Leaving Greenhalt, and traveling as the sickness came upon him. He remembered feeling oddly detached as the minstrel grew steadily more concerned, but after that there was nothing.

"Where is Stephen?"

"Young Stephen is fine, though worried about you. He will be relieved to hear that you are recovering. If you rest now, you may see him later." She turned away and drifted out of his sight.

He did not want to rest. It seemed all he had done lately was rest from injury and illness. He hated himself for displaying such weakness, and for being dependent upon the care of these strangers who were no kin.

And he feared returning to his dreams.

"I do not want to rest," he said firmly, struggling to sit

up. He managed to rise on one elbow, which shook with exhaustion.

"But you will rest," the woman said, returning with a cup brimming full with a dark liquid. "You will drink this."

He hesitated.

"Drink this," she said. "I promise, this time there will be no dreams."

He wondered if he could trust her. He gazed at her, realizing only now that she wore the silver torc that proclaimed her a healer.

He took the cup from her and drank the bitter draft in a single gulp. "No dreams," he said.

Stephen rose to his feet as the elderly healer shut the door to Devlin's chamber behind her. "Mistress Margaretha," he said. "How is he?"

Mistress Margaretha smiled. "The fever is gone, and his wits have returned."

Stephen's shoulders sagged with relief. The past three days had been torture, as they all waited anxiously to see if Mistress Margaretha would be able to save Devlin's life. As Devlin lay in fever-soaked delirium, babbling in his birth tongue, Stephen had chastised himself over and over again with the fear that Devlin would die because of his neglect. The journey along the forest trail had been even more difficult than he had feared, but he had succeeded in arriving at the keep before sunset, only to hear Mistress Margaretha say that it might already be too late.

"I knew you would save him," he said. "And I thank you."

"Give your thanks to Lady Geyra, whom I serve," the healer said tartly.

But then her face softened. "You did well, young Stephen. I had heard told that the Caerfolk were thick-skulled, but now I know it in truth. Else he would have died at once from the fracture. Still, repairing the skull and his ribs were but a small matter," she added, waving one hand as she dismissed skills that would have won her a place in any King's court. "It was the poison from the beast that caused the fever, but now your friend is finally free from its grip."

"Can I see him?"

"No. He is sleeping now, a true sleep at last. But you may see him later, when he awakes. For now, I advise you to eat, and then take your own rest. One patient is enough, I have no wish to add you to my care."

"I will do as you say," Stephen replied. In truth he was a bit light-headed, which he accounted to relief at the news that Devlin would survive after all.

Mistress Margaretha shook her head. "And as for your friend, you must convince him to take better care of himself. This is the second time in a year that he has been wounded nearly unto death. Twice now the Gods have spared him, but I would not test their mercy a third time."

Stephen had turned to leave, but as the healer's words sank in, he turned back to face her.

"Twice now, within the year? Are you certain?"

Devlin had been Chosen only four months ago. And as someone who had paid close attention to his career, Stephen knew full well this was the first time he had been seriously injured in that role.

Mistress Margaretha drew herself up to her full height and looked down her long nose at him. "Of course I am certain. Any healer worth her salt could tell you that, as soon as they laid hands on him. And how did you think he had come by those scars?"

What scars? Stephen kept his face carefully blank. "Of course," he said, his mind spinning with the implications. Just who, or what, had Devlin been before he appeared in Kingsholm? Every time he thought he finally knew the man, he uncovered another layer of mystery. How many more secrets did this former metalsmith have?

Devlin slept, without the dreams that had troubled him before. When he awoke, he felt hale and full of energy. He tried to insist on seeing Stephen, but Mistress Margaretha, the healer, would have none of it. Instead she watched him carefully as he ate a meal of soup and bread, though he felt as if he could have eaten twice as much. Then she sent for servants, who fetched a movable bath and filled it with steaming hot water. Devlin insisted on bathing and dressing himself. While he scraped several days' worth of beard off his face, he reflected on his strange luck.

He had known of the cracked ribs, but had not known that the bruise on his skull was a sign that it was broken as well. Nor had he suspected that the blood of the skrimsal would turn out to be a deadly poison. Either the skull fracture or the poison should have killed him. Would have killed him, if he had been left to the care of a village herbalist or acolyte healer.

Instead Stephen had brought him to Mistress Margaretha, a healer of the highest rank, in the service of Lord Brynjolf. So now all that remained of the battle were the patches of new pink skin that covered his hands and arms. He stretched experimentally, but his ribs gave nary a twinge.

By the time he finished shaving, he found his energy flagging, just as Mistress Margaretha had warned him it would. Still, he was well enough to sit in a chair when she finally allowed him to have a visitor.

Stephen refused to accept his thanks, and instead took Devlin to task for not revealing his illness sooner. He spent only a few minutes before being shooed out by the officious Mistress Margaretha, but Devlin did manage to make Stephen promise to convey a message of gratitude to Lord Brynjolf.

He sighed as he realized the extent of his debt to this lord.

"There now, you have tired yourself out," Mistress Margaretha scolded. He did not have the heart to tell her his weariness was more of the soul than the body, and instead allowed her to chivvy him back into bed for a rest.

The weight of his obligations bore heavily upon him. He had neither kinright nor craftright to claim the hospitality of these folk. And yet they had treated him with honor, and the services of a healer of the first rank, as if he were a great lord or a son of the house. They had saved his life.

According to the custom of his people, such hospitality had to be repaid threefold. It was a heavy burden for one man to bear. Devlin had no kin who would join with him to repay the debt. He had not even the blessing of his name to give, for his name held no power in Duncaer. And yet somehow the debt must be repaid, for the sake of his honor.

He mused upon his dilemma until he fell asleep. When he arose, the healer brought an evening meal on a tray, and promised that on the morrow he would be able to leave the room and join the household.

After he had eaten, he sat by the fire, staring into the flames as he pondered his situation. The Geas that had driven him was quiet, yet he knew it was but a matter of time before it awoke.

He heard the door open and turned his head, expecting to see Stephen. Instead he saw a tall broad-shouldered man, dressed in thigh-high riding boots and leathers. His hair was more gray than blond, and his weather-beaten face spoke of many hours spent out of doors. Though no circlet adorned his brow, Devlin knew at once who this must be, and he rose to his feet.

"Lord Brynjolf, I give you greeting," he said, managing a short bow.

Lord Brynjolf paused in stripping off his gloves and held up one hand. "Please no formalities. And it is I who should bow to you, my lord Chosen."

Devlin remained standing. "I am deeply in debt to you for your hospitality," he said.

"And I am in debt to you as well," Lord Brynjolf said, advancing toward him. "Sit, sit," he urged. "There is no reason we cannot talk like civilized men."

Devlin sat. Lord Brynjolf turned the second chair so that it faced him, and sat down.

"I would have greeted you sooner. But you were in no state for visitors, and I had matters that could not wait." He tipped his head, and regarded Devlin for a moment. "Mistress Margaretha performed wonders, as usual. I hardly recognize you as the man that Stephen brought in here."

There was something familiar about the way he cocked his head. "Stephen is nearkin to you," Devlin guessed aloud.

Lord Brynjolf blinked. "Stephen is my son. The youngest of my children, if not the wisest."

Lord Brynjolf was stocky in build, while Stephen was slender and gangling. Still, there was a certain resemblance, and Devlin realized he should have guessed it sooner. How else had Stephen known that there would be a healer here, or that they would be welcomed? And no wonder that Lord Brynjolf's guards had recognized him on the road.

"Then my debt to you is double," Devlin said, "for I owe both you and your son for my life."

Lord Brynjolf leaned forward. "No, it is I that owe you, for ridding my people of that cursed creature. Though I confess when my guards told me that my son and the Chosen One were on their way to Greenhalt, I had no hopes that you would succeed."

"I was lucky."

"That is not how Stephen tells it."

Devlin shuddered. He could imagine full well how Stephen was telling the tale. No doubt he'd already composed a song, describing Devlin's mythical virtues.

"I had no choice in what I did," Devlin said. "It was the duty of the Chosen One. Honor compelled me to act as I did. And the blow that killed the monster was a lucky one."

It was the Geas that had driven him to that last desperate attack. He would not allow others to credit him with courage or daring, when he knew he had been but a pawn of the spell, and of his own craving for oblivion.

"I would not have sent to King Olafur, had I known there was a new Chosen One. My letter to the King was but an attempt to force him to see the troubles of the borderlands. I asked him for troops, but I am not surprised that he sent none." Lord Brynjolf leaned back in his chair and rubbed his face with both hands as if weary. "In the name of the Seven, what I need is more guards. I could have destroyed the monster myself, if I had the resources. As it is, half of my best armsmen are in Ringstad, helping Lord Eynar's men fight off border raiders. Those armsmen I have left are riding the roads and watching the borders to keep my own province secure. And yet still the King does nothing."

Devlin wondered why Lord Brynjolf was confiding in him. Was he one of those who sought to win the Chosen One to his side? Was he simply trying to see how much Devlin knew of court politics? Or was he simply speaking candidly, as if to a trusted friend?

He owed this lord much, so Devlin offered candor in return. "The King does nothing because he is afraid. Afraid he will make the wrong choice and so he makes none. His council is divided, and bickers endlessly without agreeing on any course of action. The courtiers are blind to the dangers, intriguing for power while the Kingdom crumbles around them."

"You see clearly for a man who is new to the court," Lord Brynjolf observed.

"The courtiers see no reason to hold their tongues around one they presume already dead. There is much to be learned by a man who can keep his eyes and ears open."

"I begin to see why my son praises you so highly."

Devlin squirmed, uncomfortable with any praise. "It is rather Stephen's courage you should praise. Neither duty nor honor bound him to the fight, and yet he freely chose to stay and fight. He would have rowed the boat himself, had I but let him."

Lord Brynjolf shook his head. "A bold gesture, if not a wise one."

"Wisdom may be taught, but courage and a good heart may not. In time your son will gain the wisdom to match his other qualities," Devlin said, feeling the urge to defend Stephen to this man.

"It is good to see that he has a loyal friend," Lord Brynjolf said.

Devlin kept his face impassive. Friend? He had not thought of Stephen in that light. He had seen him first as a nuisance, then as a journeying companion. And now he was indebted to Stephen for his life. He was grateful, yes. But they were not friends. Devlin could not risk the burden of friendship.

"I did you no favors at the lake," he said, changing the subject.

"How so?"

"The skrimsal killed over a dozen of their kin, and yet the fisherfolk took no action of their own. They were like sheep being preyed upon by wolves, waiting for the shepherd to come and save them. If my plan had worked, and the villagers had slain the creature with arrows, then they might have learned that they were not helpless, and could work together to save themselves. But instead I killed the beast, and they made of me a legend, someone who was more than a man. The next time they face danger, they will look for another such legend to save them."

To his surprise Lord Brynjolf did not take offense. Instead he nodded gravely. "Before long, all of us along the borderlands will need to learn to defend ourselves. I only hope that we still have time to make ourselves ready."

"You have but to call on my name, and what I can do, I will," Devlin said. It was all he could promise, in payment of his debt. It was a paltry enough offer, for he knew full well that when the time came, the Geas might command him otherwise.

"I hope I never have to hold you to that promise," Lord

Brynjolf said. "But come now, enough grim thoughts. For now we can rejoice that you are well and healed, and that my son has returned safely from his adventure. That is enough for one day."

Devlin felt a sudden sympathy for this beleaguered lord. He had known that the Kingdom was breaking down. He had listened as Captain Drakken described the current troubles, and had overheard courtiers discussing the latest bad news to affect their rivals. Even Stephen, in his own way—with his songs and tales—had made him aware that the Kingdom of Jorsk was beset by troubles on all sides.

And yet never had he thought what it would be like to live in the border regions that were so afflicted, or to be one of the lords who was watching his once ordered world dissolve into chaos. Small wonder, then, that in the face of overwhelming difficulties, the common folk craved a leader that they could put their faith in, someone larger than life who could banish the darkness and restore order to their world. The Chosen One represented justice and order, and a living link to past times of glory.

Lord Brynjolf had no such illusions to comfort him, for he was too intelligent to believe in a Gods-sent savior. He knew that he could rely only upon his own efforts to save himself and his people.

Devlin repeated his vow, silently. For as long as the Gods spared him, he would help this man, and the others like him. He would repay his debt to this lord, if it was the last thing he did with his life.

Fifteen

LATE IN THE EVENING, STEPHEN PACED BACK AND forth in his father's inner chamber, waiting for him to return. For the past three days, he and Lord Brynjolf had exchanged only a few words, as Stephen had spent most of his time haunting Devlin's sickroom or waiting in the antechamber outside for word on whether the Chosen would live or die. But now that Devlin was recovering, he knew his father would expect his errant son to make an appearance, and his explanations.

Six months earlier, he and his father had exchanged angry words when Stephen insisted on leaving to pursue his destiny as a minstrel. And now he was returned, no further toward achieving his destiny than he had been on that spring day.

He still hadn't decided what he would say to his father when Lord Brynjolf appeared.

"By all the Gods, I am tired. Pour me some wine, if you would be so kind."

Stephen went over to the wooden cabinet and withdrew two glasses, which he filled with dark red wine from Myrka. His father sat down in a chair and pulled off his riding boots. When Stephen handed him his glass, he took a sip, then leaned back and sighed with pleasure.

Stephen took his own seat opposite his father, placing his glass on a low wooden table and wiping his suddenly damp palms against his trousers. Somehow his father always managed to make Stephen feel as if he were a young lad who had been caught in mischief.

But his father's first words took him off guard. "I have just seen your friend. He is not what I expected."

"He is ... unique," Stephen said, failing to come up with words that would describe the complexities and contradictions that formed Devlin's character. "In some ways, I know him like one of my brothers, and in others I don't know him at all. I am not certain we even know his true name."

His father's eyes narrowed.

"Tell me how one of the Caerfolk came to be Chosen."

"Devlin appeared on midsummer's day, as travel worn as if he had walked the length of the country. He came to the guards and asked to be sworn in as Chosen. I, uh, happened to be there," he said. No need to explain to his father that he had been under arrest at the time. "The next day I witnessed the oath. Devlin halted the ceremony, saying that the blade he had been given was false, and to prove it, he shattered it with one blow from his fist."

Stephen felt a chill run up his spine as he remembered that moment. He had seen it with his own eyes and yet still had trouble believing what had happened.

"How could he know such a thing?" his father demanded.

"He claims to have been a metalsmith. Regardless, Captain Drakken lent him her sword and he took the oath. I think even Devlin was surprised when the Gods accepted his service." Stephen thought for a moment. "After the ceremony, every weapon that the Guard possessed was checked for flaws. The Royal Armorer was kept busy for weeks replacing the weapons that had been tampered with."

"So already the Chosen One has done great service," his father mused.

It had not seemed so at the time. At the time, Stephen had been disappointed that the Chosen One was far more interested in checking the armory than he was in performing glorious deeds. But now he could see how important it had been to ensure that the weapons the Guard relied upon were trustworthy. If it came to the test, there would be no time to fix past mistakes.

"The Chosen One speaks highly of your courage," his father said.

He stared, certain his father must be joking. Devlin had never spoken highly of anything. And yet his father appeared serious.

Stephen cast his mind back to Long Lake. Already it was fading into memory, as if it had been months and not mere days ago. "I could never do what Devlin did," he said. "I offered my help only because I knew no better. I thought it would be a glorious struggle, like the songs of the past. But it wasn't. I was safely ashore, among the rocks, and yet I was so terrified I could barely aim the bow. Devlin was out in that tiny boat, alone against the skrimsal. Wounded by an arrow shot by his allies, and still he managed to defeat the creature."

"That sounds like one of your songs," his father said.

"No." Stephen shook his head firmly. "I will make no song of this. After the battle I was so wrapped up in my song making that I paid no heed to Devlin's growing illness. He needed a friend, not a minstrel, and there I failed him." He reached for his wineglass, not wanting to meet his father's eyes.

"So your travels have taught you something after all," his father said. "In these days we have little need for the services of a minstrel, but a man of courage is always needed."

They had had this argument many times before. But for the first time, a small part of Stephen agreed with his father, though he had not given up his dreams of minstrelsy. And he knew what his father would ask next.

"I will not stay here," Stephen said.

"But you must. I need you. Esker needs you. You've seen that for yourself."

"Esker has you, and Mother, and my brothers and sisters. That is enough."

His father tossed back the last of his wine, then rose and fetched the bottle. He filled each of their glasses.

"Think on it. Solveig is out with the armsmen, patrolling the borders." Solveig was Stephen's eldest sister, and their father's heir. It was a measure of his father's deep concern that he had sent Solveig on this seemingly routine task. "Harald has gone to Ringstad, to do what he may there. Your mother and Madrene are in Selvarat, practicing the art of courtly diplomacy, for what help that may bring. Your place is here. I need you."

Never before had his father said that Stephen was needed. Always before he had insisted that Stephen was too young or too foolish to venture out into the world beyond Esker. But never had he said that Stephen's talents had value, or that he might serve the province. If his father had said these words six months before, Stephen would never have left.

Stephen looked as his father, seeing that for the first time in memory his father looked all of his sixty years. The responsibilities he bore weighed heavily upon him, and Stephen had no doubt that his father could use his help.

It would be easy to give in, and to do what his father wished. But a deeper instinct told him that it would not be right. There was one that needed him more.

"I cannot stay. There are others you can rely upon. You have but to summon Marten, and he will return from Tyoga and bring his family. But my place is with the Chosen One, for as long as he will let me. Someone needs to keep an eye on him, to make sure that he doesn't destroy himself," Stephen said, trying to add a note of lightness but knowing that he had failed.

He braced himself for one of his father's fits of temper, but to his surprise his father appeared resigned, as if he had already known what Stephen would say.

"The two of you are an odd pair. Still you may be good for each other. As it is, you are not the foolish youth who ran away this spring."

"I did not run away," Stephen protested.

"As you say," his father conceded. "I will ask one promise from you. When the Chosen One is no more, you must promise to return here, to serve our people."

His father's voice was grim, as if they were already under siege. Stephen's gut tightened. Had matters gotten so much worse since he had left? Or had he simply been too oblivious to see the rising tensions? For a moment he felt tempted to change his mind, to tell his father that he would stay in Esker.

"I promise. But I pray that day is long hence."

———

Devlin remained at Lord Brynjolf's keep for another week, until Mistress Margaretha pronounced him fit to travel. He half expected that Stephen would choose to remain behind, but when he announced his intention to depart, Stephen began making arrangements as if his companionship was a matter of course.

A small part of Devlin was glad that Stephen would be along. Not just because Stephen knew the routes, but because Stephen's presence kept him from the solitary brooding he was prone to. Not that he would call the minstrel a friend, for Devlin had forsworn friendship. It was rather that if he had to have a companion on the journey, Stephen was a fair one.

Stephen's horse had lamed itself in the frantic journey to the keep, so his father provided a new mount. Devlin's horse, being of better quality and army trained, had fared better, and after a week of rest was nearly as eager for exercise as his master.

Laden with good wishes and ample provisions, they left the keep on a crisp autumn morning. They traveled through the day, and in the early evening they made camp in a clearing not far from the road. They could have stayed at an inn; they had passed one not five miles back. But Devlin had had his fill of strangers, and was just as glad that he need accept no hospitality save his own.

After dinner, Devlin built the fire back up, preparing it for the night. Stephen sat on a log across from him, idly fingering his lute. He looked up, and asked, "Devlin, who is Cerrie?"

Devlin froze, his hand in the act of placing a chunk of wood on the fire. Then he carried through with the motion before turning around.

"Where did you hear that?"

"When you were ill, you called it out. It sounded like a name, am I right?"

Devlin wondered what other things he had called out in his fevered delirium. He hoped desperately that none in Lord Brynjolf's house spoke the language of the Caerfolk.

"Who is Cerrie?" Stephen asked again, raising his head to look at Devlin.

He hesitated, wondering whether he should refuse to answer. Still, the man had saved his life. He deserved some measure of courtesy.

"Cerrie was my wife," Devlin said, returning to his bedroll, and sitting down upon it.

"Was?"

"She is dead. Killed."

"Was that when you got your scars?"

"No."

"But—"

"We will speak no more of this," Devlin said. One could push the limits of courtesy too far. Stephen had a right to his answers, but had no right to explore Devlin's pain.

Stephen played softly on his lute for a while longer. Devlin, recognizing the tune as "Harvest Fair" breathed a sigh of relief. At least Stephen was not working on a new epic.

Eventually Stephen put the lute back in its case and rolled himself in his blankets to sleep. But Devlin remained wakeful, troubled by the memories Stephen had stirred.

The night was clear, and through a patch in the trees he glimpsed the Huntress, riding high in the sky. So the seasons had indeed turned. He thought for a moment. They reckoned time differently in Jorsk. By their calendar, it was the middle of ninth month, in the fifteenth year of the reign of Olafur. Devlin was no scholar, but from the appearance of the Huntress, he knew it must be close to harvest moon, as the Caerfolk reckoned the seasons. The time of the banecats' attack.

Why had he not realized it sooner? Once he had been able to number the days and hours that had passed since Cerrie's and Lyssa's murders. Now there were whole hours that went by without him thinking of them. He felt as if they were slipping away.

He closed his hands into fists, as if he could hold the memories tightly in his grasp. The gem on the ring winked in the firelight and, releasing his hands, he pulled off the ring and held it in his palm.

If a seer had told him a year before that Devlin would become the Chosen One, defender of Jorsk, Devlin would have laughed. Who could have imagined such a thing? He was a metalsmith turned farmer, not a warrior. He'd lacked the stomach for violence and killing. His gentle spirit had been one of the things that Cerrie had claimed to love.

Would she even recognize him? If she came back to life, would she find any trace of the man he had once been? Or would he be a stranger to her?

Devlin clenched the ring in his fist and raised his arm, prepared to throw it away. A clap of thunder sounded, though the sky was clear, and he saw a light flash briefly in the woods to his right.

Holding himself absolutely still, he listened, and heard nothing. Nothing at all. The night was too quiet.

Dropping the ring on the ground next to his bedroll instead, he half rose, and pulled the axe from its sheath. Keeping his eyes on the direction where the flash had occurred, he picked a stone from the ground and tossed it in Stephen's direction. There was no response.

He tossed a second stone and a third, until he heard a muffled groan. "Stephen," he hissed.

"What?" the minstrel asked, sitting up and rubbing his eyes.

"Quiet," Devlin whispered. "There is something out there, and I do not think it means us well."

He rose to his feet, still keeping his eyes on the forest. From the corner of his eye he saw Stephen unsheathe his sword, then pull on his boots. The minstrel stood up and joined him.

"What is it?" Stephen asked, following Devlin's gaze.

"I do not know," Devlin confessed, circling around the fire so that it was at his back. His eyes were still light dazzled, and he could see only vague outlines within the trees. There was nothing overtly menacing, yet he could not shake the feeling of dread that had overcome him. For himself he had no fear, but his was not the only life at risk.

His eyes scanned the perimeter of their camp, never resting in any one spot. "Keep your eyes sharp," he ordered. "It may be nothing, but better safe than surprised."

He heard a sharp gasp behind him, then the minstrel said, "Devlin," in a quiet voice.

Devlin continued scanning the forest, wondering why Stephen had not finished his thought.

"Devlin," the minstrel repeated.

Devlin turned, and his breath caught in his throat. At the edge of the clearing stood a giant. Easily twice the height of a man, he seemed formed out of the very night itself, for he was all darkness. No light glinted off that shape, no hints of gray or white alleviated its utter blackness. The creature had a head, but no signs of eyes or other organs could be seen. It made no sound, yet somehow it exuded a sense of incalculable menace and hatred. If pure evil had a form, this was it.

Stephen began backing away slowly, until he was on the

left of the fire, by their bedrolls. Devlin was on the right, keeping the fire between himself and the creature. Behind him, he heard the horses whinnying in fear and wished he could give vent to his own fears as well.

The creature turned its head back and forth, as if considering which one of them to pursue. Then he turned toward Stephen.

"Get out of here," Devlin ordered. This was no time for foolish heroics. Stephen, his eyes fixed on the dark monstrosity, did not move. He seemed paralyzed, or under a spell.

Devlin circled the fire and grabbed the minstrel by his shirt. He pulled Stephen back just as the creature reached for him. "Run," he said, giving Stephen a firm push in the back.

Stephen took a few stumbling steps. The creature turned and reached one impossibly long limb for Devlin.

Devlin swung his axe. It passed cleanly through but instead of severing the arm, the limb simply re-formed behind his stroke. He tried again, with the same result.

His gut tightened with fear. How could he fight a creature that he could not harm? It was as if the creature was made of mist, or of the blackness of the night sky.

But there was nothing insubstantial about the blow that struck him in the chest. Devlin went flying backward, his axe dropping from his hand. He landed on his backside twenty feet away. Instinctively he threw his knives, but they passed through the creature to no effect. Scrambling to his feet, he pulled out his dagger, though he did not know what good it would do.

To his surprise, the creature did not pursue him, nor did it turn its attention toward Stephen, who was standing near the frightened horses. Instead the creature cast its head around, as if searching for something. And then it glided silently toward the blankets where Devlin had sat only moments before.

"What is it doing?" Stephen asked.

"How should I know? But be prepared to make a run for it, if we must."

The creature's arm elongated, stretching down until it touched the ground, then began pawing at the blankets. Devlin caught the glint of gold in the firelight, and suddenly realized what it was searching for.

As the creature clenched the ring within its fist, Devlin's mind raced with the implications of the act. This was no chance encounter. The creature had been sent to find and destroy the Chosen One. Somehow, the creature had homed in on the ring of his office as if it were a magical scent.

But Devlin had taken off his ring, and now the creature was confused. Dropping the ring back to the ground, the creature turned in their direction.

There was but one chance. If they ran in opposite directions, the creature could follow only one of them. Thus the other was sure to live. Devlin knew what he must do.

"When I say *now*, cut the horses loose and run for your life. In the confusion we can make our escape," he said.

"But how will I find you?" Stephen asked.

If his plan worked, there would be nothing left of Devlin to find. But he could not tell the minstrel that. Stephen had a stubborn streak of his own. Devlin thought furiously. "Circle back the way we came. We will meet at that inn we passed yesterday."

"May the Gods go with you," Stephen said.

Devlin took a few side steps, edging himself away from the minstrel and closer to the fire.

"Now!" he shouted.

Stephen slashed the ties that held the frightened horses. Screaming with terror, they ran off into the night. Stephen ran, too, in the opposite direction.

Devlin ran across the clearing, his course taking him on an angle that crossed the monster's path. He needed to make sure the monster knew which of them he was to pursue. But he did not see the obstacle that caught his foot and sent him sprawling. As he hit the ground, the dagger flew from his hand and was lost in the darkness.

Devlin rolled swiftly to his side and rose, though his right ankle protested the strain. The creature swung its head in his direction. He knew he could not let the creature kill him. Not without a fight. He had to buy time for Stephen to make his escape. Devlin looked frantically, searching for a weapon. Any weapon. But his axe was gone, and his dagger was gone as well.

There was still the fire. Hobbling a few steps, he reached in and grabbed the end of a burning brand with his bare hand.

The end he held was unburned, yet still hot enough to hurt. But this pain was comforting to one who had worked so many years with hot metal.

"Devlin!" Stephen exclaimed.

"By Kanjti's left ball," he swore, as he realized the minstrel had returned. Now Devlin's sacrifice would be for naught.

"Run for it!" Stephen urged.

He could not. His ankle was throbbing, and he could barely stand, let alone walk. "I cannot. But there is no reason for you to die as well. This creature was sent for me. Save yourself. Your people need you. There is naught you can do here."

The creature advanced. Devlin swung the flaming brand in its direction. Unlike the sword, the flames caused it to pause, and for a moment he hoped he might somehow prevail. But then the creature reached one black hand into its middle and pulled something out. With both hands it formed a ball of utter blackness, which it then threw.

Devlin ducked, but the demon missile still grazed his shoulder with such force that it tore off clothing and skin. He knew that if the missile had struck directly he would have been dead.

"Here, monster," Stephen called.

Devlin turned his head, incredulous. Stephen was jumping up and down, waving his cloak in an attempt to divert the creature. "Over here, monster! Try a minstrel for a change."

But the monster paid no heed to him, and Devlin jumped out of the way as the next missile flew. This one missed as well, but cost him dearly, for as he landed his injured ankle gave way, and he fell to the ground.

Stephen began throwing things from their packs at the monster, hoping to gain its attention. Shoes, cooking pots, and a quiver of arrows all bounced off with no apparent effect. And then he heaved a ceramic jug which broke as it hit the monster's back, dousing the creature with liquid.

The scent of kelje filled the night. Devlin, with sudden inspiration, pulled his left arm back and threw the torch. The monster burst into flames as the alcohol ignited. It screamed, a high unearthly whine, and clawed at its flesh.

Devlin dragged himself backward, crawling away from that horrible sight. And still the monster continued to burn, with a bright white light that lit the clearing as if it were day.

"By the Gods," Stephen said.

Devlin silently agreed.

As the fire burned, the monster seemed to shrink in on itself. Devlin and Stephen both armed themselves with fresh torches, but there was no need. The fire continued, blazing white-hot, until there was nothing left of the creature save a blackened stinking circle on the ground.

Sixteen

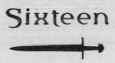

THEY BUILT THE FIRE UP HIGH AND REMAINED ON guard for the rest of that long night, but there were no further attacks. Devlin was furious that Stephen had returned to save him, but he was unable to give full vent to his anger since without Stephen's help the creature might never have been destroyed.

As punishment for his impetuosity, Stephen spent most of the next day in search of their horses. Devlin, unable to move far because of his injured ankle, had nothing to do but think about the events of the night before, and he did not like his conclusions.

He had seen magical creatures before. The skrimsal. The banecats. Ordinary creatures given extraordinary size, strength, and viciousness through magical spells. Some said such creatures were bred by mages, others that they were accidental creations, caused when natural creatures were caught up in magecraft. Though they were magic, they were also living flesh, and had weaknesses that could be exploited. When cut they bled, and thus they could be killed.

The creature last night had been different, able to

transform its substance from solid to mist and back again at will. It seemed to be a creature of pure magical energy, which meant it had been sent by a mage of great power. But which mage would have a motive to harm the Chosen One? Which mage would be able to key such a spell to the ring he wore? Devlin could think of only one man who fit that description.

Later that afternoon, his horse wandered back into camp on its own, nosing him familiarly, then gratefully slobbering down the grain that Devlin laid out. Stephen returned a short time later, having found his own horse. Apparently it had headed back in the direction of home until it was caught by a farmer.

They continued on their journey, staying in inns and farmhouses when they could. When forced to camp, they took turns standing guard. As the days passed and nothing unusual occurred, Stephen began to relax. But Devlin could not. He had a strange prickling sensation at the back of his neck, as if he were being watched.

Stephen tried on several occasions to engage Devlin in speculation about the origins of the creature that had attacked them, but Devlin refused to allow himself to be drawn in. He did not want to give any hint of his suspicions to the minstrel, lest Stephen find a way to spoil his plans. Again.

Devlin breathed a sigh of relief when the white towers of Kingsholm came into view. By then his nerves were stretched taut. He was constantly on edge, wondering when the next attack would come and what form it would take. The fact that no attack was forthcoming seemed an especially devious form of torture. A man could go mad with waiting.

They parted ways as they entered the city—Stephen to

find his friends, and Devlin to the palace. There he reported the success of his mission to an indifferent Royal Steward. His duty accomplished, Devlin was free to search for answers.

Master Dreng resided in the old city, off a once fashionable plaza whose picturesque fountain had long since run dry. Many of the residences sported the small signs of decay, rusting ironwork, missing roof tiles, or crumbling masonry. In contrast, Master Dreng's residence seemed newly built, with gleaming white stonework topped by glittering ceramic tiles in every hue of the rainbow. The effect was dazzling. And though the rest of the houses pressed close to each other, there were empty spaces on either side of the magician's dwelling.

Devlin mounted the steps, and as he approached the door slowly swung open, revealing an elderly servant whose frail, hunched form made him seem as old as time.

"Master Dreng is not receiving callers," the man intoned, his eyes fixed firmly on the floor. "Seekers of wisdom may return tomorrow, or you may leave your message with me and I will see that Master Dreng learns of your need."

The servant leaned on the door, and it began ever so slowly to close. Devlin stuck his foot in the lintel. He thought about shoving the door open, but feared the servant would shatter to pieces.

Thrusting his right hand in the gap, instead he said, "In the name of the Chosen One and the Kingdom of Jorsk, open this door or forfeit your life."

The ring on his hand sprang to life with ruby fire. It was a bit much, but it served its purpose.

There was a small gasp, and suddenly the resistance against the door was gone. Devlin pushed it open with his left hand and saw the retreating form of the servant as he scuttled away.

He stepped inside and found himself in an entrance hall. On the right, a wide stone staircase with worn carpet runners led to the upper stories. Ahead, where the servant had disappeared, there was a long hall with doorways branching off on either side. To his left was a room with scattered chairs and couches.

"Dreng!" Devlin shouted, but there was no answer.

He advanced down the hall and threw open the first door on his right. This proved a closet. The door on his left was a dining room. He continued on, finding in turn a small study, an empty room with no discernible purpose, a pantry, a small bedroom, and, finally, the kitchen, where he startled a young woman kneading bread. Making his apologies, Devlin retreated and returned to the front hall. He climbed the staircase, calling out the mage's name.

On the second floor he found three bedrooms, one of which appeared to be the mage's, and an elaborate bathing room. But there was no sign of Master Dreng. He began to feel foolish. What if the mage was not home after all of this?

At the end of the hallway was a small wooden door. Devlin opened it, expecting to find another closet, but instead found a narrow set of wooden stairs, scarcely more than a ladder. He looked up, and saw a faint light. "Dreng!" he called, as he began to climb.

As his head came up above the floor level, he saw that he was in a large room with a steeply pitched roof. Bookcases and cabinets lined the walls, while glowing white orbs set in wooden support beams provided a dim light. A large wooden table holding an empty decanter and a carelessly piled stack of books came into view next, with two stools beside it. Mounting the final stair, he looked around and realized the room covered the whole top floor of the dwelling.

"Dreng!" he called, for there was no sign of the mage.

"You needn't shout," Master Dreng replied. Devlin whirled, as Master Dreng stepped out of the shadows at the far end of the room. In his right hand he held a goblet of wine, which he raised in mocking salute. "So the Chosen One has returned safely. Again."

His voice was slurred, giving testament that the mage was well acquainted with the contents of the wine cup.

Devlin had spent the last fortnight carefully planning what he would say, but all of his cool logic disappeared with that mocking toast. In a single motion he twisted his right forearm, and threw the knife, pinning Master Dreng's right arm to a nearby post.

The crystal goblet shattered as it hit the floor, red wine running across the floor like blood. Devlin held the second knife in his left hand, so the mage could see it.

"That was just a warning," he said.

Master Dreng gaped at him, mouth open in astonishment. "Have you gone mad?"

It was a fair question. Caerfolk wisdom held that those who disturbed wizards at their work were liable to find themselves transformed into goats. Or worse. And yet Devlin saw no use in dissembling. He favored a direct approach, and if this mage took offense, so be it.

"Just how far would you go to win your wager?" Devlin asked.

Master Dreng began to raise his left arm.

"I would not move, if I were you," Devlin warned him.

"I am thinking a dead mage is just as much use to me as a live mage, and for once the Geas seems to agree. So be still and answer my question."

Master Dreng's left arm fell down by his side.

Devlin advanced slowly across the room, skirting the worktable until he stood within arm's reach of the mage. "How desperate were you to win that wager? So desperate that you had to help fate along?"

"What wager?"

"The wager on my early death," Devlin growled. "You must have been disappointed when you realized your creature had not destroyed me after all. But you made a mistake. You should have known I would come looking for you."

Master Dreng shook his head emphatically. "The lake monster? I had nothing to do with it. I've never even been to that uncivilized province."

What trick was this? "You know full well I do not mean that pathetic beast. The creature you sent was a being crafted all of darkness, that could change its form from solid to mist and back at will. The being that came looking for my ring!"

Devlin closed the distance and pressed the knife blade against Master Dreng's neck, holding the mage's bloodshot gaze with his own. He was vaguely surprised that the mage made no move to defend himself.

"You are mad. Mad or drunk. Such a creature exists only in your imagination," Master Dreng scoffed.

"Do you wish me to drag the minstrel Stephen in, to confirm what I say? No doubt he has set the encounter down already in wretched verse. But verse or plain talk, he will tell you he saw the same as I. A creature came out of the night, formed of the very fabric of darkness. And it knew exactly where to find the ring of the Chosen One."

Devlin pressed the knife blade harder, until he drew the faintest trickle of blood. "I call upon all the Gods to witness that my words are true, by my oath as Chosen One."

Master Dreng's eyes widened, then his shoulders slumped as if in defeat. "I believe you," he said. "But I did not send such a creature."

"Why should I trust in your words? What oath does a mage hold dear?"

"You stupid farmer. I did not send the creature because I cannot. I have not such power. I am only a mage of the second rank." His words held the ring of unwanted truth, and his mouth was twisted with anger and perhaps shame.

Devlin took a step back, withdrawing the knife. He had been so certain that Master Dreng was behind the attack, and yet the mage's bitter outburst had convinced him that the man was innocent.

"How can that be? You are a Master Mage, the Royal Mage of the Kingdom. I felt your power in that damned Geas spell."

Master Dreng lifted his left hand and pulled Devlin's knife out of the support post, freeing his sleeve. He held the knife in his hand, weighing the balance, then threw it so it tumbled end over end and embedded itself in the wooden table.

"The Geas spell is not mine. It was crafted decades ago by Hildigunn and Lenart, two mages of the first rank. I but mouth the words they created, and even then I have barely the strength to perform the binding ritual."

Devlin felt a faint hope die within him at these words. Deep inside, he had nourished the hope that someday the mage could be persuaded to lift the spell and free him. But if Master Dreng did not comprehend it then there was no hope that he could break it.

And now he had another problem. "So now I know my enemy is a mage of the first rank."

"Or one who holds such a mage in their employ," Master Dreng suggested.

Now his enemies were both faceless and multiplying. "Is there such a mage in the Kingdom?"

"No. There are no mages of the first rank in Jorsk. If there were, one of them would be the Royal Mage, not I."

For once the mage's mocking was directed at himself. His voice held the familiar sound of self-contempt. Devlin felt strangely guilty for forcing the mage to admit to his shortcoming.

"I apologize for disturbing you and your household. I will trouble you no more."

"No! You cannot come here, tantalize me with bits of a tale, and then leave. Come down with me to my study. My servant Johan will fetch refreshment, and you must tell me everything about your encounter with this creature. What you saw, what you heard, and how you managed to survive. If you describe it, I may be able to tell you who sent it."

As Master Dreng led the way, Devlin paused at the table and retrieved his knife, replacing it in the arm sheath. They climbed down the narrow ladder, then descended the stone stairs to the first floor. The elderly Johan appeared, bearing two wineglasses and a newly decanted bottle of a red wine from Myrka.

Devlin told of the encounter. When he described how his axe had passed through the creature, he could not repress a shudder, and took a quick gulp of his wine before continuing.

Master Dreng leaned forward in his chair, his eyes bright, his wineglass forgotten on the table beside him as he questioned Devlin over and over again about his experience, forcing him to recall every detail. The lack of sound. The appearance of the demon creature, how it rippled and flowed as it changed shape. How it had left no trail, and how—though they searched the woods—they never found the spot where the lightning had flashed and the demon had made its first appearance.

"An elemental," Master Dreng said, stroking his chin. "A creature made of darkness, just as you described. Never have I heard of one of such a size, but it is possible. Clever of you to banish it by using light."

"We did not banish it. Stephen doused it with alcohol and I set it on fire with a torch."

"I am sure that is what it looked like, but it was not burning, not in the true sense. An elemental cannot burn. What you did was to surround it with fire, which is a form of the light element. It was the light of the flames that destroyed the creature, and not burning in the sense that you know it."

Devlin shook his head. Such esoteric explanations were beyond his ken. "We killed it before it killed us," he said.

"Yes, you did." Picking up the bottle of wine, Master Dreng refilled Devlin's glass, then went to fill his own and seemed surprised to find it untouched.

"But I do not understand how it was attuned to the ring of the Chosen. Has the ring been out of your possession? Did you encounter anyone who troubled you, who might have been a sorcerer or a mage?"

"I saw no one I deemed a sorcerer, but I am hardly a judge of such things."

"No, but the ring you bear is," Master Dreng countered. "If someone near you is ensorceled, it will warn you."

"How?"

"The ring will heat up and you will feel profoundly uneasy. The nearer they are to you, the more clearly you will be able to sense them."

"I sensed no such thing before the creature's appearance," Devlin said. "But afterward...afterward, I felt as if someone were on our trail. Watching. Following. I thought it was my mind playing tricks on me. And as soon as I entered Kingsholm, the feeling disappeared."

"Curious. I must give this matter some thought. Perhaps there is something in my scrolls about elemental creatures. I seem to recall that Dunniver described them in her treatise on the properties of light and sound...." His voice trailed off, as he contemplated the possibilities.

"Just tell me who sent the creature, and I will do the rest," Devlin said.

Master Dreng suddenly turned sober. "Be very careful, Chosen One. The person who created this elemental and sent him after you is a sorcerer of great power. Greater than we have seen in generations. He will try again, and there is little I or anyone else can do to protect you."

"I will do as I may. As I must," Devlin said. In the end, he would do as the Geas commanded, for he had no other choice.

Two lines of fighters faced each other across the practice yard. Each fighter held a wooden long sword in one hand and a small round shield in the other.

"Again!" Sergeant Lukas commanded.

Each pair of fighters advanced toward each other and began to attack.

Captain Drakken watched with a critical eye, for while drilling with shields was a familiar exercise for the guards, the long sword was new. Part of her mind was absorbed in the drill, noting that Oluva showed definite signs of improvement while young Vidkun was as clumsy as ever. She watched as Sergeant Lukas moved between the fighting pairs, offering infrequent words of praise, but more often stopping the fighters to correct their technique.

When he reached the end of the line, he called, "Break," and the fighters ceased their labors. Most were sweating and out of breath. They drew apart, one going so far as to let her sword drag, which immediately drew Sergeant Lukas's wrath and the promise of a month of night watches.

"Change pairs," Sergeant Lukas called, and the fighters on the western side each advanced one place to their left, the last one running around the line to find his place at the beginning. In such a way each guard had an opportunity to practice against opponents of differing skills, sizes, and strengths.

"Now this time, try to remember what I taught you. Keep your shields raised. Slash with the sword, but don't swing wildly. And keep your footing. Understood?"

"Yes, Sergeant," called two dozen weary voices.

She knew they were tired. Knew they did not understand her current passion for relentless training and drills. Not that they hadn't trained before. On the contrary, she took pride in their training. While they might lack the fine sword technique practiced by the officers of the Royal Army, the guards excelled at their own weapons; the short sword, the cudgel, and the ceremonial spear. And they were more than capable of standing long watches without complaint, or of facing down a street riot.

But now Captain Drakken insisted that they train and drill as never before. Twenty-five years in the Guard had taught her to trust her instincts. Trouble was coming, and she was preparing to meet it as best she could. Though the King and his councilors seemed complacent, Captain Drakken knew it was only a matter of time before the troubles that afflicted the border provinces spilled over into the heartland, and then into the capital itself.

And when that time came, she and the Guard would be ready. What she really needed was a hundred new guards. Three hundred was her authorized complement, and it was scarcely enough to fulfill their duties, let alone prepare for an attack. She needed at least four hundred trained guards in uniform. Five hundred would be better. But time and time again, the King and the Royal Steward refused her the funds she needed. And thus she trained her current guards so that each could do the work of two.

But as hard as she drove them, she drove herself even harder. She had personally inspected every guard post and defensive fortification, and had met with the city leaders to draw up contingency plans. Each week she argued her case for new funds before the Royal Steward, and she lobbied the members of the court for support. And at dawn each morning she had her own weapons practice, ensuring that her skills were equal to the best of those she led.

At an age when many would think of retiring, she was preparing for war.

"The tall one at the end extends himself too far when he lunges. He is off-balance," a dry voice commented from behind her.

"Oluva has seen that as well," she replied. And indeed, a moment later, Oluva let her shield waver as if weary. When her opponent thrust his sword into the perceived opening, she danced to the side and struck him down with her shield, then placed the tip of her practice sword at his throat.

"Well done," the Chosen One said.

Captain Drakken turned slightly to face him. "You have a good eye for one who is not a swordsman."

"I have spent many an hour watching such as these practice. In time, one learns to distinguish those who are skilled fighters from those who are not."

Another enigmatic answer. Had he studied the sword or not? Who was he? A farmer? A metalsmith? And why would either have spent hours watching weapons practice? It made no sense. And yet nothing about this Chosen made any sense to her.

From the corner of her eye, she saw that the fighters had once again ceased their practice and returned to their lines. She turned her attention back to the field. "Lukas! Another quarter hour, then turn them loose," she called.

Sergeant Lukas nodded.

She turned her attention back to the Chosen One. "You wished to see me?"

"We must talk. In private."

"Come to my office. None will dare disturb us there."

She led the way across the courtyard, observing the Chosen One through casual glances. He had a few more streaks of white in his black hair, and there were lines of weariness on his face. Yet, all in all, he looked remarkably well for a man who had spent a week lingering at death's threshold, according to the testimony of the soul stone.

"May I presume you were successful?"

"Successful?"

"The lake monster," she prompted, with exaggerated patience.

"Oh, that," the Chosen One said, shrugging his shoulders dismissively. "Yes, the beast was destroyed, and the fisherfolk have reclaimed their lake."

A guard saluted them as they approached the Guard Hall. Captain Drakken returned the salute absently, then led the way up the stairs and into the building. Outside her office, her clerk looked up from the order he was copying.

"We are not to be disturbed," Captain Drakken ordered.

"Not even for the King himself," Devlin added.

The clerk looked at her for guidance. She wondered if Devlin was joking, then decided not to put him to the test. She nodded acquiescence. It was doubtful the King would come looking for her in any event.

Her office was sparsely furnished. A large desk held a bright lamp for reading reports late at night. One chair waited behind her desk, and two before it. A map of the Kingdom and another of the city—this one divided into patrol sections—covered one wall. The opposite wall held a small fireplace, and a weapons' rack.

She gestured to the chairs, but Devlin shook his head. "This will not take long."

She hesitated, then sat on the edge of her desk. "What did you have to say to me?"

The Chosen One ran the fingers of his right hand through his hair, then rubbed the back of his neck. "I seem to have acquired an enemy," he said.

"An enemy?"

Devlin nodded slowly. "On the first night of our return from Esker, we were attacked by a . . . creature. A magical being. The creature was searching for the bearer of the Chosen One's ring."

His words confused her, and she wondered if he was being deliberately obtuse. "A creature of magic? Like the skrimsal?"

"No. The skrimsal was a living being, but this was a creature forged out of the very substance of magic. Master Dreng called it an elemental."

An elemental? She had never heard of such. And yet it was no more improbable than the other strange things that had befallen Jorsk in these troubled times.

"And why are you telling me this? Since you are here, I assume you defeated this being as well?"

"I defeated the creature, but not the mage who sent it. It is probable that the mage will strike again. My presence in the palace may place others at risk, and thus I come to warn you. I did not want to speak of this publicly, lest there be panic."

Such caution was wise. Fear of a magical attack could weaken even the stoutest of hearts. And her guards would be no match for mageborn evil.

"Surely Master Dreng offered you his protection," she said.

"Master Dreng offered his regrets," the Chosen One said with a wry smile. "It seems that only a mage of the first rank could create an elemental creature, and thus good Dreng finds himself outmatched."

"So what will you do?"

"Nothing. I will wait. I will watch. Either the mage will strike again or he will not. It is up to the Fates."

She wondered how he could be so calm in the face of the new threat. Few things frightened her. In her youth she had once faced down a mob of angry peasants with only her partner to guard her back. And yet even she felt queasy at the thought of the horrors that an unscrupulous mage could inflict. If the legends of the mage wars were true, death was the least of what Devlin had to fear.

Perhaps his calmness came from the sense that he had nothing to lose. She thought again of the tangled web of stories and rumors that had been the fruit of her inquiries in Duncaer.

"There is news from Duncaer," she said casually. "The Earl of Tiernach had to abandon his plan for the New Settlements after the farmers were attacked by strange forest creatures. I believe they called them banecats."

Devlin's face was carefully expressionless. "They did not send for the Chosen One."

"How can you be so sure?"

"It is not their way."

Interesting that he referred to the Caerfolk as *they* and not *us*. Was this a sign that he considered himself a Jorskian now? Or was there something else he was trying to hide?

She fixed her gaze on her boot, which she swung idly, observing Devlin from the corner of her eye.

"You are correct. They did not send for the Chosen. It seems one of their own, a farmer, pursued the creatures into the forest and eventually hunted them down. Still, for all his efforts, the settlements were abandoned."

Her efforts proved for naught. The Chosen One showed no reaction to her words. And yet she was still convinced that he was the one in the tale. Only a giant leopard or other great cat could have inflicted those scars.

She lifted her head. "Perhaps there is something you can add to this tale?"

"How should I know aught of this farmer? I was a metalsmith, as you well know," the Chosen One replied.

She ground her teeth in frustration. She could not accuse him of being a liar. And yet she had the sense that he was not telling her the full truth.

But which truth was he hiding? The traders and couriers had brought back conflicting versions of this tale. One version said that the farmer had died while attempting to avenge his family. Another said that all present had been killed by the banecats' strike, with none left to avenge them.

And an even more chilling version had come to light, one that said the farmer had killed his own family, then been exiled to the forest for his crimes. There he had encountered the banecats, who recognized in him a kindred spirit and joined with him as he returned to take his vengeance on those who had exiled him. This she did not want to believe.

But what was Devlin hiding? What past sins were buried under his half-truths and evasions? Could it be, as some in the court whispered, that he was a traitor, in the pay of their enemies? Yet if so, how had he managed to circumvent the protections of the Choosing Ceremony?

The Chosen One had already accomplished much. If he continued to survive, he would become a powerful symbol and could be a potent ally in the struggle to restore order to the Kingdom. Yet how could she trust him when it was clear that he did not trust her? He gave nothing of himself away.

The Chosen One turned to leave. She held her breath, counting heartbeats until he reached the door.

"There is one thing more," she said, as if she had only just remembered. "A letter came for you. I have been holding it for your return."

He froze in midmotion, his hand grasping the door-frame, but he did not turn around.

"You must be mistaken."

"It was delivered to the palace, addressed to Devlin of Duncaer. The address is in Caer script. I assume that is for you."

She could tell she had taken him by surprise, as she had intended. His shoulders knotted, and his hand squeezed the doorframe until she thought the wood would crack beneath his grip. Then, with a visible effort, he relaxed and turned around.

Rising, she walked around to her desk and pulled open the center drawer. From it she withdrew a square of parchment sealed in wax. She held it out, and slowly the Chosen One advanced. He took the letter gingerly, as if it might bite.

He looked at the letter, and at the script, and his head nodded slightly as if he had confirmed something long suspected. Then he tore it open. His eyes devoured the contents in a single glance, then he crumpled the missive in his fist.

He tossed the letter into the fire and watched as the parchment began to singe. For an instant the paper unfolded in the intense heat, and she thought she saw a series of circles, or were they crowns? But before she could be certain the parchment burst into flames, and the message was lost forever.

With a last mocking glance, the Chosen One took his leave. She watched him go, half-regretting that her sense of honor had kept her from opening the letter in his absence. Next time she would not be so careful. Still she knew more than she had before. There was at least one person in Duncaer who knew of Devlin's existence... and who had the power to disturb the Chosen One's icy detachment.

Seventeen

THUNK! THE STEEL AXE SLICED THROUGH THE WOOD, cleaving it neatly into two pieces that fell away onto the ground. Devlin picked up the next piece from the stack beside him and set it on the frame. He swung the axe, and another piece was neatly divided.

The autumn morning was chilly, and frost covered the stone courtyard. The youth whose task this was sat perched on the lumber cart, huddled in his coat, his hands tucked under his arms. At first Devlin, too, felt cold, but as he settled into his labor his muscles warmed up, and he paused to strip off his coat.

He settled into the rhythm of the task, letting his mind drift. A tradesman's receipt. Murchadh had sent him a tradesman's receipt. He felt a flash of anger, and the axe cleaved through the wood and more, embedding itself in the wooden base below.

A tug was enough to remove the axe, and he resumed splitting the wood, careful not to let his emotions overwhelm him.

He had never expected to hear from Murchadh, for his friend had joined with the others in declaring Devlin forsaken. In their eyes he was already dead. Yet Murchadh had sent a tradesman's receipt. Nine stylized circles and the sign of his forge. There were no words, but it was enough. All nine golden disks had been delivered, which meant that Devlin had fulfilled his obligation.

But how had Murchadh known where to find him? One of the wool traders must have gossiped, despite Devlin's warnings. He had known that relying on such folk was chancy, but at the time it had not seemed to matter. He had been sure that he would be long in his grave by the time Murchadh received the coins and drew his own conclusions as to their source.

Devlin's confidence had been misplaced, for it was autumn, over four months after his arrival in Kingsholm. And though he had faced death thrice already, his old luck still held. Lord Haakon was not yet ready to welcome Devlin into his kingdom.

A shiver that had nothing to do with the cold ran through him as he wondered bleakly if the Lord of Death would ever be ready to take him. What if there was no death in store for him? What if this half-life was Devlin's fate, a punishment worse than any death could be?

He heard a voice behind him, but ignored it, lifting the final piece of wood into place. Then the voice called more loudly. "Devlin!"

He swung. The axe cut cleanly through the wood, and he set the axe in the chopping frame. He turned.

Captain Drakken regarded him quizzically as the youth scrambled off his perch and began stacking the kindling in the lumber cart.

"The wood offended you?" she inquired.

"My muscles needed the work."

The cart quickly filled, and he realized he had no idea

how long he had been chopping wood. At least half an hour, maybe more. It was hard to tell, for the sun had yet to banish the gray predawn mist.

She came closer, and he observed that she was dressed casually, in woolen leggings and tunic, with a long sword belted around her waist.

"I know of few souls who would brave the dawn chill for exercise," she said. Then her eyes widened. "That is your axe!"

"Of course."

"But it is a weapon, not a common tool. How can you treat it so?"

Ah. Her outrage was that of a purist. Many warriors regarded their weapons as sacred, and treated them with reverence. As a metalsmith, Devlin had no such illusions. In the end, a weapon was but a tool, no different from any other tool made of cold metal.

He lifted the axe out of the frame and wiped the blade clean with a rag from his belt. Then he ran his thumb along the edge, but as he expected there were neither nicks nor scratches. The steel held true.

"It is only an axe. What better use for it than chopping wood?"

Captain Drakken shook her head. "I do not understand you. But I must continue on my way, for my practice partner will not be pleased if I keep him waiting."

"I will walk with you, if I may. I presume the guards have a target for practicing at the bow?"

"Of course. There are several in the training yards, near where you saw the sword drills. Come, I will show you, since it is on my way."

"I thank you for your courtesy," Devlin said.

Sheathing his axe, he picked up his coat, then the

transverse bow and quiver, which he had brought with him. Turning to the servant boy, he said, "The same time tomorrow. And bring more wood."

As they walked, Captain Drakken eyed the axe in his hand and shook her head. "The axe is a common weapon among our people, but I had not heard it was used in Duncaer as such."

"Few in Duncaer would consider it a weapon at all," Devlin agreed. Even he had not. When he had forged the axe, he had intended it for use in clearing forest land in the New Settlement, where oak and heartwood were common. And so he had forged an axe blade of great size, twice again the size of an ordinary axe. The steel blade had been a testament to his skill, while the size of the axe meant that only one of his size and strength could effectively wield it. He had been well paid for his conceit. Never would he have begun the making if he had realized that the axe's true destiny was to cleave flesh and not wood.

He forced the unwelcome thought from his mind. "The transverse bow is the weapon I was trained with," he said in an attempt to change the subject. "Smaller than your crossbow, it uses lighter bolts but is more accurate."

She turned her head, and her steps slowed as his words caught her interest. "Why would a metalsmith be trained?"

"It is the law."

"All smiths must practice at the bow? There is no such law," she scoffed.

Her words puzzled him, and then he realized his mistake. For a moment he had forgotten that she was a foreigner. "It is our law," he explained. "All must choose a weapon on their naming day, and train until they can demonstrate their skill. Those who live outside the cities and the protection of the peacekeepers must join the militia and drill on the first day of each month. Only those who are crippled or have served for seven sevens in years are excused."

"Everyone?"

"Except the feeble-witted. A few choose the sword, but most will use the spear or the bow. Wooden bows are common in the country, though a city dweller may have a transverse bow made of steel." Steel was all too rare in Duncaer, for each precious bar of iron had to be imported at great cost. In Duncaer, possessing a steel axe and transverse bow were signs that he had once been prosperous.

Captain Drakken shook her head from side to side. "So all of your people are trained in the art of war? That explains much."

It was one of the things that had puzzled him about the people of Jorsk. From the earliest age, Caerfolk were taught that they must rely upon each other for protection. All drilled at their weapons so they would be ready to face any danger. In Duncaer, the skrimsal would never have escaped unscathed. If the villagers had been unable to deal with the creature themselves, they would have summoned nearkin and farkin until the weight of their numbers overwhelmed the beast.

Compared to his folk, the people of Jorsk seemed strangely passive. They relied upon others for their protection, whether it be the Guard, the Royal Army, or the Chosen One. And yet somehow these people had forged a mighty empire.

"Our skills are not infallible. If they were, Duncaer would still be a Kingdom, and not a mere province of Jorsk," he said.

"We won it. But I wonder how long we can hold it?" she mused.

For that he had no answer.

A few days after Devlin's return to Kingsholm, he attended the weekly court dinner, held in the Great Hall. Devlin took his customary seat at the head of the table on the farthest right, where the lesser members of the court gathered. The servants brought wine for all, and then King Olafur called upon Devlin to rise. Devlin stood there uncomfortably, the focus of all eyes, as the King praised his courage in defeating the giant skrimsal. It was an intensely uncomfortable experience, but mercifully it was brief, and after the formal speech, no further mention was made of the incident, for which Devlin was duly grateful.

He thought the matter well forgotten, but a week later he returned to his quarters to find that he was summoned to meet with the King on the next morning. The invitation was politely worded, but nonetheless it was a command. Devlin wondered at the reason for this summons. Could it be that the King had a task for the Chosen One? An errand that would take him far from this wretched city? He could but hope.

The next morning, he rose before dawn as was his custom, then went down to the courtyard to perform his exercises. As the rest of the palace began to stir, he made his way back to his room, summoning a chamberman with hot water so he could bathe the sweat from his body. Then he dressed carefully in the court uniform of the Chosen One.

As he left his room shortly before the appointed hour, he found a chamberwoman waiting to escort him to the

King's apartments. He followed her as she led him down the stairs and through the corridors until they reached the older section of the palace. Here the floors were not wood parquet, but marble tile, worn smooth with age.

Only the presence of a guard standing at attention in the hallway marked the entrance to the King's own apartments. As Devlin approached, the guard knocked once on the door with her fist.

"He is expecting you," the guard said, and as if on cue the door swung open behind her.

Devlin had expected to find himself in an audience room, or perhaps an office, but instead the door revealed a small parlor, scarcely larger than his own quarters. The dark-paneled walls were hung with gaily colored silk tapestries, and while there were no windows, elaborate filigreed sconces lit the room brightly. In the center of the room was a small table, where King Olafur sat opposite his daughter Ragenilda.

"Your Majesty. Your Highness," Devlin said, bowing first to the King, and then to the young Princess. He hoped his surprise was not evident in his face.

King Olafur acknowledged the bow with a brief inclination of his head. "Chosen One, this is my heir, the Princess Ragenilda."

The Princess rose from her chair and gave a brief curtsy. "My lord Chosen One," she said solemnly, her bright blue eyes fixed on his.

Devlin felt acutely uncomfortable. The King was his master, but how was he supposed to behave toward someone who was both a child and royal? He had no training for such situations.

"Princess, I am honored by your presence," he said at last, bowing again.

The Princess resumed her own seat, and the King gestured that Devlin should join them as well. As Devlin sat at the table, two servants came in, bearing bowls of fish porridge and then a platter of pastries. Glasses were filled with a pale purple liquid, and then a cup of kava was placed in front of the King. A second cup was offered to Devlin, and he seized upon it as if it were a lifeline.

He realized two things in that instant. First, the presence of the young Princess made it unlikely that the King had an errand for the Chosen One. And second, that he was expected to break his fast with the King and the Princess, as if he were accustomed to rubbing elbows with royalty. Devlin felt a trickle of sweat run down his spine, and for a moment he wished himself far from here. Anywhere would be better than this, even another confrontation with the skrimsal.

King Olafur took a sip of his kava, then took up his spoon and began to eat his porridge. The Princess did the same, and, after a moment, Devlin followed their example. The fish porridge was flavorful, but somehow in his imagination he had thought a King would have a taste for far grander fare. But perhaps the simpler food was in keeping with the Princess's presence.

"My daughter wished to meet you for herself," King Olafur said, after a few moments of silence. "I thought such an informal setting would be more to your liking."

This was an informal setting? With a guard outside the door, and at least two servants always in the room with them? He wondered what the King thought to be a formal occasion, and then realized that he did not want to know.

"It has been many years since I spoke to someone from Duncaer," King Olafur said. "So tell me, are my subjects there still loyal to the empire?"

Devlin took a sip of the rich kava, to give himself time to think. The Geas bound him to tell the truth, but he also knew there was nothing to be gained from insulting this man.

"They are as loyal as they have always been," Devlin said. The Caerfolk held little love in their hearts for the conquerors, but they were wise enough to know that rebellion was folly. As long as the Jorskians controlled the passes leading into the mountains, and their garrisons held the great city of Alvaren, there was little that the Caerfolk could do. But should the occupying army ever weaken—

"That is good to hear," King Olafur said, apparently oblivious to the true meaning of Devlin's words. "And now with your example perhaps others of your folk will choose to enter our service."

Devlin shook his head. "I doubt there is any man or woman who would want to follow in my footsteps."

A servant coughed, and he realized that his answer had been less than politic. "Only the Fates can decide who will be called to be the next Chosen One," Devlin added.

The King set his spoon down, and the servants cleared away all three bowls of porridge, replacing them with plates of rare spiny-fruit from the south. The princess began to peel hers with a small knife. Devlin kept his hand firmly on his cup of kava. He had eaten enough for courtesy's sake, and had no wish to make a fool of himself trying to peel apart the delicacy.

But his gaze lingered on the Princess Ragenilda, who had remained silent so far. She was a pretty child, with wide blue eyes and long blond hair done in elaborate braids. Her face was solemn, and she was entirely too still, too self-possessed, for one who held only nine winters to her credit. He wondered if she ever smiled, and what it would take to set her at her ease.

"Princess, was there some reason why you wished to meet me?" Devlin asked.

"Were you scared?" she asked.

"I do not understand."

Princess Ragenilda took a last bite of the spiny-fruit and wiped her fingers carefully on the linen napkin. "Were you scared?" she repeated. "When you fought the lake monster?"

"No," Devlin said.

"But they say it was as big as a tree. And it spit fire," she argued.

Devlin winced, wondering what version of the tale she had heard. He had said little in his report to the council, and after their return Stephen had declared that he would make no song of the event. But no doubt there were other minstrels who felt free to embroider the tale to suit their audience.

"It was large, yes," Devlin said. "A dozen times as long as your father the King is tall. But it did not spit fire."

"And you were not afraid?"

"I had a duty to do. I knew if I did not kill it, then it would kill me, and go on to kill others. And then I was angry, because it stole my axe."

"Really?" The Princess leaned forward, and there was a faint smile on her lips. "It stole your axe?"

"In a way, yes," Devlin said. "So I had to kill it."

The Princess giggled.

"The Chosen One showed great courage. Would that all my servants were as dutiful in their tasks," King Olafur said.

At his words the Princess's brief animation faded.

Recalled to her duty, she sat back in her chair, once again the picture of propriety. The young girl he had seen was gone, replaced by the Crown Princess of Jorsk. Devlin felt a flash of sympathy for the young Princess. The King seemed to treat her kindly; after all, he had invited Devlin simply because Ragenilda wished to meet the Chosen One. But it was a distant kindness, a formal relationship that was a far cry from the way a Caer family would behave. He wondered if she was ever allowed to escape the rigid confines of protocol and play as a child should. Perhaps matters might have been different if her mother had lived, but the Queen had died soon after Ragenilda's birth.

With the Princess silenced, the King himself seemed to have nothing else to say, and Devlin finished his kava in silence. He was grateful when the King finally arose, signaling the end of the strange interlude.

Devlin's steps slowed as he drew near the Royal Temple. He had not returned to the temple since the day of his Choosing Ceremony, but now Master Dreng had summoned him, claiming he had urgent news to relate. As Devlin entered the dark confines he felt a sense of unease, as if he were trespassing where he had no right to be. As his eyes accustomed themselves to the gloom, he saw Master Dreng conversing with Captain Drakken as they both examined a mosaic on the wall. He wondered why the Captain was here. Had the mage summoned her? Or had she simply happened by?

His boots echoed off the marble floor as he advanced. "Dreng!" he called out. "You wished speech with me?"

Master Dreng gestured with one hand, his attention still on the mosaic. As Devlin drew near, he realized that the mosaic was actually a map of the Kingdom, showing the cities and provinces in elaborate detail.

Captain Drakken nodded. "So there is a spy among us," she said to the mage.

A spy? "What are you discussing?" Devlin asked.

Both turned toward him. Captain Drakken appeared thoughtful. Master Dreng looked worried.

"My lord Chosen One," Master Dreng said, with a formal bow, bending nearly in half. "I have failed in your service and must beg your forgiveness."

What nonsense was this? "Speak plainly or not at all," Devlin ordered.

Master Dreng straightened up. "I have discovered how the elemental was able to find you," he said, gesturing toward the stone wall. He held out his right hand and opened his fist to reveal a glowing red stone. "Someone used the soul stone to key the spell, and thus the elemental had your scent, as it were. I have shielded it now, as I should have done on that day, so it cannot be used for such again."

Devlin eyed the glowing stone, which pulsed faintly as if it were a living creature. "What is that thing?"

Master Dreng blinked in surprise. "It is the soul stone."

"You said that. Now tell me, what is it?"

Master Dreng appeared puzzled. "This stone was sealed to you during your Choosing Ceremony. It is one half of a larger stone. The other half is the stone set in the ring of your office. The rings are fashioned by the court jeweler, but they have no power until they are bound to the wearer in the Choosing ritual."

Devlin cast his mind back to the day of his Choosing. He remembered there had been a glowing stone on the altar. The temple priest had placed the stone in a box or container of some sort.

"What is it for?"

The mage gestured to the map wall. "The soul stone is tied to your life essence. When you leave on an errand, it is affixed to the map wall, where it follows the track of your journey. When you return to Kingsholm it is removed, and placed back in the casket until the next journey."

"The stone tells us if the Chosen One is hale or wounded," Captain Drakken added. "So we knew that you were sorely wounded at Long Lake, and lay near death for several days. Then the stone showed your return to health. And if you were to die, the stone would tell us that as well."

Devlin's flesh crawled as he looked at that stone, and he took an involuntary step backward. He could not bear the thought that his private struggles were made plain for all the world to see. This was an unclean magic and he wanted no part of it.

"So the sorcerer who sent the creature of darkness had merely to see this map to know where I was?"

Master Dreng shook his head. "This was far more ingenious. A spell was cast to link the mage with the power of the soul stone, enabling the mage to follow the track of your soul across the ethereal plane. A cunning spell, but still it was easy to detect, which means the mage who placed it was less powerful than I. If a mage of the first rank had placed such a spell, I would have found no trace."

Devlin's mind recoiled from the horror of the thing. How could the mage speak so casually of an enemy who had the power to touch Devlin's very soul?

"So there is someone in Kingsholm who is in league with my enemy and wishes me dead. Someone in the city, or maybe even in the palace, who has access to this temple," Devlin said, fighting hard not to let his inner turmoil show.

"At least one traitor," Captain Drakken said. "Maybe more."

She looked angry at the thought. Well, security in the city was her domain, so it was no wonder.

Devlin could summon no such anger on his own behalf. Instead all his outrage was focused on the discovery of this soul stone. "What else have you forgotten to tell me? What other tricks does that cursed stone perform?"

The venom in his voice seemed to startle his companions. "There is nothing else," Master Dreng said. "Except that you can use the soul stone to summon assistance. You simply invoke the ring and focus all your thoughts upon the need for assistance. The stone in the map will change to a blue color, so we will know of your need."

"Though whether the King decides to send troops to answer that need is another matter entirely," Captain Drakken said dryly.

"And what of the Geas? Is there aught else you should tell me?"

"I have told you all I know," Master Dreng answered.

Devlin turned his head and spat on the floor, not caring that he had violated the sanctuary of this temple. "You are fools. All of you. Small wonder that the Chosen are killed like mayflies if such wisdom is all you have to offer them." They were like children, playing with magics they did not understand. Did they have any idea of what the Geas could drive him to do in their service?

He turned on his heel and began to walk away, then spun around. "Do you want to know how the Geas feels, oh mage of the second rank? Have you ever seen an iron nail pulled toward a lodestone? Imagine such a force multiplied a thousand times. When the Geas commands, I have no will. If my horse founders, I must walk. When I can no longer walk, I must crawl. The Geas does not care if I arrive at my destination a bloody, useless cripple, just so long as I obey its commands. Gods! I nearly slew two guards in Esker simply because they wished me to speak with their lord while the Geas commanded that I continue to Long Lake without delay."

He turned again and walked out of the dark foulness of that accursed temple and into the bright sunlight beyond.

Captain Drakken watched the Chosen One as he stormed angrily out. He was gone before she could think of a word to stop him. She looked over at Master Dreng, and saw that his face bore the same shock that she knew was written on her own.

"Is that truly how the Geas spell works?" She had known it was a compulsion, but not that it could be the living hell that Devlin described.

Master Dreng spread his hands apart. "I do not know. The Geas spell was meant to ensure that even if the Chosen One lacked a sense of honor or duty, he would still fulfill the responsibilities of his oath. That is how it is described in the scrolls of the masters."

"But what if the one chosen already has a strong sense of honor?"

"Then I do not know. But I fear that in this instance the Geas spell may have done far more harm than good."

Eighteen

"I STILL SAY MY PLAN WOULD HAVE WORKED. IF there had been a dozen decent archers in that village, there would have been no need for my reckless performance," Devlin argued.

"They would still have needed someone to cast the net," Stephen countered.

"Any fool could have done that," Devlin said. He reached for the pitcher and poured himself another mug of the ale.

Captain Drakken leaned back in her chair and gazed down the length of her table. To her right sat the Chosen One, and across from him the minstrel Stephen. Ranging down the table were her six lieutenants, and her most senior sergeants. Competition for seating at the head table had been fierce, once her guards had learned that Devlin had finally accepted her invitation to dine with them. In the end she'd assigned the seats by simple seniority.

The rest of the tables in the Guard's dining room were full, as all those not on duty had gathered within. She made a mental note to praise Nikulas the cook. The food had been up to its usual high standards, but his true genius had shone in the choice of beverage. From somewhere her cook had managed to procure a cask of ale brewed in Duncaer, which was served in pewter tankards to those at her table.

Upon tasting the ale, Devlin's eyes had brightened and he had been lavish in his praise of her hospitality. She had a tankard herself for the sake of politeness, though she could not see the attraction of the bitter brew. But no matter. The Chosen One was consuming enough ale for the entire table, though as yet his words were unslurred. Still, the drink had some effect. She'd wager that he'd spoken more freely in these past two hours than he had in all the months since he'd arrived in Kingsholm.

Devlin had described the battle with the skrimsal in matter-of-fact tones, assisted by cheerful observations from the minstrel. When Stephen reminded Devlin of how he had been wounded by an arrow shot by his allies, Devlin had surprised them all by bursting into laughter.

Her guards had hung on every word.

A part of her listened to his tales while another part dwelt upon the part that he did not share. They had both agreed that nothing was to be said of the elemental creature. They did not want the sender to know how nearly he had succeeded. Better that the sorcerer and his accomplice remain in the dark, while she and her guards tried to determine if the traitor lingered within Kingsholm or had already taken his leave. All had been quiet in the four weeks since Devlin's return to Kingsholm, but that did not mean the threat was gone. She would not be satisfied until she had found the traitor, and chained him in the guardhouse to await his fate.

"It is as I told Lord Brynjolf," Devlin continued. "I did the fisherfolk no service. What they needed was someone who could teach them their own strength."

"You mean they should have attacked the creature on their own?" Lieutenant Embeth asked.

"Of course," he said. "If they had but put their minds to it, they would have come up with a scheme, one like mine or perhaps better. United they could have destroyed the beast."

"But surely some of them would have been killed in the attempt," Lieutenant Didrik pointed out.

Devlin shrugged. "What of it? If one were killed, even two or three, so be it. They would have died knowing they gave their lives to save their kin. Instead the fisherfolk waited passively while more than a dozen of their own were slain. It makes no sense."

"Not everyone is accustomed to thinking in such cold-blooded terms," Captain Drakken said. "Few have the ability to command, and to make the hard decisions that need to be made in times of peril."

Devlin shook his head. "They are sheep because they wish to be. You will not convince me otherwise." He turned to Lieutenant Didrik. "Didrik, if it had been you at that lake, what would you have done?"

"Evacuated the area and sent for reinforcements," Didrik replied.

Other guards began to argue with the lieutenant, describing how they would have handled the situation. One suggested poisoning the lake, which seemed a good idea until someone else pointed out that the poison would also kill the fish that the villagers depended upon.

Devlin leaned back in his chair, his eyes half-closed as he listened to the friendly wrangling. He seemed at his ease, as if he were just another of the young officers in her command.

Around the room, the gathering began to break up into

small groups. Those who had night watch had sipped citrine instead of wine with their dinners, and now rose and took their leave. Those who remained clustered in small groups, talking. One group began a dice game at a corner table. And across the room, a half dozen of the guards began a game of darts.

She noticed Devlin's gaze wander toward those who were playing at the dartboard. He watched the game for a few moments.

She tapped his elbow, and he turned his attention back to her. "Do they play the game in Duncaer?" she asked, indicating the board.

"We have a similar game, although we do not use those small feathered things."

"Darts. They are called darts."

He nodded.

"If you do not play with darts, then how is it done?" she asked, suddenly curious.

Devlin bared his teeth in a grin. "What say you, minstrel? Shall I show them how we play the game in Duncaer?"

The minstrel looked momentarily confused, then he returned the grin. "Would you give me leave to make a few wagers first? A full purse does no one any harm."

Devlin appeared to think for a moment, then shook his head. "Letting you fleece her guards would be poor repayment for the Captain's hospitality," he said.

"Another time," Stephen replied.

Now she was truly curious.

"May I?" Devlin asked.

"Of course."

He rose to his feet and lifted the pewter tankard of ale, draining it in a single gulp. Then he banged the tankard on the table. As heads began to turn he called out, "Clear a path," in a voice loud enough to cut through the drone of conversations.

Heads turned, but no one moved. "You there, at the painted board. Clear a path," he ordered.

The minstrel rose and walked around the table, gesturing for the guards to move to the sides of the room, leaving a clear path between where Devlin stood and the dartboard. Reaching the board, Stephen pulled out the darts, and placed them on a nearby table.

Devlin lifted one booted foot to the chair, and pulled out a thin metal blade. Then he repeated the same with his other boot. Drakken rose to her feet, wondering what he would do next.

Devlin held the blades, one in each hand. She waited for him to advance to the target, but instead he stood there, and gave the room a mocking bow. "This is how we play in Duncaer," he declared.

As he straightened his hand flashed. The first knife appeared in the center of the board. Then the second. He twisted his arms and suddenly two more knives appeared. A third knife appeared in the board, and then he threw the last.

She watched as it flew through the air, tumbling end over end until it embedded itself in the target, striking so close to the first knife that the metal rang.

There was stunned silence as Stephen walked over to the board. "Dead center," he announced, as if there had been any doubt.

Never had she seen such skill. It must be twenty paces or more to the board. And Devlin had barely taken aim. Indeed, he had thrown the first knife so quickly it had not been till the knife appeared in the target that she had known what he had done.

"Praise to the Chosen One, a man of many skills," she said, lifting her wineglass.

"Praise!" the guards shouted, lifting their own glasses in turn. Excited chatter broke out as the guards clustered around the target, to witness his accomplishment with their own eyes.

"That was quite a feat," she said, resuming her seat.

Devlin shrugged, taking his own seat. "It is a common game among the peacekeepers in Duncaer. For a while in my youth it was a fashion to play."

"Where did those last two knives come from?"

"You will have all my secrets now," he said. Then he extended his left arm, turning it over and rolling up the sleeve, revealing a leather harness strapped to his forearm.

"Flex the right muscle and the knife is released," he said. "Simple."

"Convenient. An assassin's weapon."

"Or a wise man's," Devlin countered. "The hidden knife gives no insult to the host, and yet is instantly ready in time of need. If I had had these at that wretched inn I could have disarmed that clumsy boy in a heartbeat."

Stephen returned to the table, bearing the four knives. She watched as the Chosen One carefully inspected the blades before returning them to their hiding places. Then he rose and gave a half bow.

"Captain Drakken, I thank you and your guards for your hospitality."

"And I thank you for a most interesting evening," she said. She was certain the guards would talk of nothing else for days to come. "Remember that we are at your service. You are welcome here whenever you wish."

"I will remember," he promised.

After that night, the guards treated the Chosen One as if he was one of their own. A few of the younger guards openly worshiped him. They took to drinking bitter ale instead of wine, and cropped their hair short in the way of the Caerfolk. And they pestered Master Timo until he made them throwing knives, and began to practice their own skills. This she had no objection to, until one fool severely cut his hand when he flexed the wrong muscles while wearing the knife in a forearm sheath.

She was about to forbid the knives altogether when Lieutenant Didrik took matters into his own hands. He asked Devlin to teach him and the young guards the art of the throwing knives, in return for lessons at swordplay. To her surprise, Devlin agreed.

She observed him one afternoon. Over and over again he demonstrated the throwing technique, so slowly that each move could be plainly seen, and then corrected each guard in turn as they tried to copy his movements. His patience with their clumsy efforts was remarkable. It was as if he had been teaching all his life.

And he applied himself to his sword training with a grim dedication. Though slower to learn than a youth would have been, Devlin's strength and size helped make up for that lack. As did his relentless practice. Indeed the Chosen One spent most of each day training with one weapon or another. His self-discipline was contagious, and she noticed that her own guards trained all the harder for his example.

Devlin occasionally came to the Guard Hall to join them at their meals, or to spend an evening. He seemed friendly, and from time to time would join in the conversation. But there was a limit to his camaraderie, a line he would not cross. He spoke of Duncaer and his past only in the most general terms. Never did he mention any family or friends, or give even a hint as to why he had sought the post of Chosen One.

Even when she conversed with him in private, he maintained his impenetrable façade. It was as if his outburst in the temple had never happened, and yet now she realized how much his demeanor concealed. Underneath his icy surface lay an anger that burned all the more hotly for being hidden.

The quiet lasted for nearly a month, as the fall turned into winter, and she began to hope that the trouble she feared would not materialize before spring. Then early one morning, as she sat at her desk reviewing the new watch schedule, she heard a knock at the door.

"Come," she said.

She looked up to see Lieutenant Didrik. "Yes?"

"Have you read last night's watch reports?" he asked.

"I read them as soon as I came in. Lieutenant Embeth reported nothing out of the ordinary."

Lieutenant Didrik's face bore an unhappy expression. "I thought she might, and that was why I wanted to speak with you."

Now she understood the reason he looked so ill at ease. Lieutenant Embeth was senior, and she had been in command of the night watch. Lieutenant Didrik had been on duty as well, but it was the senior lieutenant who would dictate the reports of what happened.

She wondered why Didrik, normally a stickler for the

rules, had taken the step of going around Lieutenant Embeth. What could have made him so uneasy?

"Out with it," she said, when he did not seem ready to speak on his own.

"There was a killing in the old city last night, just past the twelfth hour. A cutpurse picked on the wrong target, and was killed for his pains."

She nodded. "Yes, that was in the report. Unfortunate, but there seemed no question that the dead man had been the attacker and that the citizen had defended himself."

"The citizen attacked was the Chosen One," Lieutenant Didrik said.

Captain Drakken felt her eyebrows rise. "How do you know that? And why would Embeth leave out such a thing?"

Lieutenant Didrik drew himself up. "I had city watch last night. When the incident was reported the patrol summoned me. And then when I realized who the target was, I reported to Embeth. She did not think it important."

"Did she tell you why not?" Captain Drakken asked. She would question Embeth in private later, but for now she wanted to get Didrik's side of the story.

"Dev—that is the Chosen One had just left a tavern called the Singing Fish when he was attacked as he passed a small alley. Embeth felt it was a random incident, that it was just luck that the Chosen One was the target. But I am not so sure. The attacker looked too well fed, too well dressed, to be a mere cutpurse."

So Didrik had more of a brain than she had suspected. And more courage as well, to take the risk of embarrassing a senior officer.

"I thought you ought to know," Lieutenant Didrik

added. He looked pale and uncertain as he waited to see how she would react.

"Were you able to identify this attacker? Did anyone recognize him? Perhaps another guard who had arrested him before?"

"No," Didrik said, shaking his head slowly. "We could find no one who claimed to know him. Of course, any of his acquaintances might be afraid to come forward once they realized that he had committed treason by attacking the Chosen One."

No doubt that was how Lieutenant Embeth viewed the situation. But Captain Drakken's instincts led her to side with Didrik. The attack smelled too much like coincidence. And unlike Didrik, she already had reason to believe that at least one person in Kingsholm was working to destroy the Chosen One. They may have changed from using sorcerous tools to earthly assassins, but their goal remained the same.

"You did well to come to me," she said, and she could see Lieutenant Didrik practically sagging with relief.

"Tell the clerk to draw up new orders. I want a guard on the Chosen One, night and day. The guard should be discreet, but if anything happens I want one of our own there. And make sure they are under orders to take any attackers alive if they can. We must find out who is sending them."

"Devlin is not going to like this," Didrik pointed out.

She knew he was going to hate it. For that matter, she would hate it herself. But, "It is not our duty to make him happy," she said sternly. "It is our job to secure the city and to discover if there is a traitor lurking in our midst. Understood?"

"Yes, Captain," Lieutenant Didrik said, raising his right fist to his left shoulder in salute.

As he left her office, Captain Drakken felt a sense of satisfaction. Here was her first lead in over a month. A shame that Devlin had killed his attacker before he could be questioned, but no matter. The next time they would be prepared.

Nineteen

THE SEASONS TURNED, AND THOSE COURTIERS WHO remained in the city gave up their linens and silks in favor of wool and furs. Snow fell, a rarity in Duncaer, but in Kingsholm it fell often and in great quantities, until the city was blanketed with white.

With the court adjourned for the winter, there were few formal occasions that required Devlin's attendance. Instead he busied himself in training, only gradually realizing that it was unlikely there would be a new crisis before spring.

His demonstration with the throwing knives had started a fashion, and after watching the guards' ludicrous efforts, he agreed to become their teacher. In time they ceased being a danger to themselves and gained sufficient accuracy that they could use the knives effectively, although none approached his level of mastery.

When Lieutenant Didrik had offered to teach him the long sword, Devlin had agreed mostly out of boredom. He was not used to spending idle hours, and learning the sword seemed as good a use of his time as any. The lieutenant began by teaching him practice patterns, whose elaborate movements reminded him of the hours he had spent watching Cerrie practice her own forms. The patterns were easy enough to learn, and he drilled until his muscles knew them by heart.

The practice fights were a different matter. He found himself trying to swing the sword like an axe, or use it as a hammer to bludgeon his opponent. Once, when Didrik provoked him, he threw away the sword and simply picked up the startled lieutenant by his arms, shaking him while the onlookers rolled on the practice floor in laughter. But gradually his instincts improved.

On those rare occasions when he felt the need for companionship, he would join the guards in their hall for a few hours, or wander into the old city to wherever Stephen was playing. He became a common sight, and people no longer recoiled when they realized that the Chosen One was in their midst. But neither did they make any effort at courtesy or friendship. Only the guards and the minstrel Stephen treated him as if he were a man rather than simply a title.

The night the robber attacked, Devlin had been at the Singing Fish, paying a visit to Stephen. They had dined together, swapping news and idly speculating about the latest rumors swirling around the court. Devlin had enjoyed himself, perhaps too much, for he had let his guard down. The attacker had been upon him, a garrote wrapped around his throat, before he knew what was happening.

If the attacker had been quicker, or a trifle taller, then Devlin would have perished. But as it was, the garrote had been a shade too low, and had caught on the clasp of Devlin's cloak, preventing the leather from fully encircling his neck. Instinct took over. Gasping for breath, he caught the garrote with the fingers of his right hand, then slammed his left elbow back, striking his attacker in the ribs.

The attacker moaned, and the pressure eased fractionally. Devlin took a gulp of air and flexed his left arm so the knife fell into his palm. Reversing the knife in his hand, he then stabbed backward and as he felt the knife sink in he drove it upward and twisted it sharply.

Warm blood gushed on his hand. The attacker loosed his grip on the garrote and fell onto the cobbles, screaming in pain. Devlin pulled the leather cord from around his neck and bent nearly in two as his deprived lungs sucked in air.

The attacker bled to death before the guards arrived. That should have been the end of the matter, but the next morning he discovered that Captain Drakken had given orders that he was to have a permanent escort. Every time he left his room, one of the Guard was underfoot. At first it seemed coincidence that whenever he turned he found one of the Guard lurking nearby. But then he realized that they were following him, sometimes in uniform, sometimes not. It was as if he had acquired a second shadow.

He complained bitterly to Captain Drakken, but she refused to change her orders. She was convinced that the attack had not been a random robbery attempt, but was linked to the traitor that they both suspected was in the city. Devlin agreed with her logic, but not with her methods. He took to subterfuge and evasion, trying to shake off his watchdogs. To his disgust this only inspired them to cling more tightly to his side. It became a game with them, a matter of honor to have shadowed the Chosen One for an entire watch without losing track of him.

Three days after the attack, Master Dreng sent word that he needed to speak with Devlin. This time when Devlin arrived at the mage's residence, the elderly servant let him in at once and directed him to the mage's workroom.

As Devlin climbed the ladder to the attic loft, he noticed that the room was brightly lit, in sharp contrast to his previous visit.

"Good, you got my message," Master Dreng said, as Devlin's head came into view. "I am glad you came so swiftly." Master Dreng put down the scroll that he had been reading and came over to where Devlin stood. He extended his right hand.

After a moment Devlin clasped the hand in his own, wondering why the mage felt compelled to offer the clasp of friendship. As he tried to read the mage's expression he realized that for the first time in their acquaintance Master Dreng's eyes were clear, and the hand that clasped his was steady. A remarkable change in one who was reputed to spend his entire life deep in his cups.

"I see you have acquired a new scar," Master Dreng said. "I heard rumors that you had been in a scuffle of some sorts, but from that scar on your neck it seems more serious than I thought."

"It was nothing," Devlin said, though in his heart he believed whoever had sent the first attacker would try again. And Captain Drakken believed the same, for even now one of her guards was outside, trying to lurk inconspicuously in the square as he waited for Devlin to emerge.

Master Dreng shook his head, but did not contradict Devlin. "Come now," he said, gesturing to the pile of books and scrolls on his worktable. "I asked you here to share what I have discovered about the elemental that attacked you."

"Do you know who sent it?"

"No," Master Dreng said. From the bottom of a stack of books he pulled out a small volume bound in red leather and opened the book to a spot marked by a ribbon. "But I know what it was. Listen to this. 'The element of darkness may be shaped and given form by a mind-sorcerer, according to his will. The stronger the sorcerer, the more substance he can bind. The creature of darkness will appear utterly black, and no light can illuminate it. It is most often created in the form of a man or a beast, but can change shape at will. No weapon can harm it. The only weakness is the will of the sorcerer who created it, for as his concentration wavers, the being loses form and will disappear from this plane of existence.'"

"Is that all?" Somehow Devlin had expected more.

Master Dreng closed the book with a snap. "The writer goes on to speculate that Mikaela's lightning spell might destroy such a creature, if a mage of the first rank could be found to cast it in time."

"Of what use is this knowledge to me?" Had Master Dreng called him here merely to warn him? Devlin knew full well that there was no first-rank mage in the Kingdom. If his enemies sent another such creature, it would be up to him to defend himself. Again.

"Don't you see? The elemental was created by the sorcerer, shaped by his power and will. The sorcerer was linked to his creation, so when you destroyed the creature, the sorcerer would have felt the backlash. The negative energy may have killed him, or at the very least sorely wounded him."

"So perhaps this explains why there have been no further magical attacks," Devlin mused.

"And why they have switched to earthly tools to gain

their ends," Master Dreng said, the fingers of one hand tracing a ring around his own throat.

It made a strange kind of sense. An enemy powerful enough to send such a creature after him would not have stopped with a single attack. Not unless the destruction of the creature had cost him in some way.

This did not mean that Devlin was safe. The sorcerer might merely have been injured, and was now waiting, biding his time until he could strike again. Still, it was more than he had known before.

"I thank you for this knowledge," Devlin said.

"This is but one of the reasons I wished to see you," Master Dreng said. "Give me your ring."

"Why?"

"The time for questions was before you became Chosen One. Now give me your ring."

Devlin stripped the ring off his finger and handed it to the mage. Master Dreng placed the ring in a silver bowl and set it in the center of the worktable. Then he went over to the shelves, and from a row of flasks he pulled forth a crystal bottle filled with a dark green liquid. Returning to the table, he poured the liquid into the bowl until it covered the ring.

Master Dreng held his hands outstretched over the bowl and closed his eyes. Devlin took a step backward as the mage began to chant. Green smoke rose from the bowl and curled upward to disappear among the rafters. After a few moments the chanting stopped. Master Dreng lowered his hands and opened his eyes.

Devlin stepped toward the table and peered into the bowl. The green liquid was gone and the ring lay inside, seemingly unharmed.

Master Dreng picked the ring up and handed it to him. "Put this on," he ordered.

Devlin did as he was bid. "What did you do?"

Master Dreng smiled. "I will tell you in a moment. But first, fetch the bottle of wine from the cupboard against the wall."

Devlin shrugged. So the mage wished to be mysterious. He would play along with this game for now. He walked over to the cabinet and reached for the bottle. As his hand approached, he felt the ring grow warm and begin to burn. He snatched his hand back, and the heat quickly faded.

"What was that?"

"The wine is poisoned," Master Dreng said.

"Poisoned?"

"Yes. It was a test, to see if the spell worked. A man with enemies needs to beware of many threats. The ring will now warn you of poisons or drugs."

This was a potent gift indeed. "I am in your debt," Devlin said.

"No. The debt is not yours. As the master mage for the royal house, protecting you is one of my duties. I should have done this at once, rather than waited so long."

Master Dreng picked up a scroll in one hand and began to toy with it idly. He turned his head slightly, his gaze fixed on a point in the distance. "I have been thinking much of my duty, and of my own failings, in these days since we spoke in the temple."

His words made Devlin uneasy. It had not taken him long to regret his angry outburst, and to be ashamed that he had so revealed his weakness before Captain Drakken and Master Dreng. He had tried to put that memory far behind him.

But it seemed Master Dreng had not forgotten. "I have also studied much on the Geas spell."

"There is nothing more you need to say. What is done is done," Devlin said. True, Master Dreng had placed the loathsome Geas spell upon him, but the mage had not been the one to craft it. He had merely been doing his duty, and for that Devlin could not blame him. Any resentment he harbored was more than offset by the gift of the protection spell Master Dreng had just given him.

Master Dreng's lips thinned. "It is only right that you have the same knowledge I do, since you are the one bespelled."

After a long moment, Devlin nodded.

"The Geas spell acts upon your will," Master Dreng explained. "It knows no right or wrong of its own, but it takes your own sense of justice, of righteousness you could say, and forces the Chosen One to live up to his own highest standards, without regard for mortal weaknesses."

How could this be? The Geas had already driven Devlin to acts that he would never have even considered before. And yet Master Dreng was saying that the Geas was not controlling Devlin, but rather giving shape to something that had lain buried inside him all this time. This he did not want to believe.

"You must be wrong," Devlin insisted. "What of those who have no conscience, no sense of justice? How does the Geas work on them?"

"It doesn't. Those that are unfit are destroyed during the Choosing Ceremony."

"And you have seen this happen?"

"In the five years that I have served as Royal Mage, a dozen men and women have failed the test and been destroyed," Master Dreng said. He looked vaguely ill.

Devlin felt ill as well. No wonder few had believed he would survive the ceremony.

"We say those who fail are destroyed by the wrath of the Gods," Master Dreng said. "But it is interesting to note that the rejections began only after the Geas spell was created."

So it was the spell and not the power of the Gods that destroyed the unworthy. That made far more sense than believing that the Gods cared enough about the fate of the Kingdom personally to oversee the selection of the Chosen One.

"The Geas spell has one other benefit. Its power means that no other mage can seek to bespell your will."

Devlin could not be bespelled because he had no will of his own. Not when it mattered. But he refused to believe that the spell was simply a manifestation of his own will. The Geas was an outside force that controlled him, no matter what Master Dreng might say.

Though the mage had given him a clue to controlling the spell. The Geas could not be reasoned with, but if Devlin kept his mind focused, he could try to channel its energy. Thus he had done at Long Lake, when rather than succumbing to the temptation for a suicidal attack, he had managed to control the Geas long enough to form a plan that had a chance of succeeding.

"I thank you again for your service, and I will ponder on what you have revealed," Devlin said. The next time the Geas called him to service, he would be better prepared.

The day of the winter solstice approached. In Jorsk they called it the midwinter festival and spent weeks preparing for the celebrations.

Devlin had his own preparations to make. In the week

before the solstice he ceased trying to evade his watchers,
though he continued to complain about them. He declared
his intention to tire them out instead, and led them on
seemingly pointless treks until they had explored nearly
every corner of the palace grounds and the old city. At last
he found what he was looking for, although he continued
his wanderings for another day to avoid arousing suspicion.

From the market he purchased a sheet of copper and a
set of jeweler's tools, which he used to hammer the copper
sheet into a small bowl. He then wrapped it in a heavy
woolen cloak and hid the bundle deep within the woodpile
behind the kitchen.

Most of the guards were on duty for Midwinter's Eve,
but a quarter of their number had the evening free so that
they could take the watch on the morrow. The lucky
guards had planned a gathering in their hall, and they invited Devlin to join them should he tire of the more formal
celebrations hosted by the King and courtiers.

Devlin was carefully noncommittal in his responses,
giving no hint as to his real plans.

On that day, he practiced with the bow and sword as if it
were simply another day. Then, as he had done for the past
week, he went into the Guard Hall and took off his heavy
outer clothes, hanging them up on a rack with the others.
Devlin entered the large common room and spoke for a
moment to Lieutenant Didrik, while Behra, his watcher,
took a seat near the door. When Devlin headed to the necessary, Behra made no move to follow him. No doubt he
expected that Devlin would emerge after he had washed
up, as had been his pattern before.

But this day was different. His luck held, for the

washroom was empty, and Devlin went straight to the window. He opened it, and after seeing there was no one around, simply climbed through and out into the courtyard. The cold spurred him on as he made his way to the kitchen courtyard and retrieved the bundle. Donning the cloak and pulling the hood over his head, he became anonymous, just another laborer hurrying to finish his tasks in time to enjoy the festival.

Devlin kept his head low, but the guards at the eastern gate scarcely glanced at him as he joined the jostling servants heading to join family and friends at their celebrations. He traveled with the crowd until he was certain he could no longer be seen by the guards at the gate. Then he turned, making his way to the old city. From time to time he glanced behind him, but he saw no sign that he was being followed.

He reached the temple garden just before sunset. Swiftly he climbed over the low stone wall and dropped lightly down on the other side. As he had seen earlier, the snow in the garden was unmarked. There was little reason to fear that he would be disturbed.

He made his way to the center of the garden, the snow crunching softly underfoot. There, in the center was an oak tree, sacred to Mother Teá. Kneeling before the oak tree, he scraped away the snow until he reached bare earth, and cleared a space, where he then sat.

This was not his country. It was not his earth. But he had earth, and an oak tree and the open sky above him. It would have to serve. And though the Jorskians knew it not, he was certain that the dead walked here on this night, as they did in Duncaer.

From within his coat he removed the copper bowl and

set it in his lap. Loosening his cloak, he pulled his left arm out, and then ripped the shirtsleeve off it, leaving his arm bare.

With his right hand he took the dagger from his belt.

"Haakon, Lord of the Sunset Realm, I, Devlin, son of Kameron and Talaith, once called Devlin of the Gifted Hands, greet my dead. May the burdens they carry be lighter for my remembrance."

Devlin raised the knife. "Cormack, I remember thee," he said. Holding the knife firmly, he made a shallow cut along the inside of his upper arm, and let the blood drip into the copper bowl.

As the blood dripped, he remembered his elder brother and his generous spirit. Though five years separated the two, Cormack had never complained when his younger brother insisted on following him, trying to do everything that his elder could do. Cormack had led, and Devlin had followed him, but now Cormack was gone and Devlin could not follow.

"Bevan, son of Cormack and Agneta, I remember thee," Devlin said, making a second cut parallel to the first. He thought of nine-year-old Bevan, the eldest of Cormack's children, and the one who most closely shared his father's spirit. Bevan had been so proud when he was old enough to help his father as he labored. And now Bevan, too, was gone.

"Lyssa, daughter of my heart, daughter of Cerrie my joy, I remember thee," he said, as tears welled up. He blinked them back fiercely, and his hand trembled only slightly as he made the third cut. He could not give in to his grief. Not yet. But Lyssa had been just a baby. A gift from the Gods that he had not deserved and so they had taken her from him.

"Cerrie, daughter of Ishabel and Duncan, Cerrie the proud, Cerrie the bold, Cerrie of the fierce temper, I remember thee on this day, as I do every day," he said. He drew the final cut, his knife biting deeply into his arm.

Returning the dagger to his belt, he rhythmically squeezed his upper arm, forcing all four cuts to bleed until the bowl was half-filled. Then he placed the bowl on the ground before him, and bent forward until his forehead was pressed to the ground. He held the position for a long moment, then he straightened up.

"Know that you are remembered and be at peace. Lord Haakon, I call upon you as witness. These four are innocent. I alone bear the guilt for their deaths. As kin, I claim the burden of their sins. What they left undone in their lives, I will make right with mine. Let it be so," he prayed, as the last rays of the sun disappeared below the horizon.

Only then did he bandage his arm with the torn shortsleeve and shrug back on his cloak, pulling the hood over his head.

The ground was chill beneath him, and cold seeped up into his bones as he contemplated the blood offering before him. The tears he had not given in to before now fell freely, running down his face and freezing where they fell on his cloak. He grieved quietly, for there was no sound great enough to express his pain.

"And we will meet a-gain," Stephen sang, drawing the last syllable out while his fingers strummed the final chords on his harp.

There was a round of enthusiastic applause from the several dozen guards who were lucky enough not to be on duty and their friends, who had gathered in the hall to celebrate the midwinter festival. Stephen smiled, well pleased that he had accepted the guards' invitation to join them for the celebration. He'd had offers to play in more prestigious venues, but since his return to the city he'd grown quite fond of the guards and they of him. And their honest enthusiasm was a far cry from playing for jaded nobles.

Stephen looked to his left, and caught the eye of Jenna the drummer and Thornke the fiddler, who had joined him. They were both members of the Guard, but were fairly talented for occasional musicians.

"Shall we try 'Winter's Heart'?" he asked, naming a popular dance.

The other two nodded, and as he began strumming the opening bars of the melody they joined in. Scanning the crowded room, he saw a ripple moving among the dancers. A ripple that was heading in his direction. As the dancers parted, he realized they were making way for Captain Drakken. Unlike the revelers, she was in uniform, and Stephen had a suspicion he knew the reason she was heading in his direction.

As the Captain drew near, she caught his eye and gestured for him to join her. Turning to Thornke, he said, "Play on without me, I will be but a moment."

Lifting his hands from the strings, he stood the harp upright, then rose. The music continued without him, as Thornke switched to a lively country dance. Few in the crowd seemed to notice when Stephen stepped offstage.

Captain Drakken drew him to one side, where none could hear them over the sounds of the music. "Have you seen the Chosen One?" she asked.

"He is not here."

"Has he been here tonight?"

"No," Stephen said, wondering just how much he should say. "But then I did not expect to see him."

"Do you know where he has gone?"

"No, I do not," Stephen said carefully.

Captain Drakken rubbed her chin, her eyes worried. "He gave his watcher the slip nearly six hours ago. The guards have searched the palace grounds, but there is no sign of him."

"I would not worry."

She gave a bitter laugh. "That is easy for you to say. You are not the one who has been the target of two assassination attempts in the last month. Two that I know of, that is. Damn his stubborn hide, why did he have to pick this night of all nights to disappear? Half the city is drunk, and the rest are doing their best to join them. The Guard is spread thin trying to keep order, and he picks this moment to slip his leash." She shook her head slowly. "We have lost track of him before, but never for this long. I fear the worst may have happened."

She seemed honestly distressed. Stephen hesitated. If Devlin had wanted her to know what he was about, he would have told her. Telling Captain Drakken what he knew seemed like a betrayal of his friendship. And yet if he did not tell her, she was likely to call out all the guards in search of the missing Chosen One, and should they discover Devlin, that would be an even worse betrayal.

"I did not expect to see Devlin because the Caerfolk do not celebrate the midwinter festival. For them this is the Day of Remembrance, and it is a solemn occasion," Stephen explained.

"Remembrance of what?"

"Of their dead."

Her eyes widened in surprise. "He told you this?"

"No, he did not. But I know something of the customs of his people. This is a day for private mourning. Leave him be. He will return when he is finished. And if any man has earned the right to mourn in peace, it is the Chosen One."

He turned to go, only to have Captain Drakken take hold of his sleeve. Slowly he turned to face her.

"What do you know that I do not?" she asked.

He returned her gaze steadily. "Nothing that is mine to tell you. I say again, leave him be."

Captain Drakken held his gaze for a long time, then she nodded slowly. "I will wait until the first hour after sunrise," she said.

Stephen returned to the hall and resumed his place on the stage, but his heart was not in his playing. He kept wondering if he had acted rightly. What if Captain Drakken was correct and Devlin was truly in danger? By persuading the Captain to wait, Stephen might have done his friend a grave disservice.

He told himself that he had to have confidence in his friend. Devlin could take care of himself. He had evaded his watchers purposefully because he wished to be alone, as was his right and the custom of his people.

Stephen had taken his training as a minstrel seriously, and his learning had included a smattering of the Caer tongue. Devlin had never asked, and Stephen had never found reason to tell him—especially after he had been witness to Devlin's fever-born nightmares. Stephen had understood only a fraction of what Devlin had said, but it was more than enough.

Cerrie had been only one of the names that Devlin had

mentioned. Who the others were that Devlin mourned Stephen did not know, but he had seen the depth of the pain that Devlin kept hidden from the world. He would have mourned with his friend if Devlin had let him, but Devlin had never offered. So instead Stephen did what service he could, and guarded Devlin's secrets as if they were his own.

Devlin wept until he had no more tears, and still he could not touch the bottomless well of his grief. He meditated upon his sins and his losses until he felt light headed from sorrow and the day's fasting.

He listened intently, but he heard no sounds save the beating of his own heart and the wind sighing in the oak tree above. As the night wore on, he came to realize that his dead were not going to speak to him.

Perhaps Lord Haakon had already pardoned them, and they had no need to walk this earth. Perhaps they had chosen to walk the familiar hills of Duncaer rather than journey to this foreign land in response to his call.

Or perhaps they did not come because they had no wish to speak to him. Perhaps they feared he had forgotten them. Last winter solstice he had lain half-crazed with fever from the wounds he received in the struggle with the banecats. He'd collapsed in their den, expecting to die himself, only to discover a few days later that he was still alive. And that he had missed the Day of Remembrance.

It had taken him a year, but now he had atoned for his lapse. He had fulfilled his duties to Cormack's family, ensuring they would want for nothing. And he had made his pledge to Lord Haakon, taking on the burdens of the souls that had perished before their time.

As the first rays of dawn illuminated the garden, Devlin finally felt at peace. He knew he had done all he could. All a mortal man could do, since he had not the power to restore the dead to life or to change the past. He had accepted the burden of his sins, and he would face the judgment of the Gods without fear.

He flexed fingers stiff with the cold until they could reach into his pocket and remove the flask and firestone within. He poured the alcohol on the bowl and set it alight with the firestone. The flames burned brightly, scouring the bowl.

When the flames were gone, he picked up the bowl and stored it within his cloak. Then he took a healthy swig of the kelje, feeling the alcohol warm his stomach and set his blood moving. With joints protesting his long stillness, he hoisted himself to his feet, leaning on the oak tree like an old man.

Then he began making his way back to the palace, and to those that awaited him therein.

Twenty

SLOWLY, ALMOST IMPERCEPTIBLY, THE COLD OF WIN-
ter began to give way to the warmth of spring. Like a great
hibernating beast, the empire flexed its muscles and began
to rouse itself to wakefulness.

First to appear were messengers from the provinces,
bearing tales of winter hardships. Then came the nobles
and their emissaries. And the court, which had languished
in winter doldrums, stirred to life as new alliances were
forged and old ones broken.

The palace, which had rung empty and hollow during
the winter, was filled to bursting, as nobles who had not
seen the capital in years felt compelled to make their presence felt. Even Devlin could see that there were far more
courtiers present than there had been in the previous year,
but it took Stephen to decode the message of their presence.

For the first time in many years, the nobles from the
border provinces had come in force. Nearly every province
was represented by its lord or lady.

Rikard, Thane of Myrka, came, and brought with
him Lord Dalkassar, whose life Devlin had saved in the

inn those many months ago. Devlin was invited to meet with Lord Rikard, and spent an uncomfortable half hour deflecting expressions of gratitude from Lord Dalkassar. As he left, Lord Rikard pledged his support to the Chosen One.

At the time Devlin did not recognize the significance of his words. Then came Lady Falda, who ruled the province of Denvir, which bordered Myrka on the west. Lady Falda insisted on meeting with Devlin in private, and though she did not make any pledges, the private meeting was enough to start court gossip swirling.

The next to arrive was Solveig, Stephen's eldest sister and heir to Esker. Stephen professed himself glad to see his sister, though her presence meant that he could no longer masquerade as a mere minstrel. The revelation that Stephen was of noble blood, the son of the Baron of Esker, was greeted with great suspicion. Some courtiers looked at Devlin askance, as if Devlin's well-known friendship with the minstrel was proof of a secret allegiance or hidden scheme.

Though all was calm on the surface, Devlin began to perceive a pattern in the elaborate rituals of the court. There was not one court, but three. At first glance, all were present to participate in a united court presided over by King Olafur. But if you looked closely, the illusion was shattered. The courtiers had divided into three factions.

The first was the old court, presided over by Duke Gerhard and Lady Ingeleth. Here were found most of the oldest and richest noble houses, those who formed the interior of the Kingdom and had seen little trouble in these years.

The second court was smaller, for it was made up of the

border nobles and their allies, the ones who had suffered the most or feared that they would be the next to suffer. They had come to seek changes in the King's policies, but could not agree as to the best course of action to take. Instead they jostled amongst themselves for power and influence.

And there was yet a third group, those who believed that they could not wait for the King to show leadership, but instead must take action now, with or without the support of the King and council. This was the smallest group, for few had the courage to openly display such convictions. But to his astonishment, Devlin found they were looking to him for leadership.

He had not sought power. And yet by virtue of who he was, he had somehow acquired it. Devlin was the first Chosen One in over a dozen years to survive his first quest. He had proven himself as a warrior and a force to be reckoned with. If he continued to survive and to fulfill his duties, he would become an even more potent symbol. Or so his enemies must have reasoned, for why else would they send assassins against him?

Devlin refused to be the figurehead for the disaffected courtiers. Instead he offered himself as a councilor, one voice among equals, as he would have in Duncaer. To any who asked, he gave the same message. There would be no simple answers to the problems that beset the Kingdom. They had to rely upon each other for help, and they must be prepared to make great sacrifices. Matters would get worse before they got better, and in the end they might never be able to restore all that had been lost.

Some found his message hard, and turned back to the familiar comforting platitudes offered by Duke Gerhard and the King. But there were a handful who were willing to listen, and with Devlin's help they began making plans of their own.

This day they had gathered in Solveig's chambers, which had become their makeshift council room. Solveig was very much like her father, Lord Brynjolf—plainspoken and practical, with none of her younger brother's illusions and naïveté. She had witnessed firsthand the chaos that was overtaking the borderlands and knew how difficult it would be to restore order.

In addition to Solveig, her brother Stephen had come, to offer his knowledge of history and times when the Kingdom had faced similar challenges. Then there was Lieutenant Didrik. Though officially Captain Drakken remained neutral, Lieutenant Didrik's watch schedule had been mysteriously rearranged so that he and his knowledge of military matters were at Devlin's disposal.

They had been joined by the impetuous young Lord Rikard of Myrka, whose kinsmen Devlin had saved, and the cautious Lady Falda, whose province had long been allied to that of Myrka. And the most recent to join them was Erling of Vilfort. Erling spoke little, yet he had more reason than most to wish change, for it was his home that had been destroyed by raiders, whose deeds had as of yet gone unpunished.

"We need to prove that there is a better way. We need another success. Not one that is mine alone, but a victory of the common folk," Devlin said.

"You did well against the skrimsal," Solveig said. "If you do as well again with the next crisis, we may be able to win over other lords to our side. And with enough lords, we may be able to sway one or two council votes."

It was a constant debate. There were forty great nobles

and over one hundred lesser nobles in the King's court. Only a dozen had seemed inclined to favor their views and, of these, none was a member of the King's Council.

There was so much they wished to do. Release the Royal Army from its garrisons and send units to help patrol the roads and the borders. Open the King's treasury to help those areas most afflicted. Begin arming and training the residents of the border provinces, so they could offer a first line of defense.

They were all agreed on what needed to be done. But they had no means to compel the King's Council to agree with their plans. And yet that had not always been so. By law, the Chosen One was equal in rank to the King's Champion and the First Councilor, whose authority was superseded only by the King. He was entitled to a seat on the King's Council and a voice in their deliberations.

Time had eroded both the respect given to the Chosen One and the power he was able to wield. Not since the days of King Olaven had a Chosen One sat on the council. Devlin had the rights but not the power to back up his claims. And if he tried to assert his privileges he would bring himself into open conflict with the King and his councilors—a conflict that he could only lose.

The position of Chosen One existed because of tradition, and because the King willed that the tradition be carried on. If the Chosen One became difficult, the King and his councilors could enact laws stripping him of the ancient rights associated with the office. Which would leave Devlin still bound by his oath and the Geas, yet unable to count upon the resources he needed to fulfill his duties.

And yet if Devlin did not assert at least some of his power, he would be of no use to anyone.

"The council will give you no errand. They have no use

for you," Erling said, breaking his customary silence. Till now he had been merely an observer, saying little except to profess his contempt for Lady Ingeleth and the other conservative members of the council for their refusal to help his native city.

All eyes turned toward him, and Erling flushed under their scrutiny. "I mean no disrespect, my lord, but it is what I have heard. Your earlier success is taken as an affront, and they will give you no other task. You must wait until one of the provinces asks for your aid."

Devlin nodded. Erling's words made sense, and as someone who until recently had been part of the inner circle of the court, no doubt he had sources of information that the rest of them could not match. It was why they had welcomed Erling's presence in their discussions, though until now he had offered little in the way of useful advice.

"What if the Chosen One is summoned to deal with a swamp witch or some such petty nuisance?" the elderly Lady Falda asked. "Such an errand would take time, and would serve our purposes not at all."

Devlin had to agree with her. He felt uneasy staying in this place, awaiting whatever summons would next trigger the Geas, forcing him to act. It would be a shame to give his life for nothing when there was so much more that he could do.

"Why should I wait?" Devlin asked, as the thought came to him. "Where is it written that the Chosen One must sit tamely in Kingsholm until he is summoned?"

Stephen rubbed his chin, looking thoughtful. "There is no law, but it has been the custom—"

"It has been the custom because the Chosen Ones before me had no wish to go out and seek their deaths,"

Devlin interrupted. "But I have something different in mind."

Lieutenant Didrik nodded. "I could talk to Captain Drakken. I am sure if we thought on it, we could find a reason for her to send you on an errand outside the city."

"No," Devlin said firmly. "Meaning no disrespect to the Captain, but I do not need her to invent an errand. That would defeat my purpose. I mean to show that I am willing to serve without the Geas to drive me."

"But where will you go?" Solveig asked. "Perhaps Ringstad? With spring, the border raiders will return, and I know the lord of Ringstad would be grateful for your help."

"Myrka's sea trade is bedeviled by pirates," Lord Rikard countered. "They are choking our very lifeblood."

"Do not forget the troubles in Tamarack," Lady Falda said. "The strange blights that have afflicted their crops are surely the work of some enemy rather than nature."

His advisors began to argue among themselves as they offered suggestions as to where the Chosen One's presence would do the most good. Devlin's head ached as he considered the possibilities. Northwest to Ringstad and Esker? Southeast to Myrka? South to Denvir? West to Tamarack? Should he go where there was the greatest need or where his presence would offer the most political advantage?

There were troubles on every side of the Kingdom, and he began to feel a reluctant sympathy for King Olafur. He could not help them all, so how was he to decide, knowing his decisions might mean the difference between life and death for those affected?

He realized that the room had fallen silent and looked up to find himself the center of attention.

"It is up to you. We cannot agree," Solveig declared.

Devlin sighed and ran his hands through his hair. "Let us see the map," he suggested, since his grasp of the geography of Jorsk was still somewhat sketchy.

He rose, and they gathered around a table as Solveig unrolled a map of the Kingdom. Succinctly she described each of the troubled areas, and the reasons for and against his journeying there. Her tone was dispassionate, and she gave no more emphasis to the needs of her father's ally Ringstad than she did to the troubles of Myrka far to the south.

When she had finished, Devlin tapped his finger on the one border province that had not been included in her recital. "What is happening in Korinth?" he asked.

"Nothing," she replied.

"That is not quite true," Lady Falda said. "The young Baron of Korinth complains often that his subjects are ungrateful and rebellious. But there have been no troubles reported there."

"They have the Gods' own luck," Lord Rikard said bitterly.

Something in his words raised the hairs on the back of Devlin's neck. He stared at the map, willing it to make sense. Why was this one border province spared when all the others were not?

"Korinth," he said. "I will go to Korinth."

"But why?" Lieutenant Didrik asked. "They have not asked for aid."

"Because I do not believe in luck. There is some other reason why this one province is spared the hardships that have beset the rest of the borderlands, and I will discover it."

"It is a fool's errand," Lady Falda grumbled.

"It is my choice and it is done." He could not explain to the others, but somehow he knew he had made the right decision.

"Is the King's Council meeting today?" he asked.

"This afternoon," Solveig replied.

"Then I will tell them of my decision," Devlin said.

"You cannot simply walk in there unbidden," Lady Falda said. "You must wait for the King to summon you."

Devlin smiled mirthlessly. "Oh, but I can. After all, everyone knows I am an uncouth peasant with no manners and no sense of my station."

"A disgrace to the Kingdom and to the ranks of the nobility everywhere," Stephen added in a falsetto voice, giving a wickedly accurate imitation of Lady Vendela's sneering tones.

Devlin thought for a moment. "Didrik, tell Captain Drakken that I will want to take a dozen of the Guard with me. We will call this a training mission, so have her pick a steady sergeant and those younger guards who need their skills sharpened. Tell her I will want to leave two days hence."

Didrik saluted. "It will be as you say."

"I will be ready as well," Stephen said.

Devlin blinked. He had not expected the minstrel would want to accompany him into danger. For danger there would be, he could feel it in his bones. At the very least, the assassins that had stalked him in the capital might find themselves emboldened once Devlin left the safety of the palace walls.

Not to mention whatever awaited them in Korinth. Yet if Stephen wished to come, Devlin would not forbid it. Stephen had proven his courage, and his friendship.

"Your presence would be most welcome," Devlin said.

Though normally he cared not what he wore, that afternoon Devlin donned the gray silk shirt, suede trousers, and gray overtunic that made up the formal uniform of the Chosen One. On his feet he wore not the slippers of the court but riding boots, each with a dagger showing openly in its side. As a final touch, he buckled around his waist the sword belt, with the long sword that Captain Drakken had given him on the day of his Choosing.

He had come to realize the power of symbols, for was not the Chosen One simply a living symbol of all the Jorskians hoped and feared? It was time he reminded the King and his council that they had to deal with the reality of his existence.

Lieutenant Didrik and Stephen were waiting outside his chambers when he emerged. Didrik looked thoughtful as he took in Devlin's appearance, and his eyes lingered for a long moment on the sword belt.

"Is the council in session?" Devlin asked.

"They are just about to start."

"Good. Let us see what we can add to their deliberations."

As Devlin approached the council chamber doors, the two guardsmen slanted their spears across the door, signifying that the council was now in session.

"Stand aside," Devlin ordered.

The guards looked at him, and then at Lieutenant Didrik for guidance.

"Our orders are to allow no one in," the senior guard explained.

"Your orders do not apply to me," Devlin said. "By right of my office I order you to stand aside, on peril of your lives." His right hand fell as if casually to his sword belt, but he knew no one was deceived by his apparent nonchalance.

"But—" the guard protested.

"I would do as he says," Lieutenant Didrik advised. When the guards hesitated, he added, "If there is any blame, it will fall on me."

The two sentries exchanged glances, then lifted their spears to the upright position.

"Wait here," Devlin said. He grasped the door handles and pushed the doors open.

As he entered, the councilors fell silent. Devlin's eyes swept the room. Duke Gerhard appeared slyly pleased. Lady Ingeleth looked angry. And the King himself looked as he always did, fretful and uncertain.

"What is the meaning of this intrusion?" Lady Ingeleth asked, rising to her feet. "I demand that you leave at once, or I will summon the guards."

"There is no need to summon them, for they are right outside," Devlin countered. "And surely the Chosen One has the right to speak to the King and his council? Did I not do you the service you requested last summer? At your command, I dispatched the beast that had troubled the folk of Esker. I did not expect gratitude, but I do expect the courtesy of a few moments of your time in return."

Lady Ingeleth resumed her seat. "Very well, you may speak. But we have no intention of approving your foolish scheme."

Devlin's eyes narrowed as he studied her. There was something in Lady Ingeleth's tone that made him think she knew more than she was telling.

"I see Erling has been busy," Devlin ventured.

Lady Ingeleth turned white with anger and he knew his guess had been correct. So Erling had betrayed them. He wondered what they had offered him. Vengeance? Coin to pay for all he had lost at Vilfort? It did not matter.

"Why do you mention the name of this Erling?" Duke Gerhard asked.

"Because it is clear someone has tried to betray my confidence. If not Erling then another. No matter," Devlin said, with an elaborate shrug. "I am accustomed to the treachery of Jorskians."

An older councilor hissed at the insult.

"You see, Your Majesty, it is as I said," Duke Gerhard commented. "One cannot reason with such a man."

"I did not come here to reason or to beg. Or even to argue, though a blind man could see that your present course is one of folly," Devlin said, circling around the council table and advancing toward the head where the King sat. "No, I came here to inform you that I will be leaving in two days' time."

"On what errand?" Lord Baldur asked.

"On none but my own," Devlin replied. "I see no reason to wait in Kingsholm. If trouble comes, it will come to the borderlands first. And so I will journey hence, to do what good I may."

King Olafur shook his head. "Such is against all custom. Far better that you wait here, until we know where you best may serve."

"I disagree," Devlin said. "I have idled away the winter, and now it is time to act. I have decided to take a squad of the Guard with me, to make of this a training exercise."

"So the Chosen One fears to risk his own life?" a gray-haired councilor asked.

"I will do what I must, but there is nothing that says the Chosen One need make himself an easy target," Devlin countered.

"I do not like this," Duke Gerhard said slowly.

To all appearances the Duke's words were simple caution, and support for his King's views. And yet there was something about the Duke that rubbed Devlin's nerves raw. He could not help but look for hidden meanings behind the man's every utterance, wondering how many plots were concealed behind that bland expression.

This was the tricky part. If the King forbade his leaving, Devlin could not go. And yet it was not the King he needed to convince, but Lady Ingeleth and Lord Gerhard. In the end the King would do as they advised.

Devlin reached the head of the table, close enough so that he could reach out and touch the Duke if he chose. He caught the Duke's gaze with his own.

"Duke Gerhard, often have I heard you say that the position of the Chosen One is an anachronism, and that there is no good that one such as I can do. So if my efforts are useless, what care you whether I remain in the city or roam the countryside?"

He turned then to the First Councilor. "And Lady Ingeleth, surely you have seen the factions of the court. There are many nobles who are looking for someone to lead them. Who knows what unlikely candidate they will find as the centerpiece of their schemes? Not that there is any risk that they would attach themselves to one such as I, but surely my absence from the capital during these unsettled times would do more good than harm?"

Behind him he heard a snort of laughter. So at least one councilor appreciated the beauty of the trap that Devlin had laid, though he dare not turn around to identify his unknown ally.

"You are either very wise or a fool," Lady Ingeleth said. "But I agree that there is no reason for you to remain here, where your presence may ... confuse ... those whose loyalties are unclear."

Duke Gerhard nodded. "I, too, see no reason for you to remain. But I do not know if I approve of your taking a squad of the Guard. They are sentries and lawkeepers. I do not see how their skills can serve you."

"Then give me a squad of your Royal Army as well, and we will see who can best serve," Devlin said.

The Duke nodded. "I believe I can spare them. If you would permit, Your Majesty?"

King Olafur waved his hand. "Go. Go then, and trouble us no more," he ordered.

Devlin bowed. "It is my pleasure to serve," he said, hardly able to believe that he had actually done it. His gamble had paid off. He began to back away.

As he reached the door, Duke Gerhard asked, "Where are you bound?"

"Rosmaar to start," Devlin said. "And then wherever my oath and the Kingdom's needs take me."

He reached the door, and made good his escape.

Twenty-one

⟶

IT WAS THE DAY AFTER THE COUNCIL MEETING, AND Devlin was methodically checking lists and ensuring all was in readiness to leave on the following day. It would not be a simple journey, as it had been when he and Stephen went to Esker. No, this time he would journey with over two dozen followers, and this multiplied the complexity of the journey a hundredfold.

Devlin felt dismayed at the size of the task before him. He was no war leader. How was he to decide if the guards were to be issued long swords or short swords and shields? Was it better to take fewer soldiers so they could move swiftly, or a larger force, which would reduce the risk that they would find themselves outnumbered by their foes? How was he to make these decisions? He had neither the training nor experience needed to fill this role, and yet guards who should have known what he lacked turned to him for guidance.

Devlin raised his head as Lieutenant Didrik entered the clerk's office, which Devlin had commandeered as his own.

"I have the roster of names. All are volunteers. Most of

them you will know, though there are three green recruits who joined up only this past month."

Devlin scanned the list, nodding as he saw familiar names. As he had requested, the guards selected were of the junior rank, having served less than five years. He smiled as he saw Behra's name on the list. So Behra had finally been released from duty at the gaol, his punishment for letting Devlin slip away that midwinter night.

"Sergeant Henrik is to lead? A good choice," Devlin commented. Henrik was a twenty-year veteran, and his experience would prove a steadying influence on the young guards.

Lieutenant Didrik cleared his throat. "Actually I am to lead."

Devlin leaned back in his chair. "No. Captain Drakken needs your experience here. Why else do you think I asked for the novices, those whose skills will be missed the least?"

Lieutenant Didrik drew himself erect and thumped his right fist on his chest in the Guard's salute. "I serve as my Captain commands. It would dishonor the Guard to send you forth with only a sergeant, when the Royal Army will surely send an officer with their men."

Devlin snorted. "What you meant to say is that Captain Drakken fears that without an officer to lead them, the guards will find themselves under the command of the Royal Army."

"It is not my place to speculate on the reasons behind her orders."

It was a reasonable concern. When he had first conceived this journey, Devlin had had no intention of inviting the Royal Army along. He knew well the rivalry between the army and the Guard, and that to mix the two would be awkward and potentially dangerous. Then in the

council chamber, Devlin had realized there was no other
way to gain Duke Gerhard's approval of the plan. And so
he had made the offer, and the Duke had accepted. Now it
was up to Devlin to make this work.

Perhaps it would be best to have Lieutenant Didrik
along. Should something happen to Devlin, the guards
would need a strong leader who could assume command.

"You may tell Captain Drakken I am grateful for her assistance," Devlin said.

"It is an honor to serve the Chosen One," Lieutenant
Didrik replied. It was impossible to tell if he was serious or
mocking.

Devlin glanced down at the paper-strewn desk, and began leafing through the parchments till he found the list
from the quartermaster. "Here is your first assignment," he
said, handing the list over to the lieutenant. "Make sure
each guard has drawn supplies from the quartermaster, according to this list. Each horse is to be newly shod, and I
want you personally to inspect their harness and tack.
Then go to the guards and inspect their weapons. Any that
are unprepared should have their names struck from the
list, and substitute another. Understood?"

"Yes, my lord Chosen One."

"And if you call me my lord Chosen One again, I will
take it upon myself to teach you better manners," Devlin
growled.

"The lieutenant wishes to remind the Chosen One that
he is still your master at the sword," Lieutenant Didrik said.

There was a knock at the door, then it swung open, revealing an Ensign in the blue-and-scarlet uniform of the
Royal Army.

For a moment Devlin felt unease, as he recognized the
hated uniform of his conquerors. For the Ensign wore not

the dress uniform of the court, but the field uniforms that were worn by those who had conquered Duncaer, and who now maintained control through their garrisons and fortresses.

"Ensign Greger Mikkelson," he said, entering the room, and saluting in the manner of the Royal Army, placing his hand on his heart and inclining his head. He was in his midtwenties—old still to be only an Ensign in the Royal Army, with its many officer ranks.

Ensign Mikkelson held the pose for a long moment, then straightened as he realized that Devlin had no intention of returning the salute.

"You are late," Devlin said. "I had expected you at first light."

Ensign Mikkelson blinked. "I came as soon as I had my orders, and I made all haste in doing so."

Didrik and Devlin exchanged glances. "So they could not decide who would be their sacrifice. Tell me, Ensign, what mistake have you committed? Whom did you offend to be named to this assignment?"

"I do not understand your question," Ensign Mikkelson said, drawing himself even more stiffly erect, if that were possible.

Devlin shook his head. "You will need to be a better liar if you are ever to advance beyond your present station. Didrik, show the Ensign how it is done."

Didrik's eyes danced with laughter. "It is an honor to serve the Chosen One," he said straight-faced.

"See? That is how to lie properly," Devlin said.

The Ensign said nothing, but confusion was written plainly on his face. There was no sense in tormenting him any longer, so Devlin began to give his orders.

"We will leave at noon tomorrow. If you and your troops are not here by then, we will leave without you."

"But—"

"Do not interrupt me," Devlin said. "Here is a list of supplies that each soldier will require. You will personally ensure that all is in readiness. Any soldier who lacks proper equipment or supplies will be left behind. I want fourteen soldiers and one officer, no more. Two packhorses will carry supplies, but that is all. There are to be no servants, no luxuries. Do you understand?"

"I understand," Ensign Mikkelson said stiffly.

He knew he had offended the Ensign, and it was a poor way to begin this journey. But neither did he have time for soothing ruffled sensibilities or coddling those who had not the wits to cooperate on their own.

Devlin rose from his seat and unbuttoned the collar on his tunic. "Do you see this?" he asked, the fingers of his right hand tracing the faint scar left behind by the garrote.

"Yes, sir."

"Good. My orders may seem strict, but I want you to understand that this journey is no lark. I fully expect that all of us will see fighting before we are done."

"You mean we will be attacked?"

"Of a surety. I am the Chosen One, and I cannot even go to a tavern without risking my life. This scar on my neck is a reminder of just how much my enemies wish to get rid of me. If you journey with me, you will become targets as well. And if we do not encounter assassins, then there are always outlaws, border raiders, pirates, and hellborn creatures waiting for us."

"But Korinth is a peaceful province," Ensign Mikkelson protested.

Ah. Devlin had been wondering just how much the treacherous Erling had revealed of their plans.

"Korinth is but one of the provinces I wish to inspect," Devlin replied. This was the story he had agreed on with the others. Only a handful knew the truth. And should his instincts be proven false, after journeying to Korinth there were other provinces to the south and east that could use the help of the Chosen One.

Devlin unrolled the map. "Come, see," he said. "We will begin our journey here, and then travel till we reach the coastal provinces. From there we will journey through Arkilde, Rosmaar, and then into Korinth," he said, his finger tracing the border of the Kingdom. "Beyond Korinth we will continue along the borderlands until we reach Myrka. And if any of us are still alive by that time, we will turn west toward Denvir and Tamarack."

Ensign Mikkelson swallowed hard. "This is no easy journey you propose."

"The Kingdom is crumbling around us," Lieutenant Didrik said. "We have no time for pleasure jaunts. And should the task prove beyond your abilities, no matter. We of the Guard know the meaning of service."

"Even the least of my soldiers is more than a match for any of yours," Ensign Mikkelson said hotly.

"Enough," Devlin said. "You do not have time to quarrel. It is past noon, and you and your soldiers have less than a day to prepare for the journey. If I were you, I would take this list of supplies and leave at once."

Ensign Mikkelson gave one hard look at Didrik and turned back to face Devlin. "As you command, Chosen One," he said.

After he left, Lieutenant Didrik shook his head slowly. "I do not trust him. There is going to be trouble."

A part of Devlin agreed, but as the leader of the expedition he knew it was up to him to set the tone. "It takes two to quarrel. If there is trouble, I will punish both guards and soldiers alike. There are to be no training accidents, no so-called jokes gone awry. You will give Ensign Mikkelson and his soldiers the respect they deserve, or I will send the lot of you back to Kingsholm and continue alone."

"We will not start trouble," Lieutenant Didrik said. "But—"

"There are no buts," Devlin said. "Think with your head, not your pride. If it comes to open warfare, Jorsk will need all of her warriors, both guards and soldiers, to work together. How can you expect to save the Kingdom if you cannot manage to journey in peace with a mere Ensign and a squad of soldiers?"

Lieutenant Didrik's face colored with embarrassment. "I understand. But will he?"

"I do not know. But we will give him the benefit of the doubt. For now."

Stephen watched as Devlin and Captain Drakken moved among the guards, ensuring that all was in readiness. He could not hear what they were saying, but from time to time Devlin nodded, as if he were receiving last-minute words of advice. Once he glanced toward the sun, but if he was concerned that the Royal Army troops had not yet appeared, he made no sign.

From the palace tower the noon bell began to ring, and was then echoed by the bells in the city below. Devlin walked over to the groom that held his horse. "Mount up," he ordered.

Stephen mounted his horse, while the guards, after

pausing to exchange final embraces with lovers and friends, did the same. Then Devlin led the procession from the courtyard. Stephen guided his own horse just behind Devlin's, and Lieutenant Didrik drew alongside him, followed by the fourteen guards.

Devlin's expression was unreadable, but Stephen knew him well enough to know that underneath that impassive façade he was furious that the soldiers of the Royal Army had failed to make their appearance by the appointed hour.

They wound their way through the city until they reached the great market square, with its milling throngs of vendors and city folk. Stephen let his gaze wander over the crowds, knowing it would be a long time before he saw the place again. There was movement at the far edge of the square, and Stephen caught a glimpse of a blue-and-red pennant fluttering in the breeze.

Lieutenant Didrik had seen it as well. "Chosen One, look. There to the left."

Devlin turned his head. "I see them," he said. "Ride on."

They continued across the market square, reaching the eastern gate of the city before the Royal Army troops caught up with them.

An army Ensign followed by a Sergeant carrying the army pennant rode up alongside Devlin. "My lord Chosen One, we tried—" he began.

Devlin held up his left hand to cut off the flow of words. "When I give an order, I expect it to be obeyed. This time I will let it pass, but fail me again and I will not be so lenient. Tell your soldiers to fall in behind the Guard."

"But—"

"Have them fall in behind the Guard, then return to ride with me to make your report."

"Yes, my lord," the Ensign said.

As they passed out of the city through the eastern gate, the guardsmen on duty drew stiffly to attention and saluted, which Devlin acknowledged with a nod of his head. Once outside the city, the guards aligned themselves into columns of two and the soldiers formed up behind them. A few minutes later, the Ensign returned.

Stephen, curious to hear what would be said, drew his horse up closely behind the pair, and Lieutenant Didrik did the same.

Devlin began by gesturing behind him. "You have already met Lieutenant Didrik, who commands the guards. Beside him is Stephen of Esker, who has consented to join us. This is Ensign Mikkelson, of the Royal Army."

"It is an honor to make your acquaintance," Stephen said, with his best seated bow, but the Ensign's eyes swept over him without acknowledging his presence. Then he turned back to face Devlin.

"What is the meaning of this? You said there were to be no luxuries, and yet you bring your own minstrel to record the glory of your deeds?"

Stephen cringed, waiting for the explosion.

"You should not be so quick to pass judgment on others," Devlin said in icy tones. "Stephen of Esker has proven his courage and his friendship. Twice now he has faced death by my side, against horrors that you can barely imagine. I am honored that he chooses to join us and risk his life again. Tell me, Ensign, when was the last time you drew your sword against an enemy?"

Lieutenant Didrik snickered. Stephen felt his face grow hot at Devlin's words of praise, but he knew his discomfort was nothing compared to what the Ensign must be experiencing.

"I have not had the honor of serving in combat," Ensign Mikkelson admitted in a low voice. "I apologize if I have given offense."

"It is Stephen's pardon that you must beg," Devlin said.

The Ensign turned around awkwardly in the saddle. "I crave your pardon."

"The words are already forgotten," Stephen replied, wishing to spare the Ensign farther embarrassment.

"Now, Ensign, tell me of the soldiers you have brought. What are their skills and their experiences? Have any journeyed to the borderlands before? Tell us what you know, and we will decide how best we can use them."

Devlin waved his hand, and Lieutenant Didrik drew his horse along his right side. The discussion turned to matters of military strategy, and Stephen was content to let his horse fall behind, for he had no interest in such details.

That night they camped in a fallow field, lent to them by a farmer. The guards and the soldiers set up separate camps, with their own cookfires. After they ate, Devlin called everyone together.

They gathered in a loose circle around him, the guards to his right, the soldiers to his left, each group leaving a careful space between itself and the other.

"Sit," he ordered.

He scanned their faces. The guards seemed relaxed and curious as to what he had to say. Most of them he knew, either from lessons with the throwing knives or because, like Behra, they had been assigned to shadow him.

Then he looked to his left, where the soldiers sat sullenly. He could feel the waves of resentment rising from them. Most refused to meet his eyes. All afternoon he had felt their gazes boring into his back. If looks could slay, Devlin would have died a dozen times over.

He could endure their resentment, and even their hatred. He cared little for what they thought of him. But he had to have their obedience.

Devlin turned to his right. "Guards, I thank you for presence. You have volunteered for this mission, which speaks well of your courage, if not your common sense." At this some of the guards chuckled.

Then he turned to face the soldiers of the Royal Army. "Like Ensign Mikkelson, you were ordered to take this duty. I neither know nor care the reasons why you were selected, but those who journey with me will need to understand why we go forth."

He paused, wondering how to phase his message, and decided plain speaking was best. "Who can tell me what the Chosen One is?"

"A damn fool," one of the soldiers said.

Ensign Mikkelson half rose, his head turning as he sought to identify the culprit. "Who said that?" he asked.

"Rest easy, Ensign," Devlin ordered. "I will not punish someone for speaking their mind. It is true that many would call me a fool. But that is the least part of being Chosen One. My rank makes me an easy target for all those who would strike at Jorsk, and yet at the same time it demands that I defend the Kingdom to the utmost limits of my strength and abilities. And I expect the same from each one of you, soldier and guard alike. If I give an order, I expect it to be obeyed. Failure is not acceptable, for the price of failure is death."

His eyes swept over the soldiers, trying to see if his words were sinking in. A few looked thoughtful, but most had the sullen look of men and women who had already made up their minds. "Remember that I am the Chosen One. I am your commander, and you will look to me for orders. Lieutenant Didrik and Ensign Mikkelson will serve me, but it is my orders they will pass on."

"We serve our General, Duke Gerhard," a woman objected.

Devlin nailed her with his eyes. "You serve at my command, or not at all. This is no pleasure jaunt. As the Chosen One, I invoke my power as war leader. Anyone who disobeys one of my commands will face summary justice. Do you understand?"

The woman swallowed hard. "I understand," she said, as the soldiers exchanged glances among themselves.

As Chosen One, Devlin had the power to execute both high and low justice. He could pass sentence as a magistrate, as he had done with the inn-wife. Or he could execute military justice. And *execute* was indeed the right word, for the penalty for disobeying orders during wartime was death.

"As I have told your leaders," he said, turning slowly in a circle, "I fully expect that we will see combat on this trip. You will be asked to risk your lives at my command. And if the recent history of the Chosen Ones is any guide, it is likely that many of us will perish. If any man or woman here is unwilling to journey with us, they have but to speak, and you may return to your comrades."

"They will hang us as deserters," a man objected.

Devlin shook his head. "There will be no punishment. Anyone who chooses to leave will be given written orders and a token, proving that I commanded you to return."

"Chosen One, you cannot do this," Ensign Mikkelson said, rising to his feet. "These are my soldiers, under my command."

"No. These soldiers are under my command now. As are you. And the offer applies to you as well. If you cannot carry out my orders, then now is the time for you to leave."

He drew a deep breath. Ensign Mikkelson looked troubled, but Lieutenant Didrik's face was impassive. Then again, the guards were all volunteers. Didrik had little to fear.

"Think on it this night," Devlin said. "On the morrow you will give me your decision. But mark this, I make this offer only once. Those who remain past sunrise tomorrow have committed themselves to the mission. From then on there will be no turning back."

In the end, four soldiers chose to return, including the man who had worried about being called a deserter. To each of them Devlin gave a wooden token, marked with the seal from his ring. As he watched them leave, he felt a strange regret. Those four were the only soldiers he could be certain were not plotting against him.

His eyes swept over Ensign Mikkelson and the ten soldiers who had decided to remain. He had not expected the Ensign to accept his offer. But as for the rest, he wondered at their motives. Surely at least one was a spy, sent by Duke Gerhard to report upon the Chosen One's actions and to bear witness to Devlin's mistakes. That was only to be expected, and did not worry Devlin overmuch.

What worried him was the possibility that one or more of the soldiers was in the pay of his mysterious enemies, the ones who had sent the assassins to kill him. The soldiers had no reason to be loyal to Devlin, and a full purse might easily outweigh whatever scruples they had about killing their commander.

For that matter, he could not be sure of all of the guards. Didrik was loyal. But what of the rest? How well did he

really know any of them? For all their seeming camaraderie, behind those smiling faces could beat the heart of
a traitor. Three of their number were fresh recruits. Any
one of them could be a spy, or an assassin in the pay of his
enemies.

He would have to watch his back.

Twenty-two

STEPHEN SHIVERED IN THE CHILL MORNING AIR AS he slung his saddlebags over his shoulder and approached the picket line. His horse whinnied in greeting, and Stephen rubbed the mare's nose fondly before crossing over to where his saddle had been stored with the others, covered by a tarp against the night mists. There were only a few saddles left, for most of the others had already saddled their horses and were ready to mount and leave at the Chosen One's command.

Stephen hurried back to his horse, smoothing the saddle blanket over the horse's back before placing the saddle on top. He fastened the girth, adjusted the saddle irons, and lashed the saddlebags on. Glancing around, he saw that he was nearly the last one to be finished, the guards and the soldiers each vying to show that they were the best disciplined and most efficient at their tasks.

Stephen reached down to check the girth. He gave a final tug, only to find it gave slightly. He tugged again, and heard the sound of ripping stitches, as the girth came loose in his hand.

The mare swung her head around to gaze at him reproachfully as he held the useless band in his hand.

"Blast," Stephen swore.

"Mount up," Ensign Mikkelson called out, from across the clearing.

Stephen swore again.

"Is there a problem?"

Stephen glanced to his right, where one of the female soldiers was preparing to mount a bay gelding.

"My girth has broken," Stephen said. "And I am fairly certain that I do not have a spare."

He did not know how this could have happened. He was an experienced traveler, and knew how important it was to check his horse's tack every day. And yet somehow he had missed the fraying of the girth, until it was too late.

"Devlin is going to kill me," Stephen said.

She chuckled. "I doubt it is that serious. Even the Chosen One cannot expect the tack to obey him."

He shook his head. "You don't understand. I should have caught this before. This can only be carelessness, which he will find hard to forgive."

Stephen knew from his own experience that Devlin inspected his tack and weapons every day, with almost religious dedication. This would never have happened to him.

The company began to ride out of the clearing, and Stephen looked over to find Devlin, to let him know what had happened.

"Trygg!" the soldier called out. One of the riders paused beside them. "Trygg, tell the Ensign that I have a problem with my tack, and that the minstrel has agreed to help me fix it. We will join up in a few moments."

The man studied Stephen for a moment, then nodded. "I will pass the word along."

"You did not have to do that," Stephen said, after the soldier had ridden off.

The soldier shrugged. "It is a little thing. I have a spare girth strap that should fit, and it will take us only a few minutes to repair your saddle. And the Ensign is scarcely likely to punish me for a short delay."

The last of the guards left the clearing, and in the stillness he could hear the sound of the birds, as they greeted the morning.

The soldier reached into her saddlebag and withdrew a long strip of leather. She crossed in front of his horse and came to stand beside Stephen.

"I am Freyja," she said. Up close he could see that she was young, perhaps his own age, with a broad honest face and warm brown eyes.

"I am Stephen, as you must know," he said.

"Here now, take out the old girth, and I will fit the new," she said.

He removed the old girth, and watched as she quickly fitted in the new piece of leather, using her belt knife to punch out the necessary holes. She fastened it first to the off side, then on the near side. Her movements were brisk and efficient, as if she had done this task a hundred times before. The new girth was plainer than the old, simply a wide strip of leather rather than the woven canvas he had used before. But it would more than serve, and he was grateful for her help.

"There now, give that a try," she said.

Stephen tugged firmly on the girth, but it remained in place. He tugged again harder, and the mare snorted in protest.

"May I see the old girth?" Freyja asked.

He handed her the now useless girth, and she turned it over in her hands.

"See here, how the fabric has frayed and the stitches torn loose?"

Stephen nodded. To his eye the fabric looked more as if it had been cut or torn than frayed, but there was no denying that the stitching had come loose, which had ultimately caused the girth to fail.

"It must have been weak for some time," Freyja commented. "Then the rough country and the strain of crossing the hills spelled the end of it. It would be easy to overlook, until it broke."

He knew she was being kind, trying to excuse his failure to see something that must have been obvious for days. And yet he could have sworn that he had inspected the girth yesterday and that it had been fine.

"I owe you my thanks." It had been good of her to help him, to save him the embarrassment of letting everyone see his incompetence.

"You would have done the same for me," she replied.

Stephen wondered if that were true. If this had happened to one of the guards, then he would have helped without needing to be asked. The guards had adopted Devlin as one of their own, and by extension they included Stephen within that circle. But the soldiers of the Royal Army had remained firmly aloof from him. Even now, after days of traveling together, he still did not know most of them by name.

"We should join the others," Stephen said. "I will explain to Ensign Mikkelson what happened. I do not wish to get you in trouble."

Freyja untied her horse and swung up into the saddle. Stephen did the same.

"If you wish to thank me, then join us some evening after supper," Freyja said. "A minstrel would be a welcome guest."

It was pleasant to be sought after in his own right. "I brought no instrument," Stephen said.

"You have your voice," Freyja countered. "And Trygg has a bone whistle, which he will play if coaxed."

"Your wish is my command," Stephen replied. "The first evening I am not on watch, I will join you and your friends."

Freyja grinned. "I will look forward to it."

She kneed her horse to a trot, and he followed behind, as they hurried to catch up with the others.

As they approached the river that marked the border of Korinth province, Stephen mused upon the past few weeks of journeying. He could not help thinking how different this journey was from the last time he had accompanied the Chosen One. It was good to have the companionship of others, and not to have to rely upon his and Devlin's indifferent cooking skills. And this time, though he set a good pace, Devlin did not drive himself and his companions to the edge of exhaustion.

But the real change was in Devlin himself. For a man who had often claimed he had no wish to be a leader, Devlin was proving himself an inspired commander, one who despite all obstacles was forging his disparate forces into a cohesive fighting unit.

He felt ashamed when he remembered his first impressions of Devlin. Then he had seen him as a mere peasant, one unworthy to hold the title of Chosen One. He had not been able to see past the ragged clothes and brusque manners to the man underneath.

Yet the Gods had seen what Stephen had not. None of the celebrated heroes of the past had ever had to face the obstacles that Devlin faced. A King and council who bickered and quarreled and withheld their support. A fighting force divided in half by bitter rivalries, and the ever-present possibility that one or more of his so-called protectors would try to betray him. And yet Devlin had set about overcoming each obstacle with the single-minded determination that characterized all of his endeavors. And now he had accomplished the seemingly impossible, getting the guards and the soldiers of the Royal Army to work together.

Not that it had been easy. Far from it. Those soldiers who had stayed had not done so out of love or respect for the Chosen One. Their resentment still simmered below the surface. But if he noticed their resentment, Devlin made no sign. Instead he showed himself calm and controlled, giving orders with the air of a man who expected to be obeyed without question.

As he had on the previous journey, Devlin practiced each morning and evening with his weapons. The first time he and Lieutenant Didrik had practiced with the swords, the soldiers had watched with amusement, laughing as the lieutenant defeated him in each of the three matches, earning Devlin sore ribs and a bruise on his neck.

There was no laughter the next day, as Devlin demonstrated his lethal skills with the axe, splitting the wooden target in two with one swing of the massive blade. And his keen eye enabled him to put a transverse bolt or a throwing knife in the center of the target, time after time, as if he were made of steel and not flesh and blood.

Though Devlin gave no command, the guards drilled daily with their own weapons under the watchful eye of Sergeant Henrik. After a few days some of the soldiers began to train as well, until within a week all were rising early to share in the morning practice, following Devlin's example. Even the most biased against him could see that Devlin drove himself far harder than he drove them.

Devlin divided his time equally between the soldiers and the guards, showing favor to neither group. He even alternated his meals, eating one day with the soldiers and the next day with the guards. He was seen to consult Ensign Mikkelson as often as he did Lieutenant Didrik, although since their conversations were private, it was impossible to tell which one of them he favored, or how often he followed their advice.

In Rosmaar, they had tracked down a small band of robbers who were preying on the villagers, stealing cattle and horses. Stephen had tried to view this as a glorious battle, but even he had to acknowledge that the robbers were a ragged and pathetic band, barely a dozen in all. The robbers fell neatly into Devlin's trap, caught between the bows of the mounted soldiers and the swords of the guards. A few tried to flee and were wounded, but most had surrendered, begging for mercy, and Devlin had turned them over to the local magistrate for justice.

That night the soldiers and guards had celebrated as if they had won a mighty victory instead of a mere skirmish, mingling as they swapped outrageous lies about their own daring and courageous feats. Stephen had observed it all with an odd feeling of detachment. A part of him had cheered the easy victory, and another part knew that the real test was yet to come.

As they crossed into the strangely peaceful province of Korinth, Stephen found himself wondering what form that test would take. Once he would have relished the prospect of adventure, of living in a ballad come to life. Now he was wiser, for he had learned that underneath the stirring lyrics lay the truths that all heroics had a cost in pain, fear, blood, and sacrifice.

After nearly two months of traveling, they finally crossed into the province of Korinth. They paused at the first town they came to, the town of Bruum, which lay at a crossroads. Though it was only midday, Devlin directed his troop to find lodgings, while he and his advisors retired to a tavern to discuss strategy. The Geas, which had slumbered during the journey, now chafed at him, urging him onward, although he still did not know what it was he sought.

"I say we should take the eastern road, and make our way to Baron Egeslic's keep. If there is anything awry in his province, the Baron will know of it," Ensign Mikkelson said, tapping the map with his finger for emphasis. The Ensign was an enigma to Devlin. Old for his rank, repeatedly passed over for promotion, the bitterness he often revealed was understandable. And yet he seemed to be doing his best to serve, and to uphold the high standards of the Royal Army.

"And I say we should take the coastal road," Lieutenant Didrik countered. "Rosmaar, Myrka, and Arkilde all have been plagued by coastal raiders. We should see what it is about Korinth's coast that keeps it free from harm."

Devlin leaned back in his chair and took a sip of citrine as he listened to their debate. Both men had good reasons for their arguments. And yet the final decision would be his, as it had been so many times since leaving Kingsholm. Such was the burden of command.

He had spent the first few weeks of the journey in secret dread, certain that at any moment one of the soldiers or guards would denounce him as unfit. What did he know of leading others? Devlin had never done more than supervise apprentices at their labors. He had been terrified that he would fail.

He had cast his mind over the leaders he had known, wondering how it was that they had led. Cerrie had been loved by all, so she had risen to the rank of sergeant despite her fierce temper. Captain Drakken embodied cool professionalism, backed up by two dozen years of experience. Neither example would work for him.

Then he had thought of Master Roric, in whose forge Devlin had labored for ten years. Master Roric was legendary for never raising his voice, and yet his authority was unquestioned. Master Roric had led by example, setting the highest standards for himself. And thus it was Master Roric's image that he kept in mind as Devlin began trying to wield his motley escort into a fighting command.

Slowly, gradually, the soldiers ceased their complaining and began responding to his leadership. In Rosmaar, it had been he they looked to for orders, and his name that they cheered after their victory. For there was nothing that the troops liked more than an easy victory.

But he was wise enough to know his leadership was but a fragile thing. If his plan to capture the robbers had failed, he could have lost more than a skirmish. He could have lost the respect of those he depended on. The true test would come when he asked them to face overwhelming odds, and to lay their lives on the line.

And there was at least one among them who wished him ill. During the skirmish, an arrow had barely missed him, plucking at his sleeve but doing no real harm. It could have been an accident, a careless shot gone astray in the excitement of the archer's first battle. Or it could have been deliberate. For the bandits possessed only swords, as did the guards. Only the soldiers of the Royal Army had been using bows that day.

He sighed and tipped his head forward, rubbing the back of his neck to ease the tightness. As he raised his head, he saw Didrik and Mikkelson had fallen silent and were watching him.

"I take it you still disagree?" he asked.

Both men nodded.

"We must remember our purpose, and why we came to Korinth," Lieutenant Didrik said.

"My point as well," Ensign Mikkelson said. "We are here on a training mission, and it is only proper that we inform the Baron of our presence, before making free of his domain."

Devlin kept his face still, revealing no trace of his inner conflict. The Ensign's words made sense, but logic had little to do with their presence in this part of the empire. And yet how could he argue his own case? Devlin had no proof, just vague suspicions that there was something wrong in the reports of this seemingly peaceful area. And yet, with each league that passed under their horses' hooves, he grew more and more certain that the answers he sought lay within Korinth province.

But at the moment he had a choice to make. From here

the roads diverged, and he would have to decide their course.

Olaf, the tavern keeper came over to their table. Over-awed to find himself hosting the Chosen One, the tavern keeper had banished his other customers to the far side of the tavern, leaving the surrounding tables vacant. Devlin had not protested, for if they kept their voices low, it would make it difficult for anyone to overhear them. Not that he expected to find a spy in such a backwater town, but it did not hurt to be cautious.

"More citrine?" Olaf asked. "Or perhaps you will want some wine now that you have washed the road dust from your throats?"

"Not for me," Devlin said, shaking his head with a touch of regret. Wine would be welcome, but he needed a clear head to make this decision.

Following his example, Didrik and Mikkelson requested another pitcher of citrine, although their regret was more obvious.

Olaf returned with a fresh pitcher, then lingered by the table. Clearly he felt the presence of the Chosen One and his officers represented a noble endorsement for his humble establishment, and he was only too anxious to serve them.

"A shame it is, a real shame I say," Olaf said, seemingly out of nowhere.

"What is a shame?" Devlin asked.

"The disappearance of the Assessor Brunin. That is why you are here then, isn't it?"

"Who is this assessor?" Ensign Mikkelson asked.

Olaf rocked back on his heels. "Oh my, and you don't know? Munin was the Baron's assessor. He disappeared while collecting taxes, and the Baron's men spent most of last month combing the roads for him."

"I don't understand. He disappeared last fall and they are only now beginning the search?" Ensign Mikkelson asked, in a tone that conveyed his scorn for the efforts of provincial armsmen.

"Oh no, no, not at all. The assessor made his rounds last fall with no sign of trouble. And no wonder, for who would be foolish enough to interfere with one of Baron Egeslic's officials? No, the assessor set off on his rounds this spring, and never returned. We fear the worst has happened." He leaned forward, and whispered. "And do you know what I think? I think slavers got him. Raiders from the sea came and took him away. That's what I think."

"Slavers?" Lieutenant Didrik asked. "It seems more likely a tax collector would find enemies closer to home."

Olaf blanched. "No, not one of us. No one in Korinth would dream of such a thing," he said, his face beginning to sweat. His eyes darted around, as if realizing for the first time that there were other patrons in the common room.

"I know some say that the spring tax is a hardship," Olaf said, raising his voice slightly. "But those are just fools talking. Times are hard and the Baron protects us all. We pay our coins and the Baron gives us peace. Anyone can see that."

What Devlin could see was that the tavern keeper was afraid. Afraid that his words would be reported to Lord Egeslic. His fear made no sense. Everyone grumbled about taxes, particularly when they gathered together in a tavern with strong drink. It was as constant a refrain as the weather, or speculations on the amorous adventures of those not present. And yet Olaf was clearly afraid to be heard criticizing the Baron and his taxes in public.

As if fearing contamination from their presence, Olaf began to back away, bowing nervously.

"Wait," Devlin said. "Maybe we can be of service to your Baron. Where was the assessor when he disappeared?"

"On the coast road," Olaf said, and then with a final bow he fled to the back room.

They watched him retreat.

"I take it we are to journey along the coast road?" Lieutenant Didrik asked.

"Indeed," Devlin said shortly. "I doubt we will find what the Baron's armsmen have missed, but it will do us no harm to have made the search."

"Did you see—" Ensign Mikkelson began.

"Enough discussion for one night," Devlin interrupted, jerking his head in the direction of the crowded common room. If there were informants hidden in the crowd, there was no sense in giving them any more knowledge than they already had.

Ensign Mikkelson nodded, to show that he had understood the message. "Of course, my lord Chosen One," he said. "We can make our plans tomorrow, once we have had a night of rest."

And once there was no danger of hidden listeners repeating their every word.

As they traveled toward the coast, the terrain gradually changed. The muddy roads under their horses' hooves turned to sandy dirt, and the forest had given way to grassy hills dotted with scrubby bushes.

That morning he noticed a tang in the air, a strange metallic taste. When he remarked upon it, Stephen nodded knowledgeably and said they were drawing near to the sea.

Then, as they crested a hill, Devlin looked and saw the sea spread out before him, in all its immense glory.

He rode down to the water's edge, marveling in what he beheld. The sea was vast. Endless. Dark blue waters stretched to the limits of the horizon, with rolling white-capped waves that crashed on the sandy shore, then re-treated, hissing. Dismounting, he walked into the surf and tasted the salty water, heedless of how foolish he must look.

Standing in the surf, there was nothing to meet his eyes but the vast expanse of the sea, and he felt humbled into insignificance. A mere man was nothing compared to this grandeur.

He wished fiercely that he was still an artist, that he had some way to capture and share the beauty of what he saw. But even he knew that was a foolish thought. How could anyone express eternity and limitless imagination? No metal was pure enough, no gem deep enough to reflect what he beheld. And yet he knew he had seen but a portion of its majesty. The aspect it wore on the fair spring day was but just one of the sea's many faces.

He had known that the sea existed. Had seen it portrayed on maps, and had heard accounts of travelers who had journeyed along its watery ways. His imagination had conjured up images of a large lake, one whose edges could not be seen. The reality was so much more than he could ever have dreamed.

He stood there lost in wonder, until Lieutenant Didrik's subtle coughing eventually caught his attention and re-called him to the present. Reluctantly, he turned his face from the sea and toward his duty.

The road continued along the coast, then rose along a

cliff, where it wound in and out of pine forests and grassy fields. From time to time they caught glimpses of the shore, and the oceans, until gradually the woods grew thicker and they could no longer taste the tang of salt in the air. On the second day, they passed a few scattered dwellings, then a ramshackle village, which seemed strangely lacking in people. And those folk they did see eyed Devlin and his troops with suspicion and fear. Questioning of the villagers revealed that the missing assessor had passed through here two months earlier, and that the Baron's men had come this way looking for him a month later.

On the next two days they passed through villages that looked much like the first. The inhabitants they saw were impoverished and terrified. Devlin could not understand it. The land here was good, the weather had been fair. There was no reason why the farmers could not make a living from their crops. And yet, though they appeared on the edge of starvation, there was not one word of criticism of their Baron.

The premonition that had led Devlin to Korinth province grew stronger with every league they traveled. There was something very strange happening here. And yet he had no answers, only more questions.

It was past time for politeness and discretion. At the next village he would not let the villagers evade him with half-truths and lies. This time he would persist, till he had the answers he sought.

But his plan went awry almost from the first. Someone sighted them as they approached, and Devlin saw a dozen or so people fleeing from the village to disappear into the pine woods.

"Shall we give chase?" Ensign Mikkelson asked.

"No," Devlin said. "We will wait, and speak with the cooler heads who remained behind."

He wondered what had inspired their panic. Had they been attacked by mounted riders in the past, or the slavers that the tavern keeper had mentioned? Did that explain their fears? Or was it the Baron's armsmen that they dreaded?

The village was eerily quiet as they approached. Neither barking dogs nor cackling chickens greeted their arrival. And there was not a soul to be seen.

The first cottage they came to had neither door nor shutters, and was clearly abandoned. The second was a burned-out shell. There were a dozen cottages still standing, each showing various signs of damage and of half-hearted attempts at repairs.

"This place was attacked," Ensign Mikkelson said, as his eyes swept over the damage. "Last summer or perhaps the fall."

"So it seems," Devlin said. He, too, had seen the telltale signs of damage. No storm had torn open that door, nor had rot caused that wall to fall. Those were the marks of an axe.

"I would know what has happened here," he said, dismounting from his horse. "Lieutenant. Ensign. Send out your troops and find me someone to speak with."

Mikkelson took his soldiers to search the woods for those who had fled, while Didrik and the guards began going from cottage to cottage, searching for any who had been left behind.

Stephen came over to where Devlin was standing. "I do not like this. If there have been sea raiders, then why hasn't Lord Egeslic reported this to the King?"

"A very good question," Devlin said.

From the other end of the village he heard a commotion, and a voice shouted, "We've found one!"

Devlin turned and began making his way toward the shouts. As he approached he saw Freyja and Signy emerge from a cottage, half-carrying, half-dragging an old woman.

"Put me down! Put me down!" the woman shrieked, batting ineffectually with her hands.

"Put the good woman down," Devlin said as he came near.

Freyja and Signy exchanged glances, then set the old woman on her feet. Freyja had the beginnings of a black eye, and Signy's face bore scratches. Devlin repressed a smile.

"Good woman, I would have speech with you," he said.

Feeble and stooped with age, the woman came barely up to his waist, but she drew herself up to her full height as if she were a Duchess in silks and not a cottager in a ragged wool kirtle.

"I have naught to say to you," the woman declared.

"What is your name?" Devlin asked, kneeling so he could look her in the eye.

"Nanna. Nanna Odin's-wife, though Odin has been dead these past twelve summers, the Gods preserve his soul," she said. Her voice shook, but she met his gaze without flinching.

He could see that she was afraid, but that she was too strong to give in to her fears. Her fierceness awoke a sense of kinship in him. "Nanna, I am Devlin of Duncaer, son of Kameron and Talaith," he said, introducing himself as if she were one of the Caerfolk. "And I am here because I am the Chosen One, sent by the Gods to defend the people and the Kingdom of Jorsk."

Nanna blinked and rubbed her eyes. "How can I trust you?"

He held out his left hand so the ring was in plain view. "I swear by my name and by all I hold dear that my words are true. I am the Chosen One," he declared, and the stone in the ring began glowing with ruby light until it was too bright to look at.

Nanna gasped, as did some of those who stood behind him, who had never before seen him call upon the ring's power. Satisfied that he had made an impression, Devlin closed his hand in a fist, turning the ring around so the glowing stone was held within his fist. And still the glow shone through his flesh, illuminating his very bones.

"You are here to serve the Baron?" Nanna asked, hope warring with fear in her face.

"No." Devlin shook his head. "I am here to serve the Kingdom. Now tell me, goodwife, why are the people so afraid? What has happened here that has brought such hardship on you and your neighbors?"

Nanna reached forward and clasped his right hand between hers with a grip that was surprisingly strong for one her age.

"The folk ran because they thought you were the Baron's men. There are few enough of us left here. Those who can have already left, gone to seek shelter with kin inland, or to find work in the city. There is nothing here for us. The sea raiders come as they please and take what they will. And the little they leave us, the Baron's men take for their own. A tax he calls it, to pay for our protection." Her voice quavered with indignation.

Her words did much to explain what they had seen. Caught between sea raiders and the Baron's special taxes, it was no wonder that the villages they had seen were so impoverished. And yet this was only one part of the puzzle. For what motive could Lord Egeslic have for his actions? Even a fool knew that taxes could only be pushed so far. Already the people were deserting the coastal villages. Soon they would begin to leave the Baron's lands altogether, and then who would be left to pay the taxes?

"The Assessor Brunin was here, was he not?" He had to ask, though he dreaded what he would hear.

She nodded. "Brunin was here, but we had nothing to pay him with. He swore he would send the Baron's men to turn us out of our homes. That is why the folk were so afraid when they saw you."

"Afraid enough to kill the assessor? To keep word from reaching the Baron?"

"No! No, we would not dream of such an evil thing," Nanna insisted.

Devlin wanted to believe her. And yet her own words had given ample reason to suspect that the villagers had been behind the assessor's disappearance. If not in this village, then in one of the others along his route.

"I thank you for the courtesy of your speech," Devlin said, freeing his hand and rising to his feet.

He gave her a formal bow, and watched as Behra and Signy gingerly escorted her back to her home. Then he turned to Lieutenant Didrik. "Find Ensign Mikkelson. Tell him to keep the villagers he finds apart from one another, until we can question them. See if her story matches theirs. And have the guards continue searching the cottages. There may be another here that we have missed."

"Understood," Didrik said with a salute.

In the end, they found a dozen more folk, all that was left from a village that had once boasted over a hundred souls. Those left were either the very old, or those so sunken into despair that they could not think of anywhere else to go. All those questioned confirmed Nanna's story. The assessor had been there, and he had made his threats. But he had been whole and well when he left, and after seeing the villagers, Devlin did not see any that looked as if they would have had the courage to murder a man.

Before leaving, Devlin gave Nanna a generous handful of the King's coin, enough to pay the taxes that were owed. He wished he could do more, but he knew the answers did not lie here. The solution to these villagers' problems lay with Lord Egeslic, and Devlin intended to demand a full accounting from the Baron of Korinth.

The road took them through the pine woods on the next day, and it was near sunset when they emerged into an open field. A league down the road they could see the outlines of a village.

"Shall we press on?" Lieutenant Didrik asked.

"No," Devlin said, mindful of how the folk in Nanna's village had reacted to their arrival. There was no sense in making the same mistake twice. In the darkness Devlin and his troops could easily be mistaken for the Baron's men, or for raiders.

"There is no need to panic the folk. We will camp here tonight, and tomorrow, when the sun is risen, we will make our entrance."

His company began to set up camp with the ease of long-established routine. Since the skirmish in Rosmaar they had taken to working together, and Lieutenant Didrik and Ensign Mikkelson had worked out a shared schedule of duties. Tonight it was the soldiers' turn to prepare the meal, while the guards had the less desirable chore of digging the latrine trench.

Devlin sat on the ground and leaned back on his

elbows, as he watched the activity around him. He was still troubled by what he had witnessed the day before, and bothered that he could not understand the Baron's strange behavior. Why hadn't the Baron revealed the presence of sea raiders along his coast? Why had he imposed onerous taxes upon his folk? If he needed the coin, why hadn't he petitioned the King for aid, as had the other border nobles?

He shook his head in frustration, for he felt that the answer lay just beyond his grasp. There was something he was missing. An ingredient that would make the rest take shape and make sense.

He heard a startled exclamation. Then after a moment he heard Didrik exclaim, "May the Gods preserve us."

Devlin was already on his feet when the lieutenant called his name. Lieutenant Didrik was standing next to two guards with shovels. A small crowd was forming around them.

Devlin pushed his way through the crowd. "What is it?" he asked.

The smell hit him first, a stench of rot and mold, and unclean things brought into the light. And then he looked into the half-dug latrine pit, where he saw the bloated and swollen features of a decomposing corpse, dressed in robes of silk.

"The Assessor Brunin, I presume," Devlin said.

Twenty-three

DEVLIN GAVE ORDERS THAT THE COMPANY WAS TO retreat back into the forest, while two of their number finished unearthing the body of the assessor. He steeled himself to examine the gruesome corpse, seeking clues as to how the assessor had died. Then he joined his troops in the forest. They spent a cold night, for to light fires might reveal their presence to the village.

In the predawn light the company crept through the woods to surround the village. When Devlin and his officers approached on horseback, some of the villagers began to flee, only to stop short as they caught sight of the guards and soldiers.

Magnus, the elderly village speaker, then emerged from his cottage on the arm of his daughter. His voice was steady as he bade the Chosen One welcome, but his shoulders slumped, and he had the air of a man who has seen the arrival of the troubles he has long feared.

Up until that moment Devlin had nursed a secret hope that the villagers might somehow, improbably, be innocent of the assessor's death. But Magnus's attitude proclaimed their guilt far louder than any mere words could.

Devlin, Ensign Mikkelson, and Lieutenant Didrik followed Magnus inside his home, in order to question him in private. But so far the speaker was not cooperating.

"Now I ask again. Who killed the Assessor Brunin, and why did they do this deed?"

Devlin's words were addressed to the elderly Magnus, but it was his daughter Magnilda who answered.

"I tell you we know nothing of his death. The assessor must have been killed by sea raiders or outlaws," she said defiantly. A plain woman in her middle years, her stocky frame and muscled arms spoke of one who had spent her life in hard toil. And she had a strength of character to match. For while Magnus had blanched upon learning that Devlin was the Chosen One, Magnilda had taken his appearance in stride.

"I may be a foreigner, but I am not a fool," Devlin said. "Outlaws or raiders carry weapons. A sword, a dagger, a bow, or even a spear. And they would not have bothered to hide their kill. The Assessor Brunin was strangled, and his body buried not a league from here."

"Shall I have the company begin questioning the rest of the villagers?" Lieutenant Didrik asked.

"It will do you no good. They will all tell you the same as I. They know not who killed the assessor," Magnilda answered.

Devlin kept his eyes on her father. "Are you certain this is so? There is no one here who is discontented, unhappy with their neighbors? No one who would wish to seek my favor and a purse of the King's silver for his service?"

Magnus gave a thin smile. "My people will follow my lead. There are none who have aught to say to you."

Devlin felt his frustration growing. He knew full well that everyone in this village could name the murderer, for such was the way of a small community. And yet he also knew that if this had been Duncaer, the people would never betray one another to a stranger. He would have to try a different tactic.

"Mayhap you are right. We shall see. But if I do not find the murderer, then I will have to summon the Baron's armsmen, and you will face his justice."

"And your justice is different than his? We know too well what to expect from nobles," Magnilda said scornfully.

The Baron might well put the village to the torch, destroying everything these people owned. It was his right, and from the way his people feared him, it would not be out of character.

Devlin wished fervently that they had never stumbled across the murdered assessor's body. It was the Gods' own luck that had led them to that cursed spot. And yet, how much worse would it have been for these folk if it had been the Baron's armsmen who had found the corpse?

"I am no lord," Devlin said, willing them to understand. "In my life I have been a metalsmith, a farmer, and now I serve as the Chosen One. I have seen much of hardship and sorrow in this province. But I cannot let this crime pass unpunished. You must persuade the killer to reveal himself and accept his punishment. If he does so, I swear by my name that the judgment will end with his death. There will be no further retribution."

"The Baron will not honor a promise made in his name," Magnus said.

"I do not make it in his name. I make it in the name of King Olafur, whom I serve," Devlin replied.

Magnus exchanged glances with his daughter. "Then I—"

"No, Father!" Magnilda interrupted, seizing his arm. "Say nothing."

He knew then he had won, and he could afford to be gracious. Devlin rose to his feet. "We will leave you to make your decision."

He left the cottage and went outside, followed by his officers, to find that the road outside Magnus's home was filled with villagers. They stood there silently, with hate in their eyes.

This village was farther inland than the others, which perhaps had spared it some of the sea raiders' attentions. And these folk showed fewer signs of hardship, although most looked as if they were in need of a good meal or three.

Didrik's eyes raked the crowd. "Do you think the murderer is here? Watching us?"

"Unless he has already fled," Ensign Mikkelson countered.

Devlin shook his head. "If the murderer had fled the village, the speaker would have given us his name readily enough. A shame that Magnus didn't think to tell us such a tale. We would have no means of disproving him."

"You cannot wish that a murderer would go unpunished?" Ensign Mikkelson asked.

No. Devlin wished he had never come to this cursed place, nor heard of the missing assessor.

"For all we know, the assessor brought this on himself. Or the Baron did, with his harsh taxes. If I were one of these folk, I do not know what I would have done. But now that we know the murderer is here, it is my duty to find him and see him hanged."

Devlin could not repress a shudder at the thought. If he

closed his eyes, he could still see the image of the inn-wife and her son, their faces turning purple and their bodies jerking wildly as they danced at the end of the ropes. And if ever two had deserved to die, it had been those evil creatures.

He did not know how he could bring himself to inflict the same horrors upon one of these poor folk. And yet the Geas drove him, forcing him to seek justice for the murdered official.

Magnilda opened the door and beckoned to them. "My father wishes to speak with you," she said.

Devlin entered, and found that Magnus had risen to his feet. "You must swear to me that only the one responsible will be punished. No other will suffer for the crime," he said.

"As the Chosen One, I swear this will be so, in the name of King Olafur. I call upon Ensign Mikkelson and Lieutenant Didrik to witness my oath."

Magnilda went over to her father's side, and he embraced her. Then he turned, and his eyes met Devlin's. Devlin drew in a breath as he realized the old man's intention.

"I am the one you seek," Magnus declared. "The responsibility for the killing is mine, and mine alone."

The old man's withered hands lacked the strength to wring a chicken's neck, let alone to strangle a grown man.

"And you killed him with your own hands?" Lieutenant Didrik asked.

"I am speaker of the village. The responsibility for the deed is mine," Magnus said firmly.

Devlin looked at Magnilda, who stood by her father's side, supporting his withered frame with her strong arms. And he suddenly knew whom Magnus was protecting. The father had decided to sacrifice himself for the sake of his daughter, and for his village, to spare them further pain.

"Your courage does you honor," Devlin said. "I grant you the burden of this guilt." Every man had the right to decide when he would die, and for what he would give his life.

"I have one more request. Will you tell me why you did this?" Devlin asked.

Magnus nodded. "The assessor came, with his new taxes. But we were prepared, and had managed to save enough from the fall harvest to sell this spring and earn the coins we needed. When he saw we had the coin, he laughed, and said our taxes were now doubled."

"It was unfair," Magnilda broke in. "We had already paid, and yet still he wanted more. I told him he was taxing us into our graves, and he just laughed. He said the Baron had no use for us, and that the sooner we were dead or gone, the better it would be for all. So I—"

"So you were enraged," Magnus interrupted. "As was I. I said harsh words, and the assessor promised that the Baron would hear of my disloyalty, and that the armsmen would come and drag me before the Baron's court. I knew that such a thing would mean my death, and so in a fit of rage I killed him."

He could see how it happened. The assessor had made the same threats in Nanna's village. But Nanna's people had been too cowed to defend themselves. It was the assessor's arrogance that had proved his undoing, for in this village he had encountered someone who would not back down, and whose strength was coupled to a fierce temper.

Devlin wondered whom the assessor had threatened. Had it been the speaker Magnus? Or had Magnilda been acting to save her own life? In the end, it did not matter. The crime had been done, and now he must exact punishment, according to the law.

"I would pardon you if I could," Devlin said. "But I cannot. The assessor was wrong, but that did not give you the right to kill him. You should have brought your complaints to your lord, or if you did not trust him, to the King's court."

"And who would have listened to one such as I?" Magnilda asked.

"I would have," Devlin said solemnly. But it was too late for what might have been.

"Speaker Magnus, I give you this day to make your farewells to your family and people. I will carry the sentence out tomorrow at dawn."

Magnus nodded, only a faint tremor in his hands betraying his nervousness.

Devlin's mind flashed ahead to the coming dawn. He could see it already. Magnilda crying or cursing his name. The old man's trembling courage. Devlin's own hands shaking as he forced himself to fasten the rope around that frail neck. He wanted to vomit.

"I have given you my word that the punishment ends here," Devlin said. "Know also this. When I leave here, I go to seek Lord Egeslic to confront him for his deeds. Should he prove himself guilty of a crime, I promise you that his judgment will be equally swift, and far less merciful."

"For that I thank you," Magnus said.

Stephen was stunned when Devlin and the others emerged from the old speaker's house with the news that Magnus had been found guilty of the assessor's murder and was to be executed at sunrise. He was certain it was a horrible jest. The old speaker lacked the strength to harm anyone.

Then Devlin ordered that a watch be placed on the speaker's house, and instructed the troops to camp at the outskirts of the village. The grimness in his voice convinced Stephen that this was no jest.

The afternoon wore on, and a steady procession of visitors passed in and out of Magnus's house, as the villagers made their farewells. Their mood was grim, and Ensign Mikkelson ordered a night watch as if they were in hostile country. Stephen had little appetite for the evening meal, and he saw most others felt the same.

Now night had fallen, and Devlin lit a fire near a large elm tree, some distance from the rest of the troops. A soft rain began to fall, but the tree's large leaves provided ample shelter. Ensign Mikkelson and Lieutenant Didrik joined Devlin, as was their custom in the evenings. But instead of the usual friendly banter, the three simply stared into the fire, each lost in his own thoughts.

Stephen had tried to see the speaker, hoping to discover some explanation that would make sense of it all, only to find himself rebuffed by the old man's daughter.

Eventually he wandered over and joined Devlin and his companions at the fire. There he listened as Lieutenant Didrik and Ensign Mikkelson argued over their next course of action in soft tones. From time to time they would glance across the fire at Devlin, but the Chosen One remained silent, his face mostly hidden in the shadows.

This could not be happening. How could Devlin kill a man in cold blood? A man who despite his confession, was clearly not guilty of the crime? It would be a monstrous cruelty. And yet as the evening wore on, Stephen began to despair as he realized that there would be no last-minute reprieve.

"We do not know Lord Egeslic is guilty of anything, save a poor choice in retainers," Ensign Mikkelson said. "The assessor could have been lining his own pockets, under the cloak of the Baron's authority."

"Then why are his people so afraid of him?" Lieutenant Didrik countered. "And where are the Baron's armsmen in this? Why do they not try to defend the coast road against the sea raiders? Don't they realize if they lose the road, they lose the province?"

Devlin stirred, the first movement he had made in the past hour. When he spoke, his voice was a rusty rasp as if long disused. "The longer I ponder on this, the more I wonder about these raiders, and what their true motives are. Do you not see something strange about their raids?"

Ensign Mikkelson shrugged. "The sea raiders strike where they will, and many provinces have felt their sting. We think they are from the Green Isles, but none can be sure."

"They seem well organized, for they avoid the Royal Navy. And they can strike anywhere. So why choose this land, these poor folk? Surely they know there is little wealth to be gained, and yet they attack again and again," Devlin mused.

Didrik rubbed his chin thoughtfully. "I had not thought of it in that light. But it does seem odd, as does their habit of destruction. Other provinces have reported theft and looting, but only here do we see destruction and wholesale killing."

"It is as if there are two different groups of raiders," Stephen said, thinking aloud.

"Or they are not raiders at all," Devlin said. "Tell me,

who gains if the Korinth coast is decimated, stripped bare of its population?"

"No one," said Didrik. "If the villagers are gone, there will be none left for the raiders to plunder or to pay the Baron's taxes."

"Unless that is their aim," Mikkelson said. "Say the villages are empty of life. Who will raise the alarm when the next ships bring not raiders but an invading army? Before we knew aught was amiss, they could seize the province. From their bases here they could sweep down the plains, taking the fertile south lands, and splitting the Kingdom in twain."

Such had happened two hundred years earlier, in the time of Queen Reginleifar. It had taken three years and thousands of lives to drive the invaders from Korinth. It was chilling to think that it might happen again, and there was a moment of silence as they contemplated the scale of the potential disaster.

"There is one thing more to consider," Mikkelson said. "Did not the Assessor Brunin say that the Baron would be well pleased once the villages were empty? Perhaps the Baron is somehow involved in the scheme, and that is the reason why he has burdened the people with his taxes."

Was it possible? Could the Baron really be a traitor? It seemed fantastic. And yet it would explain so much. Why the Baron had not reported the troubles in his province to the King and court. Why his people lived in such fear, and why the raiders were allowed free access along the seacoast.

"We did not hear the assessor's words. We only heard what Magnilda chose to recount to us. The Baron may yet be proved innocent," Devlin said, though from the grim tone of his voice it was clear he had little expectation that it would be so.

If Lord Egeslic was a traitor, then there was no reason to hang the speaker. Stephen felt as if a great weight had been lifted from him. "This changes everything," he said. "If the Baron is a traitor, then so was the assessor. Thus the villagers did no wrong, and you can pardon the speaker Magnus."

"No."

Stephen sucked in a quick breath. "No? But what do you mean?"

"No," Devlin repeated. "The speaker's guilt is unchanged. He will be hanged on the morrow."

Stephen could not believe it. He had thought he knew Devlin, but now he realized that he had been mistaken. The friendly face that Devlin had shown the world in these past weeks had been but a mask. This grim, unyielding man was the true face of the Chosen One.

"Who will you get to perform such a deed?"

"I will do it myself," Devlin said.

A sick sense of betrayal swept over Stephen. To think that he had admired the man. What a fool he had been. Hot anger rose within him and he leapt to his feet.

"Then you too will be a murderer," Stephen declared. Turning his back on Devlin, he stalked away.

He headed in the direction of the main camp, and its welcoming fires. A moment later he heard footsteps behind him. "I have said all I have to say," Stephen added.

"Then you will hear what I have to say," Ensign Mikkelson's voice came from behind him.

Stephen stopped in surprise. He had expected Didrik might follow him, or even Devlin. But not Mikkelson. The Ensign remained a mystery, as coldly professional and aloof as he had been on the first day of their journey.

"Walk with me," Ensign Mikkelson said, leading him in

a direction that took them away from the camp, where their words could not be overheard.

"You are acting like a spoiled child," Ensign Mikkelson said.

How dare he accuse Stephen? It was Devlin who was in the wrong. Anyone could see that.

"How can you take his part?" Stephen asked. "It is as plain as day that the old man is innocent."

"He did not kill the Assessor Brunin with his own hands, that is true. But he took responsibility for the crime."

Coming face-to-face with the awful power of the Chosen One must have terrified the elderly speaker. No doubt he would have confessed to anything. "And you believed him?"

"That he killed the assessor? No. It was probably his daughter Magnilda who did the actual deed. But the speaker took responsibility, and that is his right."

Stephen blinked. Magnilda? He remembered the glare in her eyes as she had denied Stephen the right to see her father in his final hours. Could one such as she be a murderess?

"I do not understand," Stephen said. "If she did the crime, surely she was provoked. These people are being terrified and impoverished by an unjust lord. It is only right that they defend themselves."

"They tell me your father is a lord," Mikkelson said.

"Yes," Stephen said, uncomfortable with the turn the conversation had taken.

"Then surely you have seen him and his magistrates pass judgment. It is not always easy, but it must be done."

"But this is not justice," Stephen protested. What purpose would the old man's death serve? And Devlin intended to hang him himself. How could Devlin live with himself, having performed such an act? And how could Stephen live with himself, knowing that he had called such a man friend?

"You reason like a child," Ensign Mikkelson said sternly. "Only the Baron may pass judgment on his officials. If the Baron is deemed unfair, then the villagers may petition the King's court for justice. This is the law. We cannot pick and choose who must pay for their crimes. Such would lead to anarchy. If Devlin pardoned this man, what happens the next time a farmer has a grievance with an assessor? Shall he, too, be pardoned for murder?"

"No, but—"

"There are no buts. The Chosen One is as merciful as the law allows. Far more merciful than the Baron would be. If the Baron's armsmen had found the corpse, they would have hanged Magnus and his daughter. At best, the rest of the village would merely lose their homes and property. At worst, they, too, might face execution, for having shielded the killers from justice."

Stephen shivered in the cold night air. The Ensign's words made a dreadful sense.

"But why did not Devlin tell me this?"

"Perhaps because you gave him no chance to explain. Or mayhap he felt the need to keep his own counsel, and to trust that his friends would have faith in him."

The last held the ring of truth. It was not in Devlin's nature to plead for understanding. The Chosen One made hard choices and accepted the responsibility for the consequences of his actions. Stephen had declared his friendship, but then, when Devlin needed his friendship, Stephen had turned on him in anger. He had blamed Devlin for failing him, for forcing him to see that this was no pretty ballad, where the Chosen One set all to rights with his mere presence.

"Why are you telling me this?" he asked.

"The troops must see that we stand united, or else they will lose faith and it will weaken their morale. You are his friend. Your words carry weight, as does your example. If you condemn him, the Chosen One may begin to doubt himself just when we need him to be a strong leader."

"You are an officer, while I am a mere minstrel. Surely your words would carry more weight. I have seen the respect he gives you."

Ensign Mikkelson gave a bitter laugh. "Respect? Say rather the Chosen One values my knowledge. And he chooses to keep me close so he can keep his eye on me as he tries to decide whether I am in league with his enemies."

"You must be mistaken."

"He is right to suspect me. At least one of my soldiers is not to be trusted. Who else do you think shot the arrow that barely missed the Chosen One during the skirmish in Rosmaar?"

Devlin had made no mention of a stray shot. And yet what reason would Ensign Mikkelson have to lie to him? Stephen wondered just what else had occurred that he had failed to notice.

"You have given me much to think about," Stephen said.

"Good," Ensign Mikkelson replied. He began to walk away, then stopped after a few paces and returned. "Devlin is a man in ten thousand. An officer such as we in the Royal Army have not seen in a generation. The Gods have sent him to us for a reason. I fear that we will need his greatness in the coming troubles. It is up to us to protect him. Even from himself."

Stephen had not realized the Ensign was capable of such

unbridled emotion. He stared after Mikkelson as the Ensign walked into the camp and began talking to his soldiers.

Stephen returned to the elm tree, where he found
Devlin sitting alone.

"I must apologize for my hasty words," Stephen said.

Devlin shook his head. "Say no more. On this day I hate
myself."

Devlin refused to accept Stephen's apology, for in truth
there was nothing to forgive. Devlin understood the minstrel's anger, for the same rage simmered deep inside of
him. Devlin the man pitied these poor villagers. Left to
himself, he would have pardoned the speaker and sen-
tenced the hot-tempered daughter to no more than exile.
After lecturing her on the folly of burying a body so close
to the village, in so shallow a grave.

The Chosen One had no room for such sympathies. The
Geas bound him to uphold the law and administer justice.
No matter that the justice was overly harsh. It was the law.
By the standards of Jorsk, Devlin was being merciful indeed in allowing a man near the end of his days to give his
life so that his daughter might live. But such mercy left a
bitter taste in his mouth.

He could not help thinking that a greater man would
have found a way to serve justice and yet spare Magnus's
life. One of the true Chosen Ones, who featured so prominently in Stephen's songs and stories. It was the ill luck of
these folk that it was he who must pronounce justice. And
it was he who would bear the guilt of Magnus's death.

Not that the guilt was his alone. The death of the
speaker was but one of the crimes that Devlin intended to

hold the Baron of Korinth accountable for. At the very least, the Baron was guilty of negligence, and of failing in his duty to his people. At the worst, he was a traitor.

But justice for the Baron would take time. And until the Baron could be brought to see the error of his ways, these folk would be on their own, with no one to save them should the raiders return. That, too, was an injustice, but one he could correct.

The rain stopped just before dawn, and as the sky lightened, Devlin and his officers made their way to the speaker's house.

The guard on duty came to attention and saluted. "All is quiet," she said.

Devlin nodded. With the dawn a terrible calm had descended upon him, blotting out all traces of feeling. Nothing ruled him now save an implacable sense of duty, and his oath as the Chosen One.

Ensign Mikkelson knocked on the door. "It is time," he called.

The door swung open, to reveal Magnilda, still wearing the same tunic and trousers she had worn the day before. Her eyes were swollen, but there was no trace of tears.

"You are too late," she said. "My father has escaped your justice, for he is already dead."

What trick was this?

"Take me to him," Devlin ordered.

Magnilda led him inside, and up the stairs to a small bedroom. A coarse woolen blanket had been drawn over a lifeless form. Devlin turned back the blanket, to find the pale and waxy features of the speaker. He pressed his hand to Magnus's throat, but there was no pulse in that chill flesh.

He pulled the blanket off and knelt by the bed, bending

his head down to listen, but there was no sound of breath. Rising, his eyes swept over the body, but there was no sign of violence or self-inflicted injury. Instead Magnus's features were tranquil. Peaceful.

Devlin pulled the blanket over the speaker's corpse. "Was it poison?" he asked.

"I do not know," Magnilda answered. "Perhaps. Or perhaps the Gods chose to grant him mercy, since you would give him none."

Mercy indeed if the speaker had met his death peacefully, in his sleep. And mercy for Devlin, who had been spared the task of ending the man's life.

"Who is to be speaker now?" he asked.

"I am," Magnilda replied, her body stiffening as if she expected him to challenge her right to the position.

"A good choice," Devlin said. From her expression, he could see he had surprised her, though he had spoken only the truth. Magnilda's fierce temper would be an asset for what he planned. "Gather the villagers together within the hour so I may speak with them."

"Will you not grant us time to bury my father?"

"Later. Now is the time for the living. Gather everyone from the eldest to the babes. What I have to say is for all."

"Yes, my lord Chosen," Magnilda said, her eyes bright with anger.

The villagers gathered in a loose semicircle near the elm tree, where Magnus was to have been hung. There were over a hundred of all ages, from gray-haired elders to babes in arms, strong folk in their prime and youth on the verge of adulthood. At the edges of the crowd were his troops. The soldiers looked nervous. The guards' faces gave nothing away, but their eyes constantly swept the crowd, looking for threats.

The crowd parted as Devlin approached, and he made his way through to the front.

Magnilda was standing there, wearing the silver chain of her office around her neck.

"You promised my father that the punishments would end with his death. Will you now go back on your word?"

"I said naught about punishments," Devlin answered. His eyes swept over the crowd. The folk looked sullen. Defeated. Only Magnilda had the courage to show her anger.

"Is everyone here?" he asked.

She nodded.

"Good. Now hear me," he said, pitching his voice to carry to those assembled. "I come to speak to you about the sea raiders. I have reason to believe that they will return, and that you will have to defend yourselves. Now tell me, who among you can use a bow?"

No one spoke.

"A spear?"

Silence met this query too. It was as if he was speaking in a foreign tongue. The villagers simply stared vacantly ahead, refusing to meet his eyes.

"Does any one among you have skills at knife fighting? At wrestling?" This was foolishness. "Can any man or woman here throw a rock in defense of their own lives?"

"Why should we answer you?" Magnilda said. "So you can accuse one of us of another crime? We will not fall for your tricks."

His anger boiled over, and he turned to her, turning his back on the crowd. "I have no patience for your ignorance and your foolishness. You are their leader now. So lead. Answer my question."

"I know no weapons," she said. "I have but my own hands to defend myself."

"That will serve," he said. "Now for the rest. Who has learned aught of weapons craft?"

A half dozen of the villagers raised their hands. It was fewer than he had hoped for, but it was a beginning. Devlin nodded.

"Good. Now from this day forward, all will learn weapons craft, so that you may defend yourselves. The spear to start, for it is simplest to make and to learn."

"Wherefore?" a young woman asked. "We cannot stand against the raiders."

Other heads nodded in agreement. Devlin reined in his anger. It was not their fault that these foolish folk had been bred to be sheep. But he would be damned if he left them helpless.

"You will learn because I command it. Because you wish to save your own lives, and the lives of your kin and neighbors. Because you will not willingly give up all you own. In the end you will learn because you have no choice."

"But surely I am too old," an elderly man said.

"If you cannot fight, you can keep watch. Or you will fashion weapons for those who can. Or you will care for the babes so their mothers can join in the training."

Several present shook their heads. "But surely you do not mean me," said the young woman who had objected before. She raised the baby as if the child were some magical shield.

"Everyone," Devlin growled. "You will train for an hour every day until you are proficient. Thereafter, the first day after the new moon will be set aside to practice. My own wife trained the day before she delivered our child, and she resumed training at the next new moon."

He had not meant to mention Cerrie. He ran his fingers through his hair as he tried to think of what to say next.

The villagers were silent, perhaps contemplating his words. Or perhaps they were having trouble picturing the Chosen One as someone who had once had a wife.

"You will learn to fight because you love your families," he said. "Trouble is coming. If you do not defend yourselves, there are none who will save you. You will fight because you have no other choice. Do you understand?"

"I understand," Magnilda said. "But do you think we truly have a chance to defend ourselves?"

He would not lie to her. "A chance. Perhaps. If you have the element of surprise. But even the smallest of chance is better than none at all."

He motioned, and Sergeant Henrik and Oluva stepped forward. "These are Sergeant Henrik and Oluva of the Guard. They will remain with you, to teach you what they know. And when they are finished here, they will journey on to the next village. And the next."

Lieutenant Didrik had argued fiercely against this decision, saying that Devlin would need all of his company when he finally confronted the Baron. But Devlin had overruled him. Two guards would make little difference if the Baron should see through their ruse and order his armsmen to attack Devlin's party. The villagers had far more need of their skills. He only wished he could spare more, so that the other villages could begin their training without delay.

Twenty-four

"I WILL GIVE EVERYTHING I OWN IF SOMEONE WOULD scratch my nose," Stephen declared.

Around him the soldiers and guards chuckled.

"Silence!" Devlin ordered. "You are supposed to be miserable. Try and look the part. And Stephen, enough complaining. Try to appear frightened."

Stephen shrugged, a difficult gesture since his hands were bound behind his back. "I am frightened. I keep thinking of how many things can go wrong."

Devlin raised his head and glared at the minstrel, then, nauseated by the swaying motion of the litter, lowered his head again. *I will not vomit*, he told himself for the hundredth time, as one of the bearers stumbled and the litter lurched suddenly to the left and then to the right again. He did not blame them, for he knew he made a heavy load to bear. Yet no one else could play his part.

Though he could not see the column, he knew they made a pathetic sight. Those seemingly well enough to ride wore torn and dirty uniforms, and their heads hung low, as if disheartened. Many sported signs of recent injuries, and chickens' blood had been dabbed liberally on their bandages to make their wounds seem more convincing. To all they met on the road, they gave the same story. They had found the man who had killed the assessor and had been bringing him to the Baron when they were attacked by sea raiders. Though they had managed to defend themselves, it was at grievous cost.

Anyone seeing them would conclude that they posed little threat. Or at least, that was Devlin's plan. He called it hiding in plain sight. Ensign Mikkelson called it the stupidest idea he had ever heard of. Lieutenant Didrik's opinion was less kind, although more colorfully expressed.

Yet what other choice did they have? If the Baron chose to shut the gates of his keep, Devlin lacked the troops to force him to surrender. And the Baron's keep was on a windswept grassy plain, which ruled out a stealthy approach.

As they approached the entrance to the keep, Devlin felt his stomach clench. This was the moment. By now the Baron's spies would have informed him of the approaching party. Would he give orders to admit them? Or would his armsmen bar the gate and fire on them from the safety of the ramparts?

"Tell the men to remember the plan. Do nothing until my signal," Devlin whispered to Ensign Mikkelson. The Ensign nodded, then rode down the line, repeating the message in tones too low for Devlin to hear.

Devlin risked lifting his head the barest fraction till he could see the gate. It was open, flanked by a pair of armsmen on either side. The cadence of the bearers changed, and he heard the clatter of booted feet on a wooden bridge.

"Halt!" a voice called.

Two of the bearers halted at once while two did not, and

their combined efforts made the litter sway. Devlin's nausea rose, and this time he could not contain it. He leaned over the side of the litter and retched.

"Goat turds," a woman cursed. She came over and peered at Devlin, who did his best to look pathetic.

"We come bearing the Chosen One, who seeks an audience with the Baron of Korinth, Lord Egeslic," Lieutenant Didrik said, coming up alongside the litter. His left arm was in a sling, and a bandage daubed with chicken blood was wrapped around his head.

"The Baron welcomes you to his keep," said an older male voice. This was a voice of authority, for the armswoman saluted, and the procession was allowed to pass through the gate into the open courtyard beyond.

The litter was placed on the ground, and the riders dismounted. Ensign Mikkelson and Lieutenant Didrik moved among the troops, seemingly checking on their health, but actually surveying the courtyard and surrounding walls to make sure this was not a trap.

"Bring the Chosen One inside, and our healer will see to his injuries," said the one in command.

"No," Devlin rasped, raising himself up on one elbow with a show of great difficulty. "I must fulfill my duty. I must see the Baron, so that the guilty may be brought to justice."

The muscles in his elbow quivered, and he shook as if he were at the end of his strength.

"It is his last wish," Ensign Mikkelson whispered, just loud enough for Devlin to overhear. "The Geas drives him to seek justice."

"We are sworn to uphold his orders. But if the Baron would grant us his presence, the Chosen One would be satisfied and then we could take our ease," Lieutenant Didrik said, in the tones of one who has long suffered from the whims of his commander.

The senior armsmen chewed his lip thoughtfully, then nodded. "I will go speak with the Baron and find out his will."

Devlin's elbow fell, and he sank back on the litter.

The guard Olga knelt down by his side. "Can I serve you?" she asked, her eyes bright with mischief. She tugged at the blanket that covered his torso, pulling it straight, then ran her hands along the sides of the litter to ensure that the weapons hidden beneath were in easy reach.

"Your concern warms my heart," Devlin said.

A few moments later, he heard the sound of approaching footsteps.

"Help me sit up," Devlin said.

Olga placed her arms behind his shoulder and tugged him into a sitting position. He grasped the axe in his right hand.

It was easy to spot Lord Egeslic. The young noble sported the golden circlet on his brow that was reserved for nobles of the first rank, of which he was not. He wore a purple silk tunic over green leggings, and his soft slippers made no sound on the stone courtyard. Accompanying him was the officer Devlin had seen earlier, and two ceremonial guards trailed behind.

The Baron smiled as he caught sight of Stephen, held between two of the guards. Stephen's head hung low; he made an abject sight.

"So this is the criminal? I have a very special punishment planned for him," he said, with a cruel smile.

This was it. There would be no second chance.

"Message," Devlin croaked. "Must tell Baron. Only Baron."

He tossed his head wildly from side to side, as if in the grip of delirium.

"I fear he is failing fast," Olga announced.

But the Baron's attention was for Stephen. He came up to the minstrel and grabbed his chin with one hand, forcing Stephen's head up until he could look into his eyes. "A very special punishment indeed," he drawled.

Devlin's heart froze. How long could Stephen maintain his deception before the Baron realized the truth?

"Please no! Mercy, my lord, mercy, great Baron," Stephen sobbed, his legs collapsing from under him as the guards struggled to hold him upright.

The Baron laughed.

"Message," Devlin said, this time more loudly.

"My lord," Ensign Mikkelson said, approaching with a low bow. "The Chosen One has a message that he can reveal only to you. And I fear there is very little time. . . ." His voice trailed off.

The Baron turned from his prey, slowly, reluctantly. As he drew near the litter, his face wrinkled with distaste. "Hardly an impressive sight. He looks more like a peasant than the Chosen One."

"Lord Egeslic," Devlin whispered.

The Baron drew nearer until he stood within an arm's length of the litter. "What is this message?"

"Now!" Devlin yelled, rolling off the litter and springing to his feet. Before the Baron could do more than blink, Devlin's axe was pressing against his neck.

Around them, Devlin's troops had seized their own weapons from the litters and formed a loose circle, facing outward. The Baron's armsmen took a step forward, only to be halted by the swords of Mikkelson and Didrik.

"What is the meaning of this?" Lord Egeslic demanded.

"I have come to serve justice," Devlin said. "Now tell your armsmen to drop their weapons."

"No."

He had known it would not be this easy. He raised his free arm above his head, so that his hand was clearly visible. "I am the Chosen One, and what I do here I do in the name of justice, in service to King Olafur and the people of Jorsk. I call upon the Seven Gods to witness the truth of this oath."

The ring on his finger glowed with bright ruby light.

"A pretty trick," the Baron scoffed, but his face was pale and beaded with sweat.

"Hear me!" Devlin called. "You will lay down your arms, and surrender yourselves to the King's justice. Or you will be declared traitors, and your lord will suffer the consequences."

The senior officer looked at Devlin, and then at his lord.

"You would not harm him," the officer said.

"I will what I must, to fulfill my oath. Lay down your weapons," Devlin replied, letting the grim anger he carried within rise to the surface. He met the officer's stare with his own determined glare, and it was the officer who glanced away first.

"My lord, we must do as he says," the officer said. Then he unbuckled his sword belt and laid it on the ground.

The other armsmen swiftly followed his lead. But these were only a handful, and there were sure to be more in their barracks, or scattered around the keep.

One of the soldiers cut loose Stephen's bonds, and he chafed his wrists.

"Mikkelson! Secure these prisoners, then take the rest of the armsmen into custody," Devlin ordered.

He turned his attention back to the Baron. "Lord

Egeslic, I accuse you of failing in your sworn duty to your King and your subjects. This land was given to you in trust, in return for your fealty. Yet you have failed to defend the King's realm and his people. For this, you will pay."

"You fool. You have no idea who I am, or what you have done," Lord Egeslic sneered. "I will see you destroyed for this."

"I fear no petty lordling. Save your concern for yourself. If you are lucky, you will only lose your rank."

For if he were proven traitor, the Baron would lose his life.

Securing the keep proved nearly impossible. There were too many folk, scattered in too many places. And this was their home. They knew all the passages, and the escape routes. Mikkelson managed to surprise about forty armsmen in their barracks and took them into custody. But an equal number were still missing, having either fled the keep or doffed their uniforms, blending in among the members of the Baron's household.

Some of the servants had fled as well. Devlin had watched from the walls of the keep as they scattered in a dozen different directions, frustrated because he lacked the troops to pursue them. He knew some were honestly frightened, afraid they would suffer for the Baron's crimes. But at least some of those who fled were fleeing with a purpose, no doubt to alert the Baron's allies.

He had very little time. He could not hold the keep against a besieging force. Not when he had but a dozen guards and ten soldiers, plus himself and the minstrel Stephen. Nor could he count on the loyalty of the armsmen who had surrendered. They, and the majority of the servants, had been imprisoned in the keep's storerooms. It was a makeshift solution at best.

His forces were stretched thin, between guarding the prisoners and maintaining at least a skeleton watch. That left Mikkelson and Didrik to question the prisoners, while Stephen searched the Baron's rooms for incriminating documents.

Questioning the Baron was a task Devlin had taken on himself, but as the hours turned into days he grew increasingly frustrated. The Baron's arrogance was amazing. He refused to answer questions, and gave every appearance that he regarded Devlin as simply a minor inconvenience who would be swiftly dealt with by the Baron's allies. But who these allies were, he would not reveal.

And even if Devlin had had the stomach for stronger methods of questioning, the Geas would not permit it. Not when all that could be proven against the Baron was incompetence.

It was the evening of the third day since they had taken the keep. His last session with the Baron had degenerated into an angry tirade. Slowly Devlin had realized that the Baron was deliberately provoking him. He stopped in midtirade and left without explanation. Let the Baron stew on that while Devlin took a few hours' rest. It was nearly three days since he had slept. He needed at least some rest, so his wits would be sharp.

Devlin made his way through the unfamiliar corridors of the keep. There was a guard at the bottom of the main stairs who directed him to the chambers that had been assigned to the Chosen One and his officers.

Devlin turned down the corridor and saw a figure

approach. As she drew near, he recognized Freyja, one of the soldiers. When she was a regulation two paces away, she drew to a halt and saluted stiffly.

"All quiet?" he asked.

"Yes, my lord Chosen. This wing is secure." Her voice was calm and professional.

"Good. I am going to indulge in a few hours' sleep. Leave word with the watch leader that I am to be awakened in six hours if all is quiet. If aught is amiss, wake me at once," Devlin said, repeating the orders he had given the guard below. Better that he repeat himself than risk the message going astray.

"Of course, my lord."

She held her pose, and belatedly he remembered to return her salute. Freyja was one of those who clung firmly to the formal disciplines of the army, but she seemed competent enough.

She lowered her arm and stepped aside for him to pass. He began to walk on.

"My lord! Behind you!" a voice shouted.

It took Devlin a moment to realize that the voice was speaking to him. That moment almost cost him his life. As he began to turn toward his left, he felt the sharp edge of a blade graze his right side. He threw himself to his left, landing on the floor, then rolling over to face his enemy, flexing his arms so the throwing knives were already in his hands.

Freyja stood there, a bloody sword in her hand. Her eyes were vacant, and her features held a look of sheer astonishment. The point of a sword protruded from her midsection, and blood was rapidly staining her uniform.

"Damn you," she said, though he could not tell to whom she spoke. Then she fell to her knees, her sword clattering to the floor beside her.

Ensign Mikkelson withdrew his sword, and she collapsed in a lifeless heap. A pool of blood spread out over the dark wood floor. Devlin knelt beside the body, but even as he searched for a pulse, he knew there would be none.

Devlin rose to his feet.

"Why did you kill her?"

"I had no choice. She was about to strike again. I could not risk your life," Ensign Mikkelson said.

It was a fair enough explanation. Now was not the time to point out the obvious, that Freyja's death was also convenient to whoever had given her the orders to kill the Chosen One.

"I owe you my life," Devlin said.

"It is my duty," Ensign Mikkelson replied. He looked down at the corpse and shook his head. "Freyja. I had suspected others, but never her."

"She took us both by surprise," Devlin said. It had been a very narrow escape. If Mikkelson had not been there to warn him. If Devlin had turned to his right, instead of to his left. If—

He shook his head, banishing that futile speculation. It was enough that the Gods had chosen to spare his life, so he could fulfill his promises.

He had been expecting some kind of attack for so long that this came almost as a relief. He wondered if Freyja had been behind the earlier attack in Rosmaar. Or did she have accomplices? There could still be others in his company who wished him ill.

Devlin glanced sideways at Ensign Mikkelson. Even he was not free of suspicion. Had Mikkelson saved his life because it was his duty? Or was he hoping that through this service he would gain Devlin's confidence? For all he knew, Mikkelson might have been in league with Freyja, encouraging her to attack Devlin, then killing her so as to cast himself in the light of a hero.

"If I had not come looking for you," Ensign Mikkelson mused.

"Why did you seek me out?"

The Ensign tore his gaze from the corpse. "One of the Baron's clerks has decided to cooperate and I knew you would want to be informed at once."

"Take me to him," Devlin said, banishing thoughts of conspiracies to the back of his mind. Time alone would prove whom he could trust.

He took a step, then sucked in air with a hiss as his wound chose to make its presence felt. He pressed his hand to his right side, and when he withdrew it, his hand was bloody.

"You are wounded," Ensign Mikkelson said, stating the obvious.

"It is a scratch. Nothing more," Devlin said, replacing his hand over the wound. A deeper cut would have bled more, or struck his ribs. He had been lucky indeed.

"Any wound can turn deadly. You must see a healer."

His insistence was proper. Devlin would have ordered the same, if any of his troops had been injured. And yet he did not have time for such things.

"Take me to the others, then you may summon the healer. There is no reason why we cannot talk while the healer binds this up."

Stephen watched with horrified fascination as the guard Heimdall used strips of linen to bind up the wound in Devlin's side. It was not the wound itself that horrified him, but rather the knowledge that someone Stephen had known and trusted had tried to kill Devlin. Since the day she had come to his aid and helped him repair his saddle, he had thought of Freyja as a friend. He had spent many evenings with her, sitting around the fire, as he shared his music and listened to the soldiers' stories. He felt sickened as he realized that the friendship was but a ploy on her part. He had thought her a friend, but she had only been using him, to try and win Devlin's confidence.

What a fool he had been. In hindsight it was obvious. No doubt she had deliberately tampered with his girth, then waited nearby so she could come to his aid, and win his trust. How she must have laughed at his gullibility.

It was small comfort to know that others shared his anger and sense of betrayal.

Lieutenant Didrik had reacted furiously to the news that one of the soldiers had attempted to take Devlin's life. He and Ensign Mikkelson began wrangling over how the attack could have been foreseen and prevented.

Devlin was the calmest of them all. Perhaps he had faced death so often that he no longer feared it, even when it came in the guise of a friend. Or perhaps he was simply too weary to feel anything at all—for as always Devlin had driven himself harder than anyone else, until he stood on the ragged edge of exhaustion.

Stephen suddenly realized that he had never seen Devlin truly angry. He had seen Devlin when he was frustrated, short-tempered, and merely impatient. Yet even now, when faced with betrayal by one of his own, if Devlin felt anger he did not let it show. He wondered what it would take to rouse Devlin's wrath.

Heimdall tucked in the ends of the bandage, then stepped back to admire his work. "That should serve, my lord. If you put no strain on the wound for at least a fort-night."

"Thank you," Devlin said gravely. He pulled the remnants of his bloody shirt back on and watched as Heimdall left the room.

"Enough bickering," Devlin said, as the door shut behind Heimdall. "Tell me what you found."

Devlin listened as Lieutenant Didrik recounted how they had discovered that one of the prisoners was Sigfus, the Baron's clerk. Sigfus had served the former Baron of Korinth but apparently held little loyalty for the new Baron, who had inherited five years before, upon the death of his uncle. It had taken little prompting to get Sigfus to tell what he knew.

The tale he told was fantastic, almost unbelievable. But then Sigfus had led them to a cache of documents that confirmed all he said and more.

"I have not had time to read them all, but what we have read is damning," Lieutenant Didrik said, finishing his recital.

Devlin rubbed his face with his hands, as if he were trying to wipe away the weariness. "What do we know? First, the Baron was levying taxes without permission and failing to pay the King's share to the royal treasury."

Stephen nodded. This had been the clerk's chief complaint. He had shown little dismay over the Baron's treachery, but had seethed with anger as he told how the Baron had ordered him to falsify the province's accounts.

"Next, it seems that Lord Egeslic has been in correspondence with foreign allies, and with someone in the capital. They are plotting something, and you are convinced it is an invasion. Why?" Devlin asked.

"Because of the references to Queen Reginleifar," Ensign

Mikkelson explained. "Twice her name is mentioned in the scrolls we have examined so far. And in the last scroll it says 'By summer's end, the time of Queen Reginleifar will have come again.'"

"Who is this Reginleifar?" Devlin asked. The name sounded vaguely familiar.

"Reginleifar was Queen two hundred years ago, when Korinth was invaded by troops from Selvarat. She led the bloody war against the invaders and after three years finally succeeded in expelling them," Ensign Mikkelson said.

"It is one of the most famous stories from our history," Stephen added. Over a dozen ballads in his repertoire dated from that heroic era.

"Your history. Not mine," Devlin corrected. "So you think the threat is from Selvarat?"

Stephen shook his head. "No, Selvarat is among our strongest allies now, and has been for generations. Many of the noble families have intermarried," Stephen said. "Even now, my mother and sister are there, to set the seal on an alliance."

"The raiders from Nerikaat have long troubled the western borders but have not succeeded in gaining a foothold. Yet should they send their armies by sea, they could easily overwhelm a weakened Korinth," Ensign Mikkelson said.

"Or the attackers could be from the Green Isles, where the raiders are thought to be based," Lieutenant Didrik countered.

"Enough," Devlin said. "It does not matter where they are from. What matters is when they are planning to strike and what we can do to defend this province."

"It is six weeks until Midsummer's Day," Lieutenant Didrik said. "So we have time to prepare."

Devlin frowned. "I think not. Did not Sigfus also say that Lord Egeslic was expecting foreign guests to arrive any day? Could these guests not be members of an advance party, preparing for the invasion? No doubt this explains the Baron's confidence and lack of cooperation."

"Then we must send for reinforcements. At once," Ensign Mikkelson said.

"I agree," Lieutenant Didrik added.

"From where?" Devlin countered. "Rosmaar has its own troubles. The nearest sizable force is the Royal Army garrison in Kallarne. And Duke Gerhard is hardly likely to release them, no matter what message I send."

His words held the ring of bitter truth. The Duke's animosity toward the Chosen One was well known. Any message coming from Devlin would be ignored.

Devlin rose to his feet and began to pace in the small chamber. "We must find a way to convince the King of the need to send troops. And we must make sure his allies have no chance to liberate the Baron. So we will send the Baron to the capital, under guard. They can question him, and see the proofs of his treachery themselves."

"We are to leave then?" Lieutenant Didrik asked. "What of Korinth and of these folk?"

"We are not leaving. You are," Devlin said. "You, the Baron, and the three most reliable guards you can find."

"If you stay, you will need every hand that can hold a sword," Lieutenant Didrik protested. "I cannot leave, nor can I take those you need."

"You can and you must," Devlin said. "Four swords more or less will not ensure success. Only the arrival of the Royal Army can do so."

"But why me? Why not him?" Didrik asked.

Ensign Mikkelson stiffened. "I would be glad of this honor," he said.

"No. I need you here," Devlin said. "You and your soldiers are trained as archers. They will be of more use to me here in the keep than on the road guarding the Baron."

Devlin's words made sense, and Lieutenant Didrik eventually agreed. But Stephen could not help recalling the words Ensign Mikkelson had spoken back in the village. That Devlin kept the Ensign close because he did not trust him. Today Ensign Mikkelson had saved Devlin's life, and yet even now he must wonder how far Devlin trusted his loyalties.

Devlin heard the sound of running feet, then the guard Behra burst into the Baron's chambers.

"It worked," Behra said, holding one hand to his side as he bent forward, gasping for breath. "Ensign Mikkelson is bringing their leader here."

"Good," Devlin said. "Now catch hold of yourself or get out of sight. We must show no signs of haste or panic."

"Yes, sir," Behra said. Then, with a nod, he ran off to take up his post.

Devlin, who had been pacing, now took his seat behind the massive desk that had once resided in the castellan's quarters. *Stay calm*, he reminded himself. *We must convince these envoys that Korinth is securely within our control.*

The news that Baron Egeslic had been sent to the capital to be tried for treason had worked wonders on the spirits of those left in the keep. Servants, officials, and even a few armsmen came forward to offer their services to the Chosen One and to prove their loyalty to the King.

With their numbers swelled by these new followers, Devlin and Mikkelson had conceived a plan that was one part daring and three parts desperation. The Baron's keep was to give every impression of normalcy. To that end, soldiers wearing the Baron's colors patrolled the parapets, while two others guarded the main gate.

The central courtyard was decorated as if for a celebration, with a great ox roasting on a spit, booths dispensing wine or offering games of chance, and a strolling minstrel entertaining those gathered.

From a distance one could not see the strain on the faces of these supposed merrymakers nor taste the heavily watered wine. Only Stephen entered into the pretense with any enthusiasm.

The plan was to lure the envoys into the courtyard. Once they were inside, a ring of bowmen would rise from the surrounding parapet, trapping the party and forcing them to lay down their arms. There would be sixty bowmen in all, most of whom were but servants wearing borrowed uniforms. In a fight they would be of little use, but as he had watched them rehearse, Devlin had to admit that they looked impressive.

For three days they had performed this play, with nothing to show for it. Then on the morning of the fourth day the watchers had sighted the approaching party. Devlin had been grateful. He was heartily sick of eating roast ox.

Devlin had gone to the parapets to watch the foreigners' approach, and to count their number. Twelve in all. So the clerk Sigfus had been correct. This was a delegation, not the vanguard of an invasion.

Then Devlin had retired to the Baron's chambers, pacing impatiently until Behra brought the word that the trap had been successful.

Even now, Ensign Mikkelson was escorting the foreign leader through the corridors of the keep, making sure he observed the carefully posted sentries and the many folk wearing the uniforms of the Guard or the Royal Army, engaged in purposeful duty.

There was a knock on the door.

"Enter," Devlin called.

"My lord, you have a guest," Ensign Mikkelson announced, bowing low. With a courteous wave of his hand he indicated that the foreigner was to enter the study.

Devlin's first impression was of a man of middle years, with brown hair and tawny skin, wearing the robes of a Selvarat noble. But that should be impossible. Selvarat was firmly allied to the Jorskian empire. What was one of their nobles doing mixed up in this scheme? Then again, if a Jorskian noble could turn traitor, why not one of theirs?

Devlin rose from his seat. "Thank you, Ensign. You may leave us." Then he gave a court bow. "I am Devlin, the Chosen One of Jorsk. It is an honor to make your acquaintance."

"The honor is mine," said the man, bowing with an elaborate sweeping motion of his hand. When he straightened up, there was an ironic smile on his face. "Tell me, do you greet all your guests with drawn weapons?"

Devlin shrugged and spread his hands wide. "I apologize if you were discomfited. My troops tend to be somewhat protective of my safety. I am certain they meant no offense. Please be seated. May I pour you some wine?"

At the envoy's nod, Devlin crossed over to the sideboard and poured red wine into the two goblets that had been placed there earlier. He carried them back to the desk, then placed both goblets in the center before resuming his own seat behind the desk.

The envoy took the glass on his left, but he did not drink.

Devlin took the other glass and tossed back a healthy swallow. "The vintage is not the best, but it is neither poisoned nor drugged," he said.

"The thought had never crossed my mind," the envoy said, as he took a small sip from his own glass.

"I did not catch your name?" Devlin said.

"I am called Quennel."

It was but half a name, and Devlin would wager that there was a noble title attached to the other half. If indeed Quennel was this man's given name. Still, it would serve for now.

Devlin smiled affably. He let the silence stretch between them, until at last Quennel spoke.

"I must admit, I am surprised to see you here. I would have expected to see the Baron of this keep. Lord Egeslic, I believe he is called."

Quennel said the name casually but his eyes betrayed his interest.

"The Baron has proven an unworthy steward of this province," Devlin said. "He is on his way to Kingsholm to face judgment for his shortcomings."

"Ah," Quennel replied. "Then you are in command here?"

"I have secured this province in the King's name. My troops control the keep, and even now they guard the coast." It was the truth of a sorts. Henrik and Oluva were part of his troops, and they did guard the coast. Not that two guards and half-trained villagers could do much against an invasion.

"From our reception, I assume that you intend to keep me and my party here as prisoners? If so, I must—"

"On the contrary," Devlin interrupted. "I simply wished to meet with you, to clear up this misunderstanding. Once we have spoken, you and your party will be escorted to the coast, and your weapons returned to you."

Quennel put down his wineglass and raised his eyebrows in disbelief. "Indeed? And what misunderstanding is this?"

Devlin laid both of his hands flat on the desk and leaned forward, catching the envoy's gaze with his own. "Korinth is no longer a plum ripe for the picking. Any invaders will be met with cold steel. I advise you to think carefully whether or not you wish to pay this price."

"You did all this just to warn me?"

"I have no wish to bring back the days of Reginleifar."

Quennel's face flushed, and Devlin knew he had scored a hit. So Quennel had been one of those who had been in correspondence with the Baron. Or at the very least he had been privy to the contents of those letters.

"I would prefer to avoid useless bloodshed, but do not mistake this for cowardice. If invasion comes, we will exact such a bloody toll that your followers will curse your name with their dying breaths. The choice is yours."

Quennel rubbed his chin thoughtfully. "I am a simple messenger," he said. "I have no knowledge of such a fantastic scheme. I came here merely to renew our long-standing friendship with the Barons who have ruled this province."

"Of course you know nothing of such things," Devlin said. Two could play at this game of courtly deception and face-saving lies. "But you will remember my words, and share them with those that sent you."

"Courtesy demands I do no less," Quennel agreed.

"Then we are finished," Devlin said, rising to his feet. It

was time for this envoy and his party to leave. Now, before one of the servants-turned-soldiers dropped his weapon, or someone spoke a careless word, or any one of a hundred things happened that would reveal that Devlin's proud words were but a hollow boast.

Quennel rose as well and bowed again.

"It has been a... pleasure to make your acquaintance," he said. "I hope we will meet again."

"You will forgive my discourtesy, but I do not share your hope. The next time I see you in this Kingdom, your reception will be far less pleasant."

Quennel gave a thin smile. "I concede your point." He paused, then said, "If you would, indulge my curiosity. What made you suspect Lord Egeslic's trea—er, the Baron's indiscretions?"

Devlin thought furiously. Should he imply that the Baron's treason had been well-known and try to give the impression that this trap had been planned long ago? Even as the thought occurred, he dismissed it. There was no sense tangling himself in more lies. Better to mix grains of truth in to bolster the deception.

"As Chosen One, it is my duty to secure the borderlands. Korinth is just one of my charges," Devlin said, giving the official explanation for his mission.

The envoy shook his head. "There is no need to be coy. Korinth was your true destination from the very first. The other was a story meant to placate the foolish."

Devlin kept his face very still. Such knowledge could only have come from Kingsholm. Only his allies and the members of the King's Council had known that Korinth had been his true destination all along. To everyone else he had told the same tale as he had told his troops, namely that this was an expedition to inspect all of the border provinces. His blood ran cold as he realized that Baron Egeslic's accomplice could well be a member of the King's Council. Or someone who was close enough to a councilor to be privy to their secrets. He had known there was a traitor, but had imagined it to be another petty noble, one like Egeslic, who held little power and was scheming for more. Not even in his worst imaginings had he dreamed that the traitor could be a member of the court's inner circle.

"Then let us say that the Gods led me here," he finally replied.

"As you say. A foolish question, after all," Quennel said.

"Ensign!" Devlin called, and the door swung open to reveal Ensign Mikkelson standing at stiff attention. "Ensign Mikkelson, please escort his excellency Quennel and his party back to the shore. See that their weapons are returned to them once they have rejoined their friends. Then return here and report to me."

"It shall be done, my lord," Ensign Mikkelson replied.

Devlin watched them leave, then sat down heavily in the nearest chair. He knew he should be rejoicing that so far their deception had held. But instead his thoughts kept turning toward Kingsholm and the traitor within the heart of the King's court. The more power the traitor held, the more damage he could wreak. For all Devlin knew, the invasion of Korinth was but one of the schemes that the traitor had set in motion.

He tried to reassure himself that there was no need to worry. Even as he sat and fretted, Lord Egeslic was on his way to the capital. As soon as he arrived, the King's magistrates would take on the job of determining the extent of

the Baron's treachery and discovering his accomplices.
Whoever they might be.

But what if they found no one? What if even the Baron
himself did not know the identity of his ally? Then it
would be up to Devlin to find the traitor before he destroyed the Kingdom.

Twenty-five

——————>

THEY TRAVELED ALONG THE GREAT ROAD THAT LED
to Kingsholm, and with every league that passed, hope
dimmed that they would meet the forces of the Royal
Army. Devlin's mood grew darker as the days passed and
he realized that there was to be no relief force. No rescue
for the folk of Korinth.

Lieutenant Didrik and his party should have reached
the capital over two weeks earlier. Three, if he had pressed
hard and encountered fair weather and dry roads. Even if it
had taken a week for the Royal Army to assemble the necessary troops, they should have covered more than half the
distance to Korinth.

Either Didrik had not reached the capital, or he had arrived and then been betrayed. Perhaps the traitor was indeed a powerful member of the King's Council, as Devlin
feared, someone so powerful he could persuade the council to take no action, even in the face of such treachery.

It was this possibility that had haunted Devlin. Ever
since he had spoken with Quennel, he had been unable to
rid himself of the feeling that he had made a terrible mistake by sending Baron Egeslic to the capital. He had

thought to use the Baron to expose the traitor within the capital. But instead the traitor might well shield the Baron, and then the folk of Korinth would be helpless if the invaders came.

After a fortnight of waiting, Devlin had grown so restless that he could wait no longer. Along with Ensign Mikkelson and Stephen he set out for Kingsholm, hoping that he would meet the soldiers coming from the capital. The empty roads they encountered served as but grim confirmation of his worst fears.

Devlin set a brutal pace for the journey. Each day began before true dawn and they traveled till they could no longer see the road and sometimes beyond. When their horses grew tired, Devlin commandeered fresh mounts, invoking his need as Chosen One. Their tempers grew short and they pushed their bodies to the point of exhaustion and then beyond. But after only a fortnight they crossed the River Nairne, and the city of Kingsholm came into view.

The royal road was unusually crowded for a summer afternoon, and as they approached the western gate, the crowd swelled till it blocked the road.

"What is this commotion?" Devlin asked.

"For the festival, of course," Stephen replied.

"What festival?"

"Midsummer's Eve," Stephen said, as if it should be obvious. And indeed it was, for as Devlin looked closely, he could see that these were no ordinary travelers but revelers dressed in their finest, sporting gaudy yellow ribbons tied around their sleeves or braided in their hair.

Devlin smiled mirthlessly. Midsummer's Festival. It was an ironic coincidence. A year since the day he had first set foot in Kingsholm, seeking the post of Chosen One and his own death. Now he was returning to the city, no longer a nameless stranger. He had thought he had gained respect and power during the past year, and yet perhaps that had been only an illusion.

A crowd milled aimlessly in the square before the western gate, for only a few could pass through the gate at a time.

"Ensign, clear a path," Devlin said.

Ensign Mikkelson stood in his stirrups. "Make way! Make way!" he called. "Make way for the Chosen One!"

A few of those closest to them turned to look in curiosity. Devlin's eyes swept the crowd, and those whose eyes met with his began to back away. Slowly a space around them cleared and they advanced.

The commotion attracted the attention of the guards. As soon as they recognized the party, they began using their long spears ruthlessly to push aside the folk and clear a path.

As Devlin reached the gate, he drew his horse to a halt next to the guard Patek.

"Did Lieutenant Didrik reach the city?" Devlin asked.

"Aye, that he did," Patek said.

"And what of Lord Egeslic?"

"There's strange doings at the palace. Captain Drakken left word that you were to seek her out as soon as you return. She can tell you best how things are," Patek explained. His face looked troubled.

Devlin did not need to hear any more. If the Baron had been convicted of treason, then Patek would have known of it, as would every resident of Kingsholm. Devlin's fears had come true. Justice had not been served.

He spurred his horse through the gate, leaving it to Stephen and Mikkelson to keep up as best they could.

Devlin's anger grew as he fought his way through the crowded streets. By the time he reached the Guard Hall, he could scarcely contain himself, and brushing past the startled clerk, he threw open the door to Captain Drakken's office.

The Captain raised her head from the papers she had been contemplating. There were lines on her face that had not been there in the spring, and she looked nearly as tired as he felt. But he had no sympathy to spare for her, or indeed for anyone. There was but one thing that drove him.

"What happened?" Devlin asked.

She did not hesitate or pretend to misunderstand.

"I failed. And we were betrayed," she said simply.

"Who? How?" His voice was clipped.

"Sit," she said. "It is a long story."

He remained standing. "Make it short."

Her eyes flashed briefly with anger as she stood up and came out from behind the desk to face him. "If I knew who had done this or how, I would not be sitting here," she said.

"Then tell me what you do know."

"When Lieutenant Didrik arrived, and announced that Lord Egeslic was accused of treachery, it caused great consternation in the court. Many did not want to believe such a thing. Instead of being imprisoned, the Baron was confined to apartments within the palace while the council debated whether the Baron should be tried by the magistrates or by the King and council. The evidence you had sent was placed in a storeroom under guard. My guards."

She paused.

"Go on," Devlin prompted.

"After three days it was decided the Baron would stand

before the council. The chief councilors sent for the chest of papers to review the evidence. When it was opened it was discovered that the papers were so badly water-stained that they were unreadable."

"How did this happen?"

"I do not know. I saw the chest myself as it was put in the storeroom. There was no sign of damage. And yet three days later you could see the leather was mildewed and rotting, and the papers stank as if they had lain at the bottom of a lake for a year."

"The chest was tampered with," Devlin said.

"Of course. But we cannot prove it. The council blames the Guard. Either Didrik was careless during his journey, or my own guards were careless during their watch and allowed someone to destroy the evidence. I had picked the guards personally, and they were all trustworthy veterans. They swear that no one went into or out of that room. So that puts the responsibility back on Didrik. Either way we failed. I failed—for these are my guards."

The sudden rot did not seem natural. "Could it have been magic? Some foul spell?"

"I thought that as well, but the council dismissed the idea as ludicrous and refused to allow me to send for Master Dreng to discover if it had been tampered with magically."

This only strengthened his suspicions. The actions of the council went beyond their usual bickering and maneuvering for power. There was one who had a very good reason not to want the papers examined, and that traitor was guiding the councilors' decisions.

"But what of Lieutenant Didrik's testimony? Surely he could bear witness to what he had seen?"

Captain Drakken sat down on the edge of the desk.

"They would not hear him nor any of the guards who had accompanied him. In their eyes he was guilty of negligence or worse. Some even went so far as to suggest that there never was any evidence against the Baron, and that we had destroyed the very documents that would have cleared his name."

Devlin felt a cold rage begin to build within him. Once again the courtiers had chosen to play their games of power and influence, ignoring the fact that the Kingdom was crumbling around them. "And what of the Baron?"

Captain Drakken shrugged. "He is free. An honored guest, here to enjoy the festival and to accept the King's hospitality."

This was what came of trusting others. Devlin had put his faith in the King's justice only to be betrayed. But they had done more than betray Devlin. The court had broken faith with the people of Korinth, those whom the Baron had oppressed and tormented.

He had promised those folk that they would have justice. And they would have. He would see to it himself.

"Where is the King?"

"There is a dance tonight to celebrate the end of the festival," Captain Drakken said.

Devlin nodded. "I will end this. Now."

She reached forward and caught his arm. "Wait! Do not do anything foolish. Take time for counsel with those you trust. The situation may yet be saved."

"The time for caution is past," he said, pulling his arm free. He turned on his heel and left her office.

Captain Drakken followed, still trying to talk reason, but he turned a deaf ear to her arguments. From the corner of his eye he saw that Stephen and Ensign Mikkelson had finally caught up, and they, too, followed along, as did a small knot of guards. He thought he recognized Lieutenant Didrik among their number.

But there was no time to stop, no time to acknowledge one friend or to calm the fears of others. Devlin's will was focused on one thing and one thing alone. Justice for the folk of Korinth.

His boots rang on the marble floors of the palace, and those servants he passed made haste to get out of his way. As he entered the main corridor, his gaze swept dismissively over the brightly colored banners that hung from the high ceiling. Heedless fools. No doubt they would continue their revels even as the earth crumbled beneath their feet.

The sounds of music and buzz of conversation grew louder as he approached the Great Hall. Two guards stood by the massive wooden doors.

Captain Drakken sprinted ahead, then turned to stand in front of the doors, blocking his way. "Do nothing in haste," she urged.

Devlin's eyes narrowed. For once the Geas and his own will were in perfect accord. There was justice to be done, and the path to justice lay through that door. "You will stand aside. Now."

His voice was soft, but the flat tones brooked no disagreement. Captain Drakken stepped aside, and the guards swung open the heavy doors.

The Great Hall was ablaze with light and filled with dozens of brightly garbed dancers, who laughed and chattered above the sprightly music. Across the hall, on a raised dais as if he wished to distance himself from the celebration, sat King Olafur.

Devlin strode toward the King, brushing aside those courtiers who got in his way as if they were mere insects.

Their gasps of outrage turned to shock and whispered speculation as they realized that the unshaven, travel-stained wretch invading their perfumed sanctuary was in fact the Chosen One. The laughter began to fade and the conversation grew softer, until as he reached the King, the music stopped and the room grew very still.

"Your Majesty, I have come to demand justice, and punishment for the traitor Egeslic."

King Olafur shrank back in his chair and looked around as if for support. "We have heard the charges but there was no evidence to support them. We are convinced that these were but malicious lies meant to destroy our trust in our faithful servant."

Duke Gerhard stepped from the crowd and approached the King, and in a moment he was joined by Lady Ingeleth.

"It is unseemly for you to disturb His Majesty at such a time," Lady Ingeleth said. "Have you no manners at all? No discretion?"

"Justice does not wait for your convenience, my lady," Devlin said. "I will have justice or I will know why not."

"Justice has been served," Duke Gerhard replied. "There was no basis to try the Baron of Korinth, let alone to convict him."

"Then you will convict him based on my testimony, for I have witnessed his treachery with my own eyes, and spoken with the foreign allies who plotted with him. Thus I will swear as Chosen One."

"And why should we believe your word? You have already tried once to blacken the Baron's name by sending the worthless documents," the Duke said.

Devlin raised his left hand so the ring of the Chosen One could be clearly seen. "You know full well the hellish

Geas binds me to serve the truth and to seek justice. I will swear to the truth of my words."

"The Chosen One speaks truly," Stephen said. "This I swear."

"As do I," Ensign Mikkelson said, stepping forward. "My lord General, I bear witness to the truth of Devlin's words. The Baron is a traitor."

Duke Gerhard stared angrily at Ensign Mikkelson, who returned his gaze calmly. The Ensign's words had taken great courage, for he must have known that his support of Devlin would bring down his commander's wrath.

"If he swears by the Gods—" Lady Ingeleth began.

"No," Duke Gerhard said. "It is a trick. And see how the Chosen One corrupts all who come into contact with him. Drakken. The Guard. Even my own officer is tainted by his presence."

He turned to the King, and, raising his voice said, "My King, I was holding this news till after the festival, for fear of spoiling the merriment. Yet now it must be told." He raised his arm and pointed his finger at Devlin. "This man is unfit to serve as Chosen One. He was exiled from his homeland for the crime of murdering his own family."

A shocked gasp ran through the room.

Devlin's hand fell to his sword and he took a half step forward.

"That is a lie."

"And I say it is the truth," Duke Gerhard countered. "And so say those who knew you, when you were called Devlin the Kinslayer."

King Olafur appeared horrified, as did those others whose faces swam in his vision.

"Kinslayer," he heard someone whisper.

For a moment the old guilt crashed over him and he shook his head to clear it. *I did not kill them*, he reminded himself.

"I did not kill them. You will beg my pardon. Now."

"How can I apologize for speaking the truth?" the Duke replied.

Devlin's vision narrowed until it seemed as if he and the Duke were alone. No one else mattered. He had the sense of inevitability, as if some part of him had known this moment would come since the first time he had encountered the Duke.

"Then you will defend your words with steel," Devlin said.

"Damn fool!" Captain Drakken exclaimed.

The Duke smiled. "I accept your challenge. I will meet you at dawn tomorrow."

"At dawn," Devlin replied. He knew that the Duke felt he had won by goading Devlin into issuing the challenge, to a duel that Devlin could not win. And yet, there had been no other choice.

The courtiers nearest to them began to back away, as if they feared his mere presence would somehow taint them. In a pointed lack of courtesy Devlin turned his back on the King and the Duke, then led the way from the Great Hall into the small antechamber on the left. Captain Drakken, Lieutenant Didrik, Ensign Mikkelson, and Stephen followed along in his wake as Duke Gerhard smiled triumphantly and the courtiers watched in horrified fascination.

The antechamber was empty, save for a servant setting out refreshments. "Go," Captain Drakken said, and the servant took one look and fled.

"You stupid fool," Captain Drakken said, as the door swung shut behind the servant.

Devlin ignored her, choosing instead to address Ensign Mikkelson. "That was bravely done," he said.

"I could do no less," Ensign Mikkelson replied.

"I fear your honesty will be your undoing," Devlin said. Duke Gerhard was not likely to forgive an officer who dared contradict him in public. Not when the officer had shown his loyalty to another. If he was lucky, Ensign Mikkelson had only thrown away his career.

"My father can always use an officer who is not afraid to speak the truth," Stephen said. "If you go to him, he will give you a place among his armsmen."

Devlin nodded approvingly. It was a good solution. Esker was far enough from the capital that the Ensign might be allowed to sink into obscurity.

"He goaded you into the challenge," Captain Drakken said. Her lips were thin and her face white with anger.

"What would you have me do? Ignore his words? I cannot be the Chosen One if I do not have the people's trust."

"You should not have gone there tonight. You should have waited until your temper cooled and we had time to make our plans."

He knew she was angry, and yet he could rouse no anger on his own behalf. Instead he felt the strange peace that had come over him once he had issued the challenge to the Duke. It was the peace of having surrendered to the inevitable and accepted his fate.

"There was no reason to wait," Devlin said, trying to explain. "You heard Duke Gerhard. He was merely waiting for the right moment to loose his poisonous words. If not today, then tomorrow or a week from now. In the end, it would have been the same."

"But why would he say such a thing?" Ensign Mikkelson asked.

"Because it is true. Or at least part of it," Devlin said.

"I do not believe it," Stephen declared loyally.

Captain Drakken nodded thoughtfully, while the Ensign looked at Devlin as if he had grown a second head.

Devlin ran one hand through his sweat-caked hair as he tried to think. Who could have revealed his past to the Duke's spies? Had it been Murchadh? Agneta? Or someone nameless, who had once been known to him and had heard the parts of the tale that were well-known? In the end, it did not matter.

But his comrades, at least, deserved the truth, for they had proven their loyalty to him, and risked their own lives by showing their support.

"I did not kill my family," Devlin said. "But I bear the blame for their deaths."

The guilt was his, for bringing them to that cursed land. He had known of the ancient legends of that land, but foolishly he had dismissed them, thinking any danger long past. He had been wrong, and when his family had needed him most, he had not been there.

"It was my fault," Devlin added.

"What do you mean?" Captain Drakken asked.

"The tale you heard of the banecats was true. Or at least in part. They struck without warning. The foul creatures killed my brother, his son, and my daughter. Cerrie, my wife," his voice rasped, and he took a deep breath to steady himself. "Cerrie fought bravely, but she had only a small trowel to defend herself, and it proved no match for their claws. I returned home to find their bodies," Devlin said. He blinked his eyes against the memory of that awful sight.

"If you were not there when the creatures attacked, then how did you come by your scars?" Captain Drakken asked.

"I hunted the creatures down and avenged my family's deaths," Devlin said simply. In the struggle Cerrie had wounded one of the creatures, and it had left a blood trail. It had been that trail Devlin had followed into the forest, and which had led him to the first of the evil creatures, which he then killed. Though for a time he had been sure that the pack leader had given him his death blow, before she had succumbed to her own wounds.

"But why were you exiled?" Stephen asked. "You were a hero."

Devlin shook his head. "I was alive. That does not make me a hero. And as for the exile, the Duke's informants have misled him. I was declared kinbereft, not kinslayer. Though the words sound similar enough in my own tongue."

After killing the banecats it had taken Devlin several weeks to recover from his wounds. When he had finally made his way back to the settlement, Devlin had found himself shunned. Agneta had declared him responsible for the deaths of their kin, and in his grief Devlin had agreed with her harsh judgment. He could have stayed in Duncaer, though as a man who had lost kinright and one who had no heart to follow his craft, there was nothing left for him there. And so he had wandered aimlessly, until that night, which seemed so long past, when he had first heard the tale of the Chosen One.

There was a moment of silence, and none would meet his gaze.

"Are there customs or courtesies that must be followed for this duel? Or do we simply meet at dawn?" Devlin asked. Dueling was a custom of the Jorskian court. In Duncaer lethal duels were rare indeed, for the complicated web of kinship and obligation meant that any such duel had the potential to touch off a blood feud.

"You and the Duke must each appoint an agent, who will meet and agree to the arrangements. I would be honored to serve," Lieutenant Didrik said.

Devlin hesitated. Didrik was a logical choice. And yet, given Captain Drakken's obvious disapproval, it did not seem right to involve him in making the arrangements. Captain Drakken was a warrior, one who would not recognize defeat even when it stared her in the face. She might well order Didrik to find a way to delay the duel, hoping to avoid the inevitable.

"Your offer is gracious, but you have already drawn the Duke's wrath once for me," Devlin said, not wishing to insult Didrik. "Stephen, will you serve?"

Stephen nodded. "Of course," he said, though his face was troubled. "You realize that as the challenged the Duke has the choice of weapons? Undoubtedly he will insist upon swords."

Unspoken was the knowledge that Devlin's weakest skill was that of swordsmanship. With another weapon, Devlin might have had a chance, but against a master swordsman the only question was how long it would take for Devlin to die.

"I expected nothing else," Devlin said. "I will leave you to make the arrangements."

"Wait," Captain Drakken said. "There is still much we should discuss."

He would not stay while his friends grieved for him as for one already dead. And there was nothing they could say, nothing they could do, that would change the outcome of the match.

"You have much to think on, not I," said Devlin. "What happens after tomorrow morning will be your affair. And for that you will not need me."

With that he left the room.

Captain Drakken stared angrily as the Chosen One left, though she knew her anger was as much for herself as it was for him. She should have insisted that the documents be examined as soon as Didrik had arrived, rather than delaying and giving their enemies a chance to tamper with them. Or she should have insisted that Master Dreng examine the chest, no matter what the council said. If she had been able to prove magical treachery, if she had realized that the Duke knew of Devlin's past . . .

But now there was no turning back. And Devlin of Duncaer, the strongest Chosen One the Kingdom had seen for generations, was going to throw his life away. And with him went all their work, all their hopes of rallying the Kingdom in its own defense. They would never find another to take his place.

What a waste. What a stupid, awful waste. That the Chosen One should be lost merely because Duke Gerhard envied and despised his influence. If she could, she would take Devlin's part in a heartbeat, to spare the Kingdom. She looked at the others and knew they felt the same. Yet neither Devlin nor Duke Gerhard would agree to such a substitution.

"Is there any chance he could win?" she asked Lieutenant Didrik.

"No," Lieutenant Didrik said, his eyes sorrowful. "Devlin's skills have grown greatly. He can best me two times out of three, and Ensign Mikkelson the same. But he is no match for a master swordsman."

It was as she had feared. "Then he is doomed. And with him goes the last hope for the Kingdom."

It was past midnight when Stephen knocked on the door of Solveig's chambers. Though the hour was late, he was not surprised that Solveig opened the door at once.

"Come," she said, taking him by the hand and leading him inside.

He allowed her to guide him to a padded chair, where he collapsed in a weary heap.

Solveig's long hair was unbound, and she wore a simple linen shirt and trousers. She looked much younger than a woman of nearly thirty summers, and for a moment Stephen was transported back to the days of his childhood, when as a young boy he had come to his oldest sister for advice and comfort.

"I was not there but I heard what happened," Solveig said, handing him a glass of dark red wine. "There is to be a duel?"

Stephen nodded. "All is arranged," he said. "Devlin and Duke Gerhard will face each other at the first hour past dawn, in the grand salon of arms. They will duel with swords until one yields or is killed."

But there would be no courtly honor, no Gods-sent reprieve. Devlin would not yield. Could not. It was not in him to beg for mercy. Devlin would die, spilling his lifeblood on the sands, while his enemies jeered in triumph.

Stephen took a quick gulp of wine, hoping he could drink himself into numbness or oblivion. But as he stared at the glass, the red wine seemed too much like blood, so he set the glass down on the floor in sudden revulsion.

Solveig sat down on the arm of the chair and put her arm around his shoulders. "I am truly sorry," she said. "He is a great man, and I know he is your friend."

Stephen leaned his head back and closed his eyes.

"He would not speak with me," he said. After making the arrangements, Stephen had gone to Devlin's quarters. Devlin had not even let Stephen enter, but instead made him stand in the hall as he outlined the protocol for the duel. Then he had bade Stephen good night, as if this were an ordinary night, and had firmly shut the door. Stephen had pounded and yelled, but there had been no answer. At last he had left in defeat.

Stephen could not imagine Devlin's pain upon returning to find his wife and child slain—all that had given his life meaning destroyed in that instant. Devlin had let his grief show only once, when his voice had broken as he said the name of his murdered wife. Despite the pain Devlin had managed to survive, to avenge his family's death, and to find a new purpose for his own life. Now this, too, was to be taken from him. And Devlin would not permit his friends to tell him they shared his sorrows.

"He should not be alone," Stephen said.

Solveig stroked his hair, as she had done so many times before. "He is not alone. He knows he has your friendship and that of the others."

"It is not fair," Stephen said miserably. "We made the Chosen One, and bound his will with the Geas so he can serve us. And now he must pay with his life simply because he seeks to fulfill his duties as we commanded."

A year ago, Stephen would have looked at Duke Gerhard and seen an honorable man, one outraged at the idea of a false Chosen One and the stain upon the Kingdom's honor. But Stephen was older now. Wiser. Now he looked at the Duke and saw a power-hungry noble who would brook no competition. Devlin's crime was not that of being unfit for his post. It was of challenging the Duke's authority, and this was the sin that would cost him his life.

"Life is seldom like the pretty ballads you love," Solveig said. "Court politics is about power, and the pursuit of justice is often compromised in the battle."

"I know that now," he said. In the year since he had first met the Chosen One, Stephen had learned that life could be far more terrible and wonderful than any ballad he knew. And that the true worth of a man could not be set down in song, but rather was measured both in how he acted when put to the test, and how he behaved when all was peaceful.

Devlin had taught him much. And now Stephen would learn what it was to watch a friend die. Solveig gathered him in her arms, as he closed his eyes and wept.

Twenty-six

THERE WOULD BE NO DEATH SHROUD FOR HIM. No
one to perform the ceremonies that would see him safely
to the Dread Lord's realm. No one to speak his name on
the night of the dead, or to greet him kindly in his wanderings. No children would be called Devlin in his honor, to
keep his memory alive.

Yet he felt no bitterness. He had come to this place to
die. Instead briefly, improbably, he had found friendship.
Respect from those he admired for their own courage and
loyalty. And a measure of atonement for his sins as he had
sought to help those who could not defend themselves.

Devlin was resigned to his death, but still there was one
more service that he could perform. He had learned well
the lesson of his fight with the banecats. There was much a
man could do, once he had accepted the inevitability of his
own death. Devlin's life would end on the morrow, but if
the Gods were kind, he would not die until he had dealt the
Duke a mortal blow in return.

Devlin retired to his room and sent the nervous chambermen to fetch hot water for bathing. He washed away the
dirt of travel and shaved off several days' growth of dark

beard. The face that stared back at him from the mirror was eerily calm. Donning a peasant shirt and his old frayed trousers, he took the sword from its scabbard and examined the blade carefully. He found just what he had expected. The blade was sound, free of nicks. And like all his weapons, the edge was as sharp as his skills could make it. There was no point in further honing the blade, just as there was no point in Devlin trying to learn new tactics at this last hour. Both he and the sword were as ready as they would ever be.

When Stephen came, Devlin listened attentively to the arrangements for the duel, but he brushed aside Stephen's request to talk. He could see his friend was distressed, yet there was no comfort Devlin could offer him. His friends were angry over this turn of fate, and grieved over the surety of his death. Devlin himself did not share their grief. He had sought death for so long that to him this seemed but the final step of a long journey whose destination had long been known.

But he could not allow their grief to weaken him, to distract him from what he must do. He would need to bring all his focus, indeed his entire will, to bear if he was to succeed in taking Duke Gerhard with him to the grave.

Devlin woke from a dreamless sleep in the quiet hour before dawn. He dressed himself with great care, in a linen shirt and gray trousers, over which he fastened the gray silk tunic that was the uniform of the Chosen One. He hesitated for a moment, then slipped the ring of his office on his left hand. Wearing jewelry in a duel was folly, but it would make little difference when the outcome was foreordained. And it would be good to remind the Duke and the courtiers just who and what Devlin was.

He stood in the center of the room and turned around slowly, making sure that everything was in order. His transverse bow and quiver hung from pegs on the wall. Next to them hung the great axe, and on the table below were his throwing knives and the twin wrist sheaths. Inside the closed doors of the wardrobe were his neatly folded clothes, while the chest held the few personal possessions he owned. A few metalworking tools, a sharpening stone, a fire starter, and a half dozen maps from his journeys. Little enough to show for his year of service.

Devlin's eyes lingered on the axe thoughtfully. He had no care what happened to the rest of his belongings, but the axe was a different matter.

A knock sounded.

"Enter," Devlin called.

The door swung open, and he saw Stephen standing in the hall.

"It is time," Stephen said. His face was haggard and his eyes red-rimmed as if he had spent a sleepless night.

Devlin nodded. He picked up the sword belt and buckled it around his waist.

"There is one service you can do for me afterward," Devlin said.

"Name it and it is yours," Stephen said.

"When I am dead, destroy the axe. Take it to Master Timo the smith and have him melt the steel in his forge until it is naught but a lump of metal."

"But why?"

"The axe is cursed." Once the axe had represented all of his skill, all of his pride in his craft. Yet even at the moment of forging, the axe and Devlin were already cursed, their destiny foretold. Was Devlin cursed because he owned the axe? Or was the axe cursed because he had forged it? Either way, it did not matter. The axe would be destroyed, lest he pass his unholy burden on to another.

Stephen's eyes widened. "Then why do you keep it?"

"Because it is mine," Devlin said simply. "Now come. They are waiting for us."

As they walked through the corridors of the palace toward the arms salon, Devlin noticed that there were far more servants about than was usual for that hour. They clustered at every junction of corridors and at the foot of the staircases. They did not speak, but instead watched him pass in eerie silence.

They had come to witness his death, he realized. Such lowly ones would not be privileged to witness the duel, so they had come to see him in his last minutes. He wondered where their sympathies lay. Did they see him as a common man like themselves, one who strove to uphold justice for all? Or did they believe Duke Gerhard's lies and come to witness the execution of a kinslayer?

Devlin and Stephen turned down the final corridor, and the minstrel walked past the door that led to the arms salon. Devlin halted, and after a few steps Stephen stopped when he realized Devlin was no longer following.

"Come. There is a room adjacent, where the fighters can wait in private until it is time for their match."

"No," said Devlin. He would not spend his last moments hiding. "Let us show them that I have no fear."

He led the way into the arms salon, and reluctantly Stephen followed.

Devlin blinked as he saw that the salon was filled with richly dressed courtiers, many of whom looked to be still wearing their finery from the evening before. Scanning the crowd he saw that three sides of the square were packed with spectators, but the western side held only a few folk. Among them he recognized Captain Drakken, Lieutenant Didrik, Solveig, Lord Dalkassar, Lord Rikard, and a handful of others whom he had come to know in his months in Kingsholm. Duke Gerhard was nowhere to be seen.

The crowd parted as Devlin made his way through the gallery, toward the western end. Only one man had the courage to meet his gaze.

"Chosen One, I wish you much luck," Master Dreng said.

"Good luck? Or ill?"

Master Dreng smiled. "The best of luck, of course. I have wagered on your victory."

Devlin smiled in return. "I fear I will make you a loser once again."

"You should not jest," Stephen said. "Not at a time like this."

"On the contrary, this is the best time of all. I will not have it said that the Chosen One met his death like a mewling child, afraid of the dark. Let them see the courage that comes from the service of the truth."

As they drew near their friends, Stephen touched his arm, as if for luck. "You will be remembered. Though you may fall, others will take up the challenge."

Stephen's eyes were moist and his voice hoarse, and Devlin had a sudden terrible suspicion. "You will not seek to serve as Chosen One in my place," Devlin said firmly.

Solveig gasped, and the others stared at Stephen.

"You think I am too young, too weak," Stephen said.

"No. I think you are too good. Too kindhearted for such a foul task," Devlin said. What could have put such a mad notion in Stephen's head? The minstrel would not last a month in this twisted court.

Devlin put both of his arms on Stephen's shoulders, forcing him to meet his gaze. "Your heart is good, but if you wish to honor me, do not do this thing. The path of the Chosen One is not for you. If you need to keep my memory alive then make a song of me, a dozen songs if you must, but do not throw your life away for no reason."

Stephen blinked rapidly and swallowed hard. Devlin held his gaze until Stephen nodded, and only then did Devlin release him.

"Chosen One," Captain Drakken said, extending her hand in the clasp of friendship.

He squeezed her hand in return. "Captain Drakken." There was nothing more he could say.

"My guards send their respect and wishes for your victory," she said, her mouth twisting slightly on the word *victory*. "Many wished to join me here, to show you their support, but I feared that too large a gathering might provoke an incident."

Captain Drakken was wise. The guards were well disciplined, but it would not be easy for them to watch a friend die. He knew how they felt. If it had been Didrik or Stephen or even Captain Drakken on that dueling floor, Devlin did not know if he could have forced himself to watch and do nothing.

Devlin clasped hands with Didrik and Mikkelson, and exchanged a few words with those nobles who dared risk the Duke's wrath by showing their support for the Chosen One.

A silver bell sounded.

"The King is here," Solveig announced.

Devlin nodded and unbuckled his sword belt, handing it to Stephen. He then stripped off his tunic, revealing the loose linen shirt underneath. Pulling the sword out of the sheath, he held the blade casually in his right hand, point down toward the floor.

He watched as King Olafur entered and took his seat, flanked by the members of the council. Next to appear were a pair of heralds, sounding a brassy challenge. Devlin gave a snort of disgust. Such foolishness. This was no pretty pageant for the amusement of the court, but rather a serious matter of life and death.

Stephen nudged him as Duke Gerhard and his second entered the room, accompanied by the Royal Armsmaster and a brown-robed priest. A page unlinked the silver chain so they could step onto the dueling ground.

Devlin and Stephen stepped over the chain and advanced across the room to meet his opponent. The thin layer of white sand crunched softly beneath their feet. The sand would prevent them from slipping on spilled blood, but was not deep enough that they need fear losing their footing.

They met at the north end, directly before the King and his council. The Duke and Devlin eyed each other, but neither bowed nor gave any sign of respect.

"I ask now, in the presence of the assembled court, will either of you agree to give up your quarrel?" asked the Armsmaster Koenraad.

"No," Devlin and Duke Gerhard said at the same instant.

"Then the rules of the duel are thus. You will begin at my signal, not before. This is a mortal duel, so you will fight according to the rules of honor, until one of you is killed or chooses to yield," Koenraad said. "Your Grace, do you understand these rules?"

"Yes," Duke Gerhard said. He appeared very much the bored aristocrat, impatient for these formalities to be finished so he could dispatch the challenger and return to his courtly pursuits. It was clear he saw Devlin as no threat.

"Challenger Devlin, do you understand these rules?"

"Yes. I stop when he is dead," Devlin said mockingly, in his thickest Caer accent.

There was a muffled sound as Stephen repressed a snicker. The armsmaster appeared appalled at this breach of etiquette.

His bravado had the intended effect, for Duke Gerhard's eyes narrowed and he studied Devlin, as if seeking to understand the source of his challenger's confidence.

"And now—"

"Wait," Duke Gerhard said, raising his hand to interrupt the armsmaster.

The armsmaster paused.

"Forgive the breach of ceremony, but this one is well-known for using the weapons of an assassin," Duke Gerhard said. "I would have him show that he intends to fight only with the sword, and not with any knavish tricks."

A part of him burned at the insult while the cooler, logical part of his mind reveled in the knowledge that he had indeed managed to disturb Duke Gerhard's aplomb. The Duke must think that Devlin's confidence came from the possession of some hidden weapon. How would he react when he realized Devlin had none?

Devlin handed his sword to Stephen. "I have nothing to hide," he declared. He grasped the right sleeve of his shirt in his left hand and gave a quick yank, ripping the sleeve free. Then he did the same for the left sleeve. He handed the sleeves to Stephen, and took back his sword.

"Are you satisfied, Great Champion? Or must I empty my boots, to prove them free from rocks that might trip you?"

The Duke's face was calm, but his ears were tinged with red. Koenraad looked at the Duke, then back at Devlin, and made a quick decision. "Honor is more than satisfied," he said. "Your seconds may leave the field."

Devlin did not look as Stephen made his way from the square and joined the spectators in the gallery. All of his attention was for the Duke and for what he must now do.

Devlin and Duke Gerhard moved to the center of the square and took their places as directed by the armsmaster.

King Olafur nodded. The brown-robed priest, whom Devlin recognized from the Choosing Ceremony, now stepped forward. Raising his hands to the heavens, he proclaimed, "We thank the Seven Gods for their protection, as we witness their justice proven in the trial of arms. May their will be done."

"May their will be done," echoed the spectators.

The armsmaster raised his hand high, then dropped it. The duel had begun.

Captain Drakken watched with clenched fists as the Chosen One and the King's Champion began slowly to circle each other, each seeking to gain the advantage. Duke Gerhard made the first move, a high stroke that was matched by a high block, followed immediately by a low thrust that Devlin blocked equally well, if less gracefully.

The Duke's moves were fluid, almost lazy, as he probed Devlin's defenses, looking for weaknesses. Each time Devlin managed to counter with his own sword, or evade the blow by shifting his body at the last moment. His technique was an armsmaster's nightmare, but it was working. For the moment.

"He moves well," she said. "But he uses only the one

hand." The long sword could be used as a two-handed weapon, to increase the force, and turn an ordinary strike into a killing blow. Or a very skilled fighter could switch the blade from hand to hand, confusing his opponent and enabling him to strike at both sides with equal ease. Devlin's technique showed he had been trained by the guards. The guards trained one-handed, for they normally held shields in their left hands.

The Duke's sword was a dueling weapon, easily six inches longer than the sword that Devlin wielded. And he held it in both hands, for shield training was no part of the courtly dueling rituals. This gave him the advantage of both longer reach and greater power. Combined with his long experience, it made him a deadly opponent.

The combatants met in a sudden flurry of blows and parries, and when they parted she saw a line of red staining Devlin's right side. Another moment and, as the Duke's sword slipped past his guard, he bore a matching cut on his left side.

Duke Gerhard's experience and longer reach were beginning to tell. He smiled cruelly as he pressed the attack home, wounding Devlin again and again.

"He is toying with him," Lieutenant Didrik said.

She nodded in agreement. Devlin had gained in skill, but he was no match for a man who had reigned as undefeated champion for the past fifteen years. Indeed the Duke had passed up several opportunities for a killing blow in favor of inflicting smaller wounds on his opponent. It was to be the death of a thousand cuts. Duke Gerhard intended that Devlin would suffer greatly before he died.

Devlin's bloody shirt hung in tatters, and as the Duke's sword sliced along his collarbone, the shirt split in two and fell to the ground.

A gasp ran around the room as Devlin's scars were laid bare for all to see. Even Drakken, who had seen them before, was shocked, for she had forgotten just how horrific they were. His back and left side were a maze of ridged white scars, now gruesomely outlined by the fresh red blood that dripped down from his many wounds.

Devlin grinned. "You will have to do better than these pinpricks if you wish to destroy me," he taunted. "Your pretty swordplay may be fine for the white sands, but you would not last five minutes on the battlefield. You would piss in your pants if you had to stand where I have."

The Duke's face turned dull red and he snarled a wordless reply.

At last, he had succeeded in angering the Duke. Devlin kept the grin on his lips, trying not to show how much it cost him. He was covered with sweat and his breathing was labored, and he could feel himself weakening as the small wounds combined to take their toll. If he had any chance, he must strike now, before the Duke overcame his anger and regained his icy precision. He just needed the Duke to come close enough, to be within his reach.

"Come now," he said, beckoning with his free hand. "Or are you afraid?"

The Duke whirled, raising his sword high and bringing it down in a sweeping stroke toward Devlin's neck. Devlin raised his sword, and the two blades rang with the protest of agonized metal as they crashed together. Devlin's muscles strained as the Duke's sword slid slowly down the edge of his own blade. He braced his sword arm with his left, and then, with a powerful heave, thrust his sword and the Duke away from him.

Off-balance, his right arm was extended for but an instant, but that was all it took. Duke Gerhard hooked the point of his sword under Devlin's guard, and Devlin's sword went flying.

It landed in the sand several paces to his left. He eyed the distance and took one step to his left, then another.

Duke Gerhard smiled. "So much for your fine words. Now we see what a pathetic fool you truly are," he said, as he advanced, sword extended. "The Kingdom is well rid of you."

Devlin knew he could never reach his sword in time. The Duke would kill him where he stood. There was only one weapon he had yet to try.

For the first time he let go his own will and surrendered himself to the power of the Geas. The peace that came from having no more choices washed over him.

Devlin took one more step toward the sword and stopped, turning to face Duke Gerhard directly. He waited calmly, his arms held down, hands slightly curled by his sides.

The Duke held his sword in classic attack position. He was so close Devlin could see the sweat on his brow, the triumphant gleam in his eyes.

Wait, Devlin told himself. *Wait.*

The Duke tensed his body, then began the lunge that would end Devlin's life.

At the last instant, Devlin twisted his body to the left—and then he did the unthinkable. He reached out and grabbed the blade of the Duke's sword with his right hand.

The blade sliced into his hand with a fiery kiss, cleaving muscles and sinew alike. Pain, too horrific to be borne, raced along his nerves. No mortal man could have willed himself to maintain that grip. But Devlin was in the grip of the Geas, which recognized no mortal limitations. He held on to the sword, using the Duke's own momentum to pull him forward until the Duke stumbled and fell facefirst to the ground.

As the Duke fell, Devlin's mangled hand slid off the Duke's sword. He dove to the floor and grabbed his own long sword in his left hand, rolling to his knees. As the Duke tried to rise, Devlin held the point of the sword to the Duke's neck. The Duke lay still, eyes glaring defiance and hate. Devlin's shaking hand held the sword as he rose awkwardly until he was standing over the Duke.

"Yield," Devlin croaked. He coughed, and said again, "Yield or die."

There was no sound, save the rasp of Devlin's breathing and the dripping of blood onto his boots.

"Yield now or I will slay you," Devlin said. It was the third and final chance.

"Your day will come," Duke Gerhard spat out. "And I will see you in hell."

Devlin nodded. "So be it." He raised his sword and plunged it into Duke Gerhard's chest. The point skidded along a bony rib, then sank deep into the Duke's heart.

The Duke's body convulsed, arching up from the floor. Devlin leaned on the sword, driving the point into the ground, as the Duke's body sank back and dark red blood began to flow sluggishly from the wound. The Duke's eyes were still open, and he seemed more astonished than angry as his body twitched in its death throes. After long moments, he lay still.

"He is dead," Devlin announced, relinquishing the sword. The impossible had happened. Against all odds, all expectations, Devlin had defeated the greatest swordsman in the Kingdom and proven his innocence. And yet he felt nothing, neither joy nor sorrow. It was as if all of his energy had been used up in the duel, leaving an empty husk behind.

He glanced down at his right hand, vaguely surprised to see that it was still attached to his arm. He grasped the wrist with his left hand and hugged the mangled arm to his chest, trying to stem the flow of blood.

Devlin turned to face King Olafur and the council. "By trial of arms I have proven my innocence. Is there anyone here who would deny that I am the Chosen One? Speak now, and be prepared to defend your words with steel."

He turned slowly around the room, raking the crowd with his gaze, but none stepped forward, though any fool could see that Devlin could barely stand, let alone fight another duel.

His body ached, and he wanted nothing more than to lie down on the sand and surrender to the killing exhaustion of his wounds. And yet he could not. Not before he had finished what he had set out to do.

From the corner of his eye he saw a stir, as the crowd parted, and suddenly Lord Egeslic stood alone.

"Egeslic of Korinth, you conspired with the enemies of the Kingdom and joined with them to plan an invasion. For this treachery you are condemned to die at dawn tomorrow. The Guard will take you into custody."

A low hum ran through the room, but no one challenged his verdict.

A red haze swam before his eyes, and Devlin turned back to the King and council. There was one final task. "Lady Ingeleth. Lord Rikard. Councilor Arnulf," he said, naming one member of each of the three factions of the court. "I have reason to suspect Duke Gerhard was guilty of treason as well. Captain Drakken and the guards will secure his residence, and you will oversee the guards as they search his possessions to see if there is proof of his crimes. Do you understand?"

"But surely the Duke is—" King Olafur began.

"The Duke is condemned, by the hands of the Gods," Devlin interrupted. Though the Gods had less to do with his death than did the four-foot length of steel protruding from the Duke's chest. "The evidence is there to find, of that I am sure. And with your councilors watching the guards and each other, this time there will be no mishaps."

King Olafur shrank back in his seat.

Lady Ingeleth stepped forward and bowed her head in the respect given to an equal. "I accept this charge," she said.

Lord Rikard and Councilor Arnulf echoed her acceptance.

At this Devlin's shoulders slumped, and he swayed on his feet. The energy that had sustained him drained away at the realization that he had fulfilled his duty. He closed his eyes and heard a low roaring in his ears, like the sound of the sea.

He felt a cool touch on his mangled right hand, and he nearly screamed in pain. "Lady Geyra!" a voice exclaimed, and he opened his eyes to see the shocked expression on the face of the priest.

"Quickly!" Captain Drakken said. "We don't have much time."

She was wrong. They had all the time in the world, for Devlin's task was done. He opened his mouth to speak, but no words came out, and he felt himself sinking deep into the velvety blackness.

Twenty-seven

THERE WAS THE SOUND OF VOICES RISING AND FALL-
ing as they chanted in unison, but he could not make out
the words. Slowly the fog began to clear from his mind,
and he heard voices speaking, this time quite close by.

"The luck God smiles upon him," an unknown voice
said.

"No, it is simply that he is too stubborn to die," Captain
Drakken countered.

Devlin opened his eyes, and in the dim light he saw a
wooden ceiling overhead.

"Just once I would like to awake from a fight and know
where I am," he said.

"He's awake," Stephen exclaimed, pointing out the obvious.

His friends crowded around the foot of his bed, while
an older man in the green robes of a healer came over and
laid his right hand on Devlin's forehead while with his left
he held Devlin's left wrist. "I am Master Osvald and you
are in Lady Geyra's house," he said. He held his grip for a
moment, then nodded as he removed his hands. "How do
you feel?"

Devlin thought a moment. "Surprised."

He struggled to raise himself, but his right arm collapsed under him. Master Osvald grabbed his shoulders with surprising strength and boosted Devlin to a sitting position.

His right hand would not obey his command, so Devlin grasped it with his left and brought it before his eyes. White linen bandages were wrapped from his wrist, across his palm, and then wound around his fingers. The three fingers he had left that is, for the smallest two were now missing.

He stared at the maimed limb for a long moment in silence. Never again would he craft delicate works in metal. And yet two fingers were a small price to pay for the victory he had won.

"We were lucky to save as much of the hand as we did," Master Osvald said, a touch defensively.

Devlin hastened to apologize. "I know your skills must be great, for I did not expect to awake again on this earth. The loss of the fingers is but a trifle compared to saving my life."

"The deed was not mine alone. Many here helped. And we could have done nothing, had Brother Arni not preserved your life until we were summoned." Master Osvald pursed his lips thoughtfully. "Now there is a one that missed his true calling."

"You scared us half to death," Stephen said. "I was certain Duke Gerhard would kill you. And then when we saw your injuries, I thought that he had succeeded after all."

"I did not expect to survive," Devlin confessed. "And yet I am glad that I did."

And as he said the words, he realized that they were true. He had told himself that he was resigned to his death, even looking forward to it as an end to his burdens. But he knew now that had been a lie. He no longer wished to join his family in the Dread Lord's realm. There was still a purpose for him in this world, and the pleasures that life brought. It was a strange irony. He had sought the post of Chosen One because he wished to die, only to discover in his service a reason to go on living.

"What of the Duke?"

"Duke Gerhard was indeed a traitor, as you suspected. It took two days of searching, but in the end they found a secret room in his residence. In there were papers outlining his plans." Her mouth twisted in a grimace. "The Duke knew the invasion of Korinth would throw the Kingdom into chaos. He planned to use the confusion to seize the throne."

"And he would be proclaimed a hero when he had expelled the so-called invaders," Lieutenant Didrik added.

It was a clever scheme. It might well have worked. Even if the invaders had decided to keep Korinth for themselves, still the Duke could have won much credit as the man who had held the rest of the Kingdom intact against such odds.

"And Lord Egeslic?"

"The Baron was executed, as you had commanded," Captain Drakken replied. "None of the court came to bear witness. It seems his former friends have forgotten him."

So the people of Korinth had their long-overdue justice. He had not been able to save Magnus, but those who remained would no longer be tyrannized by an unjust lord.

"What made you suspect Duke Gerhard?" Lieutenant Didrik asked.

"Many things," Devlin said. "His defense of the Baron was far too vigorous. And at the end, he could have chosen to yield. There was no reason for Duke Gerhard to choose to die, unless he knew that Lord Egeslic was sure to implicate him in the scheme."

Devlin had always known that Duke Gerhard was his enemy. That the Duke's mocking contempt was a mask for a burning hatred. Yet he had thought that hatred was for himself alone, the foreign peasant who dared stand against the Duke's power. Not until he had challenged the Duke to the duel had Devlin begun to suspect that the Duke might be the traitor they sought within the court.

"King Olafur wishes to see you, when you are well," Captain Drakken said.

"I am well now," Devlin said.

"No," Master Osvald replied. "Perhaps tomorrow. Now you will rest and regain your strength. And your friends will leave you, now they have seen for themselves that you have returned to us."

It was two more days before Master Osvald deemed Devlin fit enough to answer the King's summons. Even then he had to suffer the indignity of being conveyed to the palace in a carriage rather than on his own two feet, with a hovering attendant anxiously watching in case Devlin faltered. As soon as he reached the palace, Devlin dismissed the green-robed acolyte. The apprentice healer was reluctant to leave, but after a few strongly worded suggestions Devlin was able to make him see the error of his ways.

As Devlin approached the King's apartments, the sentry guards stiffened to attention, then thumped their fists on their chests and bowed low in the formal salute, which custom said was given only to members of the royal family and the King's Champion.

The salute made him uncomfortable enough, but when

the guards straightened up, he could see the light of hero worship in their eyes. He was reminded suddenly of the village of Greenhalt, and how those there had regarded him as a legend come to life. Surely these guards knew him better than that. In time they would treat him as they had before.

"His Majesty bids you make yourself at ease, and he will join you in a moment," the senior guard said, as the other swung open the door to the receiving room.

Devlin entered, and found himself in a small room, paneled with dark wood and an indifferent tapestry on one wall. There were a half dozen wooden chairs with brocaded seats, two small tables, and a small sideboard holding decanters of wine and other spirits. An impersonal place, fit for those who needed to cool their heels while awaiting the King's pleasure.

Gratefully he sank down on one of the chairs, stretching his long legs out before him. Master Osvald had been right. Devlin's strength was not what it had been if a simple walk from the main gate to the King's apartments could tire him out. Still, he knew that in time he would regain his strength, and the angry red scars he now bore would fade until they blended in among his many other scars, both seen and unseen.

His hand was a different matter. His right arm was in a sling, and it would be another week before the bandages came off. Master Osvald had been very vague over how well the hand would heal. Either he truly did not know, or he was trying to spare Devlin's feelings. At best, with three fingers he could train himself to hold the simpler weapons. At worst the hand might be a useless claw, and Devlin would be a cripple.

He wondered if this was the reason for the King's

summons. There was precedent for dismissing a wounded Chosen One from the royal service. The King had little reason to love Devlin, for the Chosen One had brought chaos to the court and proven the folly of the King's councilors. True, Devlin had exposed a traitor, but that was not the same as gaining the trust of the nobles. By granting Devlin honorable retirement on grounds of his injuries, the King would appear generous while ridding himself of someone who had become a thorn in his side.

And not only would Devlin need to fight to keep his position, he also had to somehow find a way to convince the King to send the army to defend Korinth. Devlin had been furious this morning, when he learned that the King had still not dispatched the army, despite the clear evidence of treachery. The news had made Devlin leave the healers' house, against their vehement objections.

He was still marshaling his arguments when the doors opened and King Olafur entered.

Devlin rose to his feet. "Your Majesty," he said, with an attempt at a half bow. Even that was too much, for as he straightened up he felt light-headed.

"Sit, please," King Olafur urged.

Devlin remained standing until the King took a seat, then he resumed his own.

"You are well? It is not too soon for you to be away from the healers' care?" King Olafur asked, gazing at Devlin with apparent concern.

"The healers did fine work," Devlin answered. "It will take time, but I am well enough to serve."

"Good, good," King Olafur said, his head bobbing nervously. His eyes darted around the room, then he leaned forward. "They have told you of Gerhard? How he was plotting to take my throne?"

"Yes," Devlin said. "Along with Lord Egeslic and his allies, whoever they may be."

The Duke's papers had contained evidence of his plans, but the foreign allies remained as yet unknown. Selvarat was mentioned, but so were Nerikaat and the Green Isles. Or it could be another country, as yet unnamed.

The papers had also contained the name of Freyja, confirming that the Duke had been behind at least two of the attempts on Devlin's life. The Duke had assured his allies that Devlin would not live to see Korinth, but he had chosen his tool poorly. For Freyja had been too cautious, biding her time until she was certain to escape unscathed.

In the end, it was the Duke's overconfidence that had proven his undoing. Even at the last, he had not seen Devlin as a real threat.

"Gerhard served me for a dozen years. I relied upon his counsel. I trusted him with my life," King Olafur complained. "Now what am I to do? Who can I trust to take his place?"

Why was the King asking for his advice? Devlin knew little of politics, and even less of how this King's mind worked. Whatever he said he must be careful, lest he give offense.

"I do not know," Devlin began. "But the army needs a General and you need a councilor. You must find someone you trust, without delay."

King Olafur shook his head sadly. "Even you can see that the court is riddled with intrigue. Two of my nobles have proven traitors. Who is to say there is not a third or a fourth?"

The thought had crossed Devlin's mind as well. "Your fears are well-founded, but you cannot let them keep you from acting. There is very little time left."

"So you think there will be war?"

"Yes," Devlin said, though he knew the King would not want to hear it. "I think war will come, sooner rather than later."

"So do I."

Devlin stared at King Olafur in amazement. He had thought the King blind, oblivious to the problems that beset his people.

"I surprised you, I see," King Olafur said.

Devlin nodded.

"I know your opinion. You think me a fool."

This was dangerous ground indeed. "I thought you illcounseled. And indeed that was so, for surely the traitor Gerhard has been playing on your fears and keeping you from acting as your own wisdom dictated."

There was a long moment of silence. "If only I had wisdom," King Olafur said softly. "I thought I was protecting the Kingdom, but instead under my rule matters have grown steadily worse. I am unworthy to wear the crown of my fathers, and my weakness will be our undoing."

The King hung his head, as if he had already resigned himself to defeat.

"That is the sound of folly," Devlin said harshly, as if he were reprimanding one of his troops. The King had been coddled enough. It was time for plain speaking.

King Olafur raised his head.

"No man knows what he can do until he is put to the test, and there is no one who knows that better than I. If a simple man can become Chosen One, then surely one of your royal blood can find the strength within him to lead his people in their time of need."

Hope warred with doubt on the King's features. "But what if I fail?"

"Far better to try and fail than not to try at all. Be bold. Lead. You will make mistakes, but you will learn from them. The only true failure is in not trying."

King Olafur rubbed his chin thoughtfully. "Harsh words, but better counsel than I have heard in a long time."

"I live to serve," Devlin said. It was a commonly uttered platitude, yet in Devlin's mouth it was the simple truth.

The King nodded slowly. "If I am to lead as my fathers before me, then it is time we returned to their ways. For centuries, the Chosen One was also the General of the Army, who led the defense of our realm in times of peril."

Devlin's heart sank. So the King intended to replace him after all.

"But Your Majesty—" he began.

"I will not be gainsaid. You are the only one I can trust, and you have proven your loyalty to the Kingdom. I will name you councilor and General of the Army."

"Me?" He had barely managed to lead his force of thirty on the expedition to Korinth, and now he was to lead thousands? It was unthinkable. And yet...

"The council will not like this," Devlin said. Many of the councilors already felt he had too much power. What would they think now that he was their equal?

"The needs of the Kingdom come first. The army needs a General, and I need someone I can trust. My councilors will accept you or they will be replaced," King Olafur replied. His voice was firm, and for the first time since Devlin had known him, the King appeared decisive.

As General of the Army, Devlin would have the power to ensure that the Kingdom was ready to meet its foes, whoever they might be. And as councilor, he could influence the King and council to the path of reason. It was all he and his friends had hoped for, when they had fought so hard for change. He was tempted to accept, but a small voice within him urged caution.

"You honor me greatly with your trust," Devlin said. "But think well before you make this decision. I am a man accustomed to plain speaking, and I will not change simply because you name me councilor."

"As long as you speak honestly, I will be well served."

"And I will insist on sending the Royal Army to Korinth. Without delay." His mind was already planning the expedition. Mikkelson could lead the relief forces, given a suitable promotion. He had already proven his loyalty; it was time to give him a rank to match his capabilities.

"I expected nothing else."

Devlin rose to his feet. "Then I accept this honor," he said, extending his left hand in the clasp of friendship. "And I swear I will serve you faithfully. Between us we will make this Kingdom strong and safe once more."

After a moment of hesitation, King Olafur took Devlin's hand in his own. "Now I see why your followers love you," he said. "You have given me hope, something I have not felt in a long time."

"I will give you more than hope," Devlin vowed. "I will give you victory."

About the Author

PATRICIA BRAY inherited her love of books from her parents, both of whom were fine storytellers in the Irish tradition. She has always enjoyed spinning tales, and turned to writing as a chance to share her stories with a wider audience. Patricia holds a master's degree in Information Technology, and combines her writing with a full-time career as an I/T Project Manager. She resides in upstate New York, where she is currently at work on the next volume in The Sword of Change series. For more information on her books visit her Web site at www.sff.net/people/patriciabray.

Don't miss the next exciting

installment in

The Sword of Change

Devlin's Honor

Coming in summer 2003

Here's a special preview:

DEVLIN OF DUNCAER, CHOSEN ONE OF THE GODS, Defender of the Realm, Personal Champion of King Olafur, Royal Councilor, and General of the Royal Army, muttered to himself as he strode through the corridors of the palace. The few folk who saw him took one look at his grim face and discovered urgent business elsewhere. It was not just his appearance that gave them pause, though his green eyes and black hair—now streaked with white—marked him as a stranger here: the first of the Caerfolk to enter into the service of their conquerors. Rather it was his reputation they fled, for it was well known that the Chosen One had little patience for fools who troubled him, and his power made him an enemy few wished to have.

As Devlin reached the chambers that served as his offices, the guard on duty took one look at his face and swiftly opened the door, forgoing the formal salute. Devlin slammed the door shut behind him.

Lieutenant Didrik looked up from his papers. "The council meeting went as we expected?"

Nearly four months ago, when Devlin was named General of the Army, Lieutenant Didrik had been detached from the City Guard to serve as Devlin's aide. Some thought the lieutenant too young for the task, but his age was offset by his proven loyalty and friendship. And Lieutenant Didrik knew Devlin well enough to recognize when he was truly angry and when he was merely frustrated, as now.

"The council sits and talks and does nothing," Devlin said, unbuttoning the stiff collar of his court uniform. "And the folk in the palace flee like frightened sheep whenever they catch a glimpse of me."

Lieutenant Didrik nodded. "It would be easier to convince them you were tame if you did not growl."

"I do not growl."

"Yes, you do."

Devlin gave a wordless snarl and began to pace the small confines of the outer office. Lieutenant Didrik remained seated, his eyes following Devlin's restless movements.

Devlin paced in silence for a moment as he tried to shake off the frustration of that afternoon's council session. Four hours, and little enough to show for it. He was not made for such. In the past he had labored as a metalsmith and a farmer. Both were hard trades, but each carried the reward of his being able to see the fruits of his labors. Now the fates had conspired to turn Devlin into a politician. No one knew better than he how ill-suited he was for the task. Court politics was about compromises and alliances, jockeying for influence and trading favors. It took skill to navigate the treacherous waters of the court, and time to get anything accomplished. Time they did not have.

Worse, Devlin's voice was but one of sixteen, and no matter whether he whispered or shouted, he could not bend the council to his will. Instead he had to reason, cajole, flatter and bargain, and try to be content with the smallest of victories.

Such as the victory he had achieved today. "There is some news," he said, dropping into a wooden chair across from Lieutenant Didrik's desk. "The council approved the proposal for recruiting trained armsmen. Word is to be sent to all the provinces at once. With luck we should have a hundred before the snows, and perhaps a thousand by springtime."

Lieutenant Didrik leaned back and smiled. "But that is excellent news. Why did you not say so at once?"

"Because it is a victory, but at a cost. I had to agree not to urge the King to train the common folk who live in the danger zones," Devlin said, running the fingers of his good hand through his short-cropped hair. He was still not convinced that he had done the right thing, and yet even those councilors who normally supported him had been united in their opposition to his proposal. To Devlin it was simple logic: make use of the people who had the most to lose in an invasion, teach them to be effective fighters rather than see them slaughtered.

However the councilors' concerns were not for the present dangers but for their future power. A peasantry that was trained in the arts of warfare would be far harder to control. The common folk might even take it into their heads to rise up against those they perceived as unjust. Devlin acknowledged the risk but argued that those who ruled wisely had nothing to fear. His words had fallen on deaf ears.

"Perhaps there will be no need. Since Major Mikkelson and his troops repelled the landing force in Korinth, there has been little trouble along the borders. It may be that the worst is over," Lieutenant Didrik said.

Devlin shook his head. "I do not believe our enemies will give up so easily."

They were still not even sure who their true enemy was. The invaders in Korinth had been a mercenary troop, in the pay of someone whom they could not even name. It was only chance that had led Devlin to discover the plot in time to repel the invasion. The Royal Army had made short work of the would-be invaders, but Devlin knew better than to suppose that this was the end of the threat.

Yet where would the enemy attack next? Devlin and his

advisors had racked their brains trying to divine the strategy behind the enemy's seemingly random attacks. Without knowing whom they were facing, they were reduced to guessing.

"The armsmen will help," Lieutenant Didrik said.

"Aye. Draw up a list of those provinces most in need and a plan to allocate the armsmen. I will want to see it tomorrow."

He closed his eyes and leaned his head back. The council sessions wearied him in a way that hard labor never had, for it was an exhaustion born of frustration and a sense of his own inadequacies. "Anyone would make a better councilor than I."

"Do not speak such folly," Lieutenant Didrik said. "Without you, the soldiers would have sat idly in their garrison rather than meeting the invaders on the shores of Korinth. And you were the one who sent the Royal Army out to patrol the highways and to survey the border fortifications."

Comforting words. But such actions were only a fraction of what Devlin had hoped to accomplish when he had accepted this position. Then he had been sure that with the King's backing he could set the Kingdom to rights. But he had not counted on the numbing effects of court politics, nor that his influence would wane as memories of his heroism faded.

Now he was left to struggle as best he could. A lesser man might have given up hope, but Devlin was the Chosen One, bound by Geas to serve the Kingdom as long as breath remained in his body. He could not conceive of surrender or of giving up. He would not rest until he had fulfilled his promise and made this Kingdom safe.

"Then we are agreed. The armsmen will be used to reinforce the border with Nerikaat," Devlin said, leaning over the map and tapping the northwestern corner of the Kingdom with one finger. "The southern provinces will have to wait until the next wave of reinforcements in the spring."

He looked up from the maps spread over his work table.

"Agreed," Captain Drakken said. Lieutenant Didrik merely nodded.

Devlin began rolling up the map. "Lieutenant, I will need to inform the senior army commanders of my decision. Send a message and ask that they meet with me on the morrow. Captain Drakken, I thank you for the courtesy of your time and counsel."

Captain Drakken dipped her head, in the show of respect between friends or equals. "I am at your service."

"And for that I am grateful."

Strictly speaking, as the commander of the City Guard, Captain Drakken was concerned with security for the palace and maintaining order within the city. The defense of the realm and disposition of provincial armsmen was more properly a matter for the Royal Army. But Devlin could count on his remaining fingers the number of folk in Jorsk that he could trust to give him honest advice, and only one of these was a member of the Royal Army. And Major Mikkelson was far from here, having been dispatched to lead the defense of the coastal province of Korinth.

Thus Devlin had become accustomed to consulting Captain Drakken, taking full advantage of her more than quarter century of experience. Once he had determined his course of action, he then informed the Royal Army officers of his decisions, allowing him to appear a decisive leader. Only he, Lieutenant Didrik, and Captain Drakken knew this for the hollow pretense it was.

He heard the sound of the outer door opening, and then footsteps, as a voice called "Devlin?"

"We are in here," he replied.

Stephen paused in the doorway. "I do not wish to interrupt ..."

"No, we have just finished our deliberations. And as I have not seen you in some time, it would be poor courtesy to turn you away."

Stephen was the first friend Devlin had made in this strange place, though it had taken him time to acknowledge that friendship and to accept its burden. Stephen had shared many of Devlin's adventures, but in these past months they had seen little of each other. Devlin had been consumed with his new responsibilities, and Stephen had made it plain that he wished to pursue his music rather than be caught up in the games of the court.

Yet somehow the court must have found Stephen, for there was no other reason for him to look so unhappy, or to have sought Devlin out in his offices rather than his private quarters.

Captain Drakken glanced at Stephen, then back at Devlin. "I will leave you now."

"No," Stephen said. "You and Lieutenant Didrik will want to hear this as well."

Devlin perched on the corner of his desk, wondering what had brought Stephen here. He nodded encouragingly.

"I played last night for a wine merchant, Soren Tyrvald."

"I know of him," Captain Drakken interjected. "He has a reputation for shrewd dealing. Shrewd, but honest."

Stephen nodded, his narrow face pale. "A respected merchant, not one to get himself involved in political schemes. Or so I would have said before last night."

"And now?" Devlin prompted.

"Last night Soren drew me aside for private speech. He claims to have heard rumors that certain nobles are objecting to your claim to be the Chosen One. That if you were the true Chosen One, the Gods would have given you the Sword of Light."

"Is that all?" Devlin asked.

"Merchant Tyrvald asked me to make sure you knew of

this rumor, and that it was likely an attempt to diminish your influence with the commoners," Stephen said. His shoulders slumped, as if he had given up some great burden.

Devlin could see that Stephen felt used, but his message was hardly unexpected. "I have heard this tale before," Devlin said. "Over a week ago it became clear that there was some new rumor circulating through the court. It took only a day before a helpful soul felt compelled to tell me what was being said."

Captain Drakken rubbed her chin thoughtfully. "It is a clever ploy, I will grant you that. At the very least, it may cast doubt on your stature. At best, they may succeed in convincing the King to have you search for the sword."

"Thus removing me from the court, and from the deliberations of the King's Council," Devlin added. He had expected this rumor to die out, but instead it seemed to be growing.

At least there was one mercy. Though he had not voiced it aloud, Devlin was convinced that those who plotted against him had yet another goal in spreading this rumor. They hoped that the Geas which bound him would compel Devlin to seek out the Sword of Light, whether he wished to or not. Some could have argued that such was his duty as Chosen One. But this time the Gods were merciful, and the Geas had not stirred from where it slept at the back of his mind.

"And how do they expect me to search for this sword?" Devlin asked, trying for a mocking tone. "There must have been dozens of copies forged over the years."

"There are no copies," Stephen said. "There was only one Sword of Light. When Lord Saemund perished and the sword was lost, they forged a new sword for the next Chosen One. The armorer felt it would be impious to make a copy, since the Sword of Light had been forged by a son of Egil."

Devlin snorted in disgust. "They say such things of

all great swords. Why not claim the Forge God himself made it?"

"It is what is said," Stephen insisted.

Devlin forbore to argue. Stephen's passion had been the lore of the past Chosen Ones, and he knew more of their history than any other in the Kingdom. If Devlin objected, Stephen might feel compelled to share more of the sword's supposed history. There might even be a song or two of its forging, which Devlin was in no mood to hear.

Still, the part of Devlin that had once been a metalsmith was intrigued. "Are there any descriptions or drawings of this sword?" he asked.

"There is a hall of portraits, little visited now, but in this hall there is a portrait of Donalt the Wise. And I seem to recall he is holding the Sword of Light," Captain Drakken said.

"Can you guide us there?" Devlin asked.

"Of course."

Captain Drakken led them from the western wing where Devlin had his offices, to the older central block of the palace. The hallways grew progressively narrower and the stones beneath their feet more worn as they made their way up to the fourth level. They traveled down a corridor with rooms branching off either side. Through the open doorways Devlin glimpsed marble sculptures, a room filled with decorative porcelains, and another room that held boxes or perhaps furniture hidden beneath white shrouds.

At the end of the corridor an archway led into a long room that ran the full two-hundred-foot length of the tower. Light streamed in from windows set high up on the three exterior walls. Devlin paused. The wall before him was covered with paintings of various sizes and styles, hung from high above down to the very floor. He turned around slowly and saw that the other three walls were equally covered. A battle scene with life-size figures hung next to a jumbled collection of small portraits. There were gilt frames, tarnished silver frames, and those of plain wood, and the mix of subjects was equally diverse.

"Where do we start?" Lieutenant Didrik asked.

Captain Drakken went over to the northern wall. She leaned forward, peering at the pictures as she walked down along the line. Then she straightened up. "Here," she said. Devlin came over, with Lieutenant Didrik and Stephen following. Captain Drakken pointed to a medium-sized portrait. "Donalt the Wise."

Donalt, often called the last of the great Chosen Ones, was shown as a man in his middle years, with long blond hair done in a warrior's braid. His features were harsh, and his blue eyes stared directly forward, as if they could see into the viewer's soul. Across his back he wore a baldric. Only the hilt of the sword was visible above his shoulder.

It couldn't be. And yet . . .

Devlin swallowed hard. "Is there a better picture of the sword?"

"My age is beginning to tell, for I had remembered this differently," Captain Drakken said. "Still, there must be another portrait in here. We should keep looking."

They split apart, one to each of the four walls. Devlin took the southern wall, the one furthest from the portrait of Donalt. His eyes scanned the pictures, but he was not really seeing them. It could not be, he told himself. His mind was playing tricks.

He craned his neck upwards, and then he saw it. A young woman who bore an unmistakable resemblance to Donalt held the sword extended in front of her as she fought off an armored warrior. Behind her, crouching next to the uncertain shelter of a boulder, was a young boy. The artist had been truly gifted, for he had managed to capture not only the boy's fear but also a sense of the woman's fierce determination. One knew that she looked her own death in the face, and that she was not afraid.

But any admiration for the artist's skill was lost when Devlin contemplated the Sword of Light, which had been depicted with equal skill. It was clearly a long sword, with a tapering blade. The grip was unusual, for instead of a single curved crossbar there was a double guard of two straight bars, one longer than the other. And in the pommel was set a stone that shone with red fire.

"The stone is wrong. It should be dark crimson, so dark it seems nearly black," Devlin whispered, though a part of him felt like screaming.

"It is dark," Stephen said, and Devlin jumped. He had not realized that the others had joined him. "The stone glows when the sword is wielded in battle by the Chosen One," Stephen explained.

But Captain Drakken had understood what Stephen had not. "How do you know of the stone's appearance?"

Devlin took a step back from the wall, and then another, although his eyes did not leave the painting.

"Because I have held that sword in my hands." He tasted bile and for a brief moment he fought the urge to vomit. But there was no denying the truth of what he saw, or of what he knew.

"How is that possible?" Captain Drakken asked.

Devlin did not answer. He turned on his heel and began to walk away. He needed to get out of here. Quickly. Before he gave in to the urge to smash something.

But he could not flee fast enough to escape his friends. Stephen caught up with him and grabbed his sleeve. "You have seen it? You know where it is?"

Devlin shook his arm free. "The sword was lost at Ynnis, was it not?"

Stephen nodded. "During the final hours of the siege, when Lord Saemund was killed."

"During the massacre," Devlin corrected. His people had their own memories of Ynnis, and none of them were kind to the Jorskians. Lord Saemund may have been the

Chosen One, but he deserved to suffer in the Dread Lord's realm for all eternity for what his troops had done. Men, women, and even children had been slaughtered, and those not killed by the soldiers perished in the flames as the army set the city to the torch. Those who survived were too few to bury the dead, and to this day Ynnis remained a ruin, inhabited only by her restless ghosts.

Still, Ynnis had been a small city, and the destruction there had not befallen the rest of Duncaer. Most Caerfolk, including Devlin, had done their best to put the siege from their minds. The war was long over, and there was no sense in brooding about the past.

But now the past had come back to haunt them.

Devlin ran his left hand through his hair, trying to think of a way to explain. "When I was a boy, my parents apprenticed me to Master Roric, a metalsmith. Like my parents, Master Roric was a survivor of the massacre at Ynnis."

"You say massacre, but that is not how it is recorded," Captain Drakken said.

"I care not what tales you tell, or what the minstrel sings," Devlin said, his clipped tones revealing his anger. "My parents were both children who were lucky to survive, for all their near kin perished on that day."

His parents had been cared for by other refugees until they reached Alvaren and found shelter with kin so distant that they could scarcely even be called far kin. And yet they had taken the children in, raised them, and in time found trades for them. But those who survived Ynnis had a special bond that kept them a closely knit community within the teeming capital city. Kameron and Talaith's friendship had ripened into love, and they had married when they became adults. When it was time to apprentice their youngest son, it was natural that they turn to one of the other survivors of Ynnis.

"Master Roric was already a journeyman smith in Ynnis during the siege. He never spoke of how he managed to survive, or of what he had lost on that day. But he did have one reminder of the battle."

"A sword," Captain Drakken said.

"A sword," Devlin agreed. "A sword so fine it was surely the work of a great master, made of steel that shimmered in the light, flexible and yet stronger than any blade I have seen before or since."

Master Roric had kept the sword in a chest, for it was both an object of great value and one that seemed to hold painful memories. From time to time he would bring it forth and let the best of his students study it as an encouragement to them in their own craft.

"So you know where the sword is?" Lieutenant Didrik asked.

"No. But I know where it was," Devlin answered.

After his uncanny revelations, the Chosen One had stalked off, and so plain was his anger that none dared follow. Captain Drakken exchanged a glance with Lieutenant Didrik, who raised his eyebrows but said nothing.

Only the minstrel Stephen seemed oblivious to the tension. His face was transfixed with wonder as he murmured, "The sword. The Sword of Light."

"He has seen the sword," Lieutenant Didrik echoed.

"But what does this mean?" Stephen said.

"It may mean nothing. Only that by some strange twist of fate, the Gods have sent us the man who can return the sword that was lost," Captain Drakken said, trying to reassure herself as much as the others.

But Devlin had worn the look of a man faced with painful memories, and she did not think he would be able to banish them as swiftly as they had come. And she could not risk this new revelation damaging the frail alliances that they had begun to build in service of the Kingdom.

"Didrik, send word to the watch commanders. I want

every guard to keep an eye out for Devlin and let me know when he is found. He may try to slip out of the city quietly, without telling anyone."

"You think he will go after the sword?" Didrik asked.

"I do not know what he will do," she answered honestly. "But I know he is angry now, and that may drive him to some foolish action, perhaps even leaving Kingsholm in the heat of his anger, ill-equipped and unprepared for a winter journey."

It took the guards less than an hour to report back that Devlin was in the practice yard, methodically destroying one wooden target after another with his great axe.

Captain Drakken spent the rest of the day busy with her own duties, inspecting the watch at the city gates, meeting with a delegation of merchants from the great square who complained about an outbreak of petty thievery, and then approving the watch schedules that Lieutenant Embeth had drawn up. But even as she went about her tasks, a part of her mind kept returning to the Chosen One and the mystery of the Sword of Light. She realized that it was only a matter of time before Devlin would have to go after the sword, for the sake of the Kingdom.

And once his anger cooled, the same thought would occur to him as well.

She worked through the dinner hour and late into the night. Each time she heard footsteps outside her office, she looked up, expecting to see the Chosen One. But he did not come. Finally, in the middle of the night watch, she decided she had let him brood long enough.

Donning her cloak against the night chill, Captain Drakken left the Guard Hall and made her way across the great courtyard to the north tower. The guard on duty at the base of the tower saluted as he saw her approach.

"All quiet?" she asked, returning the salute.

"Yes, Captain. All is at peace," the guard Behra said, in the traditional response.

Her eyes glanced upward to the battlements, and Behra's glance followed hers. "He is still up there," Behra said.

The guard opened the door to the tower, and Captain Drakken made her way inside, then up the narrow circular stairs that led to the battlements. As she opened the door at the top, she was struck by a chill blast of wind. The night air, cold enough in the protected courtyard, was positively glacial up here.

She walked the perimeter battlements until she found Devlin on the south side. He had chosen the most dangerous perch, for he sat on top of the narrow railing. She was reminded of that night over a year and a half ago, when she had sought out the new Chosen One and given him his first quest. Then Devlin had been a stranger to her, a tool that had yet to prove its value. His past had been of little interest to her, or to any other in the city.

Now they entrusted him with the safety of the Kingdom. And yet they still knew little of his people, or of his past. He had volunteered few details, and there had seemed no reason to be concerned. Until now.

His head turned as he heard her approach. In the flickering torchlight she saw that his eyes were bleak, and his face shuttered and unreadable.

"You must go after the sword," she said, without preamble.

"I know," Devlin said. "Even now, the Geas tugs at my will. Soon I will not be able to ignore its call."

He turned his face away from her. There was a long moment of silence, then Devlin asked, "Do you believe in fate?"

"No," she said firmly. "From the moment we are born, each of us makes our own path and our own luck."

"So I once thought," Devlin said. "Yet there are only a handful of folk who have seen the Sword of Light in the years since Ynnis. It passes all belief that my presence here as Chosen One is mere coincidence."

There was nothing she could say to that.

"Perhaps they were right to name me kinslayer," Devlin added, in tones so low she could scarcely hear him.

"What do you mean?"

Devlin leaned back, swung his legs around so they were on the inside ledge, then stood to face her. "If my family had not been killed, I would still be in Duncaer. I would never have become an exile, never have heard of the Chosen Ones, never been foolish and desperate enough to journey to this place. The Gods wanted a tool to return the Sword of Light." He took a quick breath, his fists clenched by his sides. "Cerrie was killed because she loved me, and because I never would have left Duncaer were she still alive."

"No," Drakken said swiftly. "You must not think that. I do not believe the Gods would be so cruel."

"Then you have more faith in the Gods than I," he replied.

"So what will you do?"

He laughed mirthlessly, and the sound made her flesh crawl, for it was the sound of a man who stood again on the edge of madness. "I have no choice, have I? The Gods set my feet on this path, and now the Geas binds me to their will, regardless of what I think or feel. I will fetch the sword, as they command. But one day I will face Lord Haakon, and I will demand a reckoning."

His eyes glittered darkly, and such was his intensity that she had no doubt that in time Devlin would demand such a reckoning, regardless of the consequences.